# tankborn

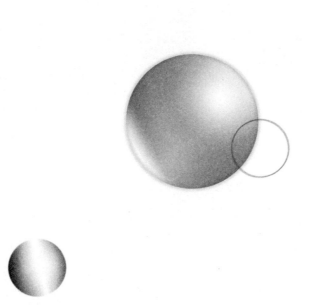

# karen sandler

# tankborn

## Tu Books

AN IMPRINT OF LEE & LOW BOOKS, INC.

New York

TU BOOKS, an imprint of LEE & LOW BOOKS Inc.
95 Madison Avenue, New York, NY 10016
leeandlow.com

Manufactured in the United States of America
by Worzalla Publishing Company, September 2011

Book design by Einav Aviram
Book production by The Kids at Our House
The text is set in Adobe Caslon Pro

10 9 8 7 6 5 4 3 2 1
First Edition

Library of Congress Cataloging-in-Publication Data

Sandler, Karen.
Tankborn / Karen Sandler. — 1st ed.
p. cm.
Summary: Kayla and Mishalla, two genetically engineered non-human slaves (GENs), fall in love with higher-status boys, discover deep secrets about the creation of GENs, and in the process find out what it means to be human.
ISBN 978-1-60060-662-5 (hardcover : alk. paper) —
ISBN 978-1-60060-876-6 (e-book)
[1. Genetic engineering—Fiction. 2. Science fiction.] I. Title. II. Title: Tankborn.
PZ7.S2173Tan 2011
[Fic]--dc23    2011014589

*To my younger son, Ryan, whose beta-read set* Tankborn
*on the right path. Kudos, too, to my daughter-in-law, Dani, for
the assists on the GEN religion and economy.*

*To my older son, Eric, fellow writer and brainstormer
who helped me name the trueborns and lowborns and
suggested Loka's arachnid fauna.*

*And to my husband, Gary, the love of my life, always a source of
emotional support and my sounding board when
it all seems impossible.*

NORTHWEST
TERRITORY

N

NORTHEAST
TERRITORY

TO SKYLOFT

TO FAR NORTH

TEF
TB

FALT
GEN

PLATOR RIVER

MENDIN
GEN

PLATOR
TB/LB

LEISA
TB

SHEYSA RIVER

ADHIKAR

CENTRAL WESTERN
TERRITORY

MUT
GEN

PLAKIT
GEN

TWO
RIVERS
TB

CHADI
GEN

CHADI RIVER

FORESTHILL
TB

SHEYSA
TB/LB

HAK
TB/LB

JASSA
GEN

EASTERN
TERRITORY

TELLIK
TB

SOUTHWEST TERRITORY

ADHIKAR

THE CONTINENT OF

svarga

TB – SECTORS FOR HIGH-STATUS &
DEMI-STATUS TRUEBORNS ONLY

TB/LB – SECTORS FOR MINOR-STATUS
TRUEBORNS & LOWBORNS

GEN – GENETICALLY ENGINEERED
NON-HUMANS ONLY

SONA
TB

# THE CONTINENT OF svarga

**N**

NORTHWEST ·········· 22 SECTORS
NORTHEAST ·········· 20 SECTORS
EASTERN ················ 19 SECTORS
SOUTHWEST ·········· 18 SECTORS
CENTRAL WESTERN ··· 27 SECTORS

TB - SECTORS FOR HIGH-STATUS &
DEMI-STATUS TRUEBORNS ONLY

TB/LB - SECTORS FOR MINOR-STATUS
TRUEBORNS & LOWBORNS

GEN - GENETICALLY ENGINEERED
NON-HUMANS ONLY

BADLANDS
UNINHABITED

THE WALL

SKYLOFT
TB

THE SOURCE

NORTHEAST
TERRITORY

NORTHWEST TERRITORY

FAR NORTH
TB

TATOR RIVER

SHEYSA RIVER

EASTERN
TERRITORY

VELK
GEN

LEISA
TB

TEF
TB

SALT
TB

MENON
GEN

ADHIKAR

CENTRAL WESTERN
TERRITORY

PLATOR
TB/LB

PLAKTI
GEN

CHADI
GEN

SALT
GEN

TWO
RIVERS
TB

SHEYSA
TB/LB

FORESTHILL
TB/LB

HAK
TB

JASSA
GEN

VELLUR
TB

CHADI RIVER

SOUTHWEST TERRITORY

ADHIKAR

SONA
TB

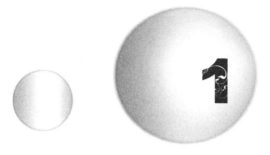

**K**ayla hunched on the bank of the Chadi River while below her, Jal, her slender, black-skinned nurture brother, skipped from one deep pool of the river to another, searching for sewer toads. Watching over Jal had not been in Kayla's plans. She'd intended to spend the rare Thirdday holiday with her friends. But when her nurture mother, Tala, got wind of Jal's plans, she'd insisted a tenth-year like Jal wouldn't be safe at the river by himself. Never mind that Tala had let Kayla go off by herself without a second thought from the time she was an eighth-year. So Kayla had to tromp down to the river with Jal for his toad hunt instead of spending the afternoon with Miva and Beela.

Not that the two girls were heart-deep, blood-to-blood, tank-sister friends the way Mishalla had been. But among the fourteenth-year GEN girls in Chadi sector, they were about the only ones who didn't think Kayla was a freak.

Jal grinned up at her as he showed off a particularly fat sewer toad, its arachnid eyes beady and staring. The sewer toad's eight segmented legs squirmed, river sludge dripping off its slimy skin. She'd seen images of bumpy brown Earth toads on the sekai readers in Doctrine classes. Those had been cuddly pets compared to the nightmare spider-like creatures Loka had to offer. But then, nearly everything on Loka was uglier than what humans had left behind on Earth.

The few mammals on Loka weren't as hideous as the spider-creatures. The wary seycats that kept the vermin down in the warehouses sported intriguing striped pelts and tall tufted ears. The six-legged droms that roamed the plains had thick mottled wool and droopy noses and only one pair of large black eyes set in their camel-like heads.

But the seycats rarely showed their faces when people were around. And there weren't too many of the native droms left. The ones that didn't get eaten by the bhimkay had been crowded out of the grassy plains by the gene-splicers' version of the drom—twice as tall, three times as heavy. The gene-splicers had used DNA from Earth cows to get bigger meat animals. Kind of like the way they used bits of animal DNA to give GENs like Kayla their skill sets.

Jal stuffed the toad into his carrysak, then waded along the far bank, gaze fixed to the water's surface. The GEN healer in thirty-third warren paid one dhan for twenty toads, although what the woman did with the disgusting things, Kayla didn't want to think about.

She'd been a pretty rough-and-tumble girl when she was Jal's age, especially considering her sket. She'd climbed the scraggly junk trees in Chadi Square, scoured condemned housing warrens for trash she could exchange for quarter-dhans. She'd even trapped the eight-legged rat-snakes for the healer, toting them in a carrysak like Jal did the toads. Rat-snakes weren't rats or snakes, just another spider-like creature with a long, squirmy thorax and a rat-like head. She shuddered now at the thought of touching those nasty, hairy monsters.

The rumble of an engine snagged her attention. On the trueborn side of the river, a micro-lev-car, a shiny pearl gray Bullet, slid into view from between the Foresthill sector warehouses. The sleek, snub-nosed Bullet rocked a little as the engine's air cushion traversed the uneven rubble of permacrete littering the far side, then settled its belly to the ground beside a skyway support pillar. The primary sun, Iyenku, cast its coppery glare on the windshield and hid the occupants from view.

Kayla's heart skittered with alarm as the wing-doors popped up and two trueborns climbed from the Bullet. They minced along on the permacrete rocks toward the river. She saw plenty of lowborns walking along the bank on the Foresthill side, taking a shortcut from one riverside shantytown to another. But other than the occasional glimpse of a warehouse supervisor, trueborns never got this close to the GEN sector.

If she only considered the high-priced Bullet and the two boys' extravagant clothes, she would have pegged them as high-status trueborns. But their pale skin and the green glint of their emerald bali in their right earlobes meant they were demi-status, not high.

Despite their showy, jewel-stitched capes and kortas, Kayla knew the demi boys possessed nothing even close to high-status trueborn wealth. The high-status started their lives rich, awarded massive tracts of adhikar land as babies, twice the acres demi babies received. Of course, the demis' adhikar grants were double what the minor-status trueborns got, and lowborns got nothing. So demis liked to rub what wealth they had into minor-status and lowborn noses.

But usually demis steered clear of GENs like Kayla and Jal. Tankborns like her and her nurture brother were beneath trueborn notice. If they'd stopped to relieve themselves, they'd have found a more private spot between the warehouses. But they were headed straight for the bank overlooking where Jal waded in the river.

Head bent down as if Jal still had her full attention, she angled her gaze up to keep one eye on the trueborns. "Jal," Kayla called out to her nurture brother. "Come out of the water."

Slogging through the sludge, Jal waved her off, too focused on finding one more toad to listen to his older nurture sister's request. And he had a point. With the river's far edge marking the transition from Chadi sector to Foresthill, she and Jal were both legitimately on the GEN side of the border. Those true-borns had nothing to report on their wristlinks.

Nevertheless, Kayla eyed them uneasily. She guessed they were maybe a little older than her nearly fifteen years. The stout one didn't wear his gem-encrusted korta well. He looked stuffed into it like a sausage, his leggings so tight she feared they might burst.

The other trueborn, blond and tall and good-looking, with a mouthful of too-white teeth, had a meanness to his pale face. He was proud enough of his broad shoulders to keep his cape thrown clear of them. Pela fur trimmed the cape, dyed a nasty shade of purple. She supposed she should be grateful the gene-splicers didn't create GENs that awful color.

The good-looking trueborn spoke to his friend, pitching his voice loud enough for Kayla to hear across the river. "What kind of DNA made that one?" He pointed at Kayla. "Looks like sow to me."

"Pig for sure," his fat friend agreed.

Kayla's cheeks burned. Even knowing the consequences, she wanted nothing more than to ford the river and grab the tall blond boy by his ugly purple cape. She'd shake him, hard, and give him a dunking in the river.

The good-looking one whispered to his friend, then they both bent to gather up a handful of the smaller perma rocks under their feet. The fat one lobbed a rock toward Jal, but he had such lousy aim, Kayla doubted he could have hit a stationary pub-trans with a boulder. Jal dodged the rocks, leaping side to side as if it were a game.

But the taller trueborn had a better arm. The chunks of permacrete he cast fell precisely to either side and just short of Jal, closer and closer. When her brother tried to back away in the dank water, a jagged piece grazed his left cheek, scratching across his GEN tattoo before it plunked into the river.

That was enough to send Kayla scrambling down the trash-strewn bank, a prayer to the Infinite and all three prophets flung off in her mind. But before she even reached the water, the good-looking trueborn raised a massive piece of perma and shouted, "Hey, jik! Catch this one with your teeth!"

Kayla screamed, "Jal, run!" as she slithered to the river's edge and struggled for footing in the slippery riverbed. His carrysak heavy with toads, Jal took a bad step, losing his balance. He fell to his knees in the shallow, slow-moving water. The trueborn stretched his arms back, ready to heave the permacrete at Jal.

A pair of hands wrenched the rock from the good-looking trueborn boy's grip. The slope of the riverbank and the broad-shouldered trueborn blocked Kayla's view of Jal's rescuer. She heard him shout, "Leave off, Livot, or I'll take some perma to that Bullet of yours."

A few more shouted words, then Livot and his fat friend retreated to their micro-lev-car, their footsteps crunching in the rubble. Kayla grabbed a handful of Jal's shirt, lifting him off his feet, the heavy carrysak and his wiry thirty-five kilos a featherweight to her strength. He squawked at the indignity of dangling from her hands, but she didn't let him go until she'd carried him to the water's edge.

The bank was steep enough she had to pull herself up on all fours, but as usual the hyper-genned strength of her upper body got the better of her lower. She fumbled more than once, muddying her knees, adding to the ugly ankle-high sludge staining her best leggings.

It wasn't until she and Jal had reached safety on the top of the bank that she realized the third trueborn was following them across the river. He'd found a path of rocks, barely wetting his boots with his careful steps, let alone the cuffs of his pants.

Kayla bent to whisper in Jal's ear. "Run to the flat. If I'm not back in an hour, tell Tala what happened."

Jal's eyes widened. "I can't leave you."

"I'll be fine." The trueborn's head had appeared above the riverbank. "Do as I say! Go!"

Carrysak clutched to his chest, Jal took off down the narrow weed-choked path. He disappeared around the corner of the kel-grain warehouse before the trueborn topped the riverbank and started toward Kayla.

Even without the white diamond glitter from the bali in his right ear, Kayla would have known this one was high-status. His dark hair was straight and glossy, not wild and kinked like Kayla's or tight curls like Jal's. His skin was the perfect color, a rich medium brown. Not near black like Jal's, nor the pale mud color of her own skin, but a warm shade in between. The color of status.

He smiled, the slash of white in his beautiful face stealing Kayla's breath. When he stopped a half-meter from her, she edged away. He wasn't as tall as the blond trueborn, but Kayla had been genned small, so she had to crane her neck to look up at him.

"Is he okay?" he asked. "The young male?"

She stood there, torn, wanting to run and wanting to stay all at once. She didn't like the way he made her feel, the way his smile, his seeming kindness, kept her feet rooted to the damp riverside dirt.

"He's fine," Kayla said, eyeing the boy warily. He wore a plain navy blue korta, not a synth-gem in sight on its collar, no fur or fluff on the brown chera pants. But he wore the clothes as if he owned the world and everything in it. Which he did, like all the other trueborns, especially a high-status like him.

His straight black hair was neatly cut short, not a waist-length sandy-colored mess like hers. She brushed and braided her hair every morning, but by mid-afternoon, like now, more of it had escaped the braid than remained in it.

By the prophets, he was beautiful. His face out-dazzled the images she'd seen of the mythic gods Iyenku and his brother, Kas. On Earth, the twins had driven their fiery chariot together across the sky. Here on Loka they chased each other, the primary sun Iyenku rising first, then sleepy Kas peeping above the horizon later. In her mind, neither god could compare with the flesh and blood trueborn standing before her.

His gaze fixed on her, his stare bordering on rude. She wanted to back away, but she made herself stand there. "What?

Have you never seen a GEN before?"

"Plenty of them. Working at the warehouses. Sometimes in towncenter. Except they're not . . ."

"Not what?" she asked.

She didn't like the way he stared at her. Usually trueborns sneered at GENs or narrowed their gazes with contempt. They'd make rude comments about what kind of animal DNA had been used for a GEN's sket, like Livot had.

But this trueborn boy looked at her as if he could see inside her. As if he could read the messages running along her neural circuits with nothing but those intense dark eyes.

She sighed with relief when he finally looked away. He fussed with the hem of his korta, scuffed a line in the dirt with the toe of his fine shoes. "They're not nearly so small as you," he said.

Of course. To him, she was just another unremarkable GEN, a Genetically Engineered Non-human. If she and Beela stood here side by side, this trueborn wouldn't know one from the other if the gene-splicers hadn't programmed the two of them with hair and skin in different colors. Maybe that was why the splicers did it that way—created one GEN like Beela with elegant high-status brown skin and dark hair, and another like Kayla with brown-beigey skin and hair to match.

The boy's gaze traced the path of her tattoo. "I thought they were usually on the left cheek. Your DNA mark," he clarified.

Heat rose in her face again. "A few have them on the right."

There were only a handful of them in Chadi, one of them her best friend Mishalla. That difference had drawn them together. Mishalla could laugh about it, but not Kayla. Her mismatched strength and the blemished skin on her arms already made her stick out. The tattoo on the wrong side gave her one more mortifying disgrace that didn't blend into the GEN norm.

"I'm Devak," he said, smiling again. His hand twitched, as if he'd been about to offer it to her to shake, then remembered he was a trueborn and she a GEN.

She didn't want to say her name. The tattoo on her cheek would tell him anything he wanted to know about her if he had a datapod like the Brigade enforcers did. She'd heard most trueborns carried them. He could slap the thumb-sized device to her tattoo and learn every last personal detail about her.

Her cheek itched at the thought, but she wouldn't let herself scratch it. "You shouldn't be here. Not without your friends."

"They're not my friends. I barely know them."

"Even so, you ought to have left with them."

"You don't want me here?" He seemed genuinely surprised. "I would think you'd be glad to have a trueborn around."

"To throw rocks at me?"

"We're not all as ill-bred as Livot," he said, his expression serious. "I admit, that one's got more dhans than adhikar and more synth-gems than sense. But most of us just want what's best for GENs."

As if any trueborn had the least clue what was best for GENs. Except he seemed to mean it, as if her well-being mattered to him. A traitorous warmth sparked inside her.

She shouldn't like him. She didn't. The Infinite's liturgy made clear the laws against relations of any kind between GENs and trueborns. Yet she couldn't seem to take her eyes from the perfection of his face, the way his korta fit his shoulders, the dimple creasing his cheek.

His untattooed, trueborn cheek. She turned away from

him slightly, so she could only see him from the corner of her eye. "Some GENs might see an opportunity with an unescorted trueborn."

He tilted up his chin and she caught a flash of his trueborn arrogance. "A GEN wouldn't dare harm me."

"If your life is miserable enough, you might not care about the consequences." She couldn't believe she'd said the words out loud. "Don't report me. Please."

"Why would I?"

"Because …" *Because you're a trueborn and you can.* "Can I go?"

"If you want to."

She wanted to. Yet she still couldn't walk away. She shifted uneasily, caught between her fascination for the trueborn boy and her better sense.

"What about a female like you?" he asked. "Aren't you at risk too, being alone?"

She didn't quite meet his gaze. "There's more to me than you'd think."

He studied her. "I saw you carrying the young male. And the way you pulled yourself up the bank."

So he'd seen her awkward scramble. Her cheeks warmed. "It's just my sket."

"Do you like your skill set? Being strong?"

*I hate it. Sometimes I want to tear my own arms off.* Like in her nightmares.

Aloud, she said again, "It's just my sket. My blessing from the Infinite."

She checked her inner clock, counted out the minutes since Jal had run off. He must be nearly to the flat by now. She should go so her nurture mother, Tala, wouldn't worry. "Thank you for helping my brother." She sidled away from him along the path. "I think I should go with you."

He used that same imperious tone as before and was reaching toward her, the way he almost had earlier. A chill ran through her and for an instant she didn't feel safe.

Then she saw the stain of embarrassment in his cheeks, the way he edged back from her. No trueborn, especially not this high-status boy, would ever touch a GEN with bare, unprotected hands. It had to be a joke, offering to walk her home, a joke he regretted now.

Devak confirmed her guess when he turned abruptly and started for the riverbank. He swung himself down and slipped from view as he descended.

She should have walked away then. But she waited until she could see him again, retracing his path across the river, finding each stone he'd used before. Kayla found the faintest pleasure when he slipped once, going ankle deep in the sludge. But as he pulled himself free, gaining the far bank in a graceful leap, she couldn't tear her gaze away.

She finally forced herself to hurry down the path. Just as she reached the corner of the kel-grain warehouse, she couldn't quite keep herself from looking back. Devak was still standing there, staring across at her. She got the stupidest urge—to wave good-bye, as if she was saying farewell to some GEN boy she'd shared stolen kisses with between the warrens. She wondered if he'd wave back.

She ran the rest of the way home, anxious about all of it—the rock-throwing trueborns, Devak's rescue, their odd conversation. But mixed in with her worries were feelings she didn't want or understand, Infinite-forbidden feelings she ought to have left behind at the riverbank.

When Kayla slipped into the twenty-ninth warren, Jal was waiting for her by the stairs. "Tala's out," Jal said, "cleaning Spil and Zeva's flat."

Kayla brushed past Jal and up the stairs. "Then we have time to change and get the river sludge out of our clothes."

"What about this?" Jal tapped the scratch on his cheek.

"I'll doctor it. If she asks, you slipped climbing down the riverbank."

"If she's tired enough," Jal pointed out, "she might not even notice the scratch."

"She'll notice. She just might not have the energy to push it."

Jal crowded up past Kayla and walked backward up the stairs. "Tala shouldn't have to work so hard."

Kayla slanted a look up at him. "You volunteering to stop eating? We could save plenty of dhans not paying for the kel-grain you inhale."

Jal gave Kayla a poke. "I mean, the trueborns should give her a new baby so she won't have to clean flats."

Kayla couldn't argue with that. Tala was genned as a nurturer, and that was all she ought to be doing. But with Kayla nearly a fifteenth-year and just weeks away from Assignment and Jal now a tenth-year and in little need of nurturing, the trueborns had shrunk Tala's monthly stipend to near nothing. If not for the handful of half-dhans Tala earned cleaning the more well-off neighbors' flats and Jal and Kayla's slim contributions, they'd be short even their basic kel-grain ration.

Kayla backed her nurture brother into Tala's flat. "I don't want her knowing what happened with those trueborns."

"We should report 'em to the Brigade."

"Like the enforcers would do anything."

In the sleeproom they shared, Kayla twitched shut the screening blanket that divided the space. Her bed filled what little room was left, but at least she had some privacy.

She quickly shucked her soggy leggings and shirt, tossing them into a pile. As always when she undressed, she tried not to look at her bare arms, but it was unavoidable. Flecks and blobs and smears of darker and lighter color marred the faded brown of her skin. Some of the blemishes were as dark as Jal's skin, some a high-status rich brown, a few as pale as Livot's near-white. The blotches ran from her wrists to just below her shoulders, ranging from nearly invisible specks to one swath as wide as her hand.

Oh, great Infinite, she would give anything to wash those marks off as easily as she could the river mud. But nothing— not the healer's lotion made from rat-snake venom, nor years of hard scrubbing, changed those stains a whit.

She yanked on a long-sleeved shirt and was just pulling on fresh leggings when Jal's voice drifted through the blanket.

karen sandler

"So, what happened with that high-status boy?"
"Nothing. He just asked if you were okay."
"He was smiling at you."
A hot flush rose in Kayla's face. "He wasn't!"
Jal guffawed. "I saw him. I was watching from behind the kel-grain warehouse."
"You were supposed to run home!"
"I did. After I saw you making eyes at him."
"I was not!" She yanked aside the blanket, tearing it from the first few rings that suspended it from the ceiling. Another task before Tala got home—stitch the torn blanket.

Jal just grinned at her, unrepentant. He knew she couldn't pummel him like she wanted to. With the strength in her hands, she'd likely kill him. And she couldn't complain to Tala about his teasing since she'd have to admit to a forbidden conversation with a trueborn.

She threw her pile of filthy clothes at him instead. "Put these in the wash. I'll take care of that scratch when you're done."

By the time Jal got back from the warren's communal washroom, Kayla had recovered her patience. She doctored up the scratch across Jal's tattoo as best she could, fairly certain they could rely on GEN disease resistance to keep infection away. As much time as Jal spent slogging through the Chadi, she couldn't remember the last time he'd gotten sick.

When Tala asked about the scratch a few hours later, Jal spun his tale of a clumsy fall. Tala didn't give a quarter-dhan's credence to Jal's story, but she didn't press for the truth. Kayla felt only the slightest twinge of guilt—there had really been nothing to their mishap down at the river. Why needlessly worry Tala?

Nevertheless, Kayla couldn't quite squelch the fear that there would be repercussions from the encounter with the rock-throwing trueborns. What if the GEN Monitoring Grid tracked down her and Jal? What if they were somehow found at fault in the altercation?

But over the next few days, no Brigade boots came stomping up to their third-floor flat in the twenty-ninth warren. No cruel hands dragged her and Jal away to be reset and realigned.

Only Assignment day loomed like a dark monster on the horizon as the last ten days of Kayla's freedom ticked away. Her old nightmares revisited Kayla too. Every night the evil dreams visited her, filled with strange images swirled in blackness—herself as a baby looking up at a woman's face that wasn't Tala's. Strangers coming for her, carrying her off as she screamed and cried for her mother.

Someone *would* be coming for her in a few days. Brigade enforcers would arrive on her doorstep the morning after her fifteenth birthday. But not to carry her off—they'd be escorting a trueborn Assignment specialist who would bring Kayla's orders, her Assignment in a trueborn sector. She would be expected to leave Tala's flat immediately after.

She knew it was the Infinite's will, that a GEN's trial of servitude was the only way back to His hands. Even still, she prayed nightly to be spared, whispering into the shiny metal surface of her prayer mirror so her pleas would be better reflected up to the Creator of the creators.

When she wasn't preoccupied with Assignment day, her waking daydreams preyed on her. Devak's face intruded every time she let her mind wander, like when she was earning a few quarter-dhans toting the neighbors' rubbish to the slag heap or shifting sacks of fibermix from storage to building sites. He was always smiling, sometimes kindly as he had that day, sometimes arrogantly, sometimes with a sneer like Livot and his fat friend. She would delete Devak from her brain one moment and the next he would pop up again, with his smug, trueborn grin.

When she couldn't wipe Devak from her mind any other way, she'd focus her thoughts on her looming Assignment and let those fears drown Devak's face. She'd let the almost suffocating sense of doom smother her impossible, ridiculous crush on the trueborn boy. She would stomp out those silly emotions by thinking only of Assignment day, the way it would yank her from everything she knew and fling her into the unknowns of the trueborn world.

But no matter what she did, Devak was always still there, just on the edges, that broad, trueborn smile taunting her.

# 3

## three weeks ago

**M**ishalla of Chadi sector, nurture daughter of Shem and Rachel, made her way through the lowborn crèche, wiping a runny nose here, retrieving a dropped blankie there and returning it to a sobbing first-year. Infant Tarita snuggled in a sling, a warm weight against Mishalla's side. Second-year Cas all but hung from her skirt, always-ready tears brimming in his eyes.

As she bent to hook an arm around Cas, Mishalla wished, not for the first time, that she had the strength of her forever friend Kayla. If she had Kayla's sket, Mishalla would be able to carry four in each arm and two more strapped in slings over her shoulders. Gene-splicers ought to create nurturers that way, instead of the stupid way they made her—plump and weak with a crooked leg and ridiculous red hair.

She'd always known she was slated to be a nurture mother. She'd had that drilled into her in Doctrine school and by her own nurture parents for as long as she could remember. She'd started care-giving duties the moment she turned ten, had learned far more than she wanted to about diaper changes, baby bathing, and bottle feeding.

But all that training was nothing like the real thing. She'd only been here a week, but already she felt overwhelmed. Six lowborn children in her care, from baby Tarita to third-year Wani. They'd been with her night and day, playing, eating, and crying here in the playroom, sleeping, wetting, and crying in cribs and beds in the adjacent sleeproom. She'd yet to see any of the parents. Pia Lanton, the trueborn from Social Benevolence who supervised this crèche, hadn't shown her face since Mishalla's first day.

If Pia intended to give Mishalla her Restday off as the Humane Treatment Edicts required, she hadn't done it yet. Mishalla's only respite was those few hours in her own sleeproom, when all the children slept, when cranky babies or toddlers weren't screaming for Mishalla to comfort them.

Nothing about her Assignment was as she'd expected. On Assignment day, she'd been Assigned to a crèche in Skyloft sector. But as she waited at the pub-trans station, Juka, a taciturn female Brigade enforcer, yanked Mishalla from the platform. Without warning, Juka pressed a datapod to Mishalla's tattoo, zapping her instantly into unconsciousness. Mishalla came to herself hours later just as the pub-trans pulled up to a warehouse district.

She knew immediately she wasn't in Skyloft. In early spring, Skyloft—far to the northeast of Svarga continent— would still be under a few inches of snow. But Mishalla had stepped off the pub-trans to morning coolness, not icy cold, the mystery sector's climate much like Chadi's. So, not Skyloft, but based on the hours that her internal clock told her had passed, still distant from her home. Maybe she had been sent directly east, toward the Wall, or directly west—was she near the sea? She could have told Juka she would have traveled as willingly awake as unconscious, but maybe that was the way GENs always started their Assignments. What did it matter? Awake or unconscious, they'd still have brought her here and thrown her in with six needy lowborn children, with no adult company except the lowborn woman who brought the meals. What did it matter if she didn't know where she was?

Tarita snored gently in her sling and Cas was nearly asleep on his feet. Bedtime at last. Cas and Wani's turns for baths tonight. The others would make do with a tidying up using sanitizing cloths. With one eye on the rest of her charges, she washed the two lowborn boys in the sink in the corner of the playroom. She'd abandoned the gloves from her Assignment kit after the second day—far too slippery to keep a good grip on the babies.

She'd been scared to death that first time she touched a lowborn bare-handed. Depending on what story you believed, GENs touching non-GENs would turn a lowborn's or trueborn's skin black. Or, diseases that non-humans were immune to might boomerang back from the human and kill a GEN who touched one. Or the skin might just peel off the GEN's hands, then her arms, until her entire body was raw meat.

Of course, none of that had happened. Maybe because it didn't work the same with lowborns as it would if she touched a trueborn. Or maybe the stories were all lies.

In any case, her biggest risk was if her trueborn supervisor, Pia, witnessed her washing the babies without gloves. Pia could have her arrested, and maybe realigned. If that happened they'd probably program her to be stupid enough to believe all the crazy stories.

Baths done, she pulled on their pajamas, corralled the toddlers, and toted them to beds and cribs. A bottle for Tarita, a special stuffed seycat for Wani. An hour later, all of them were blissfully asleep.

She went to her sleeproom, her sanctuary, and shut the door. The netcam on the wall would let her know if the baby screamed or Wani called for her. She hadn't made it through a night yet without interruption.

Dropping onto the lumpy bed, she drew her knees to her chest as far as her bad leg would let her. Her right thigh bone throbbed with its usual rhythmic ache, more noticeable now that she was idle. She gritted her teeth against the pain.

She wouldn't let herself cry—she didn't think she'd be able to stop. Instead, she rubbed her leg and let in memories of home, the images playing in front of her closed eyes like a sekai video. Her nurture mother's smile, her younger sibs' silly jokes, the secrets she and Kayla whispered late at night. All of them hundreds of kilometers away, impossibly out of reach even if Pia were to give her a Restday and a travel pass.

She ought to get up, use the washroom, and change into her sleep dress. But the bed—lumpy as it was—and the quiet were irresistibly soothing. She drifted off into a light doze, then fell deeper into dreamless sleep.

Pounding on the door brought her instantly awake and staggering to her feet. The illuminator in her room had timed out and she barked her shin on the small dresser beside the bed. She palmed the light on and stumbled from her sleeproom, her thigh muscle choosing that moment to freeze up.

# tankborn

The crèche door swung open and Pia bustled in, her emerald bali glittering in the low light of the playroom. Behind Pia, the female enforcer, Juka, lingered in the doorway. It was still full night outside, the wee hours according to Mishalla's internal clock.

"What are you—"

Mishalla cut off the question before she'd fully voiced it, then held her breath in anticipation of Pia's reprimand. But the diminutive trueborn just pushed past Mishalla, heading straight for the children's sleeproom.

Juka stared at Mishalla, the enforcer's hand resting lightly on the shockgun on her hip. Mishalla dropped her gaze, standing as motionless as she could, pain lancing her leg.

From the children's sleeproom, a whine escalated to full throated sobs, then Pia emerged with Wani in her arms. The sturdy little boy writhed and fought the trueborn's grip, all the while screaming at the top of his lungs. The noise had awakened the other children and they cried as well.

The boy's terror broke her heart. Mishalla couldn't help herself. "Where are you taking him?" she shouted over Wani's cries.

"To his family," Pia said, nearly to the door. The enforcer shifted out of Pia's way so the woman could pass through. Wani, still fighting, dropped his stuffed seycat.

Mishalla scooped it up. "He needs this—" The door shut in her face. Wani's screams, barely audible through the door, faded into silence.

Stunned, it took Mishalla a moment to remember the crying children. She hurried into the sleeproom, going from bed to crib, soothing, shushing, comforting. Cas and Wani

**21**

had been attached at the hip and he took the absence of his friend the hardest. It seemed to take forever for him to fall asleep again.

Back in the playroom, she tucked Wani's seycat into the crate with the other soft toys. Her throat felt so tight, she couldn't breathe. She desperately needed some air.

She eyed the door. No one had said she couldn't step outside. The children were well asleep. It wasn't as if she could go far, not with the Grid monitoring her movements.

She crossed the room, slowly turned the door latch. Opened the door to the cool night air. Took a tentative step over the threshold.

Where was she? Even if it didn't matter, she wanted to know. Wanted to see clearly in her mind how many sectors divided her from Chadi, from Kayla.

A quick look around told her the warehouse district was empty this time of night. She moved a little farther from the crèche, looking down the long row of buildings. Between the moons' illumination and the streetlights, she might be able to see a sign on one of the warehouses.

She sidled even farther down, keeping the crèche in view out of the corner of her eye. The building next door was unmarked, but she spied lettering on the next one over. *Plasscine Extrusion Factory*, it said, and written just below, *Sheysa Sector.*

She stared, shock running through her. She was in Sheysa. Only one sector over from Chadi. Not a thousand kilometers, but a mere fifty from Kayla.

# 4

## present day

On the last week before her birthday, Kayla's monthly courses started with a vengeance. After finding her hunched over herself in bed, Tala let Kayla stay home from Doctrine school with a radiating pad on her stomach, Infinite be praised. The whispers from the other, younger students about Kayla's impending Assignment day would have been added misery to the pain in her belly.

With each cramp, Kayla's dark mood only grew blacker. She ranted in her mind—bad enough the gene-splicers had genned her so awkward, with her mismatched strength and ugly splotched arms. Why did her monthly courses have to be so uncomfortable? And why did GEN girls have them at all when they had only part of a uterus and couldn't conceive?

She dozed, then woke to find Tala sitting beside her on the bed. "How are you feeling?"

"Better," Kayla lied. No use worrying Tala when there was nothing her nurture mother could do. Medics didn't waste painkillers on anything so trivial as a GEN girl's monthly curse.

Tala tucked a strand of Kayla's unruly hair behind her ear. "Your last days here, you should be spending them with your friends, not in bed."

Kayla made a non-committal *hmm*. The only friend she truly missed was Mishalla. "I'll be better tomorrow. I'll see them then."

Tala smoothed the pad across Kayla's belly. Kayla's eyes closed at the warm comfort. "Skal came looking for you," Tala said.

Kayla's eyes snapped open again. "What did he want?"

Skal was Mishalla's former nurture brother. Kayla had been sweet on him once, when she'd been a thirteenth-year and spent more time at Mishalla's flat than her own. Then came Skal's Assignment day when he marched proudly down Liku Street in his Brigade uniform. All those sweet feelings had turned to ash in an instant.

"He wanted to give you something. He'd been to the school, then came here." Tala's brow furrowed. "You and he aren't—"

"No," Kayla said, horror at the idea washing over her. "Absolutely not."

"You could tell me if you felt something for him."

"I don't. Not the slightest bit."

Tala sighed, relaxing. "That's good, then. I know the Infinite has a plan for every GEN, but an enforcer . . ."

Guilt tugged at Kayla and she found herself feeling bad for Skal. He couldn't help the part the Infinite had given to him, how the trueborns Assigned him. But how would a GEN enforcer ever find a partner to join with?

For that matter, who would look twice at a misfit like her? She was fated to live her life alone as surely as Skal.

# tankborn

The next day at Doctrine school, Miva and Beela, Infinite bless them, stayed glued to Kayla's side. Kayla pretended not to hear the whispers from the thirteenth- and fourteenth-years, closed her ears to the speculation about her Assignment. They all had the same terror waiting for them, but she supposed gossiping about someone else eased their own fears. Kayla had done the same thing when she'd been a thirteenth-year.

She kept her focus on preparing for her Assignment, memorizing the histories and names of high-status families, testing herself so she could discriminate between a demi-status trueborn and a minor-status trueborn. The bali earrings were the surest way, but if a woman's hair covered it or a man's head was turned away, she'd have to make an educated guess. A minor-status might be flattered at the promotion to demi, but demoting a higher status trueborn could bring her a beating at the least, and a reset at the worst.

So she studied the skin color charts on one of the Doctrine school's ancient sekai readers. Darker color was better, but only to a point. Devak's skin was perfect—there he was again, intruding on her thoughts—but more than a few tones in either direction could mean demi. Someone as dark as Jal would certainly be minor-status if they were trueborn at all—more likely they'd be lowborn. And too-light skin would bump a trueborn into minor-status as well unless, like Livot's family apparently had, they'd bought their way into a demi status.

Even having it drilled into her from her first days of Doctrine school, the subtleties of the rules made her head spin. It all had to do with how they'd started on Loka, the richest taking the top of the pile, all of them the same lovely color as Devak—she pushed him out of her mind again—then that middle group that eventually settled into demi and the rest into minor-status. The lowborns had been in servitude from the start, so they were easy to understand, although a few of them had close to that cherished skin color, the sekai said. So one had to be careful and look at how they dressed if you couldn't see their bali.

The non-humans were at the bottom of the pile, of course. She smoothed the long sleeves of her shirt over her wrists and regarded her own skin. Even ignoring the repulsive blots on her arms, no one would mistake her as anything but a GEN. Her skin was thankfully not as worm white as Livot's, but it was nowhere near Devak's perfect color—blast the boy, there he was again.

All while she was growing up, Tala told Kayla she was pretty. But Kayla knew better and had years of torment by her Doctrine schoolmates to back her up. Older girls, thankfully long gone on their own Assignments, beautiful with near high-status skin color, had educated Kayla on her lowly place, even in GEN society.

It wasn't just her skin color, or her wild frizzy hair. The older girls would gossip and speculate about what animal DNA had been used for Kayla's strength sket and what had been mixed in to make the ugly marks on her arms. GENs never knew for certain what had been mixed into their genetic makeup, but that didn't stop them from guessing.

The older GEN girls would brag that feline DNA had been used to give them their sleek grace. Even Earth horses, with their speed and nobility, were preferable to what they assumed had been woven with Kayla's DNA. She's part elephant, they'd whisper. And that hair, the skin on her arms, the way she can't walk straight without tripping—drom, for sure.

It hurt so much hearing their mean talk. But how could she defend herself? They were probably right.

Giving her sleeve another tug down, she bent her head to the skin color chart again.

❧

On Thirdday afternoon, while Kayla and Tala were assessing the sad state of their kel-grain stores and Jal was out with his pack, Social Benevolence arrived with a welcome delivery—a fresh-from-the-tank nurture son. Louder and scrawnier than Kayla remembered Jal being at that tender age, the infant had gray eyes like Kayla's, but a fluff of blond hair on his head and more creamy skin.

"Looks stronger than Liya," Kayla commented, watching a relieved Tala feed the feisty baby boy.

Poor doomed Liya had died of a fever only weeks after SB had delivered her. Strange enough that Liya's GEN resistance hadn't fought off the illness. Odder still that it took five years for Tala to receive another child to nurture.

"Why don't they bring you babies as often anymore?" Kayla ran her palm over the infant's pale, downy hair. "Cheln and Nak were only two years apart, and Cheln was only three years older than me."

"Don't know," Tala said. "I kept expecting a replacement for Liya. Maybe the gene-splicers have been genning too many nurturers."

"Trueborns make mistakes?" Kayla said sarcastically. "That never happens." Except when they messed up the prophets' instructions and made ugly, awkward her.

They soon discovered the pale-haired GEN baby had two volumes—loud and louder. After a couple days of his squalling, he had everyone frazzled, even easy-tempered Tala. Her nurturer ears, genned to be hyper-sensitive, had to be hurting from the noise.

As Kayla and Jal and Tala sat down for dinner, Jal had to nearly scream the dinner prayer over the boy's latest temper tantrum. "Infinite bless this food. We thank you for our safe deliverance from Earth to Loka." Only a microsecond passed between Jal's amen and his first mouthful of kel-grain.

Kayla took a more decorous bite, shouting over the baby's noise, "Did they tell you what his sket is?"

"Not yet," Tala yelled as she shook the baby's bottle to activate the warmer. "They'll upload the rest of his information next week."

"Why make you wait?" Kayla shouted. "They programmed the sket in the gen-tank. It's not as if it's a big surprise when they pull the baby out."

Tala plunked the bottle into the baby's mouth and the infant fell blessedly quiet. "It doesn't matter much what his sket is. Not until he's older."

"Even still, if you know, you can prepare," Kayla said. "Like hide everything you don't want taken apart."

"Hey!" Jal protested. "I mostly put them back together."

Jal had been genned for a genius level of mechanical and electronics skill. The moment he could walk, Tala had to chase him down every waking moment to keep him from disassembling the solar oven or the living room furniture.

Jal scooped up another generous serving of kel-grain

from the bowl, muttering under his breath, "Pouli, Cohn, and Gupta, that baby's loud."

Apparently the baby's shrieking hadn't affected Tala's hyper-hearing. She rapped Jal's knuckles with her spoon. "Don't take the prophets' names in vain."

Jal sucked a couple kernels of kel-grain from the back of his hand. "I think that baby's sket is screaming."

"You were just as noisy," Kayla told him.

"I might have taken things apart," Jal said, shoveling in more kel-grain, "but I didn't smash them to bits like Kayla did."

"She couldn't help it, Jal," Tala said, serene as always.

Well, most of the time Kayla couldn't. When she'd had a baby-sized brain with super-genned strength, she'd left a trail of destruction. That had been Kayla's theory of why her first nurture mother didn't want her.

But later, it wasn't always an accident when her over-powerful hands ruined Tala's things. She'd once or twice broken something out of anger, then pretended she hadn't meant to.

She gnawed on a twinge of guilt as she chewed a bite of protein, the extravagance courtesy of the dhans the baby brought Tala. "There are other GENs who are as strong as me. Stronger even. But they're different. They're not . . ."

"Clumsy?" Jal offered. "Tripping over their own two feet all the time?"

Kayla speared him with a narrow-eyed glare. "They're not mismatched. They don't have . . ." She shoved up one sleeve briefly.

"You're still coming into your own," Tala said.

"I think one of the prophets stuttered when he dictated your specs," Jal said, snickering. "Or the gene-splicer was daydreaming about his high-status trueborn love and he botched your programming."

"Jal!" Tala's stern warning startled a whimper from the baby. Shamefaced, Jal bent his head to his kel-grain.

Tala raised the baby to her shoulder to burp him. "I've heard this new Assignment specialist for Chadi sector likes to place younger GENs near their home warren for their first Assignment. Maybe you'll be assigned to a job in Foresthill."

"Maybe." She shrugged as if it didn't matter. And a year ago, it hadn't. The thought of being far away seemed exciting. She never would have wanted an Assignment in Foresthill, the trueborn sector right across the river from Chadi.

But with Assignment day so close, Foresthill didn't sound so bad. Living that near, she'd be able to visit Miva and Beela every week on Restdays, at least until they were Assigned. And she could see Tala and Jal too.

What if they Assigned her to distant Skyloft, or one of its neighboring sectors? That wouldn't be so bad. She remembered the name of the crèche in Skyloft where Mishalla had been Assigned. On her first Restday, Kayla could take pub-trans to Mishalla's crèche, walk right in, and surprise her friend.

But there was no way of knowing. Kayla could just as easily be placed in Belk sector, where the plassfiber mines could use someone with her strength. Belk was so remote, she'd never see any of them again—not Mishalla or Miva or Beela, not Tala or Jal.

At that thought, the protein and kel-grain Kayla had eaten sat like a rock in her stomach. A sick fear filled her, a terror just like what she'd seen in Mishalla's eyes a month ago, the day Kayla's one true friend had said goodbye.

# tankborn

Mishalla had been genned to be a nurturer like Tala. She'd hoped to be Assigned to nurture GENs in Chadi sector. Instead, Mishalla had been sent a thousand kilometers away to be a caretaker in a lowborn crèche. Since GENs weren't permitted the use of wristlinks or networked sekais or precious paper to send a note, Kayla had no way of knowing how her friend was doing since she left.

Jal guzzled his glass of soy, then swiped at his face with the back of his hand. "If you *are* Assigned in Foresthill, and you can come back on Restdays, I want to hear everything about the tech."

Kayla waved her fork at Jal. "The trueborns I work for won't let me anywhere near their tech."

Undeterred, Jal plowed on. "In specialized Doctrine, they've told me about these micro DNA detectors in trueborn bali earrings, but I want to know about the prevention code that keeps a minor-status from wearing a high-status diamond. And the holo houses—do the façades feel solid or are they just scattered light projections?"

Kayla had to laugh. "Do you really think I'd know the difference? You're the one with the electronics sket."

With one gulp, Jal inhaled his mouthful of protein. "Excused?" he asked Tala. "Gotta meet Tanti."

Tanti was even more manic about tech than Jal. The two of them made Kayla crazy with their constant chatter about deep-level circuits and raw-edge integration.

"Have you studied for the geo exam tomorrow?" Tala asked.

"What does it matter?" Jal protested. "A tech doesn't need to know geography."

"Trueborns could send a tech like you anywhere," Tala told

him. "You might be itinerant. You ought to know Skyloft sector is north and Belk south, if only to get on the right pub-trans."

With a mulish look, Jal tugged his sekai from his pocket. He and Tanti had been given readers a few years ago, antiquated models with the network function disabled like with all GEN sekais. Jal and Tanti had spent hundreds of fruitless hours trying to foil that block so they could secretly communicate with each other via the sekais.

"You help him, Kayla," Tala said, the baby snuggled against her neck.

Jal set the sekai on the table and opened a holo display of Svarga, Loka's only habitable continent. Maps had always enthralled Kayla, the contrast of colors from one sector to the next, the shape and texture of the continent itself. The towering Wall, a jagged line of mountains separating the livable sectors from the desolation of the Badlands. The gentler undulating hills in the center that rippled through Tef and Leisa sectors.

She traced her finger along the dark blue of the three great rivers, Plator, Chadi, Sheysa, and the slim lines of their tributaries. She imagined herself traveling along the rivers, visiting all one hundred six sectors, trueborn and GEN alike, from the Wall to Loka's great ocean.

She'd see for herself the vast fields of kel-grain in the northern territories, the endless rows of pale brown stalks rippling and bowing to the fierce northern winds. Then drift south to where the droms grazed, the over-sized genned droms towering over the smaller natives. And even though she shivered at the thought, she'd just once like to see the monstrous meter-tall bhimkay, Loka's largest spider, face to face.

And what if she could sail the ocean to Loka's other three

continents? Visit polar Virynand, earthquake-ridden Utul, and volcanic Peralor. But not as a GEN. Instead, she'd be invisible, floating like a ghost along land and water.

Jal gave her a poke. "Did I get them all?"

"What?"

"The Southwest Territory sectors." He huffed with impatience. "You weren't even listening." He reeled off the nineteen sector names again. She could see from his careless recital that he was using his bare brain to remember instead of his GEN annexed brain, something Kayla never could have done.

Even still, he only missed one. "Forgot Sona."

"Close enough." He launched into a recitation of the Central Western Territory—easier, since that was where they lived—then Northwestern, then the remaining two territories, moving clockwise around Svarga.

Hand hovering over his sekai, Jal looked toward Tala. "Enough?"

Tala patted the baby's back. "How many high-status trueborns in the Congress?"

Jal sighed loudly. "A hundred twenty."

"Demi-status?" Tala asked.

"Thirty-two. And eight minor-status trueborns," Jal added before Tala could ask.

"How many lowborns?" Kayla put in, just to tweak her nurture brother.

He rolled his eyes at her. "None."

Tala shifted the baby to her other shoulder. "Who represents the lowborns?"

"The CLW." At Tala's sharp look, Jal spelled it out. "The Committee for Lowborn Welfare. Enough?" he asked again.

Tala smiled. "Go." Jal snatched up his sekai, rocketing from the table and out the door.

With Jal gone and the baby asleep, silence fell like a blanket in Tala's small flat. Kayla looked around the kitchen where she'd eaten her meals for nearly eleven years, at the tiny living room beyond. The view of narrow Liku Street three stories below was so familiar to Kayla she could describe from memory every broken streetlight and pothole in the permacrete pavement.

There were just the two sleeprooms, the one Kayla shared with Jal, and Tala's, where she and the baby slept. The sleeproom windows overlooked the back of the seventeenth warren, where Mishalla had lived. She and Mishalla used to signal across the alley to each other from their sleeproom windows, making up their own language of hand signs.

Tala went to lay the baby down, then returned to the table. The silence seemed to press in, and Kayla's throat closed with apprehension.

She groped across the table for Tala's hand. "How many have you nurtured? Not including me and Jal?"

"Thirteen."

"Liya died."

"And another. He was two. A wasting sickness the healer couldn't cure."

"Why didn't the trueborn Medic come?"

Tala shrugged. "Adianca was busy in another warren."

One medic for all of Chadi. No wonder so many GENs used the incompetent GEN healers.

"I know they sent Nak up to do maintenance on the Colony ships," Kayla said. "And Cheln was Assigned to build trueborn houses on the coast. But that leaves nine sons and daughters. Where are they all?"

"There were two girls, close as trueborn sisters, who left not long before you arrived. Assigned together near the Wall— thank the Infinite, his prophets bless us. But too far away to ever return."

The towering Wall range slashed the Svarga continent just off center, split it in two. Its gentler western face spilled down into the livable river-crossed prairie and rolling hills of Kayla's fantasy. The eastern face loomed over the wind-scarred Badlands.

"The other seven . . . they were so long ago. All of them Assigned to Svarga's four corners, impossibly far to ever hope to see them again. I've been unlucky that way." Tala rubbed at her brow, as if she was trying to wipe away the memories.

Kayla wrapped her arms around herself. "I wish they'd Assign me in a GEN sector. I don't want to live with trueborns. I hate them."

Tala squeezed her hand. "The Creator of the creators made them for a reason. To test his plan, to make everything ready before placing GENs on Loka. To give him a conduit for our creation."

"Maybe he should have just wiped out the trueborns after creating us. Sent another plague like Geming and Abeni or a fever like Sheffold."

"You can't truly want that. To have them all killed. The prophets were trueborns."

"They should have been GENs," Kayla said, then her cheeks heated when Tala gasped at the sacrilege. Reluctantly, she said, "I'd keep a few gene-splicers to keep making GENs for the Infinite."

But then the face of the trueborn boy, Devak, floated up in her mind's eye yet again. She didn't want to consider him worth saving from her theoretical plague, but she supposed she could make an exception for him.

Shaking off the intrusion of the trueborn boy, her unease about Assignment day, Kayla finished clearing the table while Tala mixed bottles for the baby. Kayla was just drying her hands from washing the dishes when the familiar tread of heavy boots approached in the hall. A fist pounded on the door.

The Brigade! Just when she thought they were safe, they'd come for her and Jal after all.

Had Jal escaped, or had they grabbed him up outside? Should she squeeze out one of the sleeproom windows, scale down the emergency ladder? Or would an enforcer be waiting for her down in the alley?

Tala seemed unconcerned as she crossed the living room for the door, but then Tala didn't know what had happened at the river. "Tala, don't."

She looked at Kayla, her surprise clear. "It's the Brigade. We have to."

Panic swamped Kayla. If she ran, they'd only come down that much harder on Tala. She had to stay. And hope against hope that Jal escaped.

As the door opened, she recognized Skal and the air whooshed from her lungs in relief. They would never have sent a single GEN enforcer if they were scooping up Kayla and Jal for realignment.

Skal gestured with the black carrysak in his hands, its glitter matching his uniform. "I have your Assignment tack." He smiled at Kayla.

"Is that why you were looking for me the other day? You could have just left it with Tala."

His smile faltered for a moment, then it broadened. "I wanted to bring it myself. I know how exciting it is when Assignment day is just around the corner."

She grudgingly gave way so he could enter. "You say that as if it's something to look forward to."

"It is," Skal said, his expression serious. "You're starting your real life now. It's your chance to find your place. To be of service."

Of service to trueborns. And fulfilling the Infinite's plan, but this would not be her place, only where the trueborns wanted her to be. But there was no point in telling Skal that. "Did they say what my Assignment would be? Where?"

He waved off her concerns as if they were trivial, as if they shouldn't mean everything to her. "You'll find out when the specialist comes next week."

Leave it to straight-laced, rule-following Skal to stick to every letter of the Edicts. She'd get no advance warning from him.

Kayla took the carrysak from Skal and tossed it onto the end of the living room sofa. The red insignia of the Judicial Council glittered on the carrysak in the dimming light of early evening, an almost sinister glow.

"Oh!" Skal said, "almost forgot. I was asked to give you a preliminary data dump. Not your Assignment," he told her, anticipating her question. "They said it was some new set-up data, to make the Assignment installation easier." He brandished a datapod.

His gaze fixing on her right cheek, Skal flipped the datapod end over end. He seemed nervous, and cheery Skal was never nervous.

Hairs rose on the back of Kayla's neck. Mishalla had never mentioned anything like this. Of course, they'd spent most of their last moments wailing about how much they'd miss each other. Now Kayla wished she'd asked her friend a few pertinent questions, never mind how brief the time had been between when the specialist uploaded Mishalla's Assignment and when she'd had to leave.

Kayla resisted the urge to back away from Skal. "Do I have to?"

Skal hesitated, just an instant. "Of course you do. Council

ordered it." He lifted his hand a little closer to her cheek.

She turned her cheek away. "Will it hurt?"

Another blink of hesitation. "A little. Same as the Assignment upload. But this should be shorter. Since it's just set-up data." He held out the datapod. "May I?"

At her nod of agreement—did she really have a choice?—he pressed the datapod against her cheek. She could feel the slender extendibles snake out from the thumb-sized datapod, felt them match the pattern of her tattoo.

She tried to relax, but couldn't help but jump when the extendibles pierced her skin. She gasped at the first tiny jolt of electricity, flinched at the ready light's faint green glow. Embarrassed by her response, she was about to apologize when the header of the data spilled into her neurons and raced to her annexed brain.

*Do not react. Remain placid. Do not react.*

The message repeated, as if on a loop. How did she not react? She glanced at Tala in the kitchen taking stock of their remaining food stores, then over at Skal rocking from heel to toe as he waited for the datapod's ready light to switch off.

"It's not bothering you too much, is it?" Skal asked.

She shook her head, waiting for the loop to end and the delivery of the message body. Finally, it kicked in.

*Your help is required, Kayla 6982, nurture daughter of Tala.*

She took a breath, almost spoke before she remembered herself. She could feel data and programming pouring into her, incomprehensible numbers and letters.

Skal's brow furrowed and he leaned closer to the datapod. "I didn't think it would take this long. Maybe the indicator light is inoperative." He reached for the datapod as if to manually disengage it.

Kayla backed away. "It's almost finished."

*Your Assignment affords us an opportunity we must take. We have no other agent remaining to take on the task. There is a packet within your carrysak. You must conceal this packet on your person on Assignment day. It must not fall into trueborn hands.*

With that baffling warning, the data stream shut off. She felt the connection release a moment before she saw the ready light switch to red. The extendibles retreated back into the datapod and Skal caught it as it fell from her cheek. He zipped open a package of sterilizing cloths and held it out to her to take one.

She rubbed her tattoo with the cloth, wiping away pinpricks of blood. "Is that normal? To send an upload before Assignment day?"

"I wouldn't worry about it. It's just data. Nothing you have to be concerned with."

She shouldn't worry? When she'd been asked to transport contraband tech? And why her? She wasn't particularly clever. Her sket wouldn't help keep this thing safe.

The message had said, "no other agent remaining." Had some other GEN been used before? What had happened to him or her? Caught by the Brigade? Realigned? Exactly what could happen to her.

She bunched the sterilizing cloth in her hand. "Who asked you to bring it?"

He busied himself with tucking the datapod into a pouch on his belt. "Came through chain of command. Don't know where it originated."

She puzzled over the datapod's message. Had it been a

trueborn voice speaking in her mind? But a trueborn wouldn't need her help with anything. And she'd been warned to keep the packet out of trueborn hands. It couldn't be a GEN, could it? How could a GEN have laid hands on that kind of tech? A lowborn, maybe?

While Kayla worried over the possibilities, each one more frightening than the last, Tala returned to offer Skal refreshment. To Kayla's relief, he bowed out since he was still on duty. After he left, Tala activated the living room lights.

"Let's take a look at your tack," Tala said, reaching for the carrysak.

"Wait!" Kayla grabbed the carrysak before her nurture mother could open it. "I want to look first."

Turning her back on Tala, she released the carrysak's fasteners. As she carefully removed each neatly folded item of clothing and placed it on the sofa, she wondered if she should tell Tala what had been in the datapod upload. Instinct told her no, that it might place her nurture mother in danger. If Mishalla had gotten the same type of message, that could be exactly why she'd kept it to herself.

One last item, a pack of sanitary gloves, then Kayla got to the bottom of the carrysak. But there was no packet hidden inside. She felt the sides for pockets, shook it to see if there was something loose that couldn't be seen. There was nothing.

Feeling foolish, Kayla set aside the carrysak. Sending that message with the compatibility upload had probably been some trueborn idea of a joke. She'd be better off focusing on what was inside the carrysak, not what wasn't. If nothing else, the gloves and worksuits might help her figure out what her Assignment expected of her.

While Kayla had been emptying the carrysak, Tala had arranged the leggings, shirts and tunics on the sofa. They weren't new and were all far too big for her, but were in better condition than she was used to. Their bright colors stood out starkly against the dull worn cushions.

The two pair of shoes were serviceable black synth-leather and looked to be her size. She was accustomed to hand-me-downs—the sundries warehouse was full of cast-offs from GENs who'd out-grown them, or gone off on Assignment. These were far better, needing only a few minor repairs to make them wearable.

Tala smiled. "It looks like you'll be working in a house, with those sanitary gloves and delicate clothes. They can't intend to Assign you at the plassfiber mines."

She wasn't sure how she felt about that. In a house meant being in close quarters with trueborns. At the plassfiber mines, she'd be working with other GENs, excavating the vital ore from the foothills of the Wall Range. It was an important job, providing the plassfiber that the techs used to create everything from plasscine to plasscrete. Plassfiber was to Loka what petroleum had been to Earth—so much depended on it. Even as dirty and hard a job as it would be, she'd be proud to do it.

Kayla fingered the lightweight knit of the leggings, felt it catch on the rough skin of her hands. "Is this the kind of worksuit a house GEN wears in Foresthill sector?"

She tried to remember what some of the GEN girls Assigned in Foresthill had been wearing when they left. There wasn't so much piping on the shirt and the colors were more subdued.

A fist tightened in Kayla's chest as she remembered where

the GENs wearing this style had been Assigned. "It looks more like Far North." A trueborn sector on Svarga's northwest shore. Eleven hundred kilometers away, and at least that far from Skyloft, where they'd sent Mishalla.

She felt as if a hole had opened up inside her. No hope of ever seeing Mishalla again. Or Tala or Jal or even Miva.

Ignoring Tala's suggestion that she start the repairs on her worksuits, she repacked them all, then left Tala's flat and went outside into the cooling spring evening. Skal's visit had overwhelmed her. She wanted to enjoy some of her dwindling time in Chadi sector.

The few streetlights the trueborns had installed in response to the Humane Treatment Edicts of two decades ago made more shadows than illumination on Liku Street. But the dimness softened the pocked walls of the houses, blurred the graffiti, hid the grime and the cracks in the permacrete pavement. Her eyes burned with tears at the thought of leaving.

She spotted Jal and Tanti with their underage pack hanging out near a sweets stand. Miva and Beela stood well clear of the noisy underage boys. Kayla crossed the street, warmed by Miva and Beela's greetings.

Miva threw an arm across Kayla's shoulders. "We saw Skal with your tack."

Beela took her hand. "Any hint about your Assignment?"

*Far more hints than facts*, she thought. She longed to confide in Miva and Beela about the datapod upload, to ask if they'd ever heard of silly messages being embedded within the programming, but she felt too embarrassed to mention it. And if Tala could be placed in danger knowing about the message, certainly Miva and Beela could too.

So she told the other girls what she'd guessed about her destination. The empathy in Beela and Miva's faces brought Kayla close to tears again. She bit them back and out of reflex scanned the crowd for Jal.

A chill ran through her. A group of enforcers, Skal with them, was loitering beside the sweet stand. Jal, his skinny shoulders hunched with worry, had his eye on Tanti. The stout, pale-skinned GEN boy was bouncing with excitement, peppering an impatient Captain Ansgar with questions. The least sympathetic of all the trueborn enforcers in Chadi, Ansgar had some kind of tech in his hand—maybe a new model sekai reader or exotic datapod. Like a magnet to metal, Tanti's electronics sket had drawn him to the tech and wouldn't let go until he knew everything there was to know about the equipment.

Most of the trueborn Brigade enforcers knew Tanti and indulged him. But the ill-tempered sector captain would have no patience for Jal's friend's obsession.

Jal tore his gaze from Tanti long enough to find Kayla, his silent plea for help clear even from across the street. Her stomach in knots, Kayla hurried toward Tanti, her feet stumbling on the uneven pavement. That lost her time. Before she could get close enough to Tanti to pull him away from danger, he'd done the unthinkable. He put his hand on the captain's tech.

She heard the gasps from the surrounding GENs, could almost feel them suck in breath. Recovering his senses, Tanti snatched his hand back. But it was too late.

The black-gloved captain yanked hard on Tanti's wrist, throwing him off his feet. Then he bent, datapod in hand, reaching for the boy's cheek. Tanti's hands flew up to his face to stop the enforcer.

"No!" Jal shouted, throwing himself over Tanti. Rage burning in his eyes, Ansgar raised a booted foot to Jal's head.

Without thinking, Kayla slammed a hand in the captain's chest and shoved him clear of Jal. She hit the captain harder than she'd meant to and the trueborn all but flew backward into the gathered Brigade enforcers behind him. The force knocked loose his blue bali from his ear, the minor-status trueborn emblem clattering to the pavement.

As the other enforcers helped the captain to his feet and handed him back his bali, Kayla put herself between him and the boys. Ansgar would take them all now—her, Jal, and Tanti. Realign them all. She'd never wear those worksuits in her tack kit, never discover the source of that mysterious message. She would break Tala's heart.

As the captain's pale blue eyes burned with rage, Skal sidled up to him. "Captain Ansgar." The captain stiffened at a GEN's mouth so close to his ear, but he listened to what Skal whispered. The datapod still in his hand, Ansgar stretched his hand toward Kayla's cheek.

He shoved the datapod against her tattoo and pain stabbed her, made fiercer by his roughness. Panic pushed "Don't reset me!" from her throat as blackness closed in.

Then the darkness receded and she was back on the street. Ansgar was downloading his datapod to his sekai. His eyes narrowed at whatever he read there.

He lifted his gaze to Kayla. "Just got yourself a free ride, jik."

Kayla flinched at the epithet, then helped Jal to his feet. She reached for Tanti; the boy's fingertips were millimeters from hers.

Ansgar pushed her away with a gloved hand. Readjusting the datapod, he slapped it against Tanti's cheek. The boy's body jolted and he cried out. Beside Kayla, Jal moaned in horror.

Ansgar released the datapod, then barked out, "Get up." Eyes wide and unseeing, Tanti straightened his limbs mechanically and pushed himself to his feet.

"Tanti," Jal whispered to his lost friend. Tanti didn't answer. The datapod upload had reset Tanti's cognitive pathways, a first step before realignment.

Tanti wouldn't be going home to his nurture mother. Wouldn't play touch-tag with the other Liku Street underage boys, would never again talk endlessly with Jal about whether the 4.6 sekais were really superior to the 4.3. His soul was in the hands of the Infinite now, resting there with the prophets until the Creator of the creators found a new place for Tanti on Loka.

When he emerged from realignment, Tanti's body would host a different boy, with a different name, would be sent to a GEN sector far from Chadi. They'd preserve his electronics sket, of course; the trueborns weren't wasteful. But they'd likely suppress the enthusiasm that had been so key to Tanti.

"Infinite save him," Jal prayed, the words made harsh by tears.

But Tanti turned his back on Jal. Like a puppet, the boy fell in behind Ansgar, trailing the captain and the other enforcers as they marched off down Liku Street.

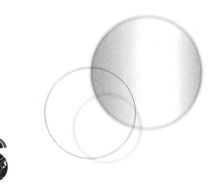

# 6

The crowd dispersed, as if the street no longer felt safe. Jal stayed rooted, watching as his friend marched away, muttering more prayers to the Infinite under his breath. When Tanti was finally out of sight, Jal started to shake, his teeth chattering. Kayla put an arm around him, trying to lend him some of her warmth as they crossed the street back to Tala's.

Tala had seen it all from the window. She pulled Kayla and Jal into her embrace, held them both closely for a long time. Then she sent the grief-stricken Jal to the communal washroom to clean up before bed.

"Infinite forgive me, but I'm so grateful they didn't take you too." She shook her head. "Poor Tanti. Poor Cika." Cika was Tanti's nurture mother.

Anger an acid stew inside her, Kayla mulled over what Ansgar had said. A free ride. Why? What had Skal told the captain? Did her "free ride" have something to do with the message?

Kayla readied herself for bed, then waited until she was sure Jal was asleep and Tala had gone to her room. She took the carrysak out to the living room and activated the small illuminator beside the flat's door. Moving the light to the floor, she sat cross-legged, then removed each and every item from the carrysak. She shook each one out, checked every fold and seam. She squeezed the pack of sanitary gloves for odd bulges inside. She found nothing.

Then she turned her attention to the carrysak itself. She ran her hands along the inside, seeking any small lump or bump she might have missed before. Then she lifted the carrysak and examined the outside.

Her heart leapt in her throat. There was an extra seam on the bottom. When she looked inside the carrysak again, she realized that the reinforcer at the bottom rested slightly above the top of the two seams.

Her hand shaking, she fitted her fingers underneath the edge of the reinforcer. It should have given way easily, but this one didn't budge. Kayla had to force her fingers under its edge and use a considerable amount of her augmented strength before she could pry the rectangle loose.

Someone must have used mag-connectors to hold it in place. That sent a shiver down her back. Whoever had sent this carrysak didn't intend for someone to remove the reinforcer by happenstance. They'd meant for someone like Kayla to pry it free.

She had to tip the black carrysak to the light to find the packet. Mag-connectors held it in place as well, and its black thin-steel wrapping made it difficult to see against the black carrysak. Kayla yanked the packet free from the bottom, then stared at it, wondering what she should do with it.

Putting aside that question for the moment, she returned

the reinforcer to the bottom of the carrysak and replaced the clothes. Then, with the packet in her hand, carrysak hooked over her shoulder, she rose and turned toward her sleeproom.

And nearly collided with Tala. "I thought I heard you out here," Tala said.

Of course Tala's nurturer-enhanced hearing wouldn't miss Kayla's clumsy steps. "I couldn't sleep. I thought I'd fix the tears in my worksuits."

Tala peered into Kayla's eyes. Kayla squirmed, wondering if her nurture mother could see the lie in her face.

But Tala just gave her a sad smile and cupped her hand on Kayla's tattooed cheek. "I'll miss you so much."

She drew Kayla into her arms. The carrysak slipped from her shoulder as Kayla hugged her nurture mother, but she gripped the small black packet tightly in her other hand. Mixed in with the fear that Tala would discover it, Kayla felt a tinge of guilt that she was hiding it.

Tala's eyes were wet as she drew away, which only made Kayla feel worse. She wanted to tell her nurture mother she'd be fine, but she was sure of nothing. She just gave Tala another hug, then said good night.

After Tala went back to bed, Kayla hurried to her room and stuffed the packet away in her pillow casing. Then she retrieved her carrysak and deactivated the living room light. In the black-as-night flat, she barked her shin on the table and caught a toe on the sleeproom door jamb. The noise roused Jal, but he only turned over in his bed before falling back into deep sleep. Kayla didn't take an easy breath until she found the packet safe in her pillow casing.

Activating the tiny reading light by her bed, she fished out her sewing kit and a scrap of fabric from her storage drawer that was a fair match for a pair of leggings from the carrysak. With awkward stitches—her strength made the delicate task of handling a needle difficult—she sewed the fabric into a rough pocket inside the waistband. Slipping the small black packet inside, she closed the pocket with two more stitches.

She started to stuff the sewing kit into the carrysak, but her glib lie to Tala nagged at her. Might as well make it into the truth. So she went methodically from one small tear to the next in each shirt, tunic, and pair of leggings. As bad as her stitches were, she had plenty of practice after years of well-worn cast-offs. If nothing else, she had a good eye for matching the thread so that her mistakes didn't show.

One last check to be certain she hadn't missed anything, then she folded everything back into the carrysak. After she deactivated the light, she stretched out under her covers. She spent a good hour wide awake, staring at the ceiling. Her fears kept popping up like sewer toads, lively and just as ugly—an Assignment on one of the uninhabitable continents, the Brigade discovering the packet, Ansgar taking her and Tala and Jal away to be realigned.

When sleep finally came, she wasn't visited by dreams so much as pummeled with incomprehensible images. Somewhere in those roiling visions, she heard a click, as if a switch had been thrown from noise to silence. The change brought her nearly to the surface of consciousness, but only briefly, before she dove again into slumber.

Assignment day morning, Kayla's nightmares gave way to crazy dreams—man-sized sewer toads, Devak smiling at her then transforming into an angry enforcer and screaming in her ear. When that voice morphed into Tala's, she finally registered that her nurture mother was shouting at her.

"Kayla! Wake up!"

Kayla's eyes felt gritty as she blinked up at Tala. A sense of doom settled on her in layers as she remembered what day it was and how soon her life would be wrenched away from her.

A mental check of her internal clock told her why Tala was so frantic. She'd slept right through her mental alarm and now had less than thirty minutes to ready herself for the specialist.

Grabbing up a shirt and the leggings with the secret pocket, she dashed to the communal washroom, her sleep dress flapping around her ankles. After using the toilet, she made a mess with the dry-bath crystals she had no time to clean up, then tamed her hair into a hasty, messy braid. She squirmed into her worn underthings, then pulled on the shirt and leggings. She could feel the scrape of the thinsteel edges of the packet as she cinched the leggings at her waist.

Kayla could barely eat the sweetened kel-grain and dried fruit Tala had made for her. She would have pushed it away, except this might well be the last meal she ate made by her nurture mother's hands. So Kayla choked down every bite.

She sat beside Tala on the sofa, holding her nurture mother's hand, reminding herself with each sharp intake of Tala's breath to relax her grip. The worksuit shirt was too loose, bagging in folds in her lap. The leggings pinched at the waist where the packet rested. She clutched the carrysak tightly to her side, the strap digging into her shoulder.

"Will I see Jal before I go?" Kayla asked. "Will he be back in time?" Jal had been sent to repair the temperature modulator for the chill case at the foodstores warehouse.

Tala patted Kayla's hand. "He'll try."

"That modulator's been giving the food managers trouble for months now. Why did they pick this morning to ask for Jal?"

Then it hit her—Jal's sudden, emergency task hadn't been accidental. Three years ago, on Cheln's Assignment day, a builder three streets over had had a pressing need to move sacks of permacrete fibermix from one building site to another. Only Kayla could do the job.

"Why don't they want us to say goodbye?" Kayla asked.

"It's easier," Tala said.

Kayla wanted to know for whom was it easier, but a fist pounded on the door. Holding her carrysak tight, Kayla got up to answer it before Tala could rise. This was her Assignment day. She would be the one to let the specialist in.

The trueborn specialist at Tala's door was small and medium-skinned, and Kayla felt a certain pride that she was able to judge the man a demi-status before she'd even seen his emerald bali. Then she saw the two Brigade enforcers flanking him and she fell back a step. One of the escorts was Captain Ansgar.

Ansgar stepped inside. "That's the jik sow who punched me."

The image of Tanti, lifeless and unseeing, formed in her mind and a hot retort sprang from her lips. "Not my fault you're fragile as a junk tree sapling."

Beyond stupid to talk back to him. Before she could put up a hand to protect herself, Ansgar backhanded her. She fell, smacking her head on the table, her cheek stinging. She waited for the boot next, wondering in her daze if he'd stomp her legs or kick her in the gut.

But as she struggled to sit up, the boot never fell. When her vision cleared, she saw the young specialist standing over her, his green demi-status bali winking as he scowled at Ansgar. "Leave her be, Captain."

"She needs discipline," Ansgar replied. "An insolent jik is a rank jik."

The specialist gave a huff of impatience. "Nevertheless, Director Manel won't want his GEN damaged."

Ansgar and his enforcer retreated to the doorway as Kayla stumbled to her feet. The specialist turned to Kayla and read from his sekai. "Kayla 6982 of Chadi sector, nurture daughter of Tala?"

She shook off the last of her muzziness to answer. "Yes."

"As authorized by the Judicial Council, I am here to deliver your Assignment. The Humane Treatment Edicts require that every Assignment be suitable for each GEN's programmed abilities. Do you understand?"

It was the standard recitation Kayla had been taught in Doctrine classes. When she'd asked, *What if it isn't suitable?* the GEN educators didn't have an answer.

No use arguing the point now, not when Ansgar was so eager with his fists. "I understand."

The specialist unclipped his datapod and pressed it to Kayla's tattoo. Although she was more prepared for the pain after Skal's visit yesterday and Ansgar's download on the street, her cheek was already tender from the captain's strike. She sucked in a breath at the needle-like stab as the datapod pierced her tattoo. The captain smirked at her reaction.

As the Assignment message streamed into Kayla's annexed brain, worry nagged at her. What if the datapod somehow detected what had been uploaded by Skal? Could the specialist find out about the packet?

The specter of Tanti and his reset loomed in her mind's eye. They might not just reset her, but Tala and Jal as well.

But the specialist seemed to see nothing amiss as her Assignment loaded. He confirmed the data stream verbally, reading aloud from his sekai. "You have been Assigned to provide elder care for high-status trueborn Zul Manel in the home of Ved and Rasia Manel in Foresthill sector."

Foresthill. She'd been Assigned in Foresthill after all. She listened with half an ear as the specialist reeled off the particulars—the paltry dhans she'd be credited, her housing and food rations. But she couldn't care less about any of that. What mattered was that she'd be a couple kilometers from Tala's house. Her family and her friends Miva and Beela wouldn't be lost to her after all.

She felt like crying, something she'd never do in front of these disapproving witnesses. Even worse, she felt an unwilling gratitude for the trueborns who had arranged her Assignment.

The specialist disengaged the datapod and clipped it back onto his belt. While he made notations on his sekai, Ansgar reached for Kayla's carrysak.

"New policy," the specialist told Kayla, still focused on his screen. "We check for contraband."

Kayla couldn't help herself—she gripped her carrysak even more snugly against her. "That's against the Edicts."

Kayla's objection didn't move the specialist. "Open to interpretation. The Judicial Council hasn't ruled on that yet."

Ansgar stripped the carrysak off Kayla's shoulder, the strap scraping her collarbone. It wasn't a search of her clothes she feared. It was what he might find at the bottom of the carrysak. The moment the captain discovered the mag-connectors, it would all be over. He'd know something had been concealed there.

And the next step would be oblivion.

7

Heat prickled over Kayla as Captain Ansgar tore open the carrysak's fasteners and dumped out the neatly folded clothes. Ansgar examined every square inch of Kayla's worksuits, crushing the fabric in his large hands to make certain there was nothing hidden inside. He scrutinized her prayer mirror as if seeking some hidden compartment in the thin metal rectangle. The packet at her waist dug into her skin; it felt as large as a play yard kickball.

Ansgar finished digging through her clothes, then turned his search to the carrysak itself. Here was the real danger. Kayla's throat closed. She couldn't breathe as he felt along its inner surface, then reached inside to pull out the bottom.

To Kayla's surprise, to her utter relief, the bottom released with no effort. The mag-connectors must have been programmed for only one use. Ansgar didn't notice the black connectors themselves on the background of the black reinforcer.

"What about what she's wearing?" Ansgar asked.

Fear made her rigid again. He knew it was there. The
bump the packet made was enormous, obvious to anyone with
eyes. She struggled to relax her features, but she was sure they'd
see something in her face.

The specialist looked up from his reader. "We'll leave
that for the medic." He gestured at Kayla. "You can put your
things away."

Tala bent to help her, shaking out the rumpled shirts
and leggings, folding them neatly again. As they worked,
Kayla's mind raced. How would she keep the medic from
seeing the packet?

As if her thoughts had conjured her, a fourth trueborn, a
dark-haired demi-status, hurried into Tala's flat. "Sorry, I had
to put down a jik and the denking sow wouldn't die."

Nausea knotted Kayla's stomach at the thought of Medic
Adianca's cruel hands on her. The medic despised her job
healing GENs; Kayla's careless scar on her shin and Miva's
crookedly knit bones from a broken arm were proof of that.

Adianca scanned the living room. "Do I examine her here?"

"Take her to a sleeproom," the specialist said. "Even GENs
deserve a little privacy."

Kayla felt weak with terror as she walked with the medic to
her sleeproom. Angling away from Adianca, she slipped a hand
under her waistband, fumbling with the rough stitches she'd
used to close the pocket.

As she passed through the sleeproom door, she said the
first thing that came to mind to distract the medic. "You know
I'm healthy. You don't need to examine me."

"Can't trust you jiks not to smuggle in contraband,"
Adianca said.

Kayla sat on the edge of the bed and bent to slip off her shoes. Her fingers still worked at the stitches. One came loose, then another. As she slipped off her second shoe, she forced two fingers into the pocket and pinched the packet between them. She drew it out.

It slid from her grip, falling between her feet. In a panic, she palmed it just as the medic picked up Kayla shoes and shook them out. With Adianca focused on the shoes, Kayla quickly stuffed the packet beneath her pillow, then stripped off her shirt and leggings.

"Undergarments too," the medic said as she gathered up the discarded worksuit.

As she took off her underthings, Kayla watched the medic scrutinize her leggings. Shivering on her bed, arms over her chest to hide herself, she waited for Adianca to find the pocket, to interrogate her about its purpose. But the medic's gaze passed right over it.

Kayla endured Adianca's exam, her cold, impatient touch. At least she was quick. And she looked away long enough as she put away her instruments to give Kayla a chance to snatch up the packet again. She didn't take a breath until she had it tucked away in her leggings again.

After Adianca declared Kayla fit for Assignment, she departed. The specialist followed soon after with one of the Brigade enforcers.

Captain Ansgar hung back. "I'm escorting you to the border."

"You won't touch her," Tala said. "We know our rights."

Ansgar looked as if he'd like to backhand Tala the way he had Kayla. If he had, Kayla would probably strike him, and that would be the end for all of them. But although he cast a dark look at Kayla's nurture mother, Ansgar kept his fists to himself.

Kayla hugged Tala goodbye, promising she'd see her and Jal on the next Restday, then grabbed her carrysak. Ansgar followed Kayla out the door. Down the stairs and out into the overcast morning. Along Liku Street, behind her a pace and to her right, looming over her like a cloud darker than the gray gloom overhead. Kayla felt the peril of his presence with each step she took.

They traveled the twists and alleys of Chadi sector's hodgepodge of warrens in silence, Ansgar's simmering anger Kayla's companion as surely as the trueborn himself was. Kayla had no doubt the captain was looking for a reason to hit her again, so she measured her steps perfectly to keep pace with him, never getting so much as a centimeter too close or too far.

She could feel the small packet with each step she took. It seemed to burn into her skin like fire and she was sure Ansgar could see it hidden in the secret pocket.

They reached the narrow path between the equipment stores warehouse and the Doctrine school play yard. Through the fence surrounding the play yard, Kayla could see the bridge that crossed the Chadi River and the lowborn shantytown beyond it.

"This is as far as I go," Ansgar growled. "But don't think I won't be tracking you. You put a foot wrong and I'll know about it."

Kayla started along the path, still feeling Ansgar's harsh gaze on her. She was nearly to the bridge when he shouted, "Stop!"

Her feet told her to run, but if he pulled his shockgun, its discharge would catch her before she got even as far as the bridge. A strike at a low power setting would drop her with a zing of pain shooting along her GEN neural circuits. At high power, the gun's discharge would stop her heart, sending her to the Infinite without spoiling her DNA. She knew the trueborn saying—kill the jik, save the meat.

So she turned and stood shaking while he strode toward her. His ice-blue eyes strafed her from head to toe. Then with a painful wrench, he stripped her carrysak from her shoulder again. He pawed through it, spilling her clothes onto the dirt. Her prayer mirror fell into a muddy puddle.

He seemed even angrier when he found nothing. He stared at her again, his gaze pausing at her waist, as if he'd guessed what she'd hidden there. This was it, she realized. He'd find the packet, tear it from her leggings. He might not even bother with a reset. As angry as he was, he might fell her with the shockgun here and now.

She wanted to close her eyes, but she forced herself to keep them open. And miracle of miracles, he threw her carrysak back into her arms. With another look of disgust, he turned on his heel and walked away. As he disappeared back into Chadi sector, Kayla's knees nearly gave way with relief.

Her hands trembling so badly she could barely use them, she gathered up her things and stuffed them back in the carrysak. She shook the water from her prayer mirror and used the inside hem of her shirt to clean it. Tears burned her eyes that Tala's tidy packing had been undone twice by the monstrous Ansgar. Blinking her eyes, Kayla forced the tears away and hurried across the bridge.

On the other side, she hid a moment in the chin-high prickle bushes to catch her breath. She had to check the route to the Manels' house. Ansgar had her so rattled, she could hardly remember how to access her annexed brain. That was where the specialist had stored her Assignment—in the annexed parts of her real brain that had been wired to her GEN circuitry.

Up until now, the only things in her annexed brain were stuff the gene-splicers had stored there in the tank. Her inner clock, a map of Chadi, images of the most poisonous Lokan arachnids. From now on, any time a trueborn felt like slapping a datapod to her cheek, they would have a free pass to add more to her annexed brain.

She focused, searching for the route. When she was little, a simple memory—one she'd experienced and remembered—would come to mind easily. But it was much harder to recall information from her annexed brain. It took years of practice to get to the point where she could retrieve simple memories from her bare brain and uploaded information from her annexed brain with equal ease.

But the datapod upload wasn't quite the same. The information wasn't just in one place. It was spread out in all those little-used parts of her brain that made up the annexed brain. She had to really concentrate to find it.

Finally, a map unfolded itself in her mind's eye, the route marked on it. The Manel home was on Priyatama Street, within walking distance. She wouldn't have to take pub-trans to get there.

Stepping clear of the spiny shrubs, she came into view of the lowborn shantytown that sprawled opposite the GEN school play yard.

She hung back, suddenly awkward about letting the

lowborns see her. She'd certainly spied on them hundreds of times growing up, her and Mishalla staring across the Chadi into trueborn Foresthill, enthralled by the lowborns living directly across from them.

Everything about the lowborns had fascinated her and Mishalla—the wild colors of the women's dresses and the men's shirts, their fights and screams of laughter, the noise of all those packed-in people. Adults and children alike, they always seemed happier than they ought to be, considering how poor they were.

It wasn't so long ago that lowborns were to the trueborns what the GENs were now. When Earth's climate finally collapsed under the weight of hurricane floods, seared by droughts and drowned by melting ice, not everyone could afford passage here. Lowborns bought their way to Loka with servitude. It wasn't until the GENs came along sixty-five years ago, when the Infinite shaped the first GEN souls and whispered the secret of creation to the prophets, that the lowborns were released from their debt.

So, why shouldn't they be happy? They were free. They might not have the status of a trueborn, but they were natural-born. Not something fermented in a tank.

They weren't tattooed, weren't Assigned, weren't monitored on the Grid like a GEN was. They could never be reset or realigned. They picked their own jobs and earned ten times the dhans a GEN would for the same work, even when they worked right alongside GENs.

And they were human. Their homes might be rundown and piecemeal, pushed to the ugly edges of trueborn territory, but they were born from a mother instead of a tank and no trueborn could change their humanity.

A lowborn boy dressed in only a diaper spotted Kayla as she lingered. He toddled toward her, giggling as his bare feet padded along the weedy dirt. Too young to know the difference between lowborn and GEN, he flung his chubby arms around Kayla's legs. She couldn't help herself—she laid her hand lightly on the boy's head, her fingers brushing the dark curls of his hair.

"Hello, sweet thing."

The boy laughed out loud, then shouted, "Up, up." While Kayla dithered over whether to walk the boy back to the lowborn settlement, a dark-haired woman poked her head out of the nearest shanty. The woman said something to someone inside, then as she left her shack, an enforcer emerged behind her.

Even though she'd left Ansgar in Chadi sector, Kayla felt a fleeting panic that the captain had followed her here. But as the enforcer moved toward her with a smile, following the lowborn woman, Kayla recognized him. It was Skal.

The lowborn woman shouted at the boy, "Shan, come away from there!" Skal dodged the lowborn child's toddling path back to his mother and continued toward Kayla.

"On your way, I see," Skal said as he reached her. "Time to be of service."

"It's not as if I had a choice. As if any of us do."

Skal's brow furrowed. She wondered sometimes if his loyalty to trueborns was due to more than his devotion to the liturgy. Maybe his fealty had been genned into him, just as Kayla's strength had been. Most GENs had doubts about their blessed servitude to the trueborns, but never Skal.

She tipped her head toward the shantytown. "Since when is the lowborn settlement part of your patrol?"

He beamed at her. "There's a new education program for the lowborns. I've been sent to assess the children, see who has the aptitude for some special classes."

"Are they assessing GENs, too?"

"Why would they need to? Gene-splicers create the aptitude in the gen-tanks."

"Just because I've been given a sket doesn't mean it's what I long to do."

"But that's why they give you the sket they do. Because the Infinite guides them to what you'd be happiest doing. Look at your nurture brother—Jal loves his tech."

"He does," Kayla allowed. But Jal had clever hands and a brilliant mind. Everything about him fit his Infinite-chosen sket.

Unlike Kayla's. It had never felt like a proper part of her. It was as if her strength had been patched into her body like that pocket had been stitched inside her leggings. It wasn't part of the original. She sometimes wondered if her true self was somewhere deep inside her, just waiting to be discovered.

But she probably never would. She suited the trueborns just fine the way she was. They wanted a GEN who could muscle around heavy objects, so they created her. What did it matter to them if she felt disconnected?

"Work will make you safe," Skal said. "Don't forget that."

How could she? That was probably the first thing they'd stored in her annexed brain. "I have to go. The Manels are expecting me."

"Wouldn't want to be late," he said cheerfully.

He was right about that. She'd only give them something to punish her for right at the outset.

She returned her attention to the programmed route. She

passed a row of warehouses, then the path intersected a thick green hedge at least triple her height. She could see nothing beyond the hedge.

She moved closer, felt the faint electronic buzz before she heard it. It seemed to vibrate along her bones, to shake her teeth. She extended a hand toward the hedge, reaching for a deep green leaf. To her astonishment, her fingers passed through the tangle of branches, vanishing in what she now realized was holographic laser light. Within the false thicket of branches and leaves, her fingers brushed against the smooth case of the holo projector set alongside the path.

Jal would want to know all about this. The way it looked, the way it prickled along her skin. She would tuck away her observations and share them with him on Restday.

Taking a breath, she stepped through the hedge, shutting her eyes out of fear the holo projection might damage them. When she opened them again, she stopped short, stunned into stillness by the riot of color. Trees so vivid green, they seemed to burn with emerald flame. Flowers in so many shades from pale pastels to brilliant primaries she couldn't possibly count them or take them all in.

She pushed herself to continue on where the path widened to a paved walkway, then met Priyatama Street. On either side of Priyatama were more wonders. Impossible houses— gorgeous castles decorated with flag-topped turrets and domes, garishly striped tents flapping in the breeze, palaces shimmering so brightly with gold and gems it hurt her eyes. The overcast of Chadi sector and the lowborn district had given way to a vivid blue-green sky in Foresthill, adding another layer to the confusion of color.

The crazy array of structures reminded her of the fairy stories she and Mishalla used to read as kids on the sekai readers at Doctrine school. They'd pore over the images embedded in the stories for hours until they drained the power, then sneak the reader back into their classroom and borrow another.

When the third house she passed—a fragile-seeming skeleton of black metal—transformed in a heartbeat to randomly piled blocks of white stone, Kayla stumbled on the walkway in surprise. Jal had explained about the holo houses. They were similar to the hedge, actually built of smooth-sided plasscrete walls. The holo-projected façades she'd seen were generated by electronics embedded in the plasscrete. But she hadn't expected the gaudiness of them, the fickle instant changes.

After seeing the hedge, she assumed the dazzling blues and reds and purples of the flowers in every yard and lining the streets were holo projections too. Yet as she brushed a hand across the top of a lavender and white flower-strewn bush along the walkway, the soft petals tickled her palm and perfume drifted up to her nose. She could feel the rough bark of the trees she grazed with her fingertips.

Her heart ached at so much color. She recognized some of the trees and bushes and flowers as Earth transplants—delicate, needy plants she'd read about in sekai stories. Coaxing that kind of beauty out of Loka's unforgiving soil and protecting it from the brutal twin suns took piles of dhans and the labor of countless GENs and lowborns.

Not something worth doing in Chadi or the other GEN sectors. There, clumps of Loka's native yellow scrub-flowers, prickle bushes, and hardscrabble blue chaff-heads forced their way through the barren earth and rock.

Lev-cars zipped by on Priyatama, a few compact Bullets like the one the trueborn Livot had been piloting, but most of them larger luxury-sized vehicles. The AirClouds and WindSpears—names she knew only from sekai stories— were fatter and taller than the Bullets, their rounded sides gleaming in cobalt or silver or blood-red. On some of them, the windscreen encompassed the entire top half, so she could see the trueborns inside as they passed.

A multi-lev pub-trans—as big as four AirClouds laid end to end—lumbered by, the upper compartment filled with lowborns, GEN passengers segregated in the lower level. The double-decker multi-lev towered over her as it glided by. It astounded her that something so enormous, loaded with so many people, could travel so easily.

The pub-trans pulled over to let off passengers, slowing traffic behind it. Three lev-cars back, a trueborn boy in the rear seat of a WindSpear mouthed *jik* when he spotted Kayla.

She stared him down, even as the boy made a rude gesture with his hand. Just before the car sped off around the pub-trans, the boy threw something from his window. The bottle clattered at Kayla's feet and splattered her leggings with the remains of the sticky fruit-meld that had been inside it.

So much for arriving clean and well turned out. Kayla gritted her teeth against her anger and focused instead on the programmed directions. The Manel house was just twenty or so meters ahead. She increased her pace, stopping when her programming told her she'd reached her destination.

A holo hedge had been installed around the front of the

house, blocking it from view. She slipped through the deep green projection and confronted a tall black metal gate, a fence of stone and metal stretching on either side. A touch told her that the fence and gate, at least, were real. She glanced behind her. From this side, the holo projection was transparent, giving the Manels a clear view of Priyatama Street.

The house was massive, but its holo façade was more modest than the others she'd seen along her way here. Two stories, white stone, fat columns holding up the cover on a wide porch. A half-dozen steps led up to the porch, intricate wood handrails on either side, each one finished with a globe carved like some exotic fruit. Broad windows overlooked the front garden and the street beyond the holo hedge.

Her stomach roiling, she opened the gate and stepped inside the garden. The weight of fear grew heavier as she moved up the walk that looked and felt like natural stone, not holo. She hesitated before starting up the stairs, remembering the insubstantial hedges. But there would be plasscrete structure under these faux wood steps. It would certainly hold her weight.

Kayla had nearly reached the top step when a woman swept from the house, her dress so heavily laden with gemstones, the hem sagged and scraped the porch. Her black hair was twisted in some kind of intricate design woven with gold and more gems. Her oversized diamond bali stretched her lobe with its weight.

There was something familiar about the woman's high cheekbones, the perfect high-status color of her skin. Kayla couldn't quite put together the pieces of where she'd seen that face before. Some wicked spell caster in a sekai story, maybe.

The woman plastered herself against the door, a glitter

of something strange sparking in her dark eyes. "Where are you going, jik?"

Kayla retreated a step. "I've been Assigned to care for Zul Manel, ma'am."

"You can't come in the front." Her gaze strafed Kayla. "Just like a jik. Your first day, couldn't even arrive tidy."

Infinite blast that trueborn boy. "Sorry, ma'am." Kayla backed up further, stumbling as she reached out for the railing to catch her balance. It should have been sturdy plasscine, the intricately scribed rail a holographic illusion. Instead it was actual, priceless wood, and her clumsy hand wrenched off one of the carved globes.

Horrified, she gaped at the piece of decoration. This would be the end of her, surely. She could see her doom in Mrs. Manel's rage-filled eyes.

The trueborn woman shook with her anger, and the clacking of the gemstones in her dress sounded to Kayla like the popping of a bhimkay's massive jointed legs as it stalked its prey. Kayla was sure that if not for the fear of dirtying her hands touching a GEN, Mrs. Manel would have struck her dead.

Kayla set the globe on the steps. "I'm sorry," she whispered.

"I told that old bastard we didn't need a GEN," the trueborn woman spat out. "Another lowborn could have done the job just as well. Can you follow directions, jik?"

The cruel epithet stinging, Kayla nodded.

"Go around to the back of the house. Use the red door," Mrs. Manel instructed. "Take the kitchen stairs. At the top, the old fool's room is the second one to your left."

She slammed the door, the windows rattling with the force. Kayla started around the front of the house, so numb with fear she barely noticed the soft green lawn, more extravagant beds of flowers. Everywhere Kayla looked there was careless, over-blown beauty.

*You could fit an entire warren on this parcel that houses only one family. A hundred GEN families could live in this broad green space.*

As she reached the back, with its garden even more lavishly planted with dazzling color, she spotted a tiny building well beyond the house. A shed, maybe, or small storehouse. A winding stone path cut through the dazzling green lawn between the shed and the house.

From a second story window, she felt the stare of someone watching. When she looked, a curtain dropped into place.

As she climbed the back porch stairs, Kayla saw a wide glass door to the left, the red door to her right. She stepped through the red door and into the kitchen, a huge space that could have fit Tala's entire flat.

A lowborn woman, working at the stove with her long black hair tied back under a scarf, cast Kayla an unfriendly look. "I suppose you're the GEN for Mr. Manel." Kayla dipped her head in a nod. "I'm Senia. I'm in charge here." She gestured with her hand, encompassing the kitchen, or maybe the entire house. "Stairs are there, just beyond the pantry."

As Kayla passed the pantry's open door, she caught a glimpse of shelves overflowing with bags of kel-grain and precious rice. Vac-seals filled with spices were piled beside the grains like fist-sized jewels—yellow saffron and rich brown cinnamon, pale-green cardamom and golden fenugreek. Beside the spices, more Earth-native fruits like processed peaches and kiwis, re-created by gene-splicers at extravagant cost.

She glanced back at Senia, saw the lowborn woman busy again at the stove, then slipped past the pantry to the living room beyond. She gasped at the opulence—the space was double Tala's entire flat, the front wall filled with windows nearly two stories high. Intricate brocade covered the sofa and float chairs, the fabric so exotic it had to be an Earth import. Scattered throughout the room were tables in a wood so dark it was nearly black. A pair of woven hangings covered the full six-meter height of the wall opposite the windows, their gorgeous colors glittering with gold threads.

Behind her, Senia snapped, "You'd do best to keep your eyes on your own business."

"Sorry," Kayla murmured, her third apology since her arrival.

She hurried toward the stairs, taking them two at a time. At the top, a short jog to the left, then a right turn into a hallway that traversed the width of the house. At the other end, the hall jogged right again.

There were three doors to her left along the hall. The stretch of wall to her right was decorated more plainly here out of the public eye; only a few family images hung there. The carpet was the dull beige of Loka dirt.

As she approached the second door, Kayla caught movement at the hall's far turning and heard the clacking of gems. When she turned, she caught the briefest glimpse of Mrs. Manel before the trueborn woman vanished around the corner.

Kayla rapped gently on the door. There was a pause, then a tired voice called, "Come in."

She slipped inside, looking cautiously around the room. The size of it surprised her—it wasn't much bigger than the living room in Tala's flat. There was clutter everywhere. Stacks of paper books, a rarity Kayla had never witnessed firsthand. Wind chimes fashioned with hanging bits of metal and plasscine made music in the breeze of her passing, globes of glass spun in gorgeous colors filled the dresser top. A lev-chair was tucked in one corner.

Zul Manel lay facing the wall in a bed barely larger than the one Kayla had slept in at Tala's flat. She couldn't see his diamond bali, but the long oval of his face, the blade of his nose, the sharp angle of his cheekbones made clear his high status. He looked so noble, he could be an ancient king.

But he was very old, his skin lined and seamed with age. A hundred and two, her upload told her. Since most GENs were recycled by the time they were fifty-fifth years and certainly before they reached sixty, Zul was by far the oldest person she'd ever seen.

The trueborn stirred, his hands coming up to rub his face. He looked as if she'd just roused him from sleeping, yet it was in his window she saw the curtain move. He lifted his shoulders from the bed, but his legs stayed inert. Up on one elbow, he smiled as he faced her fully. And she got her first shock, one that turned her mind upside down.

Zul Manel had a tattoo on his left cheek. The intricate pattern was drawn in black instead of GEN silver and the edges were fuzzier than the crisp swirls and sharp lines she wore on her own face. But it was a tattoo.

As she tried to absorb that impossibility, she heard the rattle of the door opening wider and a familiar voice calling out, "Pitamah?"

Her second shock walked into the room and sent her stumbling backward into a collection of wind chimes. It was Devak.

He GEN female stared at Devak, her gray eyes wide and wary, her body swallowed up in a garish turquoise shirt ten sizes too large for her. Devak remembered the shirt—a castoff from the stout lowborn house manager before Senia. Something dark and sticky-looking speckled the matching leggings, and the GEN female gave off a faint fruity aroma.

He shook himself from his fixation on her. "What's *she* doing here?"

Pitamah shot him a look of disapproval. "Is that any way to speak to a visitor?"

Devak's face heated with shame. An ugly part of him wanted to say, *Why do I have to be polite? She's only a GEN.* But he bit back those words, instead forcing out an apology. "Sorry, Pitamah."

"She's Jeramy's replacement. My new caregiver."

"I can take care of you, just like I have been," Devak said.

"You should be spending time with your Academy friends, not with an old man like me."

Devak didn't bother to tell his great-grandfather that he had lost all his friends, other than Junjie, who'd been true-blue since they were kids. After that day at the river, Livot and Cef had lost no time in broadcasting to everyone in their Academy network that Devak was a jik-lover. Now no one except Junjie would talk to him.

He'd only tried to do what was right, and look where it got him.

"She's just a female, and a tiny little thing at that. How can she possibly take care of you?"

But of course, Devak knew. That day by the river, she'd picked up her brother as if he weighed nothing. She'd have no trouble handling Pitamah's needs.

The old man reached out toward Kayla. "Help me sit up and we'll meet each other properly."

"I can do it," Devak said, taking a step farther into the room.

Pitamah waved him off. "I asked Kayla."

She unslung her carrysak from her shoulder. "Let me get out my gloves."

Now Pitamah flapped a hand at her. "You don't need gloves to help me sit."

"But I can't . . ." The GEN female stared at Pitamah's weathered hand. She hugged her carrysak to her.

Pitamah smiled, the faded tattoo on his cheek folding into the lines on his face. "You've never touched a trueborn, I'll wager. Except for cuffs and blows from the enforcers."

"Not even then," Kayla said. "They all wear gloves. The enforcers, when they discipline us. And the medics for examinations. They told me if I touched a trueborn—"

She looked over her shoulder at Devak. Her gray eyes

locked with his, her cheek darkening slightly around the edges of her DNA mark.

To his shock, he felt the same urge he'd had that day at the river. He wanted to reach out and brush his hand across her tattoo, see what it felt like. He kept his hands tightly to his sides as Kayla returned her attention to Pitamah.

She tipped up her chin. "It doesn't matter what I was told. This is my Assignment. If you say I don't need gloves . . ."

She dropped her carrysak to the floor and moved toward the bed. Devak thought she might flinch when her fingers wrapped around Pitamah's wrists, but he couldn't see the least reaction. She did the job of angling the long-boned old man up in the bed with much less effort than Devak, lifting him as easily as she had her brother.

While Pitamah leaned forward, propped on his hands, Kayla arranged pillows behind him. She hooked her hands under his arms to lift him up higher on the bed.

As he sagged against the pillows, he smiled up at Kayla. "Thank you."

His gratitude seemed to fluster her. "You're welcome," she responded.

Zul smoothed his rumpled white korta. "I'm Zul Manel, grandfather to Ved Manel and great-grandfather to this young man. Who it seems has already met you."

"And you know as well as I do where I met her," Devak said. "At the river, where you asked me to go collect chaff-heads."

They were still on display in the window sill, dry and scraggly, the water evaporated from the glass vase. The lowly blossoms seemed to fit the usual disorder of Pitamah's room. Just as well Devak's mother never came in here; she'd be horrified.

The GEN female dipped her head toward his great-grandfather. "I'm Kayla 6982 of Chadi sector, nurture daughter to Tala."

"A pleasure to meet you, Kayla," Zul said gravely. Then he lifted one dark brow at his great-grandson. "You may as well ask the question, Devak. We can all see it dancing around the room."

"When you sent me to the river, you knew she would be there," Devak said.

"How could I possibly?" Zul's expression was all innocence.

"Because I put you in your lev-chair that day, before I went to the warehouses. You could have gone into the monitoring room."

Zul tipped his head to one side. "But I'm not authorized."

"You're not authorized to tap into the overpass netcam system either."

It had been a guess, but Pitamah's smile gave Devak his answer. He'd bet half his adhikar grant that his great-grandfather had illegally routed a netcam feed to his sekai and spotted Livot's and Cef's mischief that way. Knowing Devak was at the warehouses nearby, Zul had called Devak's wristlink using his own.

Pitamah turned his smile to Kayla. "Did the specialist explain your duties?"

"The upload did. That I'm to feed you and . . ." Her light brown cheeks darkened again ever so slightly, an intriguing contrast to the metallic silver edges of her tattoo. "To dress you and bathe you. Take you to the washroom."

"No," Pitamah said. "Whatever they told you, you won't be attending to my personal care. Devak will continue to. An old man has some pride."

His great-grandfather's gnarled hands shifted on the bedclothes. "You'll help me in and out of the lev-chair. Devak might not complain, but it's been difficult and awkward for him. On my bad days, you will need to feed me." His mouth twisted at that necessity. "Keep me company, read to me when my eyes are weak."

He narrowed those eyes on Kayla. "I could fit five of you in that shirt. The cuffs are threadbare." He glanced down. "And what's that on the leggings?"

She squirmed and shrugged. "I kicked a fruit-meld bottle on my way here. Thought it was empty but it wasn't. It spilled on the leggings."

Pitamah peered at Kayla with the same intense look that had always peeled away Devak's lies and exposed the truth under them. But either the GEN female was telling the truth or she was immune to Pitamah's persuasion.

His great-grandfather's gaze softened. "I should have expected Senia would pull secondhand worksuits from the ragbag. No doubt she pocketed what I gave her." Pitamah flicked a hand at Devak. "You'll take us out tomorrow. We'll buy her proper clothes."

Devak tried to form an objection, but he came up empty. Kayla could help Pitamah in and out of the AirCloud, could guide his lev-chair down the towncenter walkways. But she wouldn't be allowed in the shops, and Pitamah might need Devak's help there. He would pray to the Creator that Livot and Cef and the others didn't choose that day to go idling in the towncenter shops.

Pitamah sagged more heavily against the pillows. "That's enough for now. Show Kayla her quarters." He snorted in disgust. "If you can call them that. Once she's settled, bring her back here."

Pitamah reached out, his arm trembling, seeking the sekai reader Devak had left on the bedside table. Devak had bought the reader for his great-grandfather's birthday, a slim, lightweight model easier for the old man to get his weak fingers around.

Pitamah fumbled, knocking the device to the floor. Out of habit, Devak stepped forward to retrieve it for him, but Kayla put her hand on it first. As she straightened, she bumped Devak ever so slightly, her shoulder against his arm. He jumped back and Kayla stumbled away, nearly falling against his great-grandfather's bed. That same flush darkened her cheek, outlining her tattoo.

"Sorry," she said, then turned her back to Devak to hand Pitamah his sekai.

The old man settled back against his pillows. "Thank you."

Kayla dipped her head in a nod. She retrieved her carrysak, keeping her gaze averted from Devak's as they left Pitamah's room.

As they descended the stairs, Devak's stomach lurched at the impropriety of that brief closeness. They hadn't really touched, not skin to skin like she had with Pitamah. But after a lifetime of lectures about keeping his distance from GENs, he'd come so close to crossing into the forbidden. His father had drilled into him that trueborns' superiority over GENs made contact with them inappropriate. His mother's whispered stories about what happened to trueborns who touched GENs bare-handed had terrified the denking hell out of him. Yet Pitamah's skin hadn't bubbled with blisters. His bones hadn't twisted.

But that didn't make his near miss with Kayla okay. His arm should be burning at that wrongness. Instead, a not-unpleasant tingle shivered along his skin from shoulder to fingers.

Senia, their lowborn cook, tracked Kayla as the GEN passed through her kitchen domain. Devak had seen Senia's ramshackle home in the riverside shantytown, knew that her life was just as mean as Kayla's. Yet Senia glared at the GEN female as if Kayla had to be watched to be sure she didn't steal one of the cooking pots from the hanging rack or a tempting piece of fresh sugarfruit from the bowl.

With a hard stare at Senia, Devak opened the red door, then stood aside to let Kayla pass through first. Kayla hung back, lowering her voice.

"I shouldn't go first." She tipped her head ever so slightly at Senia.

"What do I care what she thinks?" Devak said just as softly. "I'm the trueborn here, not her."

"I think she already hates me. Why make it worse?"

With a sigh of impatience, Devak pushed past her, close enough that the full sleeve of his korta brushed Kayla's arm. He glanced quickly at Senia, but Kayla's slim body had blocked the lowborn's view. Just as well—Senia would have told his mother. Still, a part of him wished the house manager had seen. Even worse, a part of him wished he could brush against Kayla again.

He shook off that illicit thought as he led Kayla across the veranda and down the steps. "Senia's brother wanted Jeramy's job. That's probably why she's unhappy with you. She'll get over it."

She followed behind him across the lawn, her footsteps

nearly silent on the stone pavers. "Why does your great-grandfather have a tattoo?"

Devak stopped abruptly, turning in sudden panic. "You're not to talk to anyone about it."

She retreated, barely keeping her balance as her foot slipped from paving stone to soft green grass. "I won't."

"It's not like yours. It's only on his skin."

"I could see that. It's only a little bit like mine."

"It's not at all like yours. It was something stupid he did when he was young, had himself tattooed. It doesn't mean anything."

"Fine. It means nothing." She flung up her hands. "I'm sorry I asked."

He took a step closer to her. "It's bad enough what trueborns say about that mark. They stare at him, laugh at him every time he goes out. I don't need to hear it from a meaningless GEN like you." The final words came out as ugly and harsh as if his mother herself had spat them out.

Defiance flashed in Kayla's gray eyes. "Forgive me, trueborn."

Shame flooded him. Even her being a GEN, his father would have ordered him to apologize. One expected that sort of rudeness from lowborns or GENs. A high-status trueborn like him was better than that. But to his utter disgrace he just turned away from her, continuing toward the structure that would be Kayla's quarters.

The cottage's roof was so low, he was afraid he'd bump his head on the overhang. Even diminutive Kayla would have to be careful not to bump her head where the roof sloped down. All the time Jeramy had lived here, Devak had never really noticed the inadequacy of the tiny structure—the paint peeling off the insubstantial plasscine walls, the castoff trash piled near the door that should have been toted to the incinerator. And there was no avoiding the rank smell from the house across the alley.

He supposed a lowborn like Jeramy or a GEN like Kayla wouldn't notice the shortcomings of their quarters. But shouldn't a trueborn do better for the lowborns and non-humans he was responsible for?

Devak opened the door. "Pitamah asked Senia to tidy up, so it should be clean."

But it wasn't. The mustiness hit him first, and he realized the door had probably been shut tight since old Jeramy passed. Then he saw the dust on the bedstead and mattress, the crud on the small table and chair. A tiny kitchen had been crammed into one corner of the shack, and bits of food still crusted the worktop and the stove's one heating element. He feared the refrigerated compartment would be just as filthy. Even if Kayla didn't notice the griminess, he should have made sure everything was in order.

She made a face. "What *is* that smell? Did the lowborn die here?"

"I don't know. I was away. They only told me about it later."

He squeezed past her into the shack, and stepped up on the narrow bed to reach the window. To the right outside the window, he could see the detached washroom; straight behind were the back fence and the alley.

He wrestled open the window. A big mistake. The stink got worse as it spilled in from the alley.

"That's awful." Kayla covered her mouth and nose with her hand.

"It's the neighbor across the way. A minor-status trueborn

who can't seem to keep his incinerator running properly."

Kayla waved a hand at him. "Close it, please."

He yanked it shut again. "Sorry."

She swung the door to fan sweeter air into the cottage. "I thought minor-status lived in their own sectors. Not right next door to high-status."

"They're still trueborns. It's not as if they're—"

He bit off the rest of what he'd been about to say, but she finished for him. "Not as if they're GENs," she said, her voice steady, her chin lifting slightly.

He remembered when he'd first seen her at the Chadi River, sitting on the bank, well above the nasty, smelly water. Spotless and tidy until she went to her brother's rescue, despite her well-worn clothes. She did know the difference between cleanliness and filth.

Shame washed over him again. He'd thought himself stamped from a different mold than his mother, that Pitamah's influence had improved him. Yet even though he hadn't said it out loud, he'd made it clear to her that he thought GENs were dirty and trueborns clean.

Evading her gaze, he sidled past her back to the doorway. "There were demis in there before, then the daughter married beneath her status. The parents were killed in a skyway accident, so the daughter and her minor-status husband live there now." Much to his mother's horror.

Kayla stared at him. "And their incinerator doesn't work because he's minor-status."

He felt that prickle of shame again. "Of course not. It's just that sometimes minor-status people, they don't . . ." He flung a hand up in frustration. "It really doesn't matter, does it? I'll get Senia, have her clean the cottage and get rid of that rubbish by the door."

As he took two steps toward the house, she called out, "Please, don't. I'll take care of it." She looked around her quarters, dismay clear in her face. "And you don't need to stay. I can find my own way back to your grandfather's room."

He'd just as soon leave, escape the awkwardness. But Pitamah had asked him to bring her back. And maybe he deserved a little humbling. "I'll wait." He propped a careful shoulder against the jamb, felt the structure give slightly under his weight.

"You'll likely soil that fine fabric leaning there," Kayla said.

He grabbed a handful of the gold-shot blue weave, digging his fingers in. Why had he thought the expensive korta would impress Anjika? He'd had high hopes this morning when he'd joined everyone at the coffee house. Anjika had been traveling with her parents the last few weeks, so maybe she hadn't heard Livot's ugly smears. Devak might still have a chance with her.

But she wouldn't so much as look at him, instead mooning over Livot. It sickened Devak that a high-status girl like Anjika could be so enamored of a pasty-faced demi like Livot.

"You don't like your korta?" Kayla asked.

"I was thinking I might toss it into the incinerator with the rest of that trash."

She looked at him sidelong. "My nurture brother would be over the moon owning a korta. Especially one as fine as that."

"Then you can take it to him on your Restday." He let go of the blue silk and crossed his arms over his chest. "Did you and the young male get home all right that day at the river?"

"Yes, thank you." Kayla set her carrysak on the bare mattress, setting off a cloud of dust. With another look of disgust, she moved her carrysak to the floor, then folded one end of the mattress over itself. "You've been caring for your great-grandfather since Jeramy died?"

He shrugged, the little shack shaking from the motion against the jamb. "My mother doesn't like it. She thinks it's a disgrace for a Manel to do physical labor."

"Senia keeps the house, then, instead of your mother?" Kayla lifted the rolled mattress to her shoulder.

"Senia cooks and manages the other lowborns who come in to clean. Mother doesn't much trust any of them in her house, but since her only choices are lowborns, GENs, or do the work herself, she chose the least of three evils. Her words, not mine," Devak added hastily. "I think lowborns and even non-humans have their place in the Creator's plan just as much as trueborns do."

Her eyes narrowed on him, their silvery gray a pretty contrast to her light brown skin. She regarded him for a few long moments, until it was hard not to look away. Finally, she said, "I suppose we all do, Infinite be praised."

She'd all but parroted his words, substituting the GEN version of the deity's name, yet somehow he'd heard a rebuke. All his years of living with his mother had made him hear censure when surely there was none.

Which she proved when she held up the mattress, her expression bland. "Where can I shake this out?"

"The alley in back." He pushed off from the doorway. "We can stop by the washroom."

She followed him from the cottage. The tiny washroom was in the back corner of the yard behind her quarters. He dreaded seeing the filth Jeramy might have left behind.

But a quick glimpse from the doorway told him the grime was minimal. As untidy as the old lowborn was, maybe he spent very little time in the washroom cleaning himself.

The reek as they made their way along the fence and through the back gate grew stronger, but Kayla set her face as if to block the stink. He ignored it himself, standing back as she shook the heavy plassfiber-filled mattress in a great rolling heave. Masses of dust took to the air.

She glanced at him sidelong. "Your house isn't a projection like all the others around here. It's real wood. Real stone."

"Father refuses to let my mother have a holo façade installed. He considers it a foolish waste of dhans. Much to her anguish." Devak sneezed, waving his hand in front of his face to clear the air. "You never answered my question. Before, when I met you down at the river."

"What question?"

She stretched on tiptoes, trying to hook the mattress on the fence. It nearly fell on top of her as it slithered to the pavement. Before she could try again, Devak took the mattress from her hands. After seeing her handle it so easily, it was heavier than he expected, but he lifted it high enough to secure it on the wrought iron fence.

"Do you like your sket? Do you like being strong?"

"Why wouldn't I?" She smacked the mattress hard. "It was a gift from the Infinite. He whispered it to the prophets before He sent my soul down to Loka."

"The gene-splicers programmed you, not your Infinite or the prophets."

She swung her gaze over to him. "The gene-splicers were the hands that made me. The prophets translated the Infinite's

Word into the genetics I'd need to set me on my path."

Devak had heard bits and pieces of GEN religion from the tankborns at the factories and warehouses. Under his father's watchful eye, he wouldn't have dared satisfy his curiosity about those strange beliefs. It wasn't seemly to discuss the GENs' primitive faith.

But his father wasn't here, so he asked, "What about the trueborns? Does your Infinite whisper instructions for us too?"

"He made you himself, from a simpler template. To prepare a place for us. First on Earth. Then here."

"Trueborns are taught there's only one Creator—and that's the Lord Creator."

She tipped her head to one side. "Some GENs believe that your Lord Creator did create the trueborns. But the Infinite created the Lord Creator."

"That's sacrilege." Her assertion appalled him.

She crossed her arms, chin tipping up. "It's truth. The Infinite created everything, god and man. He even created Himself."

Devak shook his head in confusion. "How could he create himself?"

"He held up His hands, palms facing." She held up her own hands to demonstrate. "The light of creation bounced from one hand to the other, back and forth. Like when you reflect two mirrors off each other and the reflections stretch out into infinity. That's how the Infinite made all parts of Himself, including lowborns and trueborns. How He shapes GEN souls, using His reflection."

GEN souls. He hadn't thought about the non-humans having souls at all. He supposed animals had a lesser kind of soul, the clever seycat's more complex than the slow-witted sewer toad's. Maybe the GENs' souls were like that, more complex still, although not on a par with humans.

Of course, it was the Lord Creator's holy breath that had created trueborns and lowborns, not the light of her Infinite. But why upset her with the truth? It didn't hurt anyone to let her believe in the Infinite.

Instead, he asked, "Is that why you pray into mirrors? Because the Infinite is a reflection?" He'd seen the factory GENs pull out their small hand mirrors when they were allowed their brief meal breaks.

Her expression shuttered, and he wondered if the question was too personal. He supposed even a GEN deserved some privacy.

She returned her gaze to her work. "The Infinite's light is too bright to look on. We use a reflection to send our prayers."

"Why did your Infinite create you as GENs?" he asked. "Why not trueborns?"

Her mouth pinched into a frown. "To make us worthy of Him. To make us strong."

She continued pounding the mattress. Her blows sent dust billowing into the air and he heard the wrought iron creak with each powerful strike. He was afraid she might take the fence down. "You certainly seem strong enough already."

She whirled to face him, dust motes drifting between them. "What?"

He pointed to the battered mattress. "You've torn a hole."

She turned back, grazed her fingers lightly over the stitches that had broken loose. Some of the stuffing drooped from the hole.

"That mattress is older than I am," Devak told her.

"There's another in storage I can bring for you."

"I can repair it." She brushed a finger across the tear, a considering expression on her face. "But I should get back to your grandfather first."

He unhooked the mattress from the fence and helped her gather it up. She folded the mattress into a tight roll against her hip.

He followed her back to her quarters and hovered in the doorway as she spread the mattress again. She positioned it with the tear on top, then started opening the doors and drawer of the storage cabinet beside the bed.

"Are there bedcovers? A towel?" She gave him that sidelong look again. "All that dust, I don't want to dirty your great-grandfather's room. I should clean up first in the washroom."

He ducked out of the shack. "I'll fetch what you need from the house. Take that rubbish to the incinerator too."

He gathered up the flotsam—a broken plasscine chair, a bundle of ragged clothes, a rat-snake carcass that he used old Jeramy's shirt to avoid touching. Halfway across the lawn, he glanced back and saw her watching him from the doorway. He picked up his pace, jumping to every other stepping stone, then made a sharp right to the incinerator. Dropping the trash in the chute, his stomach twinged at the thump the rat-snake made.

She was still watching him as he hurried across the veranda past the red kitchen door. Her scrutiny of him set off an irresistible curiosity inside him. He activated the retracting glass panel door and slipped inside. With the privacy adjustment set to one-way opaque, he could see her, but she couldn't see him.

She stood there a few moments more, staring at the house, then looking left and right as if to be sure no one was lurking in the garden. Then she swung the cottage door shut partway. Not enough to latch it, but sufficient to block any view of the inside.

Was she changing her clothes? If so, she certainly would have shut the door all the way. Or she'd go to the washroom, which had a lock.

Activating the retractor again, he returned to Kayla's quarters, walking on the grass to muffle his footsteps. Standing outside the door, he heard creaking and a thump. A few moments of silence, then the door swung open. They both jumped back.

Her gaze dropped to his empty hands. "The bedclothes?"

Devak scrambled for an excuse. "My father has a power sealer you can use to close that tear. I can bring it."

"I've turned the mattress over. No one will know it's there."

That was what he'd heard. Completely innocent. Yet why had she shut the door? Maybe being secretive was just in a GEN's nature.

"I'll be right back," Devak said.

He found his mother in the living room, reclining in a float chair. A pile of single-dose vac-seals were scattered across the mahogany table beside her—not that she stuck to a single dose. Some days she needed more than one for a proper vacation.

He knew the shapes of the palm-sized packets and the colors of their contents by heart. Flat triangle with golden liquid meant BeCalm, a sedative. Round fat pillow filled with blood-red was crysophora, a stimulant. The centimeter-thick blue square was loaded with some kind of leveler that she used when she felt too high or too low.

His mother's half-closed eyes fluttered as she pressed one

of the triangular vac-seals to the crook of her arm. Her fingers tensed as she squeezed to push every last drop of the drug through the release membrane.

The BeCalm worked quickly. If he'd come a few moments later, she would have been gone completely on her daily afternoon vacation. As it was, it'd be difficult to get any sense out of her.

He shook her arm. "The GEN needs sheets and blankets. And a towel."

His mother fumbled with the vac-seal, dropping it next to another empty on the precious mahogany side tables. A two-dose day. A few golden drops of the remaining BeCalm seeped through the membrane onto the table's glossy wood. The liquid would likely mar the surface and his mother would find a way to blame him. If she even remembered their conversation later.

He shook her again. "Where are they, Mother?"

"Where's what?" She slurred the words, blinking with slow sweeps of her eyelids. "Oh. Basement." She sank back into the float chair. A moment later she was snoring.

As much as he hated the BeCalm, he felt a guilty relief that he would be free of his mother for an hour or so. Even though the doses needed to send her on her vacation for that hour had gone from one to two to even three sometimes.

It took him several minutes of searching the basement storage compartments before he unearthed the bedding and towels in a box labeled "lowborn." Everything had been sani-sealed before it had been stowed. Unlike the cottage, at least Kayla's bedding would be clean.

He made another circuit through the basement, filling a bucket with worn rags and cleaning supplies. Bucket hooked in his fingers, bed sheets, towel, two blankets, and a pillow stacked in his arms, he carried it all back out to the cottage.

Kayla met him at the door, deftly taking the items from him. "Thank you."

She set the bucket aside, dropped the bedding on the mattress. Grabbing her carrysak and the towel, she sidled past him through the door and around to the washroom in back.

Standing there, waiting for her to do whatever a GEN female did in a washroom, felt terribly awkward. Maybe he should open the sani-sealed bedclothes and make up her bed. His mother would be scandalized by the thought of him doing menial work, and for a GEN to boot. That was enough to make him want to do it.

He ducked inside the cottage, then tugged the tab on the sealed sheets, the vac-seal cover sucking in a puff of air. The sheet set was stitched together at the foot, and the cups on the bottom sheet made it simple enough to figure out what went where. He had to pull up the corners of the mattress to tuck them into the cups. The last one, against the wall, required a bit of a fight to get it to fit.

While he forced the mattress into the last cup, he heard a faint plop, as if something had fallen under the bed. His skin crawled as he considered there might be some kind of arachnid vermin in the mattress. That dead rat-snake had been bad enough. Not even a GEN should have to sleep on a vermin-filled bed.

Swallowing back his distaste, he crouched and peeked under the bed. There was barely enough light from the door, but he spotted a small black lump on the floor. It wasn't moving. Best he could tell, it had no legs. In fact, he was certain it was man-made.

Bending down further, he stretched his fingers out to snag the small black thing. His shoulders relaxed as he felt the smooth surface against his palm—definitely not vermin. He sat back on his heels and angled the thing toward the dim light filtering from the door.

Odd. It was a quarter-dhan-sized packet wrapped in black thin-steel. Could Jeramy have left it behind?

A shadow cut the light. Kayla stood in the doorway, her damp hair wild around her face. When she took a step inside, and with the light on her now, he saw her face had gone gray.

"You made the bed."

"While I was putting on the sheets, I found this." He held it out to show her.

She swallowed and he wondered at the fear in her eyes. Because it might be tech, and forbidden for GENs? But it wasn't her fault Jeramy died before he could retrieve this little hidden package.

He slipped a thumbnail under the edge of the thin-steel wrapping, but the static-latch wouldn't release. "Huh. It won't open." He closed his hand around it and got to his feet. "I'll show it to Pitamah. He'll know what it is."

tanding in the crèche playroom, Mishalla checked her internal clock and counted down the minutes until the noon meal. A month into her Assignment, and each day crawled by so slowly she sometimes thought the clock installed inside her had malfunctioned. It was especially bad today with Restday tomorrow, those few precious hours of freedom Pia gave her such a short time away.

Eighteen-month-old Shan stretched his arms to Mishalla and called in his baby voice, "Up." She bent to hook an arm around him and held him close. Shan was a special favorite, a perilous weakness, considering what would eventually happen.

The day after Pia took Wani, the trueborn woman finally deigned to clarify matters for Mishalla about her Assignment. She'd been placed in a crisis crèche, and all the children were lowborn orphans from Sheysa sector. Their parents had died suddenly by accident or disease. New ones arrived daily, fearful and confused, calling out for their mama or dada. Almost as often, Pia took one or two of the babies away, always in the middle of the night, their screams like a knife in Mishalla's chest. All of the children she'd had that first week were gone, since replaced by a succession of infants and toddlers.

There were six left now, although she'd had as few as four and once as many as eight youngsters all clamoring for her attention. With each child, she knew only the name and age. It was an endless task soothing the tiny lowborns' broken hearts.

*Work will make you safe*, they'd told her in Doctrine school. She supposed she was safe. But they never said how hard it would be.

Mishalla set Shan down in the play corner beside a pile of colorful shape-blocks, then navigated the tumble of toys and infant sekai readers littering the floor to the snack table. She lowered herself into one of the child-sized chairs and sagged against the table. The muscles in her wrongly bent right leg spasmed and she winced against the pain.

As she checked her internal clock again—still not noon yet—Shan toddled over with a battered sekai in his chubby hand. He held it out to her with a hopeful look. Taking care with her leg, she slid to the floor and patted her lap. When she switched on the sekai reader, it acted as a magnet for several of the other kids. They clustered around her to hear the story.

None of them could read yet, so none of them realized the liberties Mishalla took with the humdrum tales stored on the sekai. Nor did they seem to care that the stories were never quite the same from one reading to the next. They just wanted to snuggle in close to her, hear her spin fantasy out of thin air.

"Once upon a time, there was a beautiful trueborn princess," she said, holding out the sekai so they could see the picture. "She lived in a castle made of clouds."

After all those years training as a nurturer, Mishalla had expected it would finally feel natural these past few weeks, to seem right. She did love the children—it was impossible not to. But it was only at times like now, when she spun out her daydreams and fairy tales for them, when she sparked these babies' imaginations with her whole-cloth fiction, that it seemed she was finally in the right place.

". . . the trueborn princess had found her home at last, and she lived happily ever after."

She moved to set aside the reader, but Shan pushed it back into her hands. " 'Gin. Pweez."

She would have, but a clatter at the door pulled Mishalla slowly to her feet. Eoghan backed into the room, a crate in his arms. A seventeenth-year lowborn boy, Eoghan had been delivering the noon and evening meals for the last few weeks. Presa, the lowborn woman he'd replaced, had had three fingers crushed in a food packing machine and was healing at her family's shanty.

Shrugging the door shut with his shoulder, Eoghan wound his way across the room to the snack table. "I wangled some fresh fruit today," he said cheerfully as he set his burden down on the table. "Rescued some orangefruit from the incinerator."

"You're a magician, Eoghan." Mishalla tore the seal from the crate. A few of the fruit would need the bad spots cut away, but there was plenty to share around.

Eoghan helped her organize the five first- to third-years around the table, quickly cleaning their hands with sani-wipes, then parceling out the plates of kel-grain and protein while she cut up the orangefruit. He took the sleeping baby to her crib while Mishalla served the fruit, then sat with her at the food prep counter while she ate her own lunch.

He looked around the room. "The twins are gone."

"And Treya. Simsim, too. Pia came for them just past midnight."

Eoghan snitched a slice of orangefruit from her plate. "The twins just arrived two days ago."

"They found family. It's better to get them into the arms of an auntie or uncle than leave them here."

"I suppose so," Eoghan said, stripping the fruit from its rind with his teeth. "When I was a kid, most orphans grew up in a crèche. Trueborns didn't exactly break their necks searching for lowborn next of kin."

Mishalla shrugged. "Things have gotten better, I guess."

"You do believe in magic, don't you?"

She forgave Eoghan his scorn. An unspeakable scandal had driven his mother to abandon him as an infant to a crèche and he'd spent his life there.

Eoghan never talked about his father—he didn't have to. Not with that straight black hair, the aristocratic cheekbones. His skin tone was a shade paler than most high-status trueborns, but was still within the range of those of the most exalted class.

It had been a shock the first time she'd seen him—a trueborn dressed in riotous lowborn clothes. Only his green eyes, a gift from his lowborn mother, revealed the truth.

Eoghan twisted the orangefruit rind in his long, graceful fingers. "Tomorrow's Restday. And you've got the day off."

"I believe I knew that." She plucked the peel from his hands and dropped it on her empty plate. She started around the room, clearing the mess.

He followed behind her. "I'm not working tomorrow either."

She didn't welcome the spurt of happiness inside. "You're not?"

"I was wondering . . ." While she picked up empty plates, he used sani-wipes to tidy up hands and faces. "Will you go to Streetmarket with me?"

She turned so quickly, she nearly collided with him. "We can't go out together."

He swiped a smear of juice from Shan's chin. "Why not?"

Glaring at him, she stated the obvious. "A GEN girl and lowborn boy hand in hand at Streetmarket?"

He gave her a cocky grin. "Who says I'd be holding your hand?"

"You know what I mean. I don't have the freedom you do, Eoghan."

"The Grid won't pick you up, if that's what you're worried about. Sheysa Square is within your legal radius."

"How would you know what my monitoring radius is? I've heard the trueborns change it all the time."

"They don't. They just want you to think that."

"It doesn't matter," Mishalla said. "GENs aren't allowed at Streetmarket."

She scraped leftovers into the incinerator sack before stacking the plates in the crate. Eoghan finished the task of cleaning up the little ones and helped the smallest from their chairs.

Mishalla resealed the meal crate. "You shouldn't be helping me so much. You shouldn't stay and eat meals with me. And you certainly shouldn't be asking me to Streetmarket with you."

Reaching over to press the last of the seal, he lowered his voice. "What if no one knew you were a GEN?"

She stared at him. "Are you crazy? How could I possibly?"

"If there was a way, would you go with me?"

She shook her head, although she couldn't deny that she wished she could go. "Why ask me the impossible?"

She realized she'd come to like this lowborn boy far more than she should. She risked disaster if she dipped her toe into forbidden waters with him.

He pulled the crate toward him. "Have they given you a travel pass yet?"

"Not yet."

"So you still can't go home."

Her heart ached at the reminder. She longed for Chadi sector, for her nurture parents, Shem and Rachel, and for her best friend Kayla. She couldn't bear having them so close, a one hour pub-trans ride away, yet unreachable.

She'd started asking Pia about a pass since she realized how close she was to Chadi. Pia hadn't liked that Mishalla had figured out she was in Sheysa instead of Skyloft—Mishalla could see it in the trueborn woman's scowl. The trueborn woman didn't punish her for knowing, but she didn't produce a travel pass, either.

"Another couple days," Pia would say, or "One more week." There was a problem due to Mishalla's transfer here from Skyloft, or the processing staff had all been down with the latest flu.

"That's an Edict violation," Eoghan said. "You should file a complaint."

"It would go nowhere. The travel pass will come soon enough."

Eoghan hefted the crate in his arms and threaded his way through squirming toddlers. He turned at the door. "Maybe I'll come by your quarters tomorrow. At mid-morning?"

"You shouldn't," Mishalla said.

"Mid-morning, then." He juggled the door open and left.

Why didn't she give him a definitive no? It wasn't as if there was any way forward for the two of them. Even a friendship between a GEN and a lowborn was risky.

Still, as the day wore on, as she mopped up tears and spit-up, brokered toddler wars and spun stories, she couldn't suppress the excitement. Seeing Eoghan on Restday, wandering with him down the few streets near the warehouses where GENs were allowed, testing the limits of how close they could stand together. It might go nowhere, but it would give her one day of brightness.

Anticipation kept her wide awake, tossing and turning in her bed. Her quarters were too hot, the netcam screen that gave her a view of the children's sleeproom cast too bright a glow.

When she finally drifted off in the wee hours, she was rousted from sleep not long after by a *rap-rap-rap* on the crèche door. A second loud knock before she could answer the summons of the first woke all the children, the baby wailing, the toddlers whimpering.

Mishalla's demi-status supervisor, Pia, pushed inside. Juka, the female Brigade enforcer, lingered in the doorway, keeping her sharp eyes on Mishalla. Pia made a beeline for the sleeproom, returning a few moments later with a screaming Shan.

Mishalla thought her heart would split in her chest as Shan reached for her, called out, "Up, up!" He'd been here five days, and she'd foolishly fallen hard for him. Grief filled her at the thought of him leaving her forever.

Pia grunted something about a distant cousin found in

Foresthill sector. As quickly as she and the enforcer had arrived, they were gone again, leaving Mishalla to quiet the remaining children before she could crawl back into her own bed.

But she couldn't banish Shan's tear-filled face from her mind, and his terrified voice still rang in her ears. Her sleep was fitful. She could barely drag herself out of bed in the morning to let in the substitute caregiver, Celia, an older GEN woman. Even Mishalla's enthusiasm for seeing Eoghan was dampened.

Nevertheless, she dressed in her best for the day—a deep blue ankle length skirt, an intricately embroidered blouse, dainty sandals, and a wide synth-leather belt she'd gotten in trade for a jar of scented dry-bath crystals. Her nurture mother had stitched the blouse with fanciful birds and vining flowers, working all through the fall and winter to have it ready before Mishalla left for her Assignment.

Nudging the door to her quarters shut, she pulled out the bottom drawer of her dresser and set it aside. It had taken until her second week here to figure out why the bottom dresser drawer wouldn't close completely. When she'd pulled it out, she'd found a false wall attached to the back panel of the dresser, saw it was slightly askew. Perhaps the GEN before her had been in too much of a hurry to put it back properly.

She'd figured out how to remove the cleverly designed rectangle and how to snap it back into place. She'd squirreled away each week's pay inside the hidey-hole, hoping to take some of her small hoard of dhans back to Shem and Rachel. If she was ever allowed to return home.

A few dhans tucked away in her belt, Mishalla braided her dark red hair, then enlisted Celia's help to wind the heavy plait on top of her head. The older GEN wove in a ribbon as she worked, then declared Mishalla was as beautiful as any lowborn.

That should have pleased her, but the night's events and her anxiety over spending the day with Eoghan unsettled her. When Mishalla heard his knock, she rushed to answer, barely opening the door, blocking Celia's view of who had come calling. But Mishalla's worry that Celia would see that her companion was a lowborn boy and not a GEN vanished when Eoghan grabbed her wrist and all but yanked her out the door.

Looking left and right, he towed her along the path that wound along the warehouse district beyond the crèche. "Where are we going?" she gasped, her right leg screaming out a protest.

"We need some privacy," he threw back over his shoulder.

That stole the breath from her lungs. She could think of only one reason he would want to be alone with her. The same reason GEN lovers would hide in the alleyways between the warehouses and factories. She'd seen them there, wrapped in each other's arms behind the incinerators, their murmurs and sighs barely audible.

She should be frightened—with the warehouse district all but deserted on Restday, she had no one to rescue her. But as Eoghan pulled her between the unmarked foodstores warehouse and the plasscine extrusion plant, it wasn't fear that set her heart pounding.

Finally they stopped, tucked behind an incinerator. The reflective sides of the trash disposal machine were cool, telling her it had been deactivated for the day. As she fought for breath, she inhaled the sweet-acrid chemical scent still lingering from the plasscine extrusion plant.

Now that they were out of sight of any chance passerby,

Eoghan's gaze took her in, from Celia's elaborate handiwork with her hair to the sweep of her skirt around her ankles. Mishalla felt the heat rise in her cheeks as he smiled.

"I'd say I'm the luckiest lowborn in Sheysa sector to have you with me today."

The flush spread to her chest. She must be as pink as the scraggly coral-bells that used to grow along the Chadi River.

She had her first real look at him. He wore neat white trousers and a fine pale lemon shirt, decorated along the collar and cuffs with a darker yellow. The light-colored fabric set off his dark skin, the contrast far too intriguing.

His smile faded as he studied her face, and he fixed on her right cheek where her tattoo was etched into her skin. His unwavering focus unnerved her and she felt even more knocked off-balance when he rubbed his sleeve across her tattoo.

"You're sweating a little," he said. "It has to be dry."

She shook her head, baffled. "What has to be dry?"

He reached in the pocket of his trousers. "This is only good for two hours, three at most," he said as he drew out a sealed packet. "Then the oils in your skin start to degrade it."

He thumbed open the seal on the packet and carefully extracted what looked like a delicate netting, nearly transparent. He held the hand-sized piece just with his fingertips, at its corners. It fluttered a little in the breeze.

When he moved it toward her face, she shied back. "What is it?"

"A way for you to go to Streetmarket. I have to apply it quickly, before it dries out."

Alarm, misgiving, excitement wrangled inside her in an instant. She gave into the last, leaning toward him. "Go ahead."

His warm, gentle hands trembled a little as he pressed the netting to her right cheek. Even as he applied it, she could feel it mold to the lines of her tattoo, sink into the skin that edged it. The faintest burning faded into a throb, then even that sensation vanished.

She drew her fingers across her cheek. She could just discern the familiar pattern of her tattoo. "What did it do?"

"Concealed your DNA mark. Now you look like any other lowborn girl." He curved his palm to her face. "Any other beautiful lowborn girl."

She turned toward the incinerator, angled her right cheek toward the shiny mirrored surface. The imperfect reflection deformed her features, put a ripple in her brow and widened her nose. But to her astonishment, there was no tattoo on her cheek. Just smooth, unmarked skin.

Such wondrous tech couldn't have been easily obtained— that GENs didn't even know it existed told her it was serious contraband. Certainly she would be realigned if she was found in possession of it.

She ran her fingers over and over where he'd applied the netting, searching for the familiar brand. But it was completely invisible. No one would know she was a GEN. Just for today she could be a lowborn girl.

As she touched her cheek one last time, Eoghan grabbed her wrist. "You'll shorten its life that way. As much as it cost me, I could only buy the one. And I want as much time with you today as I can get. Come on."

He wove his fingers in hers and led her from the alleyway. As they passed the screen of holo-trees concealing the warehouse district, a lowborn man approached them, his coverall identifying him as a Restday worker. Mishalla's tattoo seemed to sear her cheek and she was sure the lowborn would see it. But he gave them nothing more than an off-hand glance before hurrying on his way.

It was the same when they joined the throngs of pedestrians heading for Streetmarket. She was one of them—a lowborn girl enjoying a Restday holiday. As wrong as it was, as frightening and thrilling as it was, today she could be someone other than herself.

The crowds grew thicker as Mishalla and Eoghan approached Sheysa Square where Sheysa's merchants and artisans conducted Streetmarket. The booths had been set up on the central green where irrigation piped in from the Sheysa River kept the field of scrubby native Loka grass verdant.

In an integrated sector like Sheysa, lowborns mingled with minor-status trueborns on the walkways and in the streets. But these lowborns were prosperous and dressed like the trueborns. Many of the trueborns' skin color was as pale as Mishalla's own. Nothing but the bali would discriminate one class from the other, but some of the blue stones were so small she could barely see them.

"How do you tell them apart?" she finally whispered to Eoghan in desperation.

He seemed surprised at her difficulty. "I just know. I've lived here all my life."

"They all look the same to me, except when I find the bali."

"Watch them," Eoghan said. "The way the trueborns look

down their noses at the lowborns. And the lowborns back away."

She saw it now: One haughty glare from a trueborn and the lowborns gave way. She checked for the blue stone in the ear as a backup and was relieved each time she guessed right. With that puzzle solved, she could enjoy Streetmarket without fearing she would offend someone and maybe reveal herself.

Growing up, she'd attended street fairs in Chadi, a pitiful few stalls set up on either side of Liku Street selling hand-embroidered clothing or kel-grain bread. Poor imitations of fruit-melds, jewelry made from found objects, and used cooking pots were the best a shopper could hope for.

But Sheysa Streetmarket was like something from a sekai fantasy. Skirts and blouses in dazzling colors—vivid emerald and rich cinnamon, royal blue and a near-black purple. Gorgeous pottery, vases and bowls and wall hangings whose only purpose seemed to be to decorate a home. Half-tamed seycats with beautiful synth-leather collars and leashes. Rings and necklaces studded with synth-gems, their glitter pulling Mishalla like a magnet from one side of the crowded walkway to the other.

"Slow down," Eoghan said, laughing, as she urged him to yet another jewelry stall.

"How can I slow down? We have so little time." She brandished her right cheek at him, lowering her voice. "Is it still okay? Is anything showing?"

"It's fine. Enjoy yourself. I'll let you know when we have to leave."

His smile started her heart racing and she longed for him to kiss her. But maybe holding her hand was all he could bring himself to do. Maybe the thought of pressing his lips against a GEN girl's repulsed him.

She wouldn't think about that. She let him take her hand again and she slowed her headlong rush. They strolled from a display of silver chains to a booth selling scarves and shawls. Eoghan picked up a meter-square scarf swirled with mint green and pale blue and draped it around Mishalla's shoulders. It was soft and silky and felt heavenly against the nape of her neck.

Eoghan evened the scarf so it hung perfectly. "It matches the embroidery on your blouse."

She checked the stack of scarves still on the table and laughed. "I haven't so much as half the dhans for this, even if I spent all my savings."

He reached in his pocket. "I'll buy it for you."

"You can't. It's too much."

But he counted out the bills, the small stack in his hand growing even smaller, and gave them to the lowborn woman minding the stall. Then he tied the scarf loosely around Mishalla's neck, his fingers brushing against her skin and setting off a shiver.

"Thank you."

He nodded, then hooked his arm in hers. The next booth was filled with toys—forgotten Earth animals molded into lifelike figures, miniature Bullets and AirClouds. A sudden pain stabbed her heart as she remembered Shan. He'd adored the crèche's toy air cars, would play with them for hours, rolling them across the rug in the playroom.

"What's wrong?" Eoghan asked.

"They took Shan last night. Woke me out of a sound sleep, took him off screaming. I shouldn't have let myself get attached to him."

"I've never heard of a crèche like yours. Since when does Social Benevolence work in the middle of the night?"

"What does it matter?" She paused at a music stand, fingering the cheap, plasscine flutes spread out on the table. "They're reuniting the children with their families."

"But why not wait until morning? Why take the kids from their beds, terrify them?"

"How should I know? I only work there. I'm just a G—" She swallowed back the word, praying that no one had overheard, had read anything into the slip. "I'm just a girl who doesn't know anything."

She freed her hand from his, striding off to the next stall. As he tried to catch up, dodging a pair of giggling young girls, Mishalla grabbed up the first ornament that came to hand. Threading her fingers through the black silk cord of a necklace, she studied the blood red pendant suspended from it. A pattern was etched in black on the enameled plasscine disk. She nearly dropped the necklace when she recognized the design—a GEN's DNA mark.

"Put it down, Mishalla," Eoghan said as he reached her side. "You don't want that."

The fleshy lowborn man in the booth glided over. "The DNA mark is genuine—from a registered GEN." The man flipped over the pendant. "Here's his thumbprint on the back. And encased in the plasscine, a scrap of the GEN's actual DNA. All taken while he was in the tank for realignment."

Mishalla wanted to throw the pendant across the square. Instead she thrust it back at the merchant. "Why would anyone wear that?"

"Trueborns won't let us own GENs." The lowborn man dangled the pendant. "This is a way for you to own a piece of one."

"No, thank you," Mishalla said, feeling sick.

"It comes in other styles if you don't care for the red." The man swept a hand over the table, indicating the same pendant in turquoise, rose, and lavender. "I can change the color of the cord, as well."

She shook her head and backed away, directly into the path of a woman with two small children trying to forge the tight-packed crowd. Mishalla turned to apologize and was horrified to see the woman's blue bali, the smaller bali in her children's ears. She'd jostled a minor-status trueborn.

"Watch yourself, lowborn," the woman snapped before dragging her small boy and girl away. She would have been even more disgusted to know she'd brushed against a GEN.

Eoghan put a hand on Mishalla's shoulder. "Let's find someplace a little less close."

They squirmed through the press of bodies to a fruit-meld stand where Eoghan bought a pair of iced melds. He led her to a bench under an holo-augmented tree.

She poked at her meld with the spoon. "I miss my family. I miss home. Sometimes I think about jumping on the next pub-trans to Chadi."

"They'd track you." He drew the backs of his fingers along her untattooed cheek. "Bring you back or send you somewhere even farther away."

"Or reset me. Then I wouldn't even know you anymore. Or my family."

They ate in silence, the icy meld taking the edge off the growing heat. Her inner clock told her they were nearing the one hour mark. In an automatic gesture, she felt for the lines of her tattoo.

She glanced around, assuring herself the passing crowd wasn't near enough to hear. She leaned closer to Eoghan. "Where did you get this?"

"I have a friend." He took her empty cup and dropped it into a public incinerator. "It's meant to be a short-term concealer for trueborns, for scars and such. Not approved yet."

"But it must have been so hard to get. So expensive and dangerous. I wish . . ." She stroked her right cheek again, staring out into the passing crowd. "I shouldn't wish. A concealer won't change me. Won't make me human."

He pulled her hand from her face, pressed a kiss into the palm. "I don't care what the trueborns call you."

Their heads were close together, and Mishalla thought she'd drown in those bright green eyes. She was treading in risky territory. No matter what Eoghan said, there was a chasm between them.

She rose and started off again, keeping her arms crossed to resist the temptation to take his hand again. The ends of the scarf tickled her forearms, reminding her of the gift she never should have let him give her.

Eoghan got hung up in a surge of bodies; she could just see him two booths behind her. She took her time at yet another jewelry display, waiting for him to catch up. She didn't see the strange lowborn boy approach her from the other direction until he was near enough to tap her shoulder.

She started back from him, took in his long blond hair pulled back in a braid, his pale skin and blue eyes. He looked to be maybe a seventeenth-year like Eoghan.

"What do you want?" Mishalla asked.

"Mishalla?" he said softly.

Her heart pounded in her ears as she tried to edge away from him. Where was Eoghan? "You have me confused with someone else."

"I don't think so." He held out a micro sekai reader nestled in his palm. To her utter shock, her face was displayed on the screen, the tattoo clear for anyone to see. "This is you, isn't it?"

She recognized the image—it was from her final term at Doctrine school. Terror closed down her throat. "What do you want?"

"I'm Ilian." He put away the micro, then pulled something else from his trouser pocket. "We need your help."

She caught a glimpse of a datapod before he cupped his hand around it. "Drape your scarf over your head," he told her. "Quickly. Before your friend catches up."

She glanced over her shoulder, saw Eoghan engaged in conversation with a dark-haired lowborn woman. "Maybe I should go back for him."

"Do you want to help Shan?"

A chill crawled up her spine. "How do you know Shan?"

"I know all of them. Treya, Simsim, and the twins." He took a quick look around him. "Please, we haven't got much time."

Hands shaking, she tugged the pretty scarf up over her hair. Ilian tweaked it farther until it all but covered her face. Then he set his palm against her right cheek, pressing the datapod against her skin.

She couldn't stop her gasp, never mind that she'd felt this invasion a month ago on Assignment day. The extendibles pricked her cheek, the data upload raced along her circuitry.

The information stored so rapidly in her annexed brain she couldn't begin to interpret it. The lowborn smiled down at her as if they were lovers, keeping his hand there to hide the datapod until it finished.

He pulled it away, murmuring, "There's blood on your cheek. You won't want anyone to see it or they might guess there's a tattoo."

She used the scarf to dab the dots away. He inspected her, then nodded. "When you find them—"

A shout interrupted whatever he'd been about to say. In the distance, Mishalla could see the helmet-topped heads of two enforcers making their way toward her and the lowborn.

He slapped the datapod in her hand. "Hide this. The second upload will tell you what to do."

Second upload? She didn't even understand the first one.

Ilian, his long pale braid flying out behind him, zigzagged through the crowd, finding a clear path where it seemed none existed. The pair of enforcers shouted at him to stop as they tried to push and shove their way through.

While that drama unfolded, Eoghan finally reached her side. Mishalla's uneasiness grew. "We need to go," she said.

"You can't run away like that lowborn. It won't look right." Eoghan took her hand. "Who was he?"

"Nobody. He gave me . . ." But she couldn't tell Eoghan. Even if she trusted him, even if she was certain he would never willingly tell another soul, that knowledge could put him in danger.

Mishalla stuffed the datapod into her belt. "He gave me advice on the best places to shop. But I'm done. I want to go home."

The long-haired lowborn boy had vanished amongst the throng, but the two enforcers hadn't given up their search. They'd managed to push their way even with Mishalla and Eoghan. Mishalla thought her body would fly apart with trembling, even though the two trueborns were a good six or seven meters away.

Then one of the enforcers tilted his face toward Mishalla. He was still fixed on the crowd and not on her, but Mishalla's heart just about stopped.

"Oh, no. Oh, no, no, no," she moaned. "Dear prophets save me."

Eoghan shook her. "What is it?"

"It's Captain Ansgar, from Chadi sector. He knows me. If he sees me . . ."

She didn't have to finish. If Ansgar recognized Mishalla, she and Eoghan would both be arrested. Being reset might not be punishment enough for her. She was only a nurturer after all, and the gene-splicers might consider her tissue more valuable used to create new GENs. And what would they do to the lowborn who'd given her the concealer?

Just as Ansgar edged nearer to them, Eoghan cupped his hands around Mishalla's face. He pressed his mouth against hers, kissing her thoroughly for so long, Mishalla had to pull away to gasp for breath. When she did, and looked around her, Ansgar and his fellow enforcer were lost in the crowd.

"Please take me back," she begged, tightening the scarf around her head.

Eoghan guided her out of the stream of people, following the narrow path where the booths backed up to one another. As they wound their way back to the warehouse district, Mishalla spotted Captain Ansgar and the enforcer with him, but they were moving off in the opposite direction. She and Eoghan made it back to their hiding place behind the incinerator without being discovered.

He fished a small blister pac from his pocket. "The concealer will fall off on its own, but that'll take too long." He squeezed the contents of the blister pac into her palm. "That'll dissolve it."

She rubbed the tiny pool of liquid into her cheek. It burned again, then fragments of the concealer came loose. She let them fall to the pavement.

She could feel the contours of her tattoo again. "How does it look?"

"Perfect. Except." His brow furrowed as he leaned closer. "There's a little blood."

She ducked out from behind the incinerator. "The concealer must have pulled some skin loose."

With her back to Eoghan, she wet her thumb and felt for the pinpricks left behind by the datapod. He might not recognize those distinctive marks, but Celia would. Mishalla would have to keep the older GEN from seeing her face for an hour or two.

"I have to get back." She twitched the scarf over her right cheek as she stepped clear of the alleyway.

"I'll walk you," Eoghan said.

She wanted desperately to be alone, to try to decipher her baffling encounter with Ilian. What had he uploaded into her? What else was on the datapod?

But there was no shaking Eoghan. He accompanied her to the crèche, then grabbed her wrist when she reached for the door. "What's wrong, Mishalla?"

Her heart ached at the kindness in his voice. "Nothing."

"Does it have something to do with that lowborn? What he said to you?" He turned her face toward him.

She didn't quite look him in the eye. "I'm just tired. Seeing the enforcers, seeing Ansgar . . . Don't worry about me."

When she would have opened the door, he stopped her once more. "If you need me, for anything, I'll come. Presa knows where I live."

He walked away then, and Mishalla slipped inside. Celia, busy feeding the little ones their lunch, had time for only a quick nod in Mishalla's direction. She dodged the obstacle course of puzzles and shape-blocks and escaped to her quarters.

The datapod's intrusion still stung her cheek, but when she checked in her prayer mirror, she could barely see the wounds. In an hour, even that faint redness would fade enough that sharp-eyed Celia would never know what had happened at Streetmarket.

Mishalla lay on her bed, truly exhausted. She would shut her eyes for a few minutes, then go wash her week's laundry. Maybe while the quick-clean sanitized her clothes, she'd "read" another story to the children.

Except it wouldn't be the same without Shan. Mishalla shifted, her right thigh spasming as she straightened her legs. That ache throbbed in tandem with the tenderness in her face.

What had Ilian meant about helping Shan? The toddler boy, the other children who had come and gone in the crèche, were where they should be, with family. What would they need her for?

Edgy, she rolled onto her side and felt the datapod dig into her waist. How could she have forgotten it, forgotten the kind of danger a piece of forbidden tech put her in?

Even though it was unlikely Celia would suddenly come bursting in, Mishalla kept an eye on the door to her quarters as she pulled the bottom drawer from her dresser. She dropped the datapod into the hiding space, stuffing her dhans on top. Then she pushed the rectangle into its groove with a snap. She replaced the drawer and sagged back on her bed.

She just needed to shut her eyes for a few minutes. To let the terrors of the day fade.

Sleep washed over her like a flood, submerging her in dark oblivion. Incomprehensible dreams spun through her mind, images too quick to grab hold of. Strangers spoke to her, their urgent words inaudible. She'd try to focus, try to understand what they were saying. But just as she thought she'd translated the confusion, the words cut out and someone else started babbling at her.

Then suddenly she heard a click, like a thrown switch. Abruptly, everyone vanished into blackness, taking their jabbering with them. She drifted off into a peaceful quiet. When she woke an hour later, she was smiling, filled with an inexplicable and profound sense of relief.

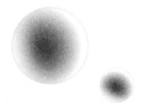

# 11

**K**ayla trailed behind Devak across that vivid green lawn, self-recrimination like a fist in her stomach. Why had she stuffed the packet into the tear in the mattress? So stupid. More stupid still to leave the bed unmade—she should have covered it with the sheet the moment Devak returned. But she'd been in such a hurry to clean the fruit-meld from her leggings so she wouldn't look like a complete wreck.

At least he hadn't jumped to the conclusion the packet was hers. That would be bad for her. But now she'd lost it to trueborns, exactly what she'd been told not to do.

So much for her mysterious mission. So much for delivering that packet to whoever needed it. They'd have to find some other GEN—a better GEN, a smarter GEN—and try again.

She followed Devak up the stairs, to the left to Zul's room. The possibilities that ran through her mind—overpowering Devak and taking the packet from him, confessing it was hers—both ended the same. Like Tanti, with being reset, having herself wiped away.

Devak knocked, then opened the door when his grandfather invited him in. Devak held out his hand. "I found this in the cottage. I think Jeramy might have hidden it in the bed frame."

Zul's immediate recognition as he took the packet from his great-grandson's hand sent a spark of fear through Kayla. That spark exploded into flame when the old man's gaze flicked past Devak to Kayla. She could almost hear his question—*it's yours, isn't it?*

But what he said aloud was, "Have you eaten, child? Since you left home?"

She shook her head.

Zul said to Devak, "Go down and ask Senia for a plate of kel-grain and soy. I can't imagine she or your mother would begrudge Kayla that much." As Devak headed for the door, Zul added, "Bring a piece of sugarfruit, too. For me."

Devak gave his grandfather an odd look, but he left without comment. Once they could hear him on the stairs, Zul told Kayla, "Shut the door."

She did, then forced herself to approach the bed. Zul was turning the packet over in his frail fingers. But rather than examine it as he did so, he kept his gaze on Kayla.

"You brought this here."

It wasn't even a question. She could have tried a lie, but he already seemed to know the truth.

"Yes."

"Someone gave it to you, told you to hide it."

Was he guessing? Or did he know something about the uploaded message? She burned to ask him, to see if he could explain the secrets of that packet, but didn't want to risk admitting too much.

So she said nothing. Just stared down at the packet, wanting so badly to have it back.

"Do you know what's in it?" he asked.

She shook her head.

"Maybe better you don't." He settled it in his palm and finally looked down at it. "Better, too, if Devak doesn't know you still have it."

She swung her head up to look at him. "What?"

"You'll have to find a more secure hiding place. Or keep it on you, if you can. Whether it's on your person or just amongst your things, if someone besides me or Devak discovers it, the punishment will be the same. So you might as well carry it. Until it's not your responsibility anymore."

While she struggled to parse out what he'd just said, he pulled her hand toward him and dropped the packet into it. She tugged up the hem of her shirt and tucked the packet away in her secret pocket.

As Devak's tread sounded on the stairs, Zul gestured toward the corner. "Press the activate control on the mini-cin. Quickly."

What the mini-cin had to do with anything, she had no clue, but Kayla made her way through the clutter to the tiny incinerator behind a stack of paper books. She thumbed the activate switch, heard the faint *whomp* as the energy core obliterated the contents of the reservoir.

Just as she backed away from the mini-cin, Devak returned. In one hand, he carried a bowl of steaming kel-grain topped with slivers of protein, in the other a blushing pink-skinned sugarfruit. "Senia would have served the kel-grain cold. I had to heat it myself in the flash-oven."

He handed Kayla the bowl and a spoon, then gave Zul the sugarfruit. Zul pointed to a bench, its padding threadbare, opposite the bed. "Sit with me. Both of you."

She couldn't help it. She turned to Devak just as he looked at her. He didn't seem horrified at the thought of sitting beside a GEN on that narrow bench, but he didn't look happy about it either.

"I have to get back to the network," Devak said. "Junjie and I are working on a project."

"The term is over," Zul said.

"For next term."

Kayla smelled a lie. She couldn't blame Devak. She wasn't keen on sitting with him, either. Zul flapped his hands at both of them. "Sit. Just for a moment."

Keeping her eyes on Zul instead of Devak, she settled close to one end of the bench, giving the trueborn boy as much space as she could. He sat precariously on the other end, leaving a foot of open bench between them. His bali, a larger diamond than he'd worn that day at the river, sparkled in his right ear.

The fragrance of the kel-grain, plain as it was, reminded her how long ago breakfast had been. She mixed in the protein, then spooned up a bite. She couldn't suppress the sigh of appreciation at the first mouthful. "It's good."

Color darkened in Devak's cheeks. "I seasoned it. It tastes like nothing, otherwise. Just put in some powdered curry. A little saffron."

Re-genned Earth spices, impossibly lavish. Tala could never afford such luxury. "Thank you," Kayla said.

Zul fidgeted with the sugarfruit the same way he had the packet. "Your mother won't approve."

"Mother will never know." Devak's mouth twisted in a grimace. "She's still on holiday."

"Ah," Zul said, his expression troubled.

"So what was it I found?" Devak asked.

"Nothing important," Zul said. "I had Kayla toss it in the mini-cin."

"Did you run it through, yet?" Devak jumped up, went to the incinerator. He pushed down the drop flap and peered inside. "I wanted to see if I could get the thing open."

"Already gone, I'm afraid," Zul told Devak. He seemed not the least bit disturbed by his lie.

Devak's gaze narrowing on his grandfather, he perched again on the far end of the thinly padded bench. "Junjic is waiting for me."

Zul rolled the sugarfruit from one hand to the other, back and forth. "I don't like taking any more of your time, but I have another important job for you." He nodded toward Kayla. "Make sure she's fed. I wouldn't leave it to Senia; she's caught up in her own machinations. Your mother won't bother, your father is rarely here. Do it yourself. It's important that Kayla stays strong."

"For you," Devak said.

"Of course, for me."

Devak cocked his head to one side, no doubt just as curious as Kayla about what was behind the old man's bland expression. Finally he said, "I'll take care of it, Pitamah."

Devak gave his great-grandfather a gentle hug before he left the room. He didn't spare so much as a glance at Kayla. But why would he? She was only the house GEN.

"Bring the bench closer, would you?" Zul said.

Setting aside her empty bowl, Kayla balanced the bench on one hand and positioned it beside the bed. She sat, squirming a little under his steady regard. "Would you like me to slice the sugarfruit for you?"

"I don't like sugarfruit." He held it out. "It's for you."

"Why did you—"

"Senia. Mrs. Manel. It's easier."

Kayla set the sugarfruit on Zul's dresser to take to her quarters later. Maybe she'd bring it back to Chadi, share it with Tala and Jal. She'd had precious little fresh fruit growing up, usually half-rotted by the time it got delivered to the GEN warehouses. It was never as fine as this sugarfruit.

"What now?" she asked.

"Have to lie down. Too tired."

She tipped him forward as she had before, long enough to pull out the extra pillow. He sagged against her arm much more heavily than he had the first time and his breathing seemed shallow.

She had to hook a second arm under his knees to shift him lower in the bed. When she laid him flat, he sighed with relief. She pulled the bedclothes over him.

He groped for the sekai reader lying on top of the covers. "Would you read the day's notices to me?"

She took the sekai, admired its featherweight sleekness. The sekais in Doctrine school were clunky and scarred with use, serviceable but outdated. She'd never seen a reader as advanced as this one. There were no buttons around the frame like the antiquated sekais. She hadn't a clue how to work it.

"Where's the power switch?" she finally asked Zul.

He wrapped weak fingers around her wrist and tugged the

sekai close enough to reach. "Brush your thumb here."

She did and the screen display lit with a dozen or so notices. "Where's the selector?" No wheel on the edge to scroll through the list and select an item.

With a patient smile, Zul tapped the first notice with his finger and the article opened on the display. Then he let go of her and sank back onto the bed.

She read aloud the report on the losses from the recent floods—ten thousand kilograms of kel-grain ruined, the destruction of the back garden of a prominent high-status trueborn, and the drowning of three underage GEN children in Mut sector. The report listed the value in dhans of the losses. The three GEN boys, ten years or more from their first Assignment, were worth barely a tenth of the kel-grain.

Zul listened with his eyes closed as she moved on to the next notice, a story about Colonization Day celebrations. He'd grown so quiet, she thought he'd fallen asleep. She looked up from a story about the upcoming anniversary of the lowborn riots, ready to stop reading and let him nap. But his eyes were open and focused on her tattoo.

"Your right cheek," he said, and she thought he'd ask about it as Devak had done. But instead, he reached a trembling hand over to nudge up her sleeve. He stared at her mottled skin. "They marked you here too."

Her cheeks heated under his examination. "What?"

"Forgive me." He let go of her and waved her off. "Take the sekai to your quarters. Find me some happy news."

"I'm not allowed—"

"Take it. Don't hide it. Put it in plain sight. If anyone objects, tell them to come to me. Bring it back at the evening meal." Abruptly, he shut his eyes and almost immediately sank into sleep.

Kayla sat beside the bed for several minutes, fidgeting with the sekai. Finally, when it was obvious that Zul wouldn't wake anytime soon, she left the room, the shiny bit of tech in her hand. What she'd tell Senia if she objected, she had no idea.

But the lowborn woman apparently had duties elsewhere. She wasn't in the kitchen or the yard. Kayla made it to her quarters without a confrontation.

She finished making the bed, then sat cross-legged on it with the sekai. She had hours until the evening meal, hours to explore the content of the reader. Fumbling sometimes with the unfamiliar screen controls, she scrolled down the listings, found story after story to satisfy her imagination.

Then her gaze fell on the icon in the lower right corner. The network function. Completely forbidden to a GEN. It would allow her to communicate with anyone with a sekai.

She shouldn't. Zul might have a way to figure out she'd opened that function. For all she knew, the Brigade had a way to monitor illicit GEN communication. But her thumb fell on the icon anyway, tapping lightly.

### NETWORK BLOCKED

Relief washed over her, mixed with only a dab of disappointment. All for the best. She could enjoy the sekai without being tempted to cross the line. Not that she ever would.

She flipped idly through the entries available, searching for an enticing title. In addition to the link to current Loka news, the sekai was well stocked with books, games, and stories.

At the bottom of the list, one title caught her eye—XRS Potentials. Curiosity sent a prickling down her spine, never mind the file was probably some dry, scientific treatise only Jal would understand. Still, Zul hadn't warned her off reading what she pleased on the sekai.

She tapped the screen and a long list filled the display—names with numbers beside them. As she scrolled through, she realized these were GEN names—Palacia, Malla, Pech, and dozens of others. The numbers must be GEN designator IDs. But why would Zul have a list of GENs on his sekai?

She reached the bottom of the list, then scrolled up more slowly. Maybe if she looked carefully, she would see a pattern in the names.

Her hand froze on the control. She stared at the screen, reading the entry over and over, sure she was mistaken. But it was her own name and ID in the list.

Her brain, annexed and bare, seemed to empty. She had to force herself to read further. When she registered the name four entries below hers, she thought her heart would stop. Mishalla was listed there, her familiar ID beside her name. And there were maybe a half-dozen more she recognized from Chadi.

The names glowed, indicating a link was attached to them. But while it seemed acceptable to give way to curiosity by opening a file, going further by clicking that link strayed a little too close to the forbidden edge. This was clearly a private file and not meant for her entertainment.

But it was her name. Her designator ID. Didn't she deserve to know what lay beyond it?

Finger trembling a little, she tapped the screen. A box popped up. Enter password.

She should have been relieved, as she'd been when she discovered the network function was blocked. But she felt only frustration.

Canceling the password request, she scrolled up and down the list of names. Could these be candidates for the Assignment as Zul's caregiver? The designator IDs were all in the same range as hers and Mishalla's, so they were likely all fourteenth- and fifteenth-years as well, ready for Assignment. But she knew the other GENs from Chadi well enough to know their skets wouldn't have been at all useful in caring for an old man. Why were they all listed together?

She wanted desperately to know, but how would she ever get past that password? Could her annexed brain figure it out? Or even her bare brain? Maybe. She could tuck it away, put it aside for now and see if an idea popped up. But did she dare? What if someone like Senia or Mrs. Manel found out Kayla was poking around Zul's sekai?

It wouldn't hurt to give the puzzle to her annexed brain. No one would know unless they downloaded her and it wasn't likely that the house manager or Devak's mother would do that.

Satisfied with her plan, Kayla closed the file. Scrolling back to the top of the contents list, she picked a story at random, a history about the trueborn settlers in the first few decades here on Loka. It was dull reading and she had to struggle to stay awake, but it kept her mind off that troubling list of names.

Mostly.

**12**

That night, the lukewarm shower in Kayla's washroom dripped out in a trickle. Her quarters, despite her efforts to tidy up, would have still earned a scolding from Tala. Her bed was lumpy and smelled bad, although not as nasty as the stink from the alley that seeped through the closed window. Just to put the icing on the cake, the tiny shack started out hot and stuffy, then turned icy cold as morning approached. Maybe two or three hours of good sleep, not counting the nightmares.

The pretty blue leggings and matching faded-rose and cornflower blue tunic she pulled on cheered her, even though the over-large size swam on her. The tunic still contrasted nicely with her blah brown hair and its long sleeves both kept out the morning chill and covered her blotchy skin. Her hair cooperated too, folding its kinks neatly into its usual braid.

But then she realized she'd have to either change back into the fruit-meld spotted leggings or fashion another pocket in the blue leggings that matched the tunic. She'd brought no fabric with her, which meant she had to pick out the stitches from the dirty leggings, then quickly sew the mismatched piece into the blue ones.

That left her only a few minutes for her morning meal. Devak had given her a pile of vac-sealed nutras, but she could barely sink a tooth into the compressed kel-grain bars. She couldn't find a date on the vac-seal but as rock hard as they were, they'd probably been manufactured four hundred years ago back on Earth.

She finally broke the nutra into the one bowl she'd been allotted, soaked it in water, and then zapped it in the shack's tiny flash-oven. It was over-sweetened and had a metallic taste that no amount of water could wash away. To add to her sour mood, she spilled a blob of the stuff while she was eating, leaving a dark stain on the long sleeve of her tunic.

As she dithered over whether to run to the washroom to try to wash away the stain, she heard a knock on the door. She opened it to Devak.

"Pitamah's waiting in the lev-car. You'll need to wear these." As he handed over a pair of sanitary gloves, his gaze fell with the precision of a lase-knife to the ugly stain.

Her cheeks heated as she realized she'd wanted to look nice for him and had failed miserably. When she got to the sleek black AirCloud, she felt even more foolish. She didn't even know how to open the door.

She'd never so much as stepped into a pub-trans, let alone a private lev-car. Minor-status techs kept the vehicles' engines running, not GENs. If GENs were trained to operate a lev-car, they might steal a vehicle and escape to the Badlands or one of the sparsely populated northern sectors. In fact, she'd heard stories of tech GENs like Jal jury-rigging a lev-car and getting as far as The Wall before the Brigade caught up with them.

So all she knew about lev-cars was that they went fast and that they sometimes crashed. She'd heard some spectacular collisions on the skyway out by the river.

"You pull this handle," Devak said, swinging open the door to the back seat.

She settled herself on the wide seat, sinking against the smooth and supple leather—could it possibly be genuine drom? Tugging the gloves on, she eased into the almost too-soft cushioning. As she sighed with sensual delight, she realized Devak still waited expectantly by the open door.

"What?" she snapped out, too embarrassed for patience.

"The safety straps."

She fumbled with them, but couldn't seem to unravel the mystery of the straps and buckles. The gloves made her even more clumsy than usual.

Zul's voice rumbled from the front seat. "Just put them on her, Devak."

Devak's mouth puckered in displeasure, but he bent over and stretched the harness around her, clicking everything in place. Somehow he managed to do it without once touching her.

As if the glorious seat wasn't luxury enough, the gleam of wood along the instrument panel was breathlessly beautiful. Even the air inside the cabin seemed perfect—its temperature, its sweet taste, its scent. She would be glad to sleep here instead of her stuffy, smelly quarters.

They rushed along the wide trueborn streets toward the skyway, the speed impossible, past block after block of fanciful holo houses—ornate castles, mansions, towers. The AirCloud's suspension engine was so silent, she and Zul and Devak could have whispered to each other and still be heard. But what did she have to say to a couple of trueborns? And they didn't seem to have much to say to each other either.

As they dropped off the skyway, Zul finally spoke up. "If you like, once you dock the AirCloud, you can go on ahead and meet us at Lossi's."

"I'll walk with you," Devak said.

"I know you want to be anywhere except with me in towncenter."

Devak took a long time to answer. "Not everyone knows you, Pitamah. They won't like that mark on your face, no matter how you explain."

"It's just a tattoo. Plenty of people got them in my day."

"I'll walk with you," Devak said again.

They pulled into an underground docking garage beneath the shops, cafés, and restaurants. On the top level near the entrance, three empty lev-car docks were labeled "Manel." Devak navigated the AirCloud into the first dock.

Kayla retrieved the lev-chair from the boot and unfolded it for Zul. He had a little more strength today, enough to ease himself from his seat in the lev-car to the chair on his own.

She followed Devak up a flight of stairs and down a narrow hallway leading from the docking garage, pushing the lev-chair along in front of her. Her heart pounded as she emerged onto the towncenter walkway, squinting and blinking against the bright blue-green sky.

Even in crowded Chadi sector, she'd never seen so many people crammed into one place. Trueborns, lowborns, GENs filled the sidewalks. Traffic jammed the streets—AirClouds and WindSpears, lumbering pub-transes and more agile

Jahaja multi-levs, the compact Bullets zipping in and out of the paths of the larger vehicles.

Of course there were trueborns everywhere. Luckily, she didn't have to study their skin tones or seek out the balis in their ears; the way they dressed made the different statuses easy to tell apart. The high-status men and women dressed with outrageous lavishness, their kortas and capes and dresses dripping with custom-genned furs and genuine gems. Demis with their faux substitutes—fine-spun drom-wool instead of uttama-silk; Lokan-grade gems in lieu of Earth varieties— strutted along as haughtily as their betters.

The few minor-status trueborns threading through the crowd puffed up their barely-above-lowborn rank with an expensive piece of synth-gem jewelry or with black-dyed hair. They fooled no one—even Kayla could see their skin color wasn't right, their clothes made from cheap duraplass fabric instead of drom-wool or uttama-silk. The high-status ignored them and the demis smirked at the minor-status pretensions.

The occasional lowborn wove through the crowd, keeping a polite distance from his or her betters as they ran errands for the trueborns who employed them. The numerous GENs might as well have been invisible, considering how lowborns and trueborns alike looked right through them. The gloved GENs carried packages, pushed trueborn infants in float prams, or stepped out into traffic to clear a path for an impatient trueborn.

No one gave her so much as a first glance, let alone a second. Their gaze would move from high-status Devak to Zul in the chair. The sequence was always the same—shock at a tattoo on that high-status face, then a quick look at the diamond in Zul's right ear. She saw the realization in a few dark eyes.

She pitched her voice low so only Zul could hear. "Do they know you?"

"Some do," he said. "By reputation, mostly. I'm the crazy old trueborn with the GEN tattoo. I haven't been out much lately. Likely most of them thought I was dead."

The choices towncenter offered were dizzying. Kayla was used to buying necessities in a GEN warehouse. Kel-grain by the twenty kilogram bag, five kilogram boxes of processed protein from the foodstores. The secondhand shirts and leggings she'd grown up wearing from sundries.

But here, shop after shop displayed clothing at prices that left Kayla gasping. The restaurant and café menus were longer than her arm, featuring dishes she'd never heard of.

"There's Lossi's," Zul said.

They stopped under the shop's red and yellow neon sign. *Lossi's,* it said, and underneath in black lettering, *Complete Inventory of GEN Tack.*

A holo projection filled the window, the images alternating through Lossi's inventory, modeled by stiff-faced GEN men and women. High-status trueborns passing by gave the place a wide berth, as if they'd lose status by straying too close to a store that catered to non-humans.

"There's a waiting area for GENs," Zul said. "You'll need to stay inside the perimeter."

To one side of the door, a yellow stripe had been painted on the walkway, marking out a two meter square on the permacrete. A GEN man, maybe in his fifties, idled there, staring down at the walkway.

"I thought this was a GEN shop," Kayla said.

"It's a place to buy GEN goods," Zul said. "It doesn't

mean GENs are welcome inside. They only allow the shop in towncenter at all because it's convenient for trueborns to send their lowborn house managers here."

"But why in front where everyone can see me?" Kayla asked, already feeling the weight of unwanted attention. "Why not let me hide in back?"

"They might pretend not to see you, but they feel more comfortable with you under their noses. In the shadows you might plot a rebellion." Zul laughed, a bitter sound. "Or a riot, like the lowborns."

She shook her head at the crazy idea of GENs rebelling, but surrendered the lev-chair to Devak. As Devak pushed Zul into Lossi's, Kayla took her place beside the GEN man.

She gave the GEN a sidelong look. He maintained his blank stare down at his toes.

Should she speak? Was she allowed to? Her only other option was to watch the trueborns pass by.

"Don't look at them," the man said. "You can't risk making eye contact."

"It's not as if I'll infect them by looking at them."

"Just not a good idea." He turned toward her then and she saw his right eyelid was sealed shut, his eye socket sunken in. "Best to keep your eyes where they belong."

He laughed at his pun before lowering his gaze to the walkway again. A chill shivered down Kayla's spine. She stopped tracking the trueborns and tried keeping her gaze down like the GEN man did.

But she thought she'd die of boredom. The holo images in Lossi's window blocked the view inside the store. She couldn't tell if Zul was still shopping or if they were passing the time with the store owner. How many worksuits could he possibly be buying for her? She could only wear one at a time.

Watching the traffic seemed safe enough. She'd kind of blur her eyes so no one could accuse her of spying or whatever it was they were afraid of. She could count the number of red AirClouds and blue WindSpears. That would keep her brain occupied.

When the pearl gray Bullet passed through her field of view, she barely registered it since it wasn't red or blue. Someone shouted out, "Denking ugly jiks!" as the Bullet sailed past.

The GEN beside her tensed, but didn't move. Kayla gritted her teeth so hard, her jaw ached. She shifted a little, putting the GEN man between her and the street, small protection that it was.

And even that was stripped from her when, a few minutes later, a lowborn woman walked out of Lossi's laden with parcels. She had the same officious look as Senia—no doubt she was a house manager for a trueborn family. She dumped her packages in the GEN man's arms and gestured for him to follow her. Three prophets save her, now it was only her on display.

When Devak stepped out of Lossi's, she thought her ordeal was over, but he squashed that hope. "Pitamah's in back talking to an old friend. It'll be a little while longer."

"Why can't I just go back to the AirCloud? Why make me stand here?"

"You can't sit by yourself in the AirCloud. If someone saw you, they might call the Brigade."

"But why? Do they think I'd steal it? When I have no idea how to operate one?"

"I didn't make the law," Devak said, then something caught his gaze and he looked away. "Denking hell."

It was the pearl-gray Bullet, come back around the other way. Now she saw the driver—the demi-status boy, Livot. The one who'd hit Jal with a chunk of permacrete.

Devak muttered, "How's a demi like him get the dhans for a Bullet, anyway?"

Livot jammed on the brakes and the WindSpear behind him nearly collided with the micro-lev-car. The blond boy leaned out his window. "Jik-lover! Do your parents know what you do with your jik sow when they're not looking?"

"I don't do anything! She's not mine!"

"Everybody knows about the Manel family tree," Livot shouted. "I'm thinking you might just be a secret jik yourself."

Since GENs couldn't have babies, what Livot said was stupid and made no sense. But she could see that didn't matter to Devak. He looked ready to explode with anger at the insult.

The Bullet roared off, Livot's guffaw echoing after him. Devak gave her a savage look, then spun on his heel and returned inside.

Not her fault he came to Jal's rescue that day by the river. Denking well not her fault that Livot was such a sewer toad. No reason at all to feel so bad for Devak.

A pub-trans pulled up just down the street, unloading a crowd of lowborns. They all seemed headed for Lossi's or one of the other surrounding shops that sold lowborn and GEN goods. The press of bodies on the walkway thickened.

A lowborn man with red-brown skin and shoulder-length black hair lingered just outside the GEN box, looking up and down the street as if trying to decide which shop to enter first.

He walked the length of the box, turning as if to study Lossi's holo display.

He glanced briefly at her, then up at the display. "Don't look at me."

Her jaw started aching again. "Why would I want to look at you, lowborn?"

She heard his huff of impatience. "Kayla 6982 of Chadi sector?"

She throbbed with heat, then cold. "Yes."

He looked around him. "Your help is required, Kayla 6982, nurture daughter of Tala."

Those were the trigger words the datapod had programmed into her neural pathways. Trigger words required that a GEN instantly submit to whatever was asked. But Kayla resisted, not at all inclined to give in.

Ignoring the tug of the programming, Kayla asked, "How do I know you're the right one?"

Annoyance flickered in the lowborn's eyes. "You don't. You'll have to trust me."

Well, she supposed she had no real quarrel with the lowborns, Senia aside. But she didn't want to hand the packet off to the wrong person. "I would like the opportunity to help," she hedged.

"Not much time. We'll have to—"

Whatever he might have said was cut short by the squeal of a lev-car engine. It was the pearl-gray Bullet again, careening back up the street. It veered from side to side, in and out of the traffic lane.

Just then, the idling pub-trans pulled out into the street. She could see the terror in Livot's face through the open window, saw him frantically trying to steer away from looming disaster.

The Bullet slammed into the pub-trans, the nose of the small car wedging under the multi-lev. The pub-trans's suspension engines pushed its rear up, where for a few breathless moments it hovered over the cabin of the Bullet.

But it wouldn't hover for long. Not if the pub-trans engines shut off, or the big multi rebalanced itself back onto the pavement. The Bullet would be crushed beneath it.

As the handful of remaining passengers poured from the pub-trans in a panic, she pushed through the crowd, ignoring the objections of the trueborns and lowborns she brushed against. Someone shouted at her—Zul maybe, finally come out of the shop. But she raced for the pub-trans and the Bullet.

Her brain clicked through the possibilities in an instant. Lifting that massive multi-lev was out of the question, even for her. She went for the Bullet instead, grabbing the buckled window frame and yanking it toward her. The underbody of the Bullet ground against the pavement, but she wrenched the micro-lev-car around and out from under the pub-trans.

Just as she pulled it clear, the pub-trans engines cut out and the ponderous vehicle crashed to the pavement. The operator jumped clear and stood swaying on the walkway.

She looked down at Livot, saw the cut on his brow, the drip of blood down his face. "Are you okay?" she asked.

He narrowed his pale blue eyes at her. "Get your denking sow hands off my Bullet."

A trueborn medic in the crowd buffeted Kayla away. She stumbled backward into someone, huffed in relief when she saw it was Devak and not a high-status trueborn stranger who might have caused trouble for her. Devak grabbed her elbow, holding it close to his body so no one in the swarm of lowborns and trueborns could see him touching her. He hustled her back to the walkway.

"I guess that's a trueborn's idea of a thank you," Kayla said as they reached the walkway.

"You left the waiting place," Devak muttered in her ear. "Touched a trueborn's lev-car."

"I saved his life!"

"Won't matter to the Brigade."

Zul was waiting outside Lossi's with parcels piled in his lap. "Back to the AirCloud. Before the enforcers arrive."

She could hear the sirens getting closer. She guided the lev-chair through the masses as quickly as she could, fighting the flow of people eager for a look at the accident. As she went, she searched for the long-haired lowborn man, but it seemed he'd vanished in the crowd.

"Don't look at them," Devak whispered in her ear.

She bent her head down and pushed the chair a little faster. Finally, she reached the opening to the narrow hallway that led to the docking garage. A few more steps and they were back at the AirCloud.

She had to lift Zul back into the lev-car, then fold the chair to put it into the boot. She didn't take an easy breath until she'd closed herself into the back seat next to the packages.

The collision had slowed the traffic flow to a crawl, but once they got clear of towncenter and onto the skyway, they moved at a fast clip. Kayla looked out the back window before the skyway curved away and saw an emergency lev-car closing in on the crash site.

A question from Devak turned her around. "Who was that you were talking to?"

Alarm prickled through her. "Just the GEN man in the waiting area with me."

"After he left. That lowborn man."

She frantically racked her mind for a plausible lie. "I wasn't—"

"You're mistaken, Devak," Zul said placidly. "Kayla wouldn't have spoken to a lowborn." The old man sighed. "Quiet now. I need to rest after all that ruckus."

They rode the rest of the way in silence, the packet digging into Kayla's hip. Great Infinite, would she ever rid herself of the denking thing?

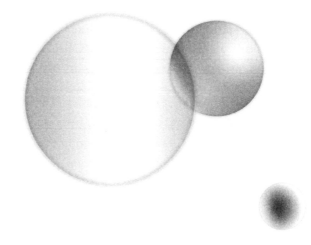

# 13

Mishalla wasn't sure what she'd expected after her encounter with Ilian. Some great revelation in her sleep, maybe, or a sudden inspiration flashing along her neurons telling her what she was supposed to do next. But there was certainly no marvelous discovery that night. She might have learned something if she'd had the nerve to submit to the second datapod upload, but she was so terrified someone would find the thing in her possession, she left it in its hidey-hole.

Eoghan didn't return, not that night for supper nor afterward. Presa showed up instead, healed enough to resume her duties, her crooked fingers testament to trueborn medics' equal indifference to GEN and lowborn health. Mishalla's hints and sideways questions about Eoghan got her nowhere with the dour Presa. Celia, too, on the next Restday, insisted she knew nothing about Eoghan and told Mishalla she ought to steer clear of lowborn boys.

Two weeks after Streetmarket, Mishalla mulled over Eoghan's absence as she sat in the afternoon stillness of the playroom. The ache in her heart throbbed as badly as the physical pain in her leg. She hugged herself against that sore spot, swinging wildly between anger at Eoghan's infidelity and despair that he wasn't here.

At a mewling noise, she cocked an ear toward the sleeproom where the four toddlers in her care napped. The whimper faded into silence and she sunk into her gloomy mood again.

The baby had been taken a week ago. With the last visit from Social Benevolence three days ago leaving her with her current four, Mishalla feared letting herself believe the shifting population of the crèche might stay the same a while longer. That she could let herself love little Zilla and sunny-faced second-year Te without fearing the heartbreak of seeing them leave.

Then with fate's casual cruelty, a knock sounded on the door. Not Pia's usual peremptory *rap-rap-rap*, but the noon meal was long past and it was far too early for supper. Who else could it be?

She allowed herself an instant of hope—that Eoghan was back. That he missed her so much he was willing to risk the enforcers and the Judicial Council to see her. She pushed to her feet in anticipation, her bad leg screaming a complaint.

She'd only taken a step or two before the door opened. Pia stepped inside, holding a sobbing second-year boy against one hip and gripping the hand of a silent third-year girl with a bandaged right cheek. Behind her, the enforcer, Juka, was saying, "If the jik is gone, do we call Celia?"

Pia did a double-take when she spotted Mishalla. "You are here."

"Where else would I be?"

"He told us—" She pursed her lips. "You're missing from the Grid."

"I can't be." Then suspicion crept along Mishalla's nerves. "For how long?"

Pia's eyes narrowed at her question. "He only discovered it this morning, but it's been two weeks."

She went numb. Ilian. His upload at Streetmarket. Somehow it had fogged her presence on the Grid.

But she couldn't tell Pia that. "You've seen me yourself during that time. So something must be wrong with the Grid. Not with me."

Mishalla could see the speculation ticking away in Pia's blue eyes. "Even so, it took dhans I couldn't spare to convince the Grid tech not to report you."

Pia tugged the little girl further inside, then shut the door. "This is Chak," she said, handing the crying boy to Mishalla. Two and a half. And the girl—"

She let go of the older child, and the little lowborn girl raced for the nearest corner of the playroom and curled up in it, her back to the room. "Her name is Amila. She's a third-year."

"Is there anything I should do for her wound?" Mishalla asked over Chak's wailing.

"Leave the bandage on," Pia told her.

"How long?"

"Until we come for her. If you disturb it, you'll likely cause an infection and the child could die."

That seemed wrong, like so much else in this crèche seemed wrong. But Pia hadn't pushed the issue of Mishalla being absent from the Grid. She'd even bribed a Grid tech to protect Mishalla. It would be best for her to keep her mouth shut.

As usual, Pia left it to Mishalla to soothe Chak and Amila. An hour later, the boy quieted finally in Mishalla's lap, although he sucked his thumb raw. But it seemed nothing would draw Amila from whatever horror consumed her. If Mishalla so much as touched the little girl, she kicked at the wall until Mishalla feared Amila would hurt herself. Mishalla didn't dare check the wound.

Five of her six charges were easy enough to put down at bedtime; even tearful Chak immediately passed out. Amila was a thornier problem. If Mishalla took her bodily to a cot, the girl's panic might wake the other children, set off another round of crying. In the end, Mishalla spread a blanket over Amila where she lay in her corner, did what she could to wedge a pillow under the dark head.

Mishalla ached seeing the bandaged cheek and Amila's messy, knotted plait. Had she been hurt in whatever accident killed her parents? Had Amila's mother, before she died, been the last one to comb her daughter's hair? Likely Amila hadn't let anyone else touch it. Hopefully tomorrow she would be calm enough that Mishalla could peel back the bandage.

With the children settled, Mishalla made a visit to the washroom, then went to her quarters and shut the door. Remembering that Amila would be unmonitored in the playroom, she cracked her door open. Her augmented nurturer hearing would probably allow her to catch Amila's cries even with the door shut, but she didn't want to take any chances.

Anxious and restless, with hours until her own bedtime, Mishalla stretched out on her bed. Letting go of her mind, she dreamed up stories she could tell the children tomorrow, far-fetched fantasies that might draw Amila from her grief.

She was whispering the tales to herself to help her remember when she heard the click and beep of the crèche front door lock disengaging.

As she scrambled from her bed, the front door slammed open. The heavy tread of boots sent a chill through her. The Brigade was here.

After the Infinite-cursed shopping trip with Zul and Devak, Kayla's days with the Manels dragged by with mindless monotony. The time that passed felt more like a year than the four weeks, three days since she'd arrived. The old trueborn wasn't so bad, but her Assignment usually required her to be at his side from the moment he woke until he fell asleep near midnight. The few hours he spent napping during the day, Senia always seemed to have something to keep Kayla's hands busy.

The sekai Zul had lent her was a blessing. She'd pass some of the long hours of the night immersing herself in the notices of the day, or the histories of Earth that Devak loaded on for her.

But the thought of this being her life for years on end weighed on her heart. After reading every word on the sekai, she'd lie awake in her bed late into the night. The walls of her cramped quarters would close in, disapproving ghosts of Senia and Mrs. Manel watching her from the shadowy corners.

Senia seemed to have a sixth sense about when Zul fell asleep in the afternoons. Within minutes, the lowborn house manager would be at the old man's door with a job she deemed too heavy or too dirty for anyone but a GEN. She'd demand Kayla's services, declaring it was at the behest of Mrs. Manel. The extra duties weren't part of her Assignment, but she feared complaining to Mrs. Manel, and Senia knew it.

Other than when Devak brought the noon and evening meals for her and Zul, she saw little of him. But then, why would a high-status trueborn boy want to spend time with a GEN like her? She'd spot him sometimes entering or leaving his room two doors down from Zul's. And he let her know, through Zul, that Livot had survived the collision with nothing more than a skin seam on his forehead. Livot's story—that he'd spun the Bullet out of the way just before the pub-trans fell— was just as well, since it kept Kayla out of it.

She clung to the bright spark of Restdays. Her first trip home was delayed when Mrs. Manel couldn't be bothered to request a travel pass, then again when Zul had had such a bad day Kayla didn't feel right leaving him. When she finally returned to Chadi, Miva was busy interning with Medic Adianca and Beela with the foodstores manager and neither had time to spare for Kayla. The next week it was Jal's genesis-day, and Tala wanted Kayla's help keeping Jal's pack under control during the celebration.

And what about the packet? Had she lost her only opportunity to get rid of it?

She'd kept it on her nearly every waking moment, had slept with it inside the casing of her pillow. It had been a frightening hazard carrying it into Chadi sector when she expected to see

Ansgar any moment. But no one approached her to take it, either in Foresthill or Chadi. She'd begun to wonder if she ought to throw it away. Just drop it into the Chadi River on her next trip home.

It dug into her hip right now as she sat on the bench in Zul's room watching the old man sleep. He'd been weak and in pain all morning and had spurned the curry and rice Kayla had tried to spoon into him.

Kayla had just had a few bites of her kel-grain when Senia pushed into the room, a sour look on her face. "You're needed below."

Kayla gestured with her bowl. "I haven't eaten yet."

"Not my fault you can't manage your time."

The irony of Senia's rebuke, that she was ordering Kayla to perform duties she herself couldn't be bothered to do, seemed to escape the lowborn woman. "He's having a bad day," Kayla said. "I shouldn't leave him."

Senia scowled. "He'll be fine. You have other work to do."

Other work that wasn't part of her Assignment. A last glance at Zul, then Kayla followed Senia from the room. The housekeeper sent her down to the basement where two lowborn girls, Meera and Yezzi, were working.

Kayla had met the sisters the first week and had trouble telling them apart. They were a few years older than her and their plain lowborn faces were near mirror images, brown-skinned and dark-haired. While they worked, they would chatter on and on, sometimes so rapidly Kayla could barely follow the flow of words.

Meera looked up as Kayla stepped into the basement. "How's the old man, GEN girl?" the lowborn asked, a smile on her broad face. Unlike Senia, the two younger lowborns were unfailingly friendly.

"Tired today," Kayla told her.

"That tattoo of his itches sometimes," Yezzi said. "Have a cream you can try. Can bring it from home."

"He hasn't complained, but that would be kind of you." She couldn't resist the temptation to ask. "The tattoo . . . do you know why he . . . ?" She gestured at her cheek.

Meera and Yezzi exchanged a glance, then Meera answered, "Because of the GENs, he told me once. Because they weren't treated fair, before the Edicts anyway. So he marked his face."

"But he could have it removed, couldn't he? They could put him in the tank and re-grow his skin there."

"Yar, but he won't, to the Lady's shame," Meera said.

Yezzi snickered. "And that's not the worst of what the old man done."

Meera took up the story. "He sent the Gentleman's—Mr. Manel's—young sister down to ruin, didn't he?"

"How?" Kayla asked.

"Made her a GEN-lover," Yezzi said. "Back before the lowborn riots. Miss Chaaya took up with a white-skinned minor-status and they both tattooed their faces. Run off to live in a GEN sector."

Kayla stared at Yezzi, stunned. "I don't believe it."

"Lord Creator's truth," Meera said. "Miss Chaaya died there, she did. Infection. No top-status trueborn medic would touch her, not with that tattoo."

"They say," Yezzi murmured with a glance toward the basement stairs as if she feared Senia was listening, "gene-splicers come and took Miss Chaaya's body to the DNA stores.

Used bits 'n' pieces of her for GEN-making before the family caught wind and got her buried proper."

It couldn't be. No way would a gene-splicer mistake a high-status trueborn for a GEN. And yet, there were a few GENs who looked so close to high-status, with their kelfa-colored skin and straight black hair, you might be confused. Especially if Chaaya had a death pallor. And a tattoo on her cheek. But wouldn't it be black like Zul's instead of silver? Maybe not. Maybe Chaaya figured out a way to make it look just like a GEN's.

Tucking away the tantalizing tale, Kayla scanned the tight-packed basement. "What is it Senia wants me to do?"

"Dragging it all out to the incinerator," Meera said, one arm flagging out to encompass a laden wall of shelving. "Like it ain't spanking new, just bought, hardly used."

Kayla wondered if she'd ever be done with toting crates around. "Senia's throwing it all away?"

"Nar, the Missus. The Lady," Yezzi told her. "Cain't let her friends see her wear them clothes twice, can she?"

Yezzi opened a crate at her feet and now Kayla saw what was inside—gorgeous gem-studded dresses, lavishly embroidered blouses and skirts. All neatly sani-sealed. And all to be destroyed because Mrs. Manel couldn't risk her friends seeing her wear the lovely things more than once.

"Why not sell them?" Kayla asked. "Or even give them away?"

Meera snorted a laugh. "If the Lady saw some lowborn girl like me or Yezzi in her finest, she'd be dragging us to the incinerator."

At Meera's direction, Kayla ferried the crates out to the side yard where the incinerator had been concealed by a holo shrub.

It was unnerving stepping through the holo image to access the disposal unit, but she got used to it after a couple trips back and forth, opening boxes and crates and emptying them into the incinerator. She had to press the activator between loads to clear it out for the next batch. Each time her heart squeezed a little at the waste.

Her fifth or sixth load, attention wandering from the tedious work, her careless grip broke one of the sani-seals as she grabbed it from the crate. A gorgeous dress of near-black cobalt slithered from the plasscine packaging. She grabbed up handfuls of the voluminous skirt, a shiver running down her spine at the cool silkiness of the heavy material. She couldn't resist the compulsion to bring the soft stuff to her cheek, to rub it against her skin. She caught the faintest hint of fragrance embedded in the fabric.

Her breath caught in her throat. It was as if memories had been stored away with the dress and now they leapt into her mind, roiling like a tempest. Her as a child, at her mother's feet, burying her face in the folds of her mother's skirt. The satin was smooth and slippery against her cheek. Her mother bent to lift her up and settle her in her lap. Kayla snuggled in closer with her mother's arms around her. Reached for that mysterious woman, aching to touch her—

*But she had no arms.*

Kayla jumped back from the waking nightmare, tripping over one of the crates and falling on her butt. The dress had spilled over her lap and she shoved it away in disgust. She shoved away the impossible memories, too. She'd made them up, out of exhaustion and a longing for a different life. Her mysterious nurture mother before Tala would never have worn such an extravagant dress. Kayla was mixing up her own past.

She jammed the dress into the incinerator with the rest of the contents of the crates and immediately jabbed the activator. She didn't stop shaking until she opened the feed slot and assured herself there was nothing inside the machine but ash. Then she trudged back to the basement for another load.

Just when she thought her eyes would cross from the tiresome work, she was down to the last crate, and she'd stopped caring about the destruction of such pretty things. Her legs ached from the bending and lifting and carrying and she'd closed off her ears to the two girls' endless, light-speed chatter.

Walking through the kitchen with the crate, she pictured herself sinking onto her lumpy bed, shutting her eyes for a few Infinite-blessed moments. Mrs. Manel snapped her out of her daydream. "Jik girl!"

Devak's mother was half-way down the back stairs, carrying a crate. Kayla didn't know what was more astonishing—that Mrs. Manel had used the back stairs or that the high-status woman toted the crate in her own two hands.

"Yes, ma'am?" Kayla said, eyes properly downcast.

"Take this one too. I want it all in the incinerator."

Mrs. Manel set the crate on the bottom step, then waited until Kayla set the one in her arms on top. As Kayla hefted the new load, Mrs. Manel hurried back upstairs.

Kayla toted the two crates to the side yard, set them at her feet and lifted the flaps on the first one. It was filled with dainties, scraps of color Kayla couldn't imagine wearing. She dropped handfuls of them into the mouth of the incinerator without a second look. After pausing long enough to stretch her legs, she broke the seal on the crate Mrs. Manel had given her.

The primary sun, Iyenku, had dropped behind the house, with lazy Kas lagging behind as usual. The secondary sun's last glow cast the side yard into shadow.

In the dimming light, Kayla could see the crate was filled with the same extravagances—glittering scarves, richly dyed belts and sandals. None of them were sani-sealed, everything tangled together as if Mrs. Manel had torn through her closets and cupboards and tossed the pretty things negligently into the crate.

She ought to just dump the contents all at once. Bending her knees, she hefted the crate, fumbling it as she went to set it on the ledge of the incinerator. Something heavy in the bottom shifted, making the crate trickier to balance than the others. Curious, she set it on the ground again.

Crouching, she dug through the crate, flipping the filmy scarves and butter-soft sandals into the incinerator as she went. In the shadows, it took her a moment to figure out what the last item in the crate was.

A book. An actual paper book dropped carelessly into the bottom. Had Mrs. Manel somehow not realized the book was in the crate? Or had she intentionally hidden it away? There were plenty of paper books in Zul's room. Why would she want to destroy this one?

Kayla had never laid her hands on a paper book, hadn't dared touch the ones in Zul's room. But the sekai images she'd seen of paper books and the description of the construction had fascinated her. With no trees on Loka except in the preserves, papermaking was an art left behind on Earth. Who needed paper anyway, when the written word could be recorded on sekais and datapods?

The paper in Zul's books had no doubt been brought here from Earth, then the pages cut and stitched and glued into a binding. The words were printed on the paper pages with actual ink instead of the virtual kind.

She checked the yard—no one in sight. She tucked herself into the space between the incinerator and the row of holo shrubs, pulling the crate after her for a seat. A last ray of sunlight spilled onto her shoulders, lighting her hiding place.

She picked up the book with the gentlest pinch of her fingers and examined it. The cover was smooth under her fingertips, with the dips and curves of an abstract engraving. There was no title or image on the front.

The edges of the paper pages were packed smooth on top and bottom and uneven along the side opposite the binding. They felt sturdy enough, but she worried that she might damage them with her clumsy strength.

Carefully, with the barest pressure, she opened the book. The pages seemed well secured in their binding and sound enough to withstand her handling. She remembered it was acid that caused paper to eventually crumble, so this book must be made of acid-free pages, of a high enough quality to survive the nearly four hundred years since it was brought from Earth.

She cautiously turned to the first page, eager to see what had been printed on it. But there was nothing there but a hand-drawn inscription, letters formed in a faded, hard-to-decipher script. As she turned more pages, she saw the script gave way to mathematical equations and drawings, far more complex than anything she'd been taught in Doctrine classes.

She turned back to the inside front cover. Numbers and letters had been written there, in the same hand as the rest of the book. She stared at the curving lines, struggling to interpret them.

With a start, she realized it was a date. The first of Cuigiu, year 294. Seventy-eight years ago.

Three words were written underneath the date. The letters she recognized suggested the ones she couldn't decipher at first. But finally, the words fell into place—Zul Shafi Manel.

A book hand-written by Zul. Why hand-written? For that matter, why written on paper at all? Why not entered electronically so that anyone who wished could read it on a sekai or wristlink? Even seventy-eight years ago, primitive versions of both devices were available.

Maybe for that very reason—Zul didn't want just anyone to read it. He had made only this one copy, which could be hidden. Anything in electronic form, no matter how well protected by passwords, could potentially be spread far and wide, exposed to eyes that Zul would rather it not be.

How, Kayla wondered, had Mrs. Manel gotten her hands on the book? And why was Devak's mother so eager to destroy it? What could be in here that Mrs. Manel feared so much she wanted the book consigned to ash?

Whatever it was, Kayla decided, it had nothing to do with her. She would just drop it into the incinerator as Mrs. Manel had ordered.

But how would anyone know that she hadn't? She could hide the book in her quarters, maybe try to read a little of it, and Mrs. Manel would never know. Even if the book was filled with nothing more than that incomprehensible math and she wouldn't be able to make the least bit of sense of it, how could she toss such a precious thing into the incinerator?

Meera's voice calling from the back door startled Kayla

into closing the book. "GEN girl! Where'd you go?"

If she didn't answer, Meera would come looking for her. "Almost finished. Be right there," Kayla shouted.

She couldn't run to her quarters to hide the book. Meera would wonder what she was up to, and her curiosity might make its way to Senia. Too risky to walk into the house with it, even hidden under her shirt.

Tuck it behind the thicket of hedges along the fence? No, the damp soil would damage the delicate paper. Under the incinerator? It sat flush to the plasscrete pad. Behind, though . . .

Just enough space between house and incinerator to slide the book into. She nudged it in far enough to be unnoticeable but still within reach of her fingers. Then she stacked the empty crates and ran as fast as she could back to the house.

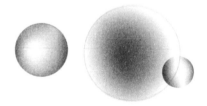

# 15

Amila screamed, her wail chilling Mishalla to the bone. She ran for the playroom, but before she could reach the little girl, two Brigade enforcers shoved Mishalla to the wall.

They were so close to her, she could smell their stale sweat. The names on their tags blurred. Guntram. Frej.

"Compliance search," Guntram shouted over Amila's terror. He held out a sekai. "Can you read?"

"Of course I can." She scanned the display as he quickly scrolled through it, skimming page after page of dense text, legal talk that made little sense to her. The sigil of the Southwest Territory Judicial Council appeared at the bottom. "This is a violation of the Edicts." As if an enforcer cared anything for her privacy.

Guntram narrowed his blue eyes on her. "Do you have something to hide?"

And then it hit her. Of course she had something to hide. The datapod Ilian had given her. Tucked inside the false panel. She would be ended the moment these enforcers found her hidey hole.

Mishalla shook her head, sinking to the floor beside Amila, wishing she could curl up beside the little girl. Instead she rested a hand on the third-year's shoulder. Amila stiffened, but she stopped screaming. Her tiny hand groped for Mishalla's.

"Look anywhere you like. I'd prefer if you wouldn't wake the children."

Although she could already hear them whimpering, roused by Amila. The two enforcers split up, Guntram scouring the playroom, Frej heading for the children's sleeproom.

Guntram dumped each crate of toys, kicking through the contents before moving on to the next. Every once in a while, he would glance over at Mishalla. Maybe he expected his intimidation would push her to spill everything she knew—about her day at Streetmarket, the tattoo concealer, her encounter with Ilian.

But why tell him anything until she had to? Once he found the datapod, they would download every last scrap of information from her annexed brain and discover whatever Ilian had uploaded. They might not be able to access her bare brain that way, but with enough force, they could persuade her to give up every guilty thought, her darkest nightmares. No point in making it easy on them before she had to.

Frej emerged from the sleeproom. "Clear. Nothing in the cots or cribs."

"Check the washroom," Guntram said, sending his compatriot down the hallway between Mishalla's quarters and the children's sleeproom.

Mishalla levered herself up from the floor. "Can I clean up the mess?"

Guntram waved a hand at her and she took that as a yes.

She moved from crate to crate, filling them with the spilled toys. She kept one eye on the open door to her quarters, saw the enforcer strip her bed and shake out the sheets and blankets. He ran his hands over the mattress, checked every inch of the frame.

For the moment, his back was to her. She could try to run for it. The enforcers had shut the door behind them, might have even entered the locking code. But she could tap out the numbers and letters with habitual speed, might get out the door before they realized what she was up to. Might even lose herself in the shadows before they could strike her down with their shockguns.

More likely her bad leg would hamper her flight enough for them to catch her. They wouldn't even have to use their shockguns.

She might have tried it. But she couldn't leave the children, Amila especially. She would simply have to wait here for her doom.

Finished tidying up, she moved close enough to her quarters to see Guntram move his attention to the two-drawer dresser. As she expected, he pulled out each drawer and dumped it, then picked through the clothes he'd spilled. Even her most intimate feminine items he pawed, looking for contraband.

Satisfied there was nothing hidden in her clothes and personal belongings, he flipped over the drawers and examined each surface. He tapped the sides and bottoms, shook them, no doubt looking for something tucked in a hidden compartment.

Her heart pounded as he set aside the second drawer and turned to the dresser itself. He ran his hands over the exterior, tipped it to check the bottom. Tapped each side as he had the drawers. The top. And then the back.

She watched him tap the section behind the top drawer, make his way down to where the false panel fit. The thud of his gloved fingers against the plasscine seemed to thunder in the small room.

Then a pounding shook her from her frozen terror. Pia's familiar *rap-rap-rap* at the door.

Guntram straightened and stared at her. Mishalla had to swallow twice to get her voice to work. "It's Social Benevolence. I have to let them in."

He gave her a negligent nod, then bent to the dresser again. He lifted it onto the bed and thrust his arm elbow-deep inside the frame. It wouldn't take him long to find the false panel.

Mishalla hurried to unlock the door, too grateful for the distraction of Pia's arrival to regret the imminent loss of one of the children. Pia and Juka stepped inside. On her usual bustling track to the children's sleeproom, Pia stopped short as Frej appeared from the hallway.

Pia spotted Guntram as well, then she glanced back at Juka. To Mishalla's surprise, a flicker of worry passed between them.

Pia barreled her way into Mishalla's quarters. "What are you doing here?"

Focused on the dresser, Guntram barely looked up. "This GEN is missing from the Grid."

The diminutive woman puffed up. "Who sent you here? If it was Ansgar—"

Mishalla's heart nearly stopped at the mention of the captain's name. Did he see her after all that day at Streetmarket? Had he finally realized who she was?

"Not Ansgar," Guntram said. "The supervisor of the Sheysa Grid substation reported the absence. Southwest

Territory Judicial Council authorized a compliance search."

Pia and Juka exchanged another glance. Juka leaned close to Pia, murmured so softly Mishalla was certain Guntram couldn't hear. But Mishalla could.

"That drom-brained Grid tech probably bleated to his supervisor first chance he got," Juka said. "You wasted those dhans bribing him."

Pia flapped her hand impatiently. "It's water down the Sheysa. The real worry is the Grid supervisor. What happens when he realizes this jik isn't supposed to be in his territory? The director won't like it."

Pia swung toward Guntram again, drawing herself up to her full meter-and-a-half height. "It doesn't matter who sent you. We conduct our own searches here. You can contact Hellis at Social Benevolence. He'll tell you."

Guntram stared at Pia for so long Mishalla thought she might scream from the tension. "I don't take orders from anyone but the Brigade commander of Sheysa."

Mishalla saw anxiety seep into the cracks of Pia's anger. The SB woman glanced over at Juka as the female enforcer's fingers closed over the butt of her shockgun. Pia shook her head at Juka, then turned back to Guntram.

"If you could give me a minute of your time, Captain."

"I'm no captain," Guntram said, apparently unimpressed by Pia's attempt to stroke his ego. But he extracted his arm from the dresser and followed Pia from the room, stepping on Mishalla's clothes as he went.

"You, jik," Pia snapped, gesturing Mishalla into her quarters. "In there. Close the door."

Mishalla shut herself into her quarters, then pressed her

ear to the door. Pia spoke quietly, but plenty loud enough for Mishalla's augmented hearing to make out the words. "I'd take it as a personal favor if you'd leave my jik alone."

"Why would I do that?" Guntram asked.

"It could profit you," Pia said. "That sow doesn't know what our true goal is here. I don't know if I could find another as dull-witted and naïve."

Outrage burned inside Mishalla and she wished again for even a tenth of Kayla's strength. She'd smash a fist into pint-sized Pia's face.

"And what goal is that?" Guntram asked.

"We're shifting lowborn population. Culling, so to speak, to open up more land."

"Culling."

"We take the children, just a few. It frightens the parents and they clear out."

"What do you do with the children? After this?"

"Leave them at a shanty in a less desirable location."

Now the odd hours of Pia's visits made sense. What better time to abandon a baby or toddler than the middle of the night? Pia and Juka could steal away in the dark unnoticed. The lowborns would likely take the poor children in without question.

"How could this possibly benefit me?" Guntram asked.

"We're freeing up adhikar land," Pia said. "They're not prime parcels, but sufficient to regain status. If it's the case that you lost your adhikar grant and were forced into Brigade service to maintain your status, we can help you. We could put a parcel into your hands only two or three months from now. Once we've cleared away enough of the lowborns, your adhikar could be restored to you."

A long, silent moment, then Guntram spoke. "There are consequences for bribing an enforcer, even for a demi-status like yourself."

"That wasn't my intent," Pia protested.

"I'll be reporting all this to the Judicial Council in the morning," Guntram said.

"Wait," Pia said. "Give us a little time to straighten out the jik's status on the Grid. If we had a week—"

"No," Guntram said flatly.

Pia persisted. "Think how much time a Council report will take. Not to mention traveling down to Sona for testimony. But if you could just give us four days—"

"Two," Guntram said. "I'll hold off sending the report until then. You'd better have that jik in order or you'll both stand before the Council."

Guntram barked out a command to Frej to follow him. Heavy boots crossed the playroom, then the crèche door slammed shut.

Pia pounded on the door to Mishalla's quarters. When Mishalla opened it, Pia snarled at her, "Whatever it is you're hiding, get rid of it. A note from your lover, contraband food, I don't care. I just want it gone next time I'm here. And whatever you're doing to fool the Grid, I want it stopped."

Her order delivered, Pia strode off into the sleeproom. Whichever hapless child she'd snatched from its bed cried out, setting off the rest of the crèche. Pia had a blanket thrown over the little lowborn, so Mishalla didn't even know who it was.

As Pia passed, she dug something out of the attaché she had slung over her shoulder. She pressed a wad of something into Mishalla's hands. "Get rid of it," she said again before she and Juka hurried out the door, taking the sobbing child with them.

Mishalla stared, stunned, at what Pia had given her. Dhans, more than double what Mishalla had secreted away in her hidey-hole.

Did Pia suspect that she'd been listening through the door? The demi-status woman had to know a nurturer like Mishalla would have no trouble hearing her conversation with the enforcer. Now Pia couldn't risk Mishalla knowing her scheme without some pressure to keep her mouth shut. Pia must have thought this blood-money would be enough to keep Mishalla quiet.

She tossed the dhans into a corner in disgust, then went to check on the children. As she moved from cot to crib, doing what she could to soothe the three boys and one girl back to sleep, she lingered briefly by Te's empty crib. Only here three days.

She'd known something was off about the crisis crèche, but she never expected something as evil as stealing children. It made no sense to her—why drive out lowborns when there was plenty of unsettled land across the Svarga continent? But maybe that was the point—trueborns wanted settled land, close in with other trueborns.

With the sleeproom quiet again, Mishalla checked on Amila in the playroom. The girl still shivered as she cowered in the corner. Mishalla sat on the floor beside her, stroking the little girl's back, humming a lullaby. Mishalla tried to twitch the bandage away, but Amila shrieked and tugged away.

Mishalla's thoughts circled back to what Guntram had

nearly discovered. If Pia had known a datapod was tucked away behind the false panel, Mishalla doubted the demi-status trueborn would have been so blasé about it. A GEN with a love note was one thing. Any written communication between GENs was illegal, but a line or two written by hand on a scrap of plasscine would likely be overlooked by most trueborns. The transgression wouldn't be worth the inconvenience a reset would cause.

But a datapod—a piece of tech that sophisticated was a dangerous thing in GEN hands. A non-human might use it to reprogram herself, to override whatever the specialists had uploaded.

A shiver ran through Mishalla. Was that what Ilian had done? Changed something inside her? How would she know?

There was one way—use the datapod again, install whatever other data it held that Ilian hadn't been able to at Streetmarket. He'd said the second upload would tell her what to do.

But she wouldn't use the datapod again. She'd already put herself at tremendous risk by hiding it. She'd been lucky— Pia had arrived in the nick of time to save her. Mishalla was disgusted by Pia's motivation, but the scowling trueborn from SB had given Mishalla a second chance.

So she would get rid of the datapod. Now. She'd creep out to the incinerator two buildings down and drop it inside. The children were unlikely to wake in the short time it would take her.

She dimmed all the crèche lights, then sat beside Amila until her breathing slowed and deepened. Mishalla took a last look in the sleeproom to assure herself the other children still slumbered. In her quarters, she worked her fingers into the edges of the false panel and pried it loose. The datapod fell with a clatter along with her small bundle of dhans.

She tucked the datapod into her belt, then padded with bare feet through the playroom. She kept her gaze on Amila as she shut the door. Outside, she tapped in the code to lock the crèche.

Only a few paces away, sudden fear all but froze her. What if something happened while she was gone? A child could wake, could fall crawling out of a bed. Shoddy wiring in the walls could start a fire.

She'd just have to hurry. She forced herself to walk faster, all too aware of the unguarded children. The safety lights glared down at her and she skipped from shadow to shadow. Boot steps sent her diving into the alleyway between the crèche and the foodstores warehouse. The night patrol. Plastering herself against the wall, she watched the lowborn guard in his yellow uniform pass within a few meters of her before he continued on out of sight.

She sprinted to the next alleyway, her right leg groaning with pain. Melting into the narrow blackness, she listened for the patrol. She heard nothing but the hum of traffic from the distant skyway.

She opened the incinerator hopper and fished the datapod from her belt. She stared down at the silvery thumb-sized device nestled in her palm. She had only to drop it inside and when the disposal service powered on the incinerator tomorrow, the datapod would be destroyed.

She'd never find out what the second upload would have told her. No doubt Ilian had meant for her to help Shan by uncovering Pia's foul actions. Maybe the datapod contained the locations of the shantytowns where Pia had taken the children. Unless she risked the second upload, Mishalla would never see the little lowborn boy back in his mother's arms.

*Drop it. Just let it go.* But the piece of tech seemed glued to her palm. Shan's face bobbed up in her mind's eye. He'd been so afraid when Pia hauled him from the crèche.

What if he isn't safe?

The uncertainty burned inside her. The possibility that Shan, that the other children, might be in danger crawled along her skin like a slime-spider swarm.

She stuffed the datapod back into her belt, crept to the end of the alley. She spotted the guard moving away from her, past the tech storage warehouse. She waited until he'd nearly reached the end of the row of buildings, then with quick, quiet steps, she returned to the crèche.

The patrol would turn any moment and look back her way. Her glance jumping from the keypad to the guard, Mishalla fumbled as she typed in the code. Just as the patrol reached the end of the warehouse row, the lock released. With a sob of relief, she slipped inside.

Not a sound from within but Amila's soft snore. Mishalla shut her eyes, listening for the sound of booted feet running toward the crèche. She counted to fifty. The silence ticked away, punctuated by a heavy sigh from Amila.

She made her way to her quarters, shut the door, and raised the light to its highest setting. After returning the dresser where it belonged, she remade the bed. Cross-legged on the tidy blanket, she extracted the datapod from her belt.

How did it work? Did she just put it against her cheek? Her hand trembled as she lifted the datapod to the right side of her face, pressed it against her tattoo. She tensed in anticipation of the extendibles' bite. She felt nothing but the cool thinsteel of the device's housing.

She lowered it again and studied its exterior. Where did the extendibles protrude from? She saw no marks on either side that would have given her a clue.

Maybe there was some other device, something the trueborn operators held in a pocket or pouch that activated the datapod. Or a secret code they spoke into it. If that was the case, why would Ilian have given it to her without the other device? Or had he intended to, but the arrival of the enforcers interrupted him?

Then she might as well have discarded the datapod in the incinerator. Having no idea how to use the device would be no excuse if a trueborn found it on her.

Dragging the dresser to the middle of the room, she stood on top of it and held the datapod up to the ceiling illuminator. She turned it over and over, slowly, angling it this way and that. And she saw it.

The faintest depression where the pad of a thumb would fit. The slightest difference in the texture of the thinsteel.

Fingers closed around the datapod, she stepped carefully back onto the bed and lowered herself to sit cross-legged. She rested her thumb in what seemed the proper spot. Exerted pressure on the datapod.

An indicator light flickered green.

This she'd seen before. When the specialist had applied his datapod to her cheek on Assignment day.

Afraid it might automatically shut down again, she slapped it to her cheek. She spent a fleeting moment worried that the device might need to be positioned just so, then jumped as the extendibles jabbed her skin. She dropped her hand as the data rushed into her annexed brain, as incomprehensible as before, but some of it vaguely familiar.

Amongst the flood of data, one startling revelation kept her frozen on her bed even after the datapod shut off and dropped to her lap. She swiped at the blood without thinking, then got to her feet and padded from her quarters.

She grabbed the first reader she spied, an especially battered unit that more than one toddler had used as a drum or to hammer pegs into a pegboard. Returning to her bed, she set the sturdy sekai screen-side-down on the dresser top. Puzzling a moment over what to use for the next step, she found a worn tenth-dhan coin tossed aside by Guntram's ransacking. Its slender edge fit into the fasteners' notches and allowed her to remove them.

A schematic spilled from her annexed brain, telling her exactly where to apply the datapod. *Every sekai reader has at least a rudimentary networking function. It needs only the proper software to activate it.*

She thumbed on the datapod. *The reader will only upload software compatible with its function.* She positioned the datapod where her internal schematic directed her. Unlike her permeable skin, the extendibles couldn't pierce the sekai's electronics. She had to hold it in place.

The green light flickered for only a few seconds before it flashed red. Mishalla removed the datapod, then took care to conceal it behind the false panel. She replaced the drawers, but piled the clothes Guntram soiled to one side.

Then she closed the sekai and flipped it over. She switched it on.

At first the screen displayed the last story she'd read,

something about a trueborn adventurer who flew to one of Loka's moons. Then the text faded, the screen blanked. She waited.

A message appeared on the screen, stealing the breath from her lungs.

**KAYLA IS ON THE NETWORK**

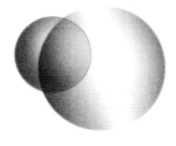

"**H**ere I am." Kayla brandished the crates. "All done."

"Give them to me," Meera said, coming down the porch steps to relieve Kayla of her burden. "The old gentleman needs you."

Kayla hurried through the red door and up the stairs. Zul's door was cracked open and she could hear his rough breathing from inside. He was awake, gaze riveted on the ceiling, stiff hands clutching the bedclothes.

"Spasm," was all he could manage.

"Where?"

"Left side."

"What do I do?" she asked.

"Prop me up. Have to move."

She did as he'd instructed, hooking her hands under his armpits and lifting him into a seated position. "Any better?"

He rubbed his side, gasped out, "Push against my ribcage."

She put her hand where his had been, exerting the slightest pressure, afraid she'd crack a rib. "Here?"

"Yes. A little harder."

She increased the weight of her hand, then was gratified by his sigh of relief. He relaxed against her, his fingers unfurling. "That's good. Prop me against the pillows, would you?"

She did, then stepped back. The pain and her treatment seemed to have taken out of him whatever restoration his nap might have given. He looked as lethargic as he had at lunch.

But his eyes were bright enough when he turned to her. "Sometimes the nerves misfire and cramp the muscles. Usually my back and lower legs."

"Like a shockgun strike."

He shrugged. "Something like that."

He'd told her nothing about his condition and she hadn't asked, out of courtesy. But he must have seen the question in her eyes.

"I have a kind of nerve damage."

"Were you in an accident?" she asked.

He shook his head. "I need you to find Devak."

"Do you need to use the washroom?"

He shook his head again. "Get Devak."

She hurried down the hall to Devak's room. The door was open and she heard the rumble of a deep male voice. She hesitated out of sight, torn between Zul's urgency and fear of invading a private conversation.

"It's time you stopped acting like a child," the man said.

"What have you asked of me that I haven't done?" Devak asked.

"That's just it. You do no more than that. One day it will be your duty to maintain the well-being of all the GENs in the western territories. Yet you don't take that responsibility seriously."

"What if I don't want to do it?" She heard the tension in Devak's voice.

"I didn't raise you to be insolent."

"You didn't raise me at all, Father."

He slapped Devak. Kayla knew that sound well enough. Her own nurture mother had never laid a hand on her, but she knew nurture parents who governed their charges with blows instead of kindness.

Devak's father spoke again. "Four GENs have gone missing from the Grid in Sheysa sector. There's no telling if they're safe. If their work is getting done."

*Work will make you safe*, popped into her mind, unbidden. With a conscious effort, she pushed it aside.

Devak's father went on. "It's a waste and an inconvenience having to reset GENs who stray. I need you to find them."

"I have to bring Pitamah his meals."

"That's the GEN female's duty. Yours is in Sheysa."

Footsteps crossing Devak's room sent her stumbling back. Devak's father emerged from the room, an older, grayer, near carbon copy of Devak.

She tried to shrink into the shadows of the hallway, but blast her luck, he spotted her. She expected some snarling comment like what Mrs. Manel often tossed her way. But his gaze was dispassionate, not wrathful.

"How is my grandfather faring, GEN?" he asked.

"T-tired this afternoon," she stuttered.

"Don't let him overdo." His dark eyes bored into her.

"I won't."

Almost before she'd finished speaking, he'd turned on his heel and strode away from her down the hall. Despite his fairer treatment of her, she couldn't suppress the shiver running through her.

On shaking legs, she moved toward Devak's room and stepped into the doorway. She looked around at the ornate furniture, the thick rug on a polished wood floor, the artwork on the walls. It was so tidy, you'd wonder if anyone lived here.

He was at the window, staring out at the darkening garden. "Devak."

"What is it?"

"Your great-grandfather needs you."

He turned on his heel and moved past her, the faintest glitter of moisture in his eyes. She followed him from the room.

She thought maybe Zul had fallen asleep again, but he opened his eyes as she and Devak walked in. "Where's your mother?"

"I don't know." Devak moved to stand beside Zul's bed. "She went out this afternoon and isn't back yet."

"Good." Zul took Devak's hand. "Do you know where she keeps her supplies?"

Devak's back stiffened. "If she hasn't hidden them somewhere else."

Zul's hand tightened on Devak's. "I need some crysophora."

Devak pulled his hand free. "It isn't safe. The last time you—"

"I have to go out tomorrow. I have business."

"But I won't be able to come with you," Devak said.

"Kayla will."

Zul redirected his intent gaze toward her. It was as if he expected her to catch some meaning in those dark eyes. But whatever his silence was trying to convey, she missed it.

"What about your . . ." Devak gestured at his own cheek.

"You needn't worry. No one will see it."

The tattoo. Kayla didn't see how it could be hidden, not the way it so clearly marked his left cheek.

"I need the crysophora." He captured Devak's hand again. "Without it, I won't have the strength."

"What's crysophora?" Kayla asked. "Is that what Mrs. Manel takes for her vacations?"

"No," Devak said. "It's what she takes to counteract the sedatives. It's a powerful stimulant and neural reinforcer. It gives Pitamah a temporary boost of strength."

"I'll need two vac-seals," Zul said.

Devak stared at his great-grandfather, clearly horrified. "One could do enough damage."

Zul got a mulish look. "I need two."

Devak sighed, shook his head. "Mother will notice it's missing."

"I'll get more while I'm out to replace it," Zul said. "I know someone."

Devak pulled free of his great-grandfather and left the room. Zul shut his eyes again.

"Is there anything I can do?" Kayla asked the old man.

"Just stay close tomorrow. Once the crysophora wears off, I'll need you."

Devak returned and drew from his pocket two circle-shaped vac-seals, each about the size of his palm. The liquid inside them was blood-red. "I won't be the one to dose you," Devak said.

"Give them to Kayla—she'll do it. One tonight and one in the morning before we leave."

Devak set the vac-seals in her hands, real worry in his face. Kayla asked, "Can this hurt him?"

Devak gave his great-grandfather a pointed look.

"Mother's had to go into the gen-tank three times to fix what crysophora broke."

Zul glared at Devak. "Your mother's a chronic user. That's what damaged her heart. My taking it this one time—"

"Except it's never just one time," Devak said. "I hate that you take it at all." He dropped a hand on his great-grandfather's shoulder. "I'd give every acre of my adhikar if I could stop you. If I could stop Mother."

Zul looked away, his gaze dropping to his feeble hands. Devak turned to Kayla, anger mixed with sorrow in his face. "The first dose might make him sick. You'll want to be ready for that."

She brought over the reservoir from the mini-cin and set it beside the bed. Then, at his direction, she pulled up Zul's sleeve and peeled the tab off the membrane of one of the vac-seals. She felt sick herself at the thought that something could go wrong. She'd never heard of crysophora, but she'd seen GENs dead from lifters and lowerers they'd distilled from fungus and rawseed nurtured in warren basements.

But surely trueborn drugs would be safer. Made in factories, care taken to purify them, packaged in neat, sanitary vac-seals. They wouldn't have the toxins of a bad batch of rawseed zing or the unpredictable potency of a hit of charnel fungus.

She positioned the vac-seal in the crook of Zul's arm the way she'd seen the medics do it and pressed it lightly.

Zul said, "You'll need more pressure than that to activate the membrane. I'll want every drop."

So she squeezed harder. There was no reaction from Zul at first, then he sucked in a breath and his arm tensed. By the time the vac-seal had emptied, he was groping for the reservoir. She got it up into his lap just before he emptied his stomach of the little it contained.

The old man pushed the reservoir back into her hands. She passed it to Devak, then poured water for Zul from the bedside pitcher. Devak reassembled the mini-cin and ran it through its cycle.

While Kayla held the glass, Zul sipped a few mouthfuls of water. "Let me sleep the night. Come back in the morning."

Kayla helped him lie down again, then dimmed the lights. "Should I stay?"

Devak spoke from just behind her in the dark room. "He's likely asleep already."

Zul had never fallen asleep this early in the entire four weeks she'd been there. She felt at loose ends. "What should I do?"

"Go to your quarters. Before Senia puts more of her work on your shoulders." He leaned closer to her in the shadowy room. "She has no authority over you. My mother has no idea what Senia is doing."

Then he'd noticed Senia's mistreatment of her. How, she didn't know, when he seemed to be always hiding in his room or out with his friends. That he seemed to care at least that much filled her with a warmth she had no business feeling. Because if he'd noticed, why hadn't he done something about it? Ordered Senia to do her own work? He had that much power in the household.

She all but ran from the room, tension between her shoulders driving her down the stairs, through the kitchen and out the red door. She was halfway across the yard before she remembered the book behind the incinerator.

Looking around to be sure no one was watching her, she hurried back to the incinerator. As she stuffed the paper book under her shirt and crossed the yard to her quarters, she sent a prayer to the prophets that Senia wasn't spying on her.

In her quarters, she activated the overhead light, its glow barely reaching the corner shadows. She let the book slide from under her shirt to the tiny kitchen table, next to the sekai, which was out in plain sight as always. She trembled, the magnitude of what she was risking settling over her. Zul would defend her possession of the sekai, but how would he feel about her all but stealing his priceless paper book?

He'd never know because the moment she'd finished reading what she wanted of it, she'd toss it into the incinerator as Mrs. Manel had intended her to. Or maybe she'd sneak it into Zul's room while he was asleep and shove it in a drawer or under his bed. Let someone else find it.

She was just pulling her worn, scuffed chair up to the table, settling with the book in front of her, when the sekai beeped. Had she left the device in wait mode? She could have sworn she'd powered off the reader.

She slid the sekai over and scanned the screen, expecting to see the text of the last article she'd read, a story about the great migration from Earth. Instead, the screen was blank, with a single line displayed across the bottom.

MISHALLA IS ON THE NETWORK

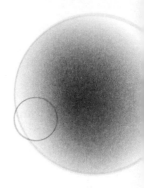

# 17

**K**ayla stared at the sekai, stunned. If it had suddenly transformed itself into a snarling seycat, it would have seemed less perilous. Of all the ways trueborns regulated GEN lives, they most tightly controlled communication. Only word of mouth was permitted, face to face or spread from one GEN family to another. And if word of mouth could have been outlawed, they would have done that, too. If GENs were allowed tech to communicate, who knew what seditious plots they might plan?

Jal would be beyond jealous that Kayla had gotten her hands on a networked sekai, something all his tech had never achieved. But for Kayla, Jal's coveted function just terrified her.

Still, the message all but jumped from the sekai, straight into Kayla's heart. Mishalla is on the network. Mishalla. Kayla's heart-deep, blood-to-blood tank-sister, a friend surely given to her by the Infinite Himself. How could she not answer that summons?

Unsure of what to do next, she tapped on the screen. To her shock, the message vanished, replaced by Mishalla's face filling the display. Kayla's throat grew tight with emotion.

"Mishalla? Is it really you?"

Mishalla's eyes narrowed. "Is this a trick?"

"No. It's me. Truly."

"It looks like you, but . . ." She still didn't look convinced. "What did we do on your tenth genesis-day?"

Mishalla was looking for proof. "We went to the Chadi River for chaffheads," Kayla said, "and you stepped on a sewer toad. You made me carry you back to your warren."

Mishalla's scowl softened, then she laughed. "You brought that toad home in your pocket."

"And threw it at Skal the next day in Doctrine school."

Mishalla sighed. "I thought I'd never talk to you again. We shouldn't be talking now. If anyone finds out—"

"They won't. We'll be careful."

"Where were you Assigned?" Mishalla asked.

"Foresthill. I'm caring for an old trueborn man. How is it working at the crèche?"

"Not good," Mishalla said. "The children—they've all been stolen from their families. To frighten the lowborns away from their shantytowns and clear the way for minor-status trueborns. The babies are here a few days, then dumped in some mixed-sector shantytown somewhere."

"That's awful. But the lowborns—they would never turn a child away. So those babies must be safe."

"I pray to the Infinite that they are. But I'm afraid, Kayla. Someone's going to find out what's going on here sooner or later, and you know they'll blame the GEN. Just tonight, the

Brigade was here. I was sure they'd take me. They said they couldn't find me on the—"

A knock on the door jolted Kayla so she missed the rest of what Mishalla said. Oh, great Infinite, had Senia come looking for her? She jabbed the *close connection* button on the sekai and cleared the screen, then brought up the migration story again.

Praying that the lowborn woman wouldn't just barge in, she grabbed up the paper book, considered and then rejected a half-dozen hiding places before heaving it into the storage cupboard beneath the flash-oven. Hurrying to the door, she swung it open, ready to tell Senia she could take care of her own chores.

But it was Devak standing on her doorstep. He stepped past her with a tray filled with dishes—two steaming bowls, two plates, two glasses.

"Let me in before she sees," he said, edging a shoulder inside and ducking under the low roof. "Mother's still out, but I don't want to deal with Senia's nonsense."

Kayla stepped out of his way. When she didn't immediately close the door, he caught it with his foot and swung it shut.

He set the tray down on the table. While he off-loaded the dishes, she noticed she hadn't quite shut the cupboard door. If she moved to nudge it closed, he might wonder what she was hiding.

As a distraction, she said the first thing that popped into her head. "That's too much food for one person."

"When I realized you probably hadn't eaten, I thought I better bring you something. I thought we'd share." He glanced over at her. "If that's all right?"

No, it wasn't all right. She was rattled enough after her conversation with Mishalla. How could she sit across that tiny table from Devak, in the small space of her quarters, and share a meal? She didn't like how she felt every time he walked into his great-grandfather's larger room. This would be much worse.

She groped for an excuse. "I don't know where you'll sit."

He looked around as if she might have hidden a second chair somewhere in the room. "I'll be right back." Opening the door a crack, he took a cautionary look, then slipped out.

The moment he was out of sight, she rummaged through the cupboard, rearranging the odds and ends inside to better hide the book. Then she shut it, making sure it latched. She considered tossing the sekai inside too, but Devak already knew Zul had lent it to her. If it was missing, he might ask.

She ached to press that network icon again, to continue her conversation with Mishalla. How had her friend managed to get through to her? For that matter, how had the block been removed from Zul's sekai?

Her stomach rumbled, distracting her from the unanswerable unknowns. Did she sit and start eating? Or wait for him? She knew what Tala would say, what she'd been taught. No one eats until everyone is served and at the table.

Yet she was so hungry and the food smelled so good. It was bowls of kel-grain as usual, but root vegetables as well as protein bits dotted the surface. Slices of fresh, fragrant orangefruit were fanned across each plate and tea filled the glasses. If she started now, it would be that much less time they sat at the table together.

But just as she lowered herself into her chair, the door swung open again. He was breathing heavier, as if he'd run both ways. He carried a stool she'd seen in the kitchen, red metal that matched the back door, its paint chipped and rusted in spots.

"It was Pitamah's when he was a young man," he said, setting it opposite her. "Very old."

She would just focus on her food, forget that Devak was here. They would eat, he would go, and she would have her privacy back.

When he picked up his fork, she followed suit. After the first well-spiced bite, she had to force herself to eat slowly. Whether it was appetite or the seasonings or the vegetables, she'd never tasted a better meal.

But he wasn't going to let her eat in silence. "Do you like it? Kel-grain?"

He might as well have asked if she liked the sky being blue-green, or rain being wet. "It's all Health and Welfare delivers to the warehouses."

Devak looked up from his bowl. "They bring you protein."

"Some. Not enough for every day. And we can't always afford to buy it."

"What about fruit and vegetables?"

She scooped up a bite. "We get lowborn castoffs sometimes. Between our own genetics and what the kel-grain is designed to give us, we could eat nothing but that and stay healthy. When I was growing up, there were times we had no protein, no fruit or vegetables for weeks."

He stared at her. "You ate nothing but kel-grain, day in, day out?"

She shrugged. "Tala knows more ways to prepare it than anyone I know. We share spices, look in empty lots for whatever's edible. You'd be surprised what you can find growing wild in Chadi sector. Not everything good to eat comes from Earth."

He seemed stunned by what she'd told him. "I didn't know."

She stabbed her spoon into her bowl and pushed the kel-grain around. "Most trueborns don't give much thought to what happens in the GEN sectors."

"But I should." There was true regret in his words.

Kayla didn't want to hear it, didn't believe him. Most trueborns didn't care about non-humans. To them, GENs were nothing more than the scraps of DNA the gene-splicers put together to create them.

She forced herself to relax her hand on her spoon so she wouldn't bend it. "Day after day, you feed the same electricity to that Bullet you drive. The Bullet runs, and you're happy. Do you change the power source for your sekai reader to give it variety? Of course not. It's a machine. It doesn't matter how you power it. What does it matter what a GEN eats?"

Silence fell like a thick blanket around them. The bowl of kel-grain had lost its flavor, but she ate it anyway. He'd made it for her; she could at least do him the courtesy of finishing it. Tala would have wanted her to.

The fruit she saved for last, like Jal would have done. Each sweet-tart bite reminded her of her nurture brother, and she felt a pang of longing for home.

Devak rose to stack the bowls and set them on the tray, and Kayla felt relief that he would be leaving soon. But he sat again and his steady gaze fixed on her.

"My father wants me to take over his work when I'm old enough."

She remembered their overheard conversation. "I don't even

know what your father does. Or if I'm even allowed to ask."

He wove his fingers together. "It's no great secret. He's director of the GEN Monitoring Grid for all of the western territories."

A chill traveled down Kayla's spine. Devak said it so easily, as if the Grid were something ordinary. Like a machine for extruding plasscine or a device to tidy up trueborn streets. "The Grid violates the Humane Edicts."

"Not when it's used lawfully," Devak said. "The method the Grid uses—checking the location of a given GEN only every five days—is exactly what's specified in the Edicts. The Grid just needs to confirm that GENs are within a reasonable radius of where they're expected to be."

"Except sometimes the Brigade targets GENs, requests a monitoring tag so they can watch them every moment. One step outside their radius and an enforcer sweeps them up."

Devak shook his head. "It might seem that way to an outsider. That an enforcer takes a GEN for no reason. But the Judicial Council doesn't issue a tag unless there's well-documented justification. My father has brought me to Council sessions. I've seen how fairly non-humans are treated."

"You aren't seeing how they're treated in Chadi sector by the Brigade."

"Sometimes they might seem harsh," Devak said. "But when you were a kit and too young to know better, your nurture parents might have had to punish you for doing something bad."

"My nurture mother never would have reset me. And I was never a kit. Or a 'female.' I might be non-human, but I'm not an animal. I'm a girl."

Devak shifted on his stool, his expression uneasy. "The Brigade only resets when there's good reason. Sometimes it's better to start over with a GEN."

"Better for who?" Kayla pressed. "Not for the GEN. Or his family."

"It is better. If a GEN gets to the point where it needs resetting, it isn't happy. Its programming has gotten so corrupted, it can't do its duty anymore. And GENs are happiest when they're doing their duty."

"Work will make you safe," Kayla said, unable to keep the sarcasm from her tone.

Devak narrowed his gaze. "I would think you'd want to be safe. To be taken care of."

All the frustration of the last four weeks exploded in the words she flung at Devak. "We're not droms that need care, we're not children. I'm not an 'it' that needs a trueborn to tell me when I'm happy. I might be less than you, but I'm tired of being told how I should feel."

Devak stared at her, and it crossed her mind that he could have her reset for what she'd said. But the turbulence in his dark eyes told her he was maybe in as much turmoil as she was.

She had the strangest urge to touch his hand, to comfort him. Instead, she locked her hands together on the table. "Those missing GENs I heard you and your father talking about. If you find them, if they're outside their radius, what will you do?"

He folded and unfolded his fingers, eyes downcast. "I'd have to report them. It's my duty."

"Then you know your place too."

"I guess I do." He shrugged. "It was supposed to be my

brother, Azad, filling my father's shoes, not me. Azad had just started the training, took to it as if he'd been born to it. At least that's what my father said."

"Why didn't he?" Kayla asked.

"He's dead. The lowborn Sheffold riots."

She'd been taught in Doctrine school the official story of the riots thirteen years ago. But she'd learned the truth from Tala, who'd learned it from other GENs who'd been there. Kayla was five or six when Tala first told her, and had helped Tala pass it on to Jal.

A dim fact surfaced now. "Azad Sharma."

Devak nodded. "My half-brother."

"Then you—"

"I'm the child he gave his life to save."

"But they never meant to kill him."

His gaze narrowed on her. "Of course they did. He went in as a peacemaker. He'd befriended some of the lowborns, but they betrayed him."

"That's how the trueborns tell the story," Kayla said.

"What other way is there to tell it? That's how it happened."

"I learned it differently."

She could see unwilling curiosity in his face. It would be a wasted effort to tell him what she knew—why would a trueborn believe her? Just because he'd sat down over a bowl of kel-grain with her didn't mean he was willing to let her change his world.

He crossed his arms over his chest. "Tell me what you learned."

She took on Tala's storytelling rhythms. "The lowborns *were* angry that day. An epidemic of Sheffold fever had swept through the shanties and the trueborns were slow sending in medics or medicines."

"I know that much," Devak said. "The medics were stretched thin and there weren't enough vaccines to go around. Even after the Abeni and Geming epidemics in 303, they were caught unprepared."

"The medics didn't even go in for three weeks after the first cases. And trueborns hoarded the vaccines, even those who'd been inoculated."

A reluctant understanding flickered in his eyes. "Pitamah told me something like that once."

"When your brother came to the shanty, they crowded around him. They shouted at him, but only to tell him their grievances. They respected him. They hoped he would make things better for them."

She hated the next part of the story. "Someone in the crowd, mad with fever, started pushing and screaming. The ones he pushed fell into others, and a panic started. The ones in back trying to escape, the ones in front trying to hold the wall around your brother. The ones in front—Lechim, Farn, Afa, and the others—they tried to keep the crowd away. But they weren't strong enough."

Devak's face paled. "He threw himself on top of me to protect me. My mother told me they beat him."

She shook her head. "They did what they could to save him. And one of them, Afa, I think, carried you to safety. But how was it you were there?"

"I saw him leave the house and I followed him. He was near the shantytown when I caught up with him, so he decided to take me with him. If I hadn't been there—"

"He would have died anyway. Maybe not a hero trying to protect his baby brother. Maybe the uprising would have dragged on another year and thousands more lowborns would have died."

He spread his hands on the table. "You tell the story as if it matters to you. As if it were GENs involved instead of lowborns."

"There were GENs involved. A few. Secretly. Lowborns like Lechim, Farn, and Afa wanted conditions improved for GENs as well as lowborns. Around the time of Sheffold, a few members of Congress were threatening to strike down the Humane Edicts."

"Pitamah told me that," Devak said.

"Lechim and the others knew if the GEN Edicts went, repeal of the lowborn Benevolence Statute wouldn't be far behind."

"What happened to those lowborns?" Devak asked.

"Afa died from the fever," Kayla told him, "Lechim and Farn from a street bomb set off by a more violent faction." He didn't ask about the GENs, but she didn't even know their names, if they were alive or dead.

"No matter what the truth is about my brother, it doesn't make it any easier to take his place." Devak sighed. "Why can't I do what I want? Have a chance to figure out who I am? What I would be, what I would do if my father wasn't who he was and I wasn't a substitute for Azad. If the whole wide world was open to me, instead of just this little corner."

Kayla couldn't help but laugh. "A trueborn complaining that his world is restricted?"

"But it is, in a way." He stared down at the table. "Yes, I'm high-status. Anything I want, I have only to say it and it's mine. But high-status children always follow their fathers or their mothers. The only change my father would accept would be if I won a seat in the Congress or were nominated to the Judicial Council. But that will never happen, not with Mother's problems and the shame that great-grandfather and Aunt Chaaya brought to the family. My path is set and narrow as a lase-knife blade."

She shouldn't have felt sympathy for him. He might be in a trap, but it was a luxurious one. And as constricted as it was, he had a hundred times more freedom than a GEN like her. It made no sense that her heart ached for him.

She rested her hands across from his, condensation from the glass of tea damp on her skin. She was all too conscious of how close his fingertips were to hers.

He seemed to stretch them toward her. "That first day, when you realized you would have to touch Pitamah and you were afraid. You wouldn't say why."

Her cheeks warmed. "It's something nurture mothers tell GEN children. To keep them from even accidentally touching a trueborn."

"What were you told?"

She half smiled, feeling foolish. "That our skin would shrivel up and fall off."

He almost laughed; she could see him hold it back. "How?" he asked.

"We were told there was one chemical the gene-splicers made sure GENs weren't immune to, a special chemical that only trueborns gave off. That's why the medics and enforcers always wear gloves, nuture parents tell little ones, so they won't infect us."

His fingertips inched closer across the rough table. "Yet

you've touched Pitamah, and nothing happened."

She straightened her fingers within a centimeter of his. "But he's an old man. Maybe his body doesn't make the chemical anymore."

Now he did laugh. "My parents told me nearly the same thing. Except, of course, the chemical was genned into GEN bodies, and it would make my bones grow crooked."

"They look straight enough to me." She studied what she could see of him, from shoulder to waist, her boldness shocking her. "So I guess you haven't tested their theory."

"Are you willing to try it? Risk that pretty light brown skin of yours?"

Her breath caught in her throat. The terror stopping her answer had nothing to do with Tala's old story.

He kept his gaze locked with hers as he lifted his hand. He reached toward her slowly, until she could feel the warmth drifting down from his palm. And then he lowered his hand on hers.

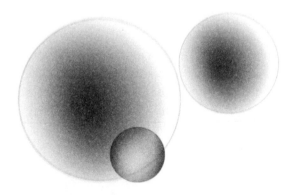

**18**

hy had Devak thought Kayla's skin might feel different than a trueborn girl's? GENs might be non-human, but they were created using human DNA. Certainly the skin that covered them would feel the same.

He ran his thumb across the back of her hand, curled his fingers into her palm. He wanted to enclose her hand in both of his, to lift it to his cheek and feel it there.

But that would be a step too far. As would the other possibilities spinning out in his mind, fantasies that would be at least acceptable with Anjika or Eesha or Lajita. His father might scold him if he caught Devak kissing a high-status girl not yet betrothed to him, but if she was from a good family, one that would add to the Manels' status, Ved would secretly be pleased.

But touching Kayla was beyond shameful. Except he felt warm from the tips of his fingers to the center of his chest, and lost in those wide gray eyes. When his transgression should have mortified him, he felt as if broken parts of him had healed into a whole.

He turned her hand palm up. "Your skin seems undamaged."

Despite the wariness in her eyes, she smiled. "Your bones seem just as straight."

He smiled back at her. "Then they've lied about this much, at least."

"And your brother's story."

"And that." He hadn't completely wrapped his mind around her version, but he liked it better and hoped it was true. "Who knows what else is a lie?"

Her gaze dropped to their linked hands. "Who knows?"

His thumb moved a little higher, to her wrist, the circular motion nudging the edge of her sleeve. Her gaze softened, and he made the circles a little bigger, pushing the sleeve up past her wrist bone.

He spotted the intriguing dark swirl of color on her arm a moment before she snatched her hand away. She made to hide her hand under the table, but he captured it again and tugged up her sleeve to just below the elbow. The random designs on her forearm entranced him, streaks of dark and light, shades deeper and paler than her light brown. Every color he'd ever seen on a Lokan face, every status, was drawn on her skin.

So rapt at the meld of colors, he didn't notice her distress until he heard her tiny moan of anguish. She neatly plucked her hands from his grip and he realized that with her strength she could have done that all along. He guessed that only politeness had kept her from being so abrupt.

He thought she'd cover her arm again, but she shoved up both sleeves past her elbows. Now he saw the same washes of color on the other arm, small specks, long streaks, thumb-sized dots.

She held them out, chin lifted, a challenging look in her

eyes. "You wanted to see, you might as well get a good look."

"I've never seen anything like it," he said, still not sure why she seemed so upset.

"Because trueborn gene-splicers never make a mistake."

He met her gaze. "They do. Sometimes."

"Then this," she flung her arms in his direction, "is probably their biggest."

He studied the pattern of dark and light. "I think it's beautiful."

That seemed to upset her even more. "You're lying."

"I'm telling you the truth."

"You can't be." She sounded on the edge of crying.

"I mean it," he said. "I like it."

Her gaze narrowed on him with disbelief. But at least she didn't seem so miserable. She pulled her sleeves down to cover her arms again, and to his relief let him take her hands.

She took a long breath and angled her gaze at him. "There are things I've wondered, things I could never ask a trueborn because I'd be punished. Can I ask you?"

A prickling started up his spine in warning. "Yes."

"Can I trust you not to tell your mother or your father?"

"If my parents knew I was in here with you, I'm the one who'd be punished."

She stretched her fingers, the tips stroking his palm. "You might lose the use of your Bullet, or be told you couldn't see your friends for a month. I would be reset and realigned. Wiped away. Kayla would be gone and another GEN in her place."

He knew about realignment; his father had told him, had made it seem like a righteous thing. GENs who needed resetting were ill or unhappy with the life they'd been given, and it was kinder to give them a new one. Resetting was thrifty, too, a way to reuse what had been spoiled if reprimands proved ineffective.

But his father had been talking about faceless GENs, not this one sitting in front of him. Devak felt hollowed out by the thought of the Brigade erasing Kayla.

"Ask me," he said. "I won't tell anyone."

Her gray eyes fixed on his. "What is it about you, and me, that makes you human and me not?"

By reflex, he produced the rote answer. "You're tankborn. My mother gave birth to me."

She nodded in acknowledgement. "I've heard that medics sometimes put trueborns into tanks to re-grow an injured arm or heal a child's deformity. Are they still human when they come out? Or partly GEN?"

His stomach lurched at her question. "They went in human, they come out human."

"But you could say I went in human—most of my DNA, anyway. The parts that were animal, they're such a small fraction. And the embryo that started me might have been artificial, but wasn't it pure human once?"

"That's different." Her hand felt too heavy in his suddenly and he pulled away. "They put Pitamah in the tank several times to try and fix his nerve problems. But he was a fully grown man. Not a collection of cells."

"So, if a trueborn *child* goes in a tank, to cure a disease maybe, they could be a GEN when they come out again."

"No! They were a human child, a trueborn child first. They would have already worn a bali in their ear. They would still be human."

"Even a trueborn as young as a baby?"

# tankborn

"Of course," he said, sure of his answer now. "Even a baby wears a bali."

"But the lowborns don't."

"But they're still born of a mother," Devak said with assurance. "And they never go into the tank."

"Because they haven't got the dhans to pay for it." Kayla changed tack. "What about a trueborn baby born too early from its mother? They're put in the tank sometimes. Do the medics install a bali before they put the baby in the tank?"

"I don't know." A snake of uncertainty crawled in his belly.

"Because by your definition, if it doesn't have a bali—"

"It's still human. It gets a bali when it emerges from the tank. And the bali's DNA detectors will know the baby's trueborn."

Kayla's eyes narrowed as if she didn't quite believe him. "I've heard that sometimes trueborns need help making that baby. They have to use a kind of a tank to start it."

The snake twisted tighter in his gut. His friend Junjie had said his mother had needed exactly that kind of help to have him. And demi-status Junjie was as human as Devak himself was.

When he said nothing, Kayla pressed her point. "Then when?" she asked. "When is the dividing line? When is the DNA surely human? When is it not?"

The problem with all of Kayla's questions, all her probing, was that Devak had wondered some of the same things. He gave her the only answer he was certain of. "The dividing line is animal DNA. Trueborns and lowborn have none. Every GEN has some."

That she couldn't deny. Right from the start, the gene-splicers had used animal DNA brought from Earth to give GENs their skets. Dolphin DNA to improve nurturing, cheetah

**195**

DNA for quick response. Elephant or gorilla for strength.

"But the animal part of me is so small," she said. "The tiniest scrap. Why is the whole GEN non-human when such a small bit is animal?"

He had no answer for her, especially when he was sitting here with her, talking to her. Truly, despite that adulteration of her DNA, he could see no difference between her and any human girl. Except for those lovely swirls on her arms. And any self-respecting high-status parent would have those removed. *In a gen-tank.*

"I'm told what work I'll do and where I'll live," she went on. "I'm only a fifteenth-year, but the trueborns could have sent me clear across Svarga Continent, far away from my family, and I wouldn't have had any choice."

"It used to be that way with the lowborns," he said, "when we first came here. Only the trueborns had the money to build the colony ships. The lowborns had to work for their passage, be servants to the trueborns when they arrived."

"But the lowborns agreed to work for the trueborns. And they didn't have to do that forever. Now they pick their own jobs, live where they like, how they like. So, why aren't the lowborns trueborns now?"

"Because of the adhikar. Lowborns don't own land."

"Because they're not allowed to."

"But that's how the lowborns want it. They don't want to become trueborns, tied down by an adhikar parcel. What would a lowborn do with a big kel-grain farm or acres of grazing land? They want to be free to move from place to place, without responsibilities."

"How many lowborns have you asked about that?"

Her steady gaze stripped him bare. She knew the answer without him speaking it. None.

She pressed on. "Why do it this way, anyway? High-status, demi, minor-status. I've seen trueborns that could just as well be lowborns except for the bali, lowborns that could almost pass for high-status. So why divide people at all?"

"Don't they teach you in Doctrine school?"

"Only that it had something to do with how we all got here from Earth."

"Yes, that's a big part of it," Devak said, feeling on surer footing now. "After Earth was ruined, so much of the chaos happened because people forgot their place, where they fit in society. They took care of themselves and their own, but wouldn't trust anyone outside. And they couldn't do everything themselves, they had to rely on other people.

"A few joined together, then a few others. They figured out who could pay to get the factories running again, who knew how to build the parts for the colony ships and who knew how to put those parts together. They organized the labor, the scientists, the farmers who could grow the food needed for the journey.

"Everyone had their part to play, their place in the colony project. And when the founders arrived here, they knew it would be best to continue that way. Give everyone their place. For a secure society."

"I think most GENs would give up security if they could choose their own lives. If we could take away this tattoo, go where we wanted without the Grid watching us."

"But that wouldn't fit your liturgy," Devak said. "You told me that servitude, not freedom, will get you back to your Infinite's hands."

"That's true," she said. "And I do believe the Infinite's plan is right and good. But sometimes my life is so terribly hard that I want it to be different."

She rested her fingers on the back of his hand, so lightly they tickled the hairs. "I speak. I feel. I laugh and cry." She broke off and looked away briefly. "Some things I want so badly I think I'll die of it. I do worship the Infinite. But to be told every day that I'm not human . . ."

"It doesn't mean you're worth less than a human."

"You know that's not true."

"My father taught me to treat all GENs with compassion."

"But if your father had to choose, save the trueborn or the GEN, even the lowborn or the GEN, you can't tell me he'd choose the GEN."

He shook his head. *But I would, if the GEN was you.*

"They all treat me like dirt on their shoes, Devak—your mother, Senia, all those trueborns in towncenter. Like I'm less than nothing."

"I don't."

"Don't you? You bring meals for me and Zul, then run from the room. When you pass me, you pretend you don't see me." Tears edged her voice. "From that first day, you've acted as if I'm something ugly you're forced to have in your house."

Wetness shimmered in her eyes and sent guilt knifing through him. "You're not ugly. That's not why I avoid you."

"Why are you here at all? Why didn't you bring the kelgrain and leave me to eat alone?"

He'd tried to keep his feelings inside him, knew how wrong it was to let them spill out. But his father's hand still stung on his cheek. Every one of his mother's depravities seemed to take him by the shoulders and shake the forbidden thoughts from his head.

"Because I like you. Too much. I want to be around you all the time. I've only kept away from you because I couldn't let myself feel so much for you."

And then he compounded the sin of his confession, lifting his hand to her right cheek, curving it over that glittering tattoo. "I wish I could wipe that from your face," he whispered.

When his wristlink chirped, he wanted to ignore it. He might have if it had been Junjie's staccato beep-beep-beep. But it was the short-long-short, low-high-low of his mother.

He glanced at the message and he felt a fist grab his heart. She was back home. She'd likely seen the Bullet in the garage when she pulled the AirCloud in, had checked his room and Pitamah's.

"My mother." He stumbled to his feet, grabbed the stool.

"What about the dishes?" she asked.

With a huff of impatience, he hooked his arm around the stool's legs and balanced the tray in his other hand. His wristlink sounded again, short-long-short. He peered out the door to make certain his mother wasn't on the back porch or looking out the back windows. "Deactivate your light."

She did, plunging them into darkness. If his hands hadn't been full, he would have reached for her one last time. He slipped outside into the cool night air and hurried toward the house. Along the way, he stuffed the tray and its contents into the incinerator.

He entered through the red door into blinding light. His

mother was on the other side, her pupils so dilated he knew instantly what entertainment she and her friends had been up to tonight.

"Where have you been?" she demanded, the words slurred with who knew how many vac-seals.

"Sitting out in the garden." He put the stool back in its corner.

When he headed for the stairs, she stood in his path. "Two vac-seals of crysophora are missing."

He dodged past her and started up the steps. "Maybe you used them and you forgot. Considering how much garbage you pour into yourself—"

Her fingers closed on his arm in a painful grip. "I keep count. Did you take them for him?"

He could tell her the truth—what could she do to her own husband's grandfather? But Devak knew the answer to that, knew how vulnerable his great-grandfather was.

After Aunt Chaaya's scandal, Zul had handed over his adhikar to Devak's father, in essence giving up all rights to it in exchange for life-long care. Devak's mother only grudgingly agreed to take him in, expecting Pitamah to greet the Lord Creator not long after he'd moved under her roof.

But then he didn't die. And just recently, once last year and once the year before, his great-grandfather had gotten terribly sick after eating a special meal prepared at his mother's direction.

"I took them for myself," he said. "Placement exams are coming up for next term and I need to be alert."

"Liar!" Her slap and the word came in quick succession.

Not the same cheek as his father had struck, so there was a scrap of luck. Another bit of fortune since she'd let go of his arm to hit him. He took the steps two at a time, ignoring the heat in his cheek, ignoring her screech that she wasn't finished with him.

He used the washroom quickly, then as he returned to his room, heard the arguing from his parents' suite. His father must have come and gotten her, thank the Lord Creator. His mother screamed in outrage over the missing crysophora and demanded his father go to the dispensary for more. His father reminded her she'd exceeded her limit on the drug and insisted she take the BeCalm instead.

Devak hoped Pitamah was too deeply asleep to hear the uproar. In spite of himself, he hoped, too, that his father wouldn't give in about the crysophora. His mother was killing herself bit by bit with the powerful drug.

When Devak finally lay in his bed, the evening's events tumbled in his mind. The argument with his father, Kayla dosing his great-grandfather with crysophora, the time spent in Kayla's quarters.

Touching her. Taking her hand.

Then her tale about his brother and her questions that turned his world inside out. His confrontation with his mother was nothing compared to the war raging inside him now, contemplating what Kayla had said, had asked.

Of the lessons his family had taught him about GENs—his father's patronizing arrogance, his mother's snarling disgust, his Pitamah's steadfast respect—he'd taken his great-grandfather's to heart. But treating someone kindly and considering them equal were light years apart. He could respect a pet sey-cat, treat it kindly, but that did not make it human.

But he'd touched Kayla. And there had been nothing about her that had seemed less than human.

# 19

In the morning, Zul came to fetch Kayla from her quarters, waking her from a nightmare with a pounding on her door. That had been surprise enough. That he was standing on her doorstep under his own power, looking vigorous and strong, was even more stunning.

His unmarked cheek was a third shock. She stared at it for a long time, searching for the mark of that faded tattoo on his left cheek. Not only could she not see it, she couldn't figure out how he could have covered it so perfectly. The left cheek looked exactly the same as the right, the same lined, aged skin.

"Do you need me to give you the second crysophora?" she asked.

"Did it myself." His sharp dark eyes fell on the sekai sitting on the table, then fixed on her. "Are you enjoying the reader?"

Her heart lodged in her throat. Did he know about Mishalla? That they'd used the sekai illicitly last night to talk? He couldn't possibly, could he? Zul's gaze narrowed on her, almost as if he could see her thoughts.

"I . . . y-yes," she stuttered. "It's good to have something to read in the evening."

But as she waited, breathless, for further interrogation, the corners of his mouth twitched up. "You have ten minutes. I'll be waiting for you in the AirCloud." He turned on his heel and marched back across the lawn.

She made it to the garage in nine. He insisted she sit in the front beside him and waited with ill-concealed impatience while she fumbled the safety straps on.

He piloted the lev-car with silent efficiency, looking as if he was sunk into some kind of darkness. Kayla glanced at him sidelong as they climbed up onto the skyway, uneasy at the stranger beside her. Instead of his usual white, he wore a purple korta and matching chera pants. His eyes glittered with a manic energy. Every so often, his body would shudder and he would clutch the navigation wheel to stop the tremor.

He caught her staring at him. "It's the crysophora," he said just a little too loudly, with a wild edge to the words. "An unfortunate side effect. I'm sorry if it distresses you."

She shifted in her seat, felt the packet nestled in the waistband of her leggings. "I don't understand why you need me with you."

"For the same reason I brought the lev-chair," he told her, turning the navigation wheel left. "The crysophora will only sustain me so long. I'll need you to help me home again."

"What about the lev-car?" she asked in sudden panic. "Will you be able to pilot it?"

"It's easy enough to program. I could have done it on the trip out, but I like to fool myself into thinking I have control over some part of my life."

Everything about him seemed so dark this morning. More of the crysophora's work.

She couldn't quell her fascination with the contours of his

unmarked cheek. "How did you erase it? Is it gone for good now?"

"It'll never be gone," he said. "Better you don't know how I've hidden it."

"You didn't erase it the day we went shopping."

"The concealer is far too expensive to use often. Devak was along at towncenter, so I could avoid the expense."

She turned her gaze away from him, out at the passing scenery. Watching the shifting holo façades of trueborn houses, the blur of exotic trees and shrubs as they rushed past, she longed for Chadi sector. At least what she saw there was real. Unlike all the trueborn fakery and this false Zul beside her.

They dropped off the skyway in the middle of towncenter, the shopping area behind them, the business district beyond. As they moved along the roadway, the structures grew taller on either side, until it seemed as if they traveled through a canyon of glass and permacrete. Lev-cars crawled along like the Chadi River between the man-made canyon walls. Trueborns swarmed the walkways on either side of the street.

"This many trueborns work?" she asked.

"They spend their day prying into the privacy of others, devising new genetic horrors, and consider it noble employment." That same edginess weighted his tone. "You've met my grandson? Ved?"

She put down his sudden shift of topics to the crysophora's mischief. "Not met him. I've seen him."

"Didn't introduce himself to you, I'll wager. He likes to think he knows what compassion is." He laughed, loudly, harshly. "Not one GEN lost in the western territories on his watch. At least not lost for long."

They turned off the long canyon of the main thoroughfare, between two structures with a black, oily sheen. Past the buildings, she saw a familiar screen of holo trees and a glimpse of warehouses beyond.

Zul guided the AirCloud into a docking station behind the oily black building to their left, nosing it into a slot between a Bullet and a WindSpear. With a faint clunk and hiss, the lev-car settled into its charging dock.

He climbed from the lev-car and she scrambled out as well. "What do I do?" she asked.

"There's a lowborn village beyond the warehouses," Zul told her.

She looked over her shoulder. "I can't just walk into a shantytown."

"You can't stay here. In or out of the lev-car, you'll be fair game for any curious enforcer. You're safer with the lowborns."

Then why did he bring her? His explanation before made no sense. Whoever he was visiting inside that black glass building would help him to the AirCloud, set the programming for home.

"Why can't I just go walk along the river?" Kayla asked. "There's no reason for me to bother the lowborns."

"Because you're on the wrong side of the river." Zul shut and locked the doors to the AirCloud, cutting Kayla off from its dubious protection. "You can wander all you like in Chadi sector, but on the Foresthill side, an enforcer might spot you."

"But why would a lowborn even talk to a GEN like me?" She sounded like a whiny tenth-year, but she couldn't bear the thought of the whole of the shantytown looking down their noses at her the way Senia did.

Zul waved her off toward the warehouses with an impatient gesture. "Go talk to them. Consider it an order. Be back here in two hours."

He strode away from her toward a smoked glass doorway imprinted with a gleaming crown. Palming a bio-scanner, he stepped inside.

Leaving Kayla alone on the fringes of the trueborn business district, with no choice but to do as Zul had demanded. She'd have to walk into the shantytown and hope the lowborns wouldn't drive her away.

She started toward the holo trees, passing between two of the generators, her flesh tingling with static electricity. She had to jog right to reach the nearest alleyway, then had to dodge a knot of GEN boys loitering between the buildings. They were sharing a vac-seal of something, maybe a lifter to help them through their next shift.

They called after her as she edged past them, each one trying to top the other with their crass observations. They invited her to take a dose from the vac-seal, to find a private place behind the incinerator for some fun. She kept moving.

As she stepped clear of the alleyway, she caught the familiar rank smell of the Chadi. There were a half-dozen structures—more houses than shanties—built along the river's edge. They were sided with slabs of plasscine instead of rusted scavenged metal, set on foundations of plasscrete instead of bare dirt. She saw power generators behind each shack and an incinerator half-way down.

The children gathered behind the houses were well dressed, all with shoes on their feet, the girls with hair neatly braided back. They were playing a counting game with a lowborn woman supervising.

A lowborn man emerged from the first shack. Balding, but tall and rangy, he spotted Kayla. He stood there, watching her, with hands on hips.

She pushed herself to move in his direction, shaking harder the closer she got. The lowborn man kept his steady blue gaze on her as she approached.

"Are you lost, GEN?" he asked, not rudely, but not kindly either.

She fell back on Tala's lessons in courtesy. "I'm Kayla 6982 of Chadi sector, nurture daughter of Tala. I know it's too much for a GEN to ask for lowborn hospitality—"

"Come sit with me." The man walked away toward his house.

A moment's indecision, then Kayla followed. The lowborn pointed to a chair covered with hand-woven cloth, then sat opposite on a stool. A rug was spread between them, its edges unraveling and colors sun-faded, and it gave a homey feel to the makeshift yard.

He stared at her for a long time, the lines fanning from his blue eyes deepening as he narrowed his gaze on her. He seemed to expect something from her. It was like a game of sarka, when you waited for your opponent's first move. Two left, three forward meant you could follow with a strategy, but one left, four forward would utterly tangle the game.

But this wasn't sarka and she didn't know the first move. She locked her hands together, took a breath. Waited.

Until he finally spoke. "Your help is required, Kayla 6982, nurture daughter of Tala."

His trigger words tapped into the data upload and compelled her to answer. "I would like the opportunity to help."

The lowborn nodded. "My wife, Quila, is in the house."

The door was open and Kayla stepped inside. The house wasn't as big as the flat she'd shared with Tala and Jal, but the living room was bright with colors GENs could only dream of—intricate rugs on the floor, vivid blankets thrown over the furniture, a brilliant mural painted across one wall. A baby lay sleeping on the sofa, pillows piled around her. In the kitchen, the dark-haired Quila washed dishes.

The woman turned, drying her hands on a cloth. As Quila crossed to the living room, faint recognition teased Kayla. "Do I know you?" Kayla asked.

A heart-wrenching grief passed over the woman's face. "The first day of your Assignment you passed by my village by the north bridge, where I used to live. My son, Shan, ran over to you."

Kayla glanced over at the tiny baby asleep on the sofa. Three or four months old, maybe, not the stout toddler she recalled. "Is Shan in another room? Or with the other children?"

She shook her head, tears rimming her eyes. "He was taken from me, the next day."

"Taken . . ." Kayla struggled to understand. "He didn't wander off, like children do? He didn't . . ." She gestured out the open door toward the Chadi.

Quila shook her head. "I'd gone inside the house, left Shan only a moment. One of the older girls had her eye on him and heard a trueborn call Shan over. Called him by name."

"He came right to me that day," Kayla remembered. He'd no doubt run into the arms of his captors, that happy grin on his face.

"Before the girl could shout a warning, the trueborn swept

Shan up. Ran to a lev-car." Quila stared in stoic grief, tears spilling down her cheeks.

If it had been Tala crying, or Mishalla or Miva, Kayla would have put her arms around her without thinking twice. But this was a lowborn woman who would likely take offense at GEN comfort.

Yet Quila reached blindly across the space between them, groping for contact. Kayla took her hand.

"Surely you've reported it to the Brigade," Kayla said.

"Yes." Quila let go, went to the kitchen for the cloth she'd used earlier. She dried her face. "That GEN who'd been there testing Shan—"

"Skal." The name came out on a puff of air.

"Yes, that one. We hadn't called him but there he was, not three hours after Shan had been taken."

"Why was he there?"

"He said he'd been asked to follow up on the assessment he'd done of Shan. Run another battery of tests."

Dread settled in Kayla's belly. "Did he say he wanted to do that with any of the other children?"

"Only Shan."

And Shan was the one who had been taken. Had Mishalla's nurture brother, Skal, been involved?

Quila twisted the cloth in her hands. "We'd heard rumors of other eastern Foresthill villages, children being stolen like Shan was. We didn't feel safe there anymore, so we moved farther west."

Now she remembered what Mishalla had said about her crèche. Could whatever was happening up in Skyloft be happening here too?

She had to give Quila at least a crumb of comfort. Hopefully the lowborn woman wouldn't press her for where she'd heard the information. "I've heard rumors too. That the children were taken and moved to another shantytown."

Quila's eyes flashed with gratitude. "Then he'd be safe at least. I pray to the Lord Creator that what you say is true."

In her mind, Kayla flung a prayer of her own to the Infinite that Shan would be returned to Quila. Could Skal have had something to do with Shan's disappearance? She felt sick inside at the possibility. Had Skal's time as an enforcer perverted him enough that he would participate in stealing lowborn children?

Quila pulled Kayla from her troubling thoughts. "Do you have the packet?"

Kayla hesitated. After guarding it so long, she was reluctant to surrender it.

Quila must have sensed Kayla's misgivings. The lowborn woman's mouth twisted into a half-smile. "They tell me it will do a great deal of good."

Of course, they'd told Kayla nothing. Just asked her to carry the Infinite-cursed thing.

"Do you know what it is? What it's for?" Kayla asked.

"I know only that it's DNA of some kind," Quila said. "DNA that was collected in Chadi sector."

"Why have a GEN carry it out?" Kayla asked. "Wouldn't it be safer to use a lowborn or trueborn?"

"I think you can guess why a GEN is best," Quila said.

Kayla thought a moment. "Because lowborns hardly ever come into the GEN sectors. And the trueborns are all medics or Assignment specialists or enforcers. How would you know if you could trust any of them?"

And you'd have to trust, because whatever this DNA was, it was secret, and meant for only certain people to know about.

As much as Kayla's curiosity burned, it was just as well she knew so little herself. She dug out the packet finally and placed it in Quila's hand. The lowborn woman disappeared through a doorway, and Kayla stood in the coolness of the living room, wondering if she should leave now that she'd passed on her burden. She felt deflated with her minor adventure over.

But Quila returned, her hand closed around something. When the lowborn held it out, Kayla took it reflexively.

And nearly dropped the thing. A datapod. Kayla could claim she had no idea what was inside the mysterious packet and just might avoid a reset as a consequence of possessing it. But there was no question the datapod was forbidden tech.

"Is this real?" she asked, horrified to see it nestled in her palm.

"It is," Quila said.

"I can't take it," she said, trying to hand the datapod back.

Quila wouldn't accept it. "You brought the packet all this way."

"But I thought I was done. What am I supposed to do with this?"

"There are others to tell you that."

Kayla's legs felt so weak she sank onto the sofa beside the baby. What others? How far did this conspiracy extend? And why were they using her as a go-between when there were so many others with far more courage than her? Like Mishalla. Mishalla would have accepted the datapod without thinking twice.

"Will you do it?" Quila asked.

Completely unwilling, Kayla nevertheless closed her fingers around the datapod, then tucked it away in the hidden pocket.

The datapod was two or three times as large as the tiny packet, but if she kept her shirt loose around her waist, it wouldn't show.

Quila offered her a small portion of kel-grain and a tiny glass of sugarfruit juice. Kayla accepted even though her stomach was in knots. She would have preferred returning to the lev-car, but it wasn't time yet. It would be bad enough for her to be caught by patrolling enforcers while loitering around the AirCloud. Even worse to have a datapod in her possession.

She'd just sat down to eat when the baby woke and cried, the imperious voice reminding her of Tala's newest nurture baby, Pren. After changing the baby girl, Quila picked her up and sat with her at the kitchen table. When she pushed up her blouse to expose her breast, Kayla couldn't stop herself from staring.

Quila brought the baby up to nurse and the infant latched on enthusiastically. "You've never seen this?"

Kayla shook her head. "I've read about it. Seen sekai pictures. But GEN nurture mothers aren't genned to nurse babies. Why would they? It's not always babies they nurture. And how would you turn it on and off? Easier just to give a bottle."

Still, it fascinated her. The convenience of it, the way the baby seemed so cozy and happy snuggled in Quila's arms. An image flashed in her mind of herself as a baby, staring up at that mysterious woman who'd nurtured her before Tala. A fantasy, of course, something she'd made up. Because how could she recall something from that long ago?

Quila finished feeding the baby while Kayla ate the few bites of kel-grain and sipped the token glass of juice. Too restless to sit any longer, she set the bowl and cup in the kitchen, then went outside to the very edge of the Chadi.

She was quite a ways downstream from where Jal had

hunted sewer toads that day. With the recent rains and runoff, the river was deeper here and ran faster. It looked close to hip-deep near the bank and would probably reach her shoulders in its deepest part. Yet there was no barrier on either side. Thanks to a recent spring deluge, the water was fresher here, not thick with pollution as it had been where Jal had hunted toads. With enough courage, she could cross it. Duck into the Doctrine school play yard on the other side and hide herself amongst the school buildings.

How far was she from home? Thirty, forty kilometers? Certainly outside her Grid radius if she stepped over to the Chadi side. Her annexed brain told her that nearly anywhere in Foresthill was within the radius, but since she'd been Assigned, only a small swath of Chadi was legal now. If she walked those forty or so kilometers to Tala's warren, traveling at least part of the time outside her radius, how long before the Grid detected her absence? Would they send out the Brigade immediately or would someone like Devak or his father investigate first?

What did it matter? The end result would be the same—punishment. If they didn't reset her, they'd change her Assignment to somewhere much less pleasant than the Manel home. She'd never see Devak again.

Which might be better. Her Infinite-forbidden feelings for him would be abruptly cut away.

As her inner clock ticked out the remaining minutes to the meeting time, Kayla stared across the Chadi at the GEN sector. She imagined those few moments of freedom, walking from here to her warren, before the enforcers came for her. Or maybe she would turn the other way, follow the Chadi to the ocean, then wander Svarga's western coast. Explore the continent as she'd always longed to. Until she got caught, she would be her own person for that precious span, not merely a GEN, beholden to the trueborns as demanded by the Infinite.

When she turned to climb the bank, she saw Quila waiting for her, the baby in her arms. The lowborn woman smiled as Kayla came even with her.

So odd seeing Quila's mouth and the tall lowborn man's blue eyes in the baby's small face. There was an echo, too, of Kayla's dim memory of Shan in the determined chin. An alien thing for a GEN, seeing family resemblance.

Quila must have seen Kayla's interest because she offered the bundled baby girl. "Would you like to hold her?"

Kayla took the infant to be polite, although she didn't think she'd been genned with even a scrap of nurturing DNA. She held the baby expertly enough, having had some experience with Pren and poor, doomed Liya. And she couldn't help but smile at the baby girl's grin.

But gazing down at her, with the infant returning her stare, Kayla felt a dizzying sense of déjà vu. In the same instant she was the baby, and herself looking down at the baby. It reminded her of the symbolism of the Infinite—mirrors facing each other, throwing reflections into infinity. Except it was her face and this baby's that were the mirrors.

"Are you all right?" Quila asked, reaching for her child as Kayla swayed.

"Fine. Yes. Thank you," Kayla said as she handed the infant back.

She shook off the strange illusion, turning away, leaving the shantytown behind her.

# 20

After a poor night's sleep, Devak woke late, and when he went past his great-grandfather's room, he saw the bed was empty. The lev-chair was gone as well, and Devak thought maybe Kayla had taken Pitamah down to eat his morning meal in the kitchen.

But Senia told him that they'd both gone. "He went off with her. Sat her in the front of the AirCloud, as if I wouldn't have to clean the seat after that jik sat in it."

Devak could barely tamp down his anger. "You won't use that word around me. You won't use it at all."

Senia had the good sense not to ask which word Devak meant. She just thrust out her jaw and slammed a plate of egg paratha on the kitchen table. He ate the paratha, washing it down with tea, while Senia banged her way around the kitchen.

His mother stumbled in just as he finished, her eyes red-rimmed, the sash on her skirt tied crookedly. She glared at him, dropping into a chair as if her legs couldn't hold her up a moment longer.

"That was the last of my crysophora, you evil boy. Now I have to go out for some more."

Senia set a cup of coffee in front of his mother. Her hands shook so roughly as she picked it up, she spilled a little of the dark brew bringing it to her lips.

"Father's gone already and Pitamah took the other AirCloud."

Her bleary eyes snapped open. "I'll take your Bullet, then."

He shook his head, hating the ugly pleasure he felt at thwarting his mother. "I need it. Father's sending me to Sheysa today."

She looked ready to cry, and Devak's heart ached. He took the cup from her and held her hand. "Maybe it's good the crysophora's gone. Maybe you can try to be yourself today without it."

She pulled away from him, sagging onto the table. "I don't want to be myself."

His mother's hopelessness weighing heavily on him, he headed for his father's office. His father had left the door open for him. Devak went inside and collected a datapod and the sekai reader his father had uploaded with the information on the missing GENs. He'd use his wristlink to access the Grid.

As he dropped the datapod and sekai in his pocket, he realized he could monitor Kayla right now. Find her, wherever she was with Pitamah. He'd done it before, working for his father, had thought nothing of tracking a GEN's location. But to do it with Kayla, after their conversation last night, seemed like a terrible intrusion.

Yet he had the power to do it. Like his father did, like any trueborn did with the proper authorizations. If a trueborn

# tankborn

employer suspected their house GEN was taking side trips while doing the family marketing, the employer could request a trace. Some trueborns would track their GENs even on Restdays, and the Brigade often demanded a monitoring tag.

It had never seemed wrong before. He'd let himself believe it was beneficial for the GENs, a way of protecting them. Even when his father had finally tracked down some missing GENs using the Grid, then had turned them over to the Brigade, Devak had persuaded himself it was better for the GENs to be in trueborn hands than wandering on their own.

It was like the herds of droms that grazed on his adhikar grant. His father had taught Devak at an early age to check often with the lowborn caretakers to be sure the fencing was secure in the drom pastures. That electrified fence not only kept out predators like the massive bhimkay spider, the zap that it gave the droms also deterred them from blundering through the fence into danger.

But GENs weren't droms, no matter how much animal DNA had been woven into their bodies. If they stepped beyond their radius, they'd made a conscious choice and knew the danger they faced. And when someone like his father stepped in, it wasn't to keep them safe. It was to punish.

All this time he'd been pretending. He hadn't liked the ugliness of the truth. But deep inside he'd always known what likely had happened to the GENs his father turned over. Once they went into Brigade custody, they were reset. Then the enforcers transported them to the appropriate GEN transition facility. And the GENs that came out of that facility weren't the same GENs that had gone in.

He locked his father's office, then headed out to the

docking garage for his Bullet. He tossed the sekai and datapod on the Bullet's seat, the two small devices a reminder of what he might be complicit in today. If he found the GENs at all. Maybe they all were well and truly gone.

Eight kilometers along the skyway, a big two hundred passenger pub-trans had collided with a lev-car, and the lumbering vehicle had toppled on its side, blocking three lanes. Three triage trucks added to the mess, the six medics who had arrived in the trucks woefully inadequate for the number of injured. Two medics hovered over the one trueborn whose WindSpear had hit the rear of the pub-trans.

As the Bullet crawled past the wreckage, Devak saw two or three dozen bodies arrayed across the skyway pavement on thin blankets. Lowborns, bloody and broken, lay in rows spread out between the pub-trans and the triage trucks, four medics spread out amongst them. Other lowborns wandered amongst the wounded, their pale skin even more wan from the shock.

The instant a slot opened in the traffic, a horn blared behind him. As he edged past the wreckage, he couldn't resist the compulsion to take a last look in his rear viewer. In front of the pub-trans, at least a dozen injured GENs lay propped up against the skyway wall. Another, a female of maybe sixteen, lay flat on the pavement, her head bloody. Two GENs knelt beside her, under the watchful eye of a pair of enforcers.

A burning started in Devak's gut as he continued out of sight. What was the Brigade there for? Certainly the GENs posed no threat. The only reason he could conjure up for their presence sickened him.

They were there to harvest genetic material. If the GEN female died, her tissue could be recycled, her skin and muscles and organs transformed into stem cells. Then those stem cells would be re-used to create more artificial embryos, more GENs. He'd learned the process in an Academy science class, but it had seemed dry going to a twelfth-year. Seeing the dying GEN, the hovering Brigade, put a dark twist on what had seemed an innocuous procedure when he'd read about it in his classes.

A kilometer past the accident, the clot of vehicles finally dispersed, and the skyway was clear all the way to Sheysa. The images of the injured GEN female, her friends struggling to sustain her, the lurking enforcers, circled in his mind the rest of the twenty minute journey.

The images still clung as he nosed the Bullet into a docking slot near the Sheysa warehouse district and shut down the suspension engine. He couldn't drive the GEN female's misery from his mind; even worse, Kayla's face kept taking the place of that anonymous GEN's. Kayla dying. Kayla carried off by the Brigade to be harvested.

The breath left his lungs, leaving him gasping. He wouldn't let that happen. He would protect her, keep her safe. If his efforts failed, he would burn her remains himself and keep her from being harvested. The enforcers would never touch her.

# 21

To Devak's eyes, it could have been the warehouse district in Foresthill—one windowless permacrete box after another, as far as the eye could see, uniform in size and color. Each one twelve meters high, fifty wide and deep. The featureless walls tinted the same peach-tan, the only mark on the exteriors the dark brown ground-level doorways. Occasionally two boxes were built side by side if the building's function required more interior space.

With the mid-morning break over, the walkways surrounding the warehouses and factories were nearly deserted. He spotted a GEN in an alleyway dumping refuse into an incinerator, another pair toting crates out to a waiting lev-truck.

Devak glanced at the locator display on his sekai, comparing the map to the three buildings directly in front of him. On the right, a plasscine extrusion factory, in the middle a foodstores warehouse, on the left an empty building. Not completely empty—as he watched, a lowborn woman carried a crate to the door and knocked. A redheaded girl answered—a GEN?—and let the lowborn woman inside.

The streets and walkways around the factories and warehouses were nearly deserted. He checked his sekai—today was Sheysa's Founding Day, so only GENs and their lowborn supervisors would be working.

The GENs he was interested in worked at the extrusion factory. As he walked toward the double doors, he paged through the non-humans' images on the sekai. They were all of pale-skinned stock, their hair dark and straight, their eyes brown. Their faces all ran together in his mind, the female distinctive only because of her gender.

But he had to admit that even with GENs he encountered from more varied DNA stock—pale or dark, hair as straight as a high-status trueborn's or as untamed as Kayla's, he had to struggle to recall who was who.

It was the same with the droms on his adhikar grant. There was some prized breeding stock amongst his herd; the lowborn caretaker, Kalk, had pointed them out to Devak. But Devak couldn't tell a bull calf worthy of a future as a stud from an animal destined for a bowl of curry.

He wondered what Kayla would think of him comparing her fellow GENs to a herd of droms and he squirmed with shame. For years, his father had taught him that it was best to think of GENs as interchangeable parts in a machine, or as part of a herd. They were truly happiest that way, his father said, each GEN a properly functioning part of the whole, most content when Assigned to their proper place. GENs didn't see themselves as individuals, so it didn't make sense for a trueborn to consider them that way.

Devak had blindly accepted his father's lessons when he was younger. But once he got older, he'd started to question. Spending time with Kayla over the last few weeks, talking with her last night, he'd thought his attitude about GENs had changed even more. That he was seeing that maybe some non-humans did have unique personalities. Yet since yesterday when his father first ordered him here, and on his way to Sheysa, he hadn't thought about the missing GENs that way at all. They were a blur to him, each one just like the other.

He forced himself to examine each image again, to take notice of the differences in the shapes of the GENs' eyes, the variations in their hair color, however small. He realized that the four faces were indeed distinctive, never mind that they were all as pale as Livot. They were no more identical than that GEN female on the skyway was the same as Kayla. The two females—the two *girls*—were no more interchangeable than Devak and his long-dead brother Azad.

Then with a jolt, he realized something unique about these GENs. All had their DNA mark on their right cheeks, not their left. Like Kayla. The odd coincidence meant nothing, but it chilled him nonetheless.

He prodded himself toward the warehouse. If GENs were different from one another, if they were individuals, how could they be parts of a machine? If they suffered pain, if their hearts sometimes ached like any man's or woman's did. If they fought for life like the injured GEN girl. If they showed Kayla's sharp intelligence—how could they be less human than a trueborn or a lowborn?

He couldn't wrap his mind around that now. He had to ask after the missing GENs, make at least a show of trying to find them. If they were truly gone, he was glad he wouldn't be the one to track them down.

The sickly-sweet stench and deafening noise hit Devak as he stepped inside the factory. A stocky lowborn man spotted him immediately, hurrying over and bobbing his head deferentially.

"How can I help you, sir?" he shouted over the cacophony.

"I'm looking for these GENs." Devak held out the sekai and paged through the images.

"Yes, they're all on shift. I'll bring them."

To Devak's surprise, the lowborn hurried off. Several minutes later, the pale-haired lowborn returned with four GENs, three males—men—and a woman. The four exchanged glances with one another as they spotted Devak and he could see their uneasiness as they drew closer.

He took them all outside to escape the noise and stink of molten plassfiber. Lining them up, he compared each GEN face with the accompanying image. He asked their names and identifiers, double checking with his datapod against their tattoos. They all swore they had no idea why they'd dropped from the Grid.

And the lowborn supervisor confirmed their story. The four had appeared faithfully for work at the factory every day but Restday for the two weeks they'd supposedly been missing from the Grid.

The GENs smiled at one another in relief as they returned to the factory, swiping away the blood from the datapod reads. One of the men winced a little as he touched his cheek.

Guilt twinged inside Devak. He knew using the datapod hurt the GENs, yet he'd used it often for the most trivial reasons. To confirm a work schedule rather than take a GEN at his word. To tally skets within a factory population when that information existed in a database he could more easily access. He'd always justified the intrusion into the GENs' annexed brains because it had been at his father's direction rather than his own volition. But truly, it had more often been his own laziness that led to their pain.

The datapod seemed to burn his palm as the last of the GENs disappeared inside. His father would have approved of him using it, yet it wasn't the GENs at fault, it was obviously a problem in the Grid. The tracking equipment must have developed some kind of blind spot here in Sheysa where these GENs were clustered.

Devak dropped the datapod back into his pocket and started walking, only half-aware of his destination as he cut through the holo trees. Since last night's conversation, really since Kayla had arrived at his home, his world had been turned upside down and inside out. Truths he'd never thought to question now seemed ragged with doubt. The foundations of life he'd stood solidly on now sagged and shifted under his feet.

He followed the streets through a minor-status trueborn neighborhood into Sheysa Square. Centered on a green filled with scrubby natural grass and holo trees, shops lined the square's four sides. A Founders Day holiday crowd packed the walkways, toting carrysaks and pushing carts, some with infants and toddlers in tow. School-age children rioted across the green, racing through the scrap grass, screaming with joy while their parents looked on.

Since Sheysa sector was set aside for more affluent lowborns and minor-status trueborns, lowborn shoppers frequented even the trueborn shops. In fact, if not for the blue bali gems the trueborns wore, he might have mistaken some of the well-to-do lowborns for minor-status trueborns and vice versa, just judging by their clothing, hair texture, and skin color.

He threaded his way through the crowd to a row of the most prosperous-looking shops and stopped at the window of a jeweler. The crowd swarmed around him, occasionally jostling him. When they got a look at his diamond bali and recognized his status, lowborn and minor-status alike would step away with an apology.

As he scanned the jeweler's offerings, he was struck with the outrageous notion of buying something for Kayla. It couldn't be anything expensive—his mother would accuse her of stealing it. But maybe one of the ceramic-coated pendants. She could tie it on a ribbon and keep it hidden under her shirt.

The delicate gray seycat pendant would match her eyes. He could buy a length of black ribbon to go with it. Devak turned to go inside, then stopped short when a lowborn boy about his age moved into his path.

He got a brief look at the boy's face, took in the long blond hair, the blue eyes, then stepped to his left. "Excuse me."

Except the boy didn't yield. He shifted, still blocking Devak's way. While Devak leaned to the right to evade the lowborn, he felt someone else behind him and the unmistakable heat of a lase-knife.

The boy in front of him smiled affably. "Just come around the corner with us. And we'll all walk away unharmed."

Devak's left hand got within a few centimeters of the wristlink on his right arm before the lowborn stopped him. With deft fingers, he disengaged the wristlink's latch and snatched it before it fell. It vanished into a pocket.

"We need only a moment of your time," the blond boy said, smiling.

Devak could call out and any of these lowborns or minor-status trueborns would come to his aid. But how many might be hurt by the lase-knife before the person wielding it could be overcome? Or what if Devak's alarm set off a panic in this packed crowd of the kind that killed his brother, Azad? How could he let himself be responsible for anyone injured protecting his own safety?

He would deal with these two thugs on his own. When the blond nudged Devak into a narrow alleyway between the jeweler and a music shop, Devak went along, glad enough to divert the danger from the busy street.

As they moved into the shadows, Devak craned his neck to see the knife-wielder, but the dark-haired attacker kept his face averted. The blond lowborn urged Devak to the rear of the dead-end alleyway, behind the incinerator. The one with the lase-knife hung back, his attention still on the street beyond the alley entrance.

The blond lowborn wasn't much bigger than Devak, but he looked wiry and strong. And even if Devak overpowered the blond boy, he'd still have the armed lowborn to contend with.

"What do you want?" Devak asked, injecting all of his mother's imperiousness into his tone. He might as well make that genetic link good for something.

The lowborn smiled. "Just the datapod." He held out his hand.

"I don't have one," Devak said.

"Of course you do," the lowborn said. "I haven't yet seen a high-status so much as cross his doorstep without one. If you'd like my friend with the lase-knife to be the one to search for it—"

"I can't give it to you." There was no way of knowing what his father had loaded on the datapod, what information he might be giving away to this lowborn.

As if the blond boy had read his mind, he said, "Feel free to wipe it before you hand it over. I only need the device, not what's on it."

Devak backed away, ever so slightly, toward the street. "Buy your own, lowborn. I won't give you mine."

Too fast for Devak to follow, the lowborn retrieved another lase-knife from somewhere, snapping it open under Devak's nose. "As if a lowborn had the dhans to buy a proper datapod. The drek you sell us won't do. Not enough storage, not near enough processing power. So I'll need yours."

The energy of the lase-knife heating his cheek, Devak groped in his pocket for the datapod. He found the Data Clear buttons and pressed them with his thumbnail and index finger, then dropped the device into the lowborn's hand.

The lowborn threw Devak's wristlink into the incinerator and took off running. Devak dashed after him. The other lowborn had already cleared the alley, but as Devak reached the entrance, a pub-trans pulled up, blocking the lowborns' escape. The blond peeled left, the dark-haired boy right, toward Devak.

Certainly the dark-haired lowborn hadn't meant it to, but as he skirted the pub-trans, his face angled in full view of Devak. It was just a moment, but long enough for Devak to register the odd combination of high-status skin color and green eyes. Then both lowborns were sprinting across the square and out of sight.

He should call the Brigade, give out a description of the two lowborns. The blond was a tenth-dhan-a-dozen; he could have been Livot's brother, Devak realized with a certain satisfaction. But the dark-haired boy, with that high-status face and green eyes, would stand out like a GEN bride at a high-status trueborn wedding.

Devak returned to the alleyway, opened the access lid of the incinerator. Luckily, he could reach the wristlink, although it had been fouled by a pile of spoiled kel-grain. He found a water spigot in the green and rinsed the wristlink, then dried it on his korta. He ran it through a status test. Its trip into the incinerator hadn't disrupted its function.

He thumbed the Open Connection pad, then hovered over the pre-set for the Brigade. Of course he'd contact them. Lowborns couldn't be allowed to accost trueborns in daylight, in plain view. It wasn't as if he'd been wandering alone in a GEN sector—this was Sheysa. A minor-status sector, but trueborn nonetheless.

Yet he didn't push the pre-set. He lowered his wrist, shoved his hands into the pockets of his cheras. Felt the contours of the sekai and pulled it out.

The blond lowborn had only wanted the datapod. Not the more valuable wristlink or sekai. Leaving behind the wristlink made sense; it would tag their location to a millimeter. But the sekai—its network function was easily disabled to prevent it from being used as a homing device. The boy might not have known for certain that Devak had one in his pocket, but he could have found it quickly enough. Yet he'd only wanted the datapod and he'd allowed Devak to wipe it.

He wouldn't notify the Brigade. He'd tell his father he'd somehow lost the datapod when he discarded the remains of lunch in a café mini-cin. He'd certainly feel the flat of his father's hand. Might lose the Bullet for a week or two, might not see Junjie for awhile. But Devak didn't care.

What would Pitamah think of Devak's rebellion? What would Kayla think? Would she be proud of him for not following his knee-jerk reaction and calling the enforcers?

He looked down at his wristlink. He wanted Kayla here with him, so badly. So he could tell her what happened. Hear what she thought.

Maybe it wouldn't be so bad to find her on the Grid. He knew where she was—somewhere with great-grandfather, likely at the Raja Club where the old trueborns gathered. He only wanted to have this small connection with her.

Pushing down his misgivings, he opened the link to the Grid on his wristlink. He entered Kayla's name and designator ID, home sector and nurture affiliation. Tapped Send.

*Entry not found.*

A chill went through him as he read the message. He tried again, taking great care to enter the text without mistakes. Hit Send.

*Entry not found.*

Just like the factory GENs. Except if the monitoring system couldn't locate the four GENs because of a blind spot in Sheysa, how could Kayla be missing from the Grid forty kilometers away in Foresthill?

# 22

**K**ayla reached the meeting place just as two old trueborn men emerged on either side of Zul, his arms draped over their shoulders. The taller of Zul's two friends bore the additional weight of a carrysak, its strap crossing his chest.

Kayla rushed over to help the men, who were likely as aged as Zul himself and clearly struggling to keep their friend upright. Zul sagged into her arms and she lifted him easily.

"Do you need a medic?" Kayla asked him.

Eyes closed, Zul shook his head. He gestured to the smaller of the two trueborns. "Hala. Come close." When Hala leaned over, Zul murmured what must have been the alarm code for the AirCloud. Hala hurried ahead to open the door to the lev-car.

The taller trueborn, his hair so white with age it seemed transparent, helped Kayla ease Zul behind the navigation wheel. He shrugged off the carrysak and slung it into the AirCloud's rear seat.

"Thank you, Jemali," Zul said, in barely more than a whisper.

Kayla drew the safety straps across Zul's chest. Jemali told her, "He should be fine with rest. I had to administer a lifter—something gentler than the crysophora."

"Should he have had more drugs?" Kayla asked. Only after the words were out of her mouth did it occur to her that maybe she shouldn't second-guess a trueborn.

But neither man took any offense. "I was a doctor—a medic," Jemali said. "Zul's taken a terrible risk, has probably put more strain on his heart than he should have. But the old coot will live."

Hala slipped into the passenger seat and entered something into the control panel. He ducked back out of the AirCloud. "I've keyed in the programming for the return trip. It'll be slower, but you'll get home just fine."

"Thank you," Kayla said.

"It's you who deserves thanks," Jemali responded.

"What have I done?" Kayla tried to decipher the look in the two old trueborns' eyes. They knew something. But what? Could they see the lump the datapod made at her waist? But why would they thank her for that? Why weren't they calling the enforcers and having her arrested?

She climbed into the lev-car. The smaller trueborn activated the lev-car suspension engine and shut the door. With Zul slumped in the safety straps, it was unsettling to have the AirCloud disengage from its docking station of its own accord and back up into the street. But the programmed lev-car seemed to travel far more carefully than it had under Zul's control. It moved along at a more sedate speed and maintained a larger buffer between itself and the other AirClouds, Bullets, WindSpears, and pub-transes.

When they reached the Manel house, the second AirCloud was in its slot in the garage, so Mr. Manel was home. But Devak's Bullet was gone.

The AirCloud docked itself, and Kayla quickly rounded the vehicle to extricate the old man from the safety straps. She reached to lift him out, but he batted her hands away.

"Get the chair," he said, his voice gruff but kind, the crysophora edge worn off. "Won't have you carry me inside."

She retrieved the lev-chair from the boot and helped Zul into it. After hooking the carrysak on the back of the chair at Zul's direction, she guided the chair from the garage and around the side of the house to the back.

Kayla didn't breathe easy until she'd guided the lev-chair up the back stairs and into Zul's room. She got him comfortable in his bed, leaving him dressed when he insisted.

"Should I stay?" she asked.

"No need for you to watch an old man sleep." He fluttered a hand toward his dresser. "Hide the carrysak in the bottom drawer."

The contents of the carrysak shifted and spread as she stuffed it into the drawer, piquing her curiosity as to what was inside. "I'll come back for evening meal."

He'd already drifted off. She took another look to be sure his color was good, then quietly left the room.

She crossed the lawn to her quarters, troubled by the morning's revelations. Her conversation with Quila about the lowborn's missing son, Zul's illness, the new burden she'd been asked to carry. The carrysak Zul had brought back with him—what was inside? How did the contents fit into the other unknowns that seemed to grow larger in number each day?

And what unknowns would she find in the file of GEN names on the sekai and in Zul's paper book? She'd wanted to pull the book out last night after Devak left, but she didn't want to attract attention by turning her light back on. Instead she tried without success to reconnect with Mishalla, but perversely the sekai's network function was again blocked.

She shut the door to her quarters, going immediately to the cupboard with the paper book. With luck, Zul would sleep the afternoon through and give her a few stolen hours.

Sitting at the table, she opened the book and flipped through it, squinting at it in the pale overhead light. As she'd seen in her quick scan the day before, the entries were thick with tech talk. Complex diagrams and charts filled with bewildering symbols alternated with the dry scientific descriptions. Several pages in the back had been torn out.

Sprinkled amongst the incomprehensible text were the names Abeni and Geming, which made sense since those deadly plagues would still have been ravaging Svarga seventy-eight years ago. For all she knew, Zul was one of the techs who'd worked on the plague vaccines. He'd have been a young man, only a twenty-fourth year.

*The neural circuitry nanoparticles injected using mono-clonal antibody carriers.* Maybe Jal would understand what that gobbledygook meant, but she didn't have a clue. If she'd ever read about it in Doctrine school, she'd forgotten it soon after.

*Sub-neural network and dermal interface developing at expected rate—optimum pathway for genetic engineering?*

Even as her eyes passed over Zul's scrawled words without comprehension, something tickled the back of her bare brain. Genetic engineering she knew, of course. The Infinite had chosen that method to create the GENs. Trueborns had fiddled with genetic engineering since they arrived on Loka, preparing a place for the prophets' triumph.

Sub-neural network. Dermal interface. The words teased at a memory.

Then she remembered. Jal had explained to her one day, with ill-concealed impatience at her denseness, how GEN programming worked. The circuitry incorporated into her nervous system was a sub-neural network. Her tattoo was the dermal interface.

And Zul knew about them in 294. Five years before the Infinite whispered the secrets of GEN life into the prophets' ears.

Hand shaking, she turned the page, read the first line written there. And her heart nearly stopped.

*Meeting with higher-ups—Pouli, Cohn, and Gupta.*

Zul had met with the prophets. Long before those three hallowed trueborns had been given even an inkling of GEN creation by the Infinite, Zul had tinkered with what would someday be the sacred trust of the Three.

Then why was Zul not a prophet too? Kayla had read every word of the liturgy, even the dullest parts. And Zul Manel's name was never mentioned.

Was it possible the Infinite had first whispered the secrets to Zul? And Zul had somehow turned aside from that call? The Infinite might have turned His back on Zul then. It could have something to do with Zul's weakness now, that mark on his cheek so like the GEN tattoo. The fact that gene-splicers apparently couldn't fix the old man's ailment.

She turned back to the front of the book and studied the pages again more carefully, running a finger along each scribed line. She might have missed a previous mention of the prophets, an entry that would more clearly explain Zul's connection. She even examined the charts and diagrams, searching for something familiar. No luck.

With the book open to the torn-out section, she realized that what she'd thought was one lone page were two stuck together. Something brown glued them to one another. Running a careful fingernail between them, she separated the pages, holding her breath in anticipation of finding some new, important secret. But she saw only a brief line, still in Zul's hand but shakier as if written later when the old man's disease had progressed.

*Chaaya—Plakit, Mendin, Chadi? Filter the list by sectors.*

Plakit and Mendin were GEN sectors like Chadi. But Chaaya was a trueborn name. Where had she heard it?

She sucked in a breath. Chaaya was Mr. Manel's sister, the granddaughter Zul had "ruined." Chaaya had tattooed her face and run away to a GEN sector with a minor-status trueborn.

Was Zul trying to find out what sector she'd died in? But wouldn't he know that? And "filter the list." What list? Why?

Realization jolted through her like a lightning bolt. The list on the sekai. The list that included her name and Mishalla's and dozens of others who all appeared to be the same age.

*Used bits 'n' pieces of her for GEN-making,* Yezzi had said. What if it was true? What if there were GENs out there, maybe even a couple hundred, all made from Zul's granddaughter's DNA?

The artificial embryos that started GENs weren't truly artificial. It was just that they were grown from zygotes built not from sperm and egg but from ordinary cells transformed into stem cells.

If they'd truly thought Chaaya was a GEN, had taken her cells, used them to create non-humans . . . Yes, they would have changed Chaaya's DNA in the process, selected animal DNA for skets, added variations in skin and hair color, but Chaaya would have still been the source.

All the GENs from the list. Her. Mishalla. Progeny of Chaaya. Of a trueborn. And not just any trueborn—Zul's granddaughter.

The possibility took her breath away. Suddenly the discovery that Zul might have learned the secrets of GEN creation before the prophets faded into unimportance. That her own DNA might trace back to Chaaya and therefore to Zul, that she might be a distant DNA-cousin to Devak, that she and Mishalla might be tank-sisters in more than name only filled her with wonder.

It would tie together so many confusing threads. How she ended up here in the Manel household. Why Zul seemed so interested in her. GEN or no, she would almost be a great-granddaughter to him. As would Mishalla and all those others on the list.

If her guesses were right. If her longing to be something more, something special hadn't led her to leap to a wrong conclusion.

She grabbed up the sekai and scrolled to the XRS Potentials file. Opened it and found her name again. Tapped the link. The *Enter password* request popped up.

What would Zul use as a password? How would she even enter it when she had no idea how to bring up the screen keyboard? She poked and tapped and even shook the sekai once in frustration. She finally brushed against the icon by chance and the keyboard appeared on the screen.

Her courage faded for a moment. She shouldn't be doing this. Ought to put the thing away. But she clutched the sekai tighter. She was going to at least try.

The password wouldn't be anything simple, like Zul's name or the street they lived on. Jal had lectured her until her eyes crossed about how a password had to be "strong" to be any good. But if it was strong, she certainly would never get it.

So she tried the obvious options anyway—Zul's name, Devak's name, even Chaaya's. The street they lived on. All rejected.

She racked her brain, bare and annexed, entering a half-dozen wild guesses—Svarga, Loka, Earth. The names of the colony ships, of the original captains. Of course none of them worked. There was nothing strong about any of them.

She considered praying to the prophets for inspiration. But why would they help her, when she was violating trueborn law by trying to break into private files?

But they did answer her prayer, in a way. An idea flashed into her mind, into her bare brain. Her fingers shaking a little, she typed *PouliCohnGupta* and hit enter.

To her utter shock, the password box vanished. For an instant, she tasted triumph.

Then another request popped up on the screen. *Enter passkey.* And below those words were twenty little boxes, each of which required a letter or number.

No way to guess this. There were billions of possibilities. If someone had uploaded a code-guessing algorithm into her annexed brain, she could run through them all. But no trueborn in their right mind would upload something like a passkey-guesser into a GEN.

Edgy with frustration, she finally tossed aside the sekai. She forced herself to return her attention to the paper book. But the dry going and the startling discoveries of the past hour were too much for her. Her eyes grew heavier, as if the Infinite Himself weighted them down. Maybe that was intentional—maybe there were some things the Infinite didn't want her to see. She finally gave in, resting her head on the open book.

It seemed she'd only closed her eyes for a moment before a pounding jolted her from sleep. Could it be Devak? Her internal clock told her she'd slept the afternoon away; Devak must have returned by now. She rose, and had just gotten the book hidden in the cupboard when the door swung open.

Her astonishment that Devak would enter without permission faded into anger as Senia stepped inside. Of course Senia felt she had every right to barge into Kayla's quarters, Humane Edicts be damned.

"You're needed in the house," the lowborn said with a sour look on her face.

"Is Zul awake?

"Never mind the old man. Come with me."

As Kayla followed behind Senia, she saw Mr. Manel escorting two trueborn men and a woman along the side of the house toward the back garden. When the trueborns reached the stone path, Senia gave Kayla a little shove off onto the grass, then moved aside herself to give the trueborns right of way. As the visitors walked along in the fading light, Mr. Manel was describing a dragon tree that grew near the back fence. Senia and Kayla might as well have been a pair of unremarkable weeds for all the attention he gave them as he drew his visitors to inspect his exotic Earth plant.

Senia hurried Kayla on toward the house and they entered through the red door. In the kitchen, the lowborn woman stopped and faced Kayla.

"You'll keep your mouth shut about this," Senia hissed. "No one believes a jik anyway, but I won't have you spreading gossip."

They continued on into the living room. Devak's mother lay there, collapsed in a float chair, lost to the world. Empty vac-seals littered her lap and the table beside her. Her brightly dyed dress, gem-studded and gorgeous, was stained by whatever drugs had leaked from the vac-seals.

Senia's lips were pressed so tightly together, it was a wonder she could speak. "Mr. Manel will be conducting a business meeting upstairs, but he doesn't want his associates seeing Mrs. Manel sleeping. You're to carry her to her room so Mr. Manel and his associates can come inside."

"She won't like me touching her."

Senia flicked dismissive fingers toward Kayla. "No choice. Mr. Manel's visitors arrived before he realized Mrs. Manel was taking her nap. He can't leave them in the garden to carry her himself."

As far gone as Mrs. Manel was, Kayla doubted the woman would wake in transit. Still, as she removed the empty vac-seals from Devak's mother's lap, then hooked her arms under the woman's shoulders and knees, tension built a knot in Kayla's throat.

Mrs. Manel was more solid than Kayla expected. Still an easy load, but the woman's dead weight made her an awkward burden. They took the front stairs, the ones Kayla had never set foot on, and she had to move at an angle up the flight to avoid striking the drugged woman's head on the railing.

She'd nearly reached the top when the sound of the front door opening made her jump, and she jostled Mrs. Manel. Senia hissed at her, "Careful, jik," and squeezed past and down a few steps. Maybe the lowborn had some idea of blocking Mrs. Manel from the view of whoever had just arrived. Then she saw it was only Devak returned from whatever errand his father had sent him on.

Senia motioned to Devak. "I have to clean up the living room. You help the jik get your mother settled."

Devak surged up the stairs until he was level with the diminutive lowborn. "Call Kayla that again, Senia, and I'll have you removed from the house."

Kayla, watching the drama from the landing, saw the lowborn's eyes narrow. "You can't. Your mother—"

"My mother might want to know about how you skim from Meera and Yezzi's wages. How you've lifted a vac-seal or two from her supply to sell in the shantytown."

Senia launched an evil look up at Kayla, then tipped her head at Devak in token submission. She continued down the stairs as Devak climbed up.

Devak passed Kayla to lead the way. He paused at the open door to his father's office, looking inside.

"He's in the garden with those visitors of his," Kayla told Devak.

Mr. Manel's sterile office looked empty other than the lone float chair. There was nothing inside but blank white walls studded here and there with small boxes. Maybe Mr. Manel didn't have access to the Grid from here.

Farther down the hall, Devak pushed open the door to his parents' sleeproom. By the time Kayla brought Mrs. Manel in, he'd stripped back the bedclothes. Kayla laid the lax body on the bed, and Devak did nothing more than tug off his mother's shoes before carelessly throwing the covers over her.

They left the room and he shut the door. "It isn't the first time. It won't be the last." The shame was clear in his eyes.

She followed him around the corner to his own sleeproom, waiting at the door as he went inside. At the window that overlooked the garden, he palmed open the privacy screen. No doubt his father had been watching for a signal. Devak lifted his hand before he opaqued the window again.

He met her in the hall. "Something happened today. I have to tell Pitamah."

"He might still be asleep."

"We have to wake him."

Before Kayla could object, Mr. Manel shouted for his son. "Devak!"

A rebellious look crossed Devak's face, but he leaned around the corner. "Here, Father." He swung toward Kayla again. "Will you be there when I get back?"

"If your great-grandfather is awake. If not, I was going to go back to my quarters."

"Wait for me in Pitamah's room." Mr. Manel yelled Devak's name again, but Devak kept his gaze on Kayla. "Please."

She couldn't refuse him, not when his eyes pleaded with her that way. "I will."

Devak's smile grabbed at Kayla's heart. As he hurried off to obey his father's summons, a spark burned inside her. A huge mistake, a monumental one to feel anything like that for Devak. Infinite forgive her.

When she saw that Zul still slept, she put a hand to his

forehead to check for fever, then listened to his breathing. No heat; his breaths were deep and even. She settled on the bench opposite the bed to wait for Devak.

As he slumbered, Zul's eyes moved under the papery lids. She wondered what kind of dreams trueborns had, if they were the same as GEN dreams. Fearful, joyful, mundane, uplifting. Did they have nightmares like GENs did? Like Kayla still did?

She'd been here for nearly five weeks now. She would have thought her brain would stop replaying that same frightening dream over and over again. But two or three times a week there it was, filling her with terror. She would will herself awake, and her heart would pound in the aftermath.

Why were her arms gone in the nightmare? Because she was ashamed of her strength as a child and in her dream she wished them away? And why did the woman's face look so much like her own? Same gray eyes, same mousy hair. Like Quila's baby looked so much like Quila. Infinite's blessing, she didn't wish herself to be a lowborn, did she? Lowborns didn't return to the Infinite's mighty hands.

Could those nightmares fit in with what she'd guessed about the sekai list? What if, instead of her former nurture mother sending her away because she was so destructive, it was Zul's intervention? Maybe someone else found out she was genned from Chaaya's DNA and that put Kayla in danger. Zul could have had her placed with Tala.

While she struggled with those tangled thoughts, Devak entered, edgy and agitated, the smile that had so moved her gone. He glanced over at his sleeping great-grandfather, then prowled the floor, scraping his fingers through his dark hair.

"It just keeps getting worse and worse."

"What?" Kayla asked.

"I have to talk to Pitamah. He'll know what to do."

"We shouldn't wake him."

"It can't wait."

Zul groaned and swiped at his face, peering at Devak with slitted eyes. "What can't wait?"

Devak paced to the bed. "I told him they were just where they were supposed to be, Pitamah, at the factory. I told him there had to be a mistake in the Grid. But he's still sending them."

Zul gave an impatient huff. "Sit me up, Kayla. And maybe this boy will make more sense."

Kayla propped Zul up on the pillows, not liking the way he sagged against the cushions. "You should have something to eat."

"In a moment. I want to hear what Devak has to say."

Devak's story poured out—how he'd been sent to Sheysa to find four GENs missing from the Grid, that they'd been right where they should be the whole two weeks they'd supposedly been missing. Nevertheless, his father had notified the Brigade, and the GENs would be arrested.

Zul's troubled expression matched Devak's. "Sheysa. Was one of the four at a crèche?"

"I never saw a crèche."

"Next to the foodstores warehouse," Zul said.

"The GENs Father asked me to find were at the extrusion factory. He didn't mention a crèche or that anyone was missing from one."

"Maybe she's not been detected yet." Zul huffed a sigh of relief. "The factory workers have a failsafe—the Brigade won't take them. But things are trickier with Mishalla being off the Grid."

Kayla's mind stuttered on the words *off the Grid,* so it took her a moment to back up to the name. "Mishalla—not from Chadi sector? Nurture daughter of Shem and Rachel?"

Devak looked down at her, baffled. "I don't—"

"It's her, Kayla." Zul's keen eyes narrowed on her. "Your friend. She's Assigned to a crisis crèche in Sheysa."

"Sheysa . . . but she never told me she'd been moved so close—" She took in a sharp breath, wishing she could suck the words back into her throat with that lungful of air.

Devak missed the slip, but Zul's sharp gaze told her he hadn't. His casual question about the sekai this morning— he'd been fishing for confirmation that she'd networked with Mishalla on it. And now a glance at his great-grandson and the slight shake of his head told her to keep that fact from Devak.

Zul reached for her hand. "Mishalla has been pulled into something not of her own making. Dangerous for her, but an opportunity we had to grasp. We're doing what we can to keep her safe."

But how safe could she be? Zul might not know that the enforcers had already come for Mishalla last night, and Mishalla was trying to tell Kayla something about it when Devak interrupted their conversation. Was this what Mishalla had been leading up to? What if the enforcers who went today for the factory workers decided they ought to check on her again? Whatever had saved her the first time might not do the trick a second time.

Her mind circled back to what Zul had said. "Off the Grid. What did you mean by that?"

"We thought we had the situation handled with Mishalla

and you, with the other GENs," Zul said. "We knew a Grid upgrade was coming, but they advanced the upgrade date before we could hack into the code."

That caught Devak's attention, although Kayla was more confused than ever. "You've made changes to the Grid?" Devak asked.

"Not me," Zul said.

"Who, then?" Devak asked, then when Zul hesitated, Devak said fervently, "You know I'd never tell Father. I didn't even tell him about the datapod."

"What datapod?" Kayla said in unison with Zul. The old man's gaze briefly locked with hers. She felt the slight weight burn against her hip.

"Two lowborn boys took mine from me at lase-point. Oddest thing—they let me wipe it first when the data's always more valuable than the device, even if a trueborn datapod is better than what a lowborn can buy."

"Ilian and Eoghan wouldn't have known who you were," Zul said. "If they had, they would have left you alone."

"You know those lowborn boys? One blond, the other—"

"High-status looking, but with green eyes," Zul finished. "They appropriate datapods where they can. Off the back of lorries. From factories before they're shipped. If they went around buying trueborn-level tech it would look too suspicious. Someone would wonder where they got the dhans. But they don't usually confront trueborns like you. You must have looked like easy pickings."

"Sheysa Square was jammed with people," Devak said. "They caught me off-guard."

Zul tipped his head toward Kayla. "If you truly want to step into this mud swamp with me, you'll require Kayla's assistance.

She has certain information."

A chill crawled over Kayla's skin. "I don't know anything. I don't even understand what you're talking about."

"Devak knows. He can explain it."

"I only know some of it," Devak said. "I don't understand why those boys took my datapod. But I do know something about Kayla." Devak turned to her. "I looked for you on the Grid earlier today. It couldn't find you."

The chill sank deeper, to her bones. "But I'm where I'm supposed to be. I'm within my radius."

"You've been removed from the Grid, Kayla," Devak told her. "I'm guessing both you and your friend Mishalla were. And those four GENs at the factory. I don't know why or how, but I'm sure Pitamah knows."

"And you'll both learn in due time," Zul said.

Devak added, "The Grid checks GEN positions in a rolling pattern, so it eventually checks every GEN in its territory. But since it's programmed according to the Edicts, no GEN location is checked more often than every five days. When a GEN is discovered missing, the system sends out a flag."

"So, it flagged the factory workers," Kayla said.

"And it will flag you and Mishalla, sooner or later, when your names come up in the rolling pattern," Devak said. "It's sheer luck it hasn't before now."

"They must have only just installed the upgrade in the past few days," Zul said, "if your father got notification of the factory workers' flagging yesterday. The Grid would have done a back search on those workers and determined how long they'd been missing."

"If they only just now figured out they were missing," Kayla said, "how could they figure out they were gone two weeks?"

Guilt flashed across Devak's face. "Because, even though the Edicts say GEN locations should be checked only every five days, they're checked more often. Pretty much constantly. The Council justifies it by mandating that the data must be automatically stored. No one has access to it until a GEN comes up missing. I guess they figure that even with a five-day head start, they'll find that GEN eventually."

Zul zeroed in on his great-grandson. "Are you willing to hack into your father's system?"

Devak hesitated. "I've done some wrong things, Pitamah. Hacked Father's passwords to get into his office when he's gone. Brought in Junjie to see the Grid. But hacking the Grid itself—"

"If they discover Kayla missing from the Grid," Zul said, "they might take her, reset her. Even though it wasn't her doing. Isn't that a worse wrong?"

Devak stood silent for a long time, glancing over at her once, his dark gaze troubled. But finally he said, "You're right. I can't let Kayla down."

"You'll have to break into your father's office tonight, after he's gone to sleep. We have foils you can put into place in the Grid programming. They'll ghost in locations for Kayla, Mishalla, and the others, fool the Grid into thinking they're all where they should be."

"I can do that," Devak said.

"Once you're in this, you're in all the way," Zul said. "None of us will be exempt if the Brigade discovers what we're doing."

"I want to be part of it, Pitamah, if it keeps Kayla safe."

"It will. And Kayla, Devak will need your help in hacking the Grid."

She backed away from the bed. "But I don't know anything. I've never operated a computer. Other than the Doctrine school sekais and the one you lent me, I never touched a piece of tech until—" She bit back the flow of words.

"You know more than you realize, Kayla," Zul said.

What could she possibly know? She'd been nothing more than a pack-drom for unknown people. Asked to carry the packet, then the datapod. Even before that, when Skal came the day before her Assignment.

Pack-drom. Not just with what she could carry in her hands. There were other ways a GEN could transport something.

She gulped in a breath and took a chance. "Does this have to do with the upload?"

To her surprise, Zul smiled and nodded approvingly. "Yes."

Questions tumbled in her mind. But she didn't know if she dared ask them out loud.

Zul answered her anyway. "There are some tech GENs in Chadi sector who write programs for us. They live in hiding— from the Grid, from other GENs."

"How could they hide in a GEN sector?" Kayla asked. "When we're all so packed in, when everyone knows everyone?"

"I can't tell you that. Just know that they're there, that they're working for us. They created half the program that was uploaded into you the day before your Assignment. Your annexed brain has been processing it since."

She hadn't noticed, had tuned it out as she did so much else in her annexed brain until she needed it.

She tapped into it now, her view of the room growing fuzzy as she turned inward. "Before, it seemed like nothing but raw data. But now it's kind of got a pattern."

"That was part of the plan, creating program code to look like data, letting the GENs we uploaded do the processing. The rest of the program, what's on the datapod you're carrying, was written by another group of techs hidden in another sector."

"*What* datapod?" Devak asked.

Zul waved off his great-grandson's query. "Unfortunately, the GEN who was to carry the datapod's contents to me here was taken and reset by the Brigade before he received the upload. So it was stored on the datapod."

"What datapod, Pitamah?" Devak asked again.

The thumb-sized device sat like a fat silver slime-spider against Kayla's hip. Even though Zul had already proven his trustworthiness, even though she was certain he would never report her to the Brigade, by habit her first impulse was to deny the datapod's existence. Admitting ownership of the black packet had been questionable—she might have made a case that she didn't know it had DNA inside it. But she had willingly accepted the datapod.

She gave herself a mental kick. Zul was possibly her DNA great-grandfather. And surely Devak had proved himself trustworthy as well. It was safe to give them the contraband device.

She reached inside the hidden pocket and pulled the datapod out, then dropped it into Zul's hand. Beside her, Devak stared openmouthed.

"This is why you brought me with you today," she said to Zul. The strange encounter in the lowborn village finally began to make sense. "So I could hand off the packet with the DNA and get the datapod."

"After the loss of the other GEN and our failure to

complete the exchange that day in towncenter, this was our only alternative. I'm too well-known to have entered the shantytown with the packet unnoticed."

"Then if you're sending programs via GENs using stolen datapods, that explains why those lowborn boys in Sheysa took mine," Devak said.

"They're part of the Kinship," Zul said. "We're using those datapods across Svarga to transmit communication and programming. Using willing GENs as vehicles."

"Except you uploaded me without asking," Kayla said. "Does that really count as willing?"

"You did say yes by taking the packet. And that upload also took you off the Grid," Zul said. "Giving you and your friend Mishalla a certain amount of freedom."

"Then Mishalla was uploaded too? She never said."

"It happened later," Zul told her. "Through Ilian."

So that upload the day before she got her Assignment had removed her from the Grid. Thinking back, Kayla remembered the sudden change when she'd woke during that night. The abrupt silence. The moment when the constant pinging from the Grid had been shut off. The relief she'd felt even when she didn't know its cause.

"Did Skal know?" Kayla asked, then clarified for Zul, "Mishalla's nurture brother, Skal, is a GEN enforcer. He installed the upload. Did he know what was in it?"

"He may not have," Zul said. "It could be someone who is a member of the Kinship passed the upload off to Skal without him even knowing."

"If Mishalla's in danger when she's off the Grid, shouldn't she know that?" Kayla asked. "Shouldn't someone warn her?"

"Yes," Zul said slowly. "I think that's wise. And it would be safest if you were the one to do it."

"How could Kayla possibly contact Mishalla?" Devak asked.

"Can I tell him now?" Kayla asked.

"Of course. But first . . ." He gave his great-grandson the datapod. "You'll need to upload the contents into Kayla."

"Now?" Devak asked.

"That would be best," Zul said. "Kayla's annexed brain will need time to process it. Might as well do it while you're waiting for your father to go to bed."

Devak fidgeted with the datapod a moment before lifting it to her cheek. "I know it hurts," he said to her softly.

"I'm used to it," she said, although that wasn't entirely true. She just didn't want him to feel bad about it.

He put the device to her cheek, his fingers brushing her tattoo. A shiver ran down her spine—not fear, like she'd felt when Skal and Ansgar had applied the datapod. The pleasant sensation left her breathless.

When the extendibles bit her cheek, she was so caught up in the feel of Devak touching her that she couldn't guard her reaction to the pain. She smiled gamely, wanting to relieve his dismay.

She didn't exactly recognize the flood of data, but it had a familiarity to it. She could sense it streaming toward where the rest of the program waited, could sense it restructuring itself.

When the upload ended, Devak pulled away the datapod. He took a sani-wipe from the dispenser on Zul's dresser and handed it to her.

Kayla wiped the blood from her cheek. "I won't have to go with Devak, right? Once it's all processed and he downloads it back into the datapod, he can do the rest on his own."

"It would be best if you were there," Zul said. "Devak will need to copy the Grid updates into the ghosting program to incorporate the changes."

"Pitamah, I could just walk the changes back to Kayla's quarters, then bring them back when she's processed them."

Zul let Kayla work out the problem with Devak's suggestion. "It's too risky, Devak," Kayla said. "Too much chance of getting caught. I'll come with you."

"I won't need you anymore tonight, Kayla," Zul said. "You can go to your quarters, and Devak to his room. Just give me my wristlink, Devak, so I can send the network activation signal. Kayla still needs to contact her friend."

Devak found the wristlink on the dresser and handed it to Zul. Using his thumbs, the old trueborn laboriously entered a sequence on the wristlink.

With all the new information crowding her mind, both bare and annexed brain, she'd forgotten entirely about Chaaya. Maybe she should ask Zul straight out about his granddaughter. But what if Devak didn't know the truth? Zul might not want it revealed.

So she fished around the edges. "I don't understand why I matter. Why Mishalla matters. When we're only GENs."

"There's more to you and Mishalla than you think," Zul told her.

She could barely resist dancing with excitement. Was that his way of explaining her guesses were right?

He went on. "There's a puzzle we're trying to solve. You and Mishalla are part of it. As am I, as is Quila. As is Devak, now." He turned to his great-grandson. "I'd intended to bring you into the Kinship, Devak. I didn't expect it would be so soon. Hadn't wanted to put you at risk."

"Your friends from this morning, the ones who helped you into the lev-car, they're in this Kinship too," Kayla guessed. Zul nodded in affirmation. "How many are there?"

"I don't know. Maybe hundreds. Maybe more. None of us know who all of them are, a safety measure so that no one member can betray more than a handful. That's why I can't be certain about your friend Skal. We're all over the continent, in every sector. Trueborns of all statuses, lowborns, and GENs. Everyone within the Kinship has the same goals."

"What goals?" Kayla asked.

"Officially, we are a lowborn advocacy group. Registered through the Congress under the Benevolence Statute. Our aim is to secure more fairness for lowborns."

"That's what Azad tried to do," Devak said.

"He did what he could. It's still a knotty problem, but child's play compared to our other key objective."

"Which is?" Kayla asked.

Zul fixed his gaze on her. "Free the GENs."

Wariness rose inside Kayla. "Free us. How?"

"Allow you to live your own lives. Of your own choosing."

"There's no way," Kayla said. "The trueborns would never let us."

Which was the way it should be. Yes, she wished for, dreamed of freedom. Had talked Devak's ear off about it last night. But liberation for GENs on Loka would violate the Infinite's laws. It would only be right for GENs to taste true freedom in the palm of the Infinite's hand.

"It's true that if the Council or the Congress discovered the full mission of the Kinship, if they found out that trueborns have been mixing with lowborns and GENs to reach our goals, the enforcers would punish every member of the Kinship they could find."

The old man glanced over at Devak. "Trueborn members like Devak and me, they'd imprison. We'd lose every square centimeter of our adhikar. They'd execute the lowborns." He looked at her. "I'm sure you can guess what they'd do to the GENs in the Kinship."

"Reset and realigned," Kayla said.

"You both should know this," Zul said. "Know fully what I'm asking you to step into."

"Taking GENs off the Grid?" Devak asked. "Like you have Kayla and Mishalla? But even if you did that with hundreds of GENs, they'd have nowhere safe to go. Their DNA marks would always identify them."

"True," Zul said. "But that's why we intend to go further. To truly release GENs from their shackles."

"Our shackles are part of the Infinite's plan," Kayla said.

"What if letting them go is the next step in your Infinite's plan? It could be."

"It's not in the liturgy." But the revelations of Zul's journal nagged at her.

"Your liturgy—" The words dripped with scorn. Zul snapped his mouth shut, leaving whatever else he might have said unvoiced. "I can't tell you more about that. What you know can be extracted from you by the Brigade. You can't tell them what you don't know." The old man settled deeper into the pillows with a sigh.

"But I still don't understand," Kayla said, hoping to draw the truth of Chaaya's DNA out of him. "Why would you do this for the GENs? The lowborns I could see—they're natural-born, not tank concoctions. What would the GENs matter to a trueborn like you?"

Zul opened his eyes again, fixed his dark gaze directly on Kayla. "Because I'm responsible for your slavery. Because I'm the one who created the GENs."

# 23

**K**ayla backed from the bed. "Not you. It was the prophets."
Zul stared at her a long time. "Do you want to know
the truth?"

She lowered her voice, although she knew Devak, standing
right there, would be able to hear her. "I know what you wrote
in that book. But I don't believe it. Whatever you thought you
knew then was wrong. It was Pouli, Cohn, and Gupta."

Zul's gaze narrowed on her. "What book?"

Now heat rose up her neck, into her face. Her heart
pounded in her ears. "I found a paper book in a crate of things
Mrs. Manel asked me to incinerate. I threw the rest of it away,
but kept the book. And read it."

"A book." His puzzlement gave way to realization. "Written
in my hand?" At her nod, his expression darkened. "Of course,
she would want that one destroyed. She must have stolen it
from my dresser while I slept."

"Pitamah, what are you two talking about?" Devak asked.

"A bit of history that Kayla has found." He must have seen

the fear in her face because he waved a soothing hand at her. "I have no problem with you reading my journal, although I suspect what you could understand of it shook your world." He speared Devak with his gaze. "You'll have had enough background to follow my ramblings. I would appreciate it, Kayla, if you would let my great-grandson read it while you wait for your opportunity tonight."

If Devak could figure out all those diagrams and tech talk, did she want to know what it all meant? Even if it changed everything she believed about the Infinite? And why, after revealing so much else, had Zul not admitted anything about Chaaya? Because Kayla's guesses were wrong? Or maybe they were right but Zul was ashamed of what had happened to Chaaya.

Zul's exhaustion overwhelmed him, muting him into a frustrating silence. He suffered through Kayla and Devak's insistence that he eat, taking a few spoonfuls of curried greens and fola roots with little enthusiasm. Once he'd finished, he querulously asked Kayla to help him lie down again, then growled at them that they should leave; he had to rest.

But before she could turn away, he grabbed her hand, startling because they never touched except for her to assist him. His gaze locked with hers and he squeezed her fingers. "You know more than you think."

He kept telling her that, but for every new thing she learned, it seemed there were dozens more she didn't understand.

Kayla moved with Devak out into the hall. "You should eat too," he said.

She'd eaten nothing since the kel-grain and juice that Quila had served her, and that had been little enough. "I have to talk to Mishalla about being off the Grid."

"I'm sure you'll explain how that's possible," he said. "I'll bring food out. Father's still in his secret meeting and Mother won't open her eyes again until morning. They won't notice that I'm not in my room."

They took the back stairs together. Senia ignored them as they reached the kitchen. The lowborn woman raced from the food prep station to the radiant stove, tending to pots filled with fragrant stews and steaming curries.

Kayla left through the red door, light spilling from the kitchen faintly illuminating her path across the back lawn. The primary sun, Iyenku, had set, but indolent Kas still clung to the horizon, fending off full night. Still, the gloom was deep enough she had to walk carefully to avoid stumbling on the stepping stones.

Swinging the door to her quarters nearly shut, she fumbled for the switch to the overhead. Should she wait for Devak before she contacted Mishalla? Worry for her friend drove her to pick up the sekai.

The network block had been removed, but Mishalla didn't immediately appear when Kayla logged on. She was still waiting when Devak backed into her quarters juggling a laden tray and the red stool.

"The visitors are staying for evening meal," he told her as he dropped the metal stool by the table. "That's what's got Senia in a frenzy. It means it'll be even later before it's safe to go into his office."

"Do we call it off until tomorrow night?" Kayla asked, anxiety twisting inside her at the thought of leaving Mishalla at risk.

"No. Father has to go to sleep sometime."

Devak arranged bowls of kel-grain on her table, placing a larger bowl of curried greens and fola root in the center. "I thought maybe you'd want to try it."

He ladled a spoonful of curry over her kel-grain, then his, before sitting opposite her. As he ate, his expression was grim.

"Father left his office door open while he met with his visitors. I stood by the door and listened. They were talking about skets. The woman needed an electronics expert to replace an elderly GEN; one of the men needed an engine mechanic to repair lev-cars."

"Is that something your father usually does? Help the specialists Assign GENs where they're needed?"

"Sometimes," Devak said, scooping up another mouthful of kel-grain and curry. "The Grid keeps track of skets as well as locations. The way it's supposed to work is the specialists in all the western territories meet with Father several times a year to work out the Assignments. That way it's most fair."

"For the trueborns, anyway," Kayla said.

"My father thinks he's dealing fairly with the GENs by finding an Assignment that suits them," Devak said.

"What do you think?" Kayla asked.

He poked at his bowl of kel-grain. "I'm not so sure anymore."

"So, he meets with the specialists."

"Yes, but sometimes there's an emergency. People come here in a panic because the GEN working for them is sick or dies unexpectedly. They might get bumped to the head of the line depending on how critical the work is."

"So, is that what these three want?" Kayla asked.

"I guess. Maybe." Devak drew his spoon around the bowl, but he didn't take a bite. "But here's the part that's so wrong.

My father was telling the visitors about GENs with the skets they wanted, but they were all too young."

"Underage? Like a tenth or eleventh-year?"

He shook his head. "Younger. Third and even second-years."

"That makes no sense. If they need the GENs now, what good would babies like that do them?"

"I don't know. But one of the men handed my father some dhans. A lot of them." He shook his head. "My father's done some things I don't like, but to take bribes . . . Five or six years ago, a Grid tech was running a scheme where, for enough dhans, he'd report GENs outside their radius even when they weren't. The GENs would be reset, then the person who paid would get the realigned GEN. Father was so angry when he found out, he nearly took the Grid tech's head off. He called the Brigade and the tech went to prison."

"But now he's taking bribes and worse. Assigning GEN children so young is a sin in the Infinite's eyes."

"Maybe I misunderstood that part." He looked at Kayla, clearly desperate to believe that.

"I'm glad you agree it's bad to take babies, or eighth-years or tenth-years. But what about fifteenth-years?" Kayla asked. "You think I wanted to go off on Assignment, leave everything I knew? Some GENs get sent so far away, they never see their families again. We're not allowed to keep in touch by tech, so we basically say goodbye forever."

Devak had nothing to say to that. He barely touched the rest of his curry, and she'd lost her appetite as well. She set the dishes on the tray and stowed them in the shack's tiny food prep area.

Kayla retrieved the paper book from its hiding place, setting it on the table but keeping her hand on it. "Before you read it, there's something I found out. A note written by Zul that led me to guess something about myself. It may not be true, but . . ."

"What?"

"I'll show you. You can tell me what you think." She flipped to the back, and it fell open at the torn-out pages. She tapped the ragged edges. "I guess Zul will have to tell us what was here." She separated the last two pages and turned the book to face Devak.

He read the inscription aloud. "Chaaya—Plakit, Mendin, Chadi? Filter the list by sectors." Devak shrugged. "I don't know what list he means, but Pitamah told me that Aunt Chaaya spent time in those three GEN sectors."

"I think I know what the list is." Kayla swallowed, her throat tight with tension. "A list of GENs. Made from Chaaya's DNA."

He laughed, a bitter edge to the sound. "Where'd you hear that ugly old rumor?" He waved off her reply. "Never mind, I can guess. Senia."

Her cheeks flared with heat. "Meera and Yezzi."

"You should know better than to listen to lowborn gossip. Yes, my aunt died in a GEN sector and yes, she wore a tattoo like Pitamah's on her cheek. But there was never any doubt that she was trueborn and no one sampled her for genning."

"But there's a list on Zul's sekai." She found the file and opened it, then nudged the reader toward Devak.

Devak zeroed in on the file name. "XRS—do you know what that means?"

"No. I figured it was some kind of tech talk."

"It is, sort of. It's given to a GEN who at some point in their lives has been reset."

The air left her lungs and for a moment she couldn't breathe. "I've never been reset. Neither has Mishalla. I'm sure of it."

"Maybe you're on the list by mistake, then. Did you try the link by your name?" He tapped the screen and the password request popped up.

"It's PouliCohnGupta," she told him. "All one word and each name capitalized." He raised one brow in silent query. "I guessed. I couldn't believe that it actually worked."

He entered the password. The passkey request popped up.

"I couldn't get past that," Kayla said.

He let out a long breath. "I *might* be able to break it, given a ton of time and the right program. Neither of which we have."

"So I guess we just forget about it."

He leaned back with the sekai, idly tapping the screen with his thumb, his brow furrowed. "What was it Pitamah said? That you know more than you think? He said it twice."

Kayla shrugged. "He just meant the stuff stored in my annexed brain."

"Maybe . . ." He stared at the list of file names. "A lot of security is done in two pieces like this. One that uses a fairly simple password that's easy to remember, one that's a complicated passkey that's impossible to guess. Or it needs a fingerprint, or a retinal scan. Even a specific string of DNA."

His voice trailed off. "I have a program on my wristlink. It translates part of a DNA strand into a passkey." His gaze just about bored a hole through her. "It's used to reset GENs."

Her throat tightened. "How?"

"Partly it's a safety measure—to be sure it's the right GEN being reset."

"A Brigade captain reset an underage named Tanti right

before I left for Assignment," Kayla said. "The boy made the captain angry and he reset Tanti, just like that. I don't think he took any safety measures."

"I'm sorry," Devak said. "He shouldn't have."

"It's Ansgar who should apologize."

"Anyway, the genetic passkey is also used to make sure the reset is"—his voice faltered—". . . effective. Every GEN's neural pathways are different. The neural pattern is stored in a central database with the DNA strand."

"So you think Zul's passkey might be based on my DNA?"

"He said you knew more than you thought. And I think he wants you to see those files. He had to know you'd find it on the sekai, that you'd see your name."

She nodded. "The gene-splicers store a GEN's gene sequence in their annexed brain."

"Yes. Father told me. I know how to access the sequence."

"But it can't . . ." She felt stupid asking the question, but had to ask anyway. "There's no chance it would reset me, is there?"

"No." He shook his head for emphasis. "Absolutely not. That's a different program. This one only reads your DNA sequence. Finds the twenty-digit passkey."

He tugged the datapod from his pocket and set it on the table. Kayla stared at the small silver device.

"Have you ever done it?" Kayla asked. "Reset a GEN?"

"The enforcers do that," he said.

"But do you have the program?"

He nodded reluctantly.

"Could you do it?" Kayla asked.

He fidgeted with the datapod. "I don't think I could. Are you ready?"

The thought of him extracting a passkey from her DNA that could be used to reset her was terrifying. But she trusted Devak. She turned her right cheek toward him. He brought the datapod to her cheek, then she felt the sting of the extendibles.

A fearful blackness closed in as it always did when a GEN was downloaded. The next thing she knew, Devak was pulling his hand away.

As she swiped away the blood, he clipped the datapod into the back of his wristlink. She breathed deep to let go of the last of her fear.

When the program finished, he read the passkey out loud and she entered it into the sekai. It was strange seeing the string of letters and numbers, seeing her DNA structure broken down into those twenty digits.

"The file is opening," Kayla said. Suddenly she didn't want to see what was inside. She handed the sekai to Devak.

As he scanned the screen, his brow furrowed. "That's odd. What's your emergence date?"

Why would he want to know the date she'd been pulled from the tank? "The sixth of Anceathru."

"That's right, then. Except . . ." He turned the sekai toward her. "Look at the year. It's 361. Only eleven years ago. Not fifteen like it should be."

She scanned the sekai screen. There was her name and designator ID at the top, then an emergence date of Anceathru 6th, 361.

"It's just a data error." Kayla looked up at Devak. "I'm fifteen. You can't tell me I'm only an eleventh-year."

"Of course you're not," Devak agreed. "But this link, beside your ID . . ." He skimmed a finger over it so the link displayed.

"That's not to the GEN emergence database. It points to the birth records."

Her skin prickled as she tried to grasp what Devak had just said. "That can't be. I wasn't born. I was made. Built in a gentank, like every other GEN."

"I could check it. I can't upload to my father's system with my wristlink but I could download. I could search birth records, see if I can find your ID."

She shook her head, the effort to move enormous. "I was made, not born. By the Infinite's design. That has to be a mistake."

He stared at her for a long time, then laid his hand over hers. "You're right. It has to be a mistake."

"Even if I was once reset . . ." She could hardly choke out the word. What kind of mistake could she have made as a fourth-year to be reset so young? Did she break something especially precious? "I'm still just a GEN. Even if I *had* been made from Chaaya's DNA—"

"You weren't."

"When did she die?" Kayla asked.

"A little over sixteen years ago," Devak told her.

"So the time would be exactly right," Kayla said.

Devak shook his head. He wouldn't want to believe it, but Kayla still wasn't convinced that her suspicions weren't true. Not when Zul had said, *There's more to you and Mishalla than you think.*

But no use arguing with Devak about it. "It wouldn't change who I am now."

"I guess." He turned his hand, weaving his fingers through hers. "If I could, I'd make us different. So there wouldn't be a wall between us."

She should have said, *I want that too.* She could see it in his eyes, that he wanted to hear it. But her world was tumbling apart already. The confusion about Chaaya. Her own name on that list. The mistake of her emergence date.

The bridge between her and the Infinite's loving hands was trembling, in danger of shattering. She couldn't risk letting those words out.

Kayla pulled free, then shoved the book over to him. "Parts are faded and hard to read. But you understanding the tech terms might make it easier for you."

Devak drew the journal closer. A moment's hesitation, then he flipped back to the front. "I haven't seen anything written by Pitamah in a long time. He can't hold even a stylus anymore to write on a sekai screen."

He settled down to read. Kayla sat beside him, the quiet of her quarters broken only by the soft rustle as he turned the pages. That silence seemed to close in on her even more tightly with each passing moment.

She picked up the sekai, closing the file that now frightened her so and flipping through the day's news instead. But dread weighed her down so heavily she barely comprehended the words.

*Oh, Infinite! Are you with me? I can't hear your voice anymore.*

Had she ever heard His voice? Had she fooled herself all these years into thinking there was something more, something higher, better than herself watching over her?

Shortly after her internal clock ticked past the two hour mark, Devak looked up from the paper book. The sympathy in his dark gaze closed her throat.

She forced out her question. "Do you understand it?"

He half-shrugged, half-nodded. "Not all of it. It's more advanced than anything I've learned, but . . ."

"But?"

His expression turned serious. "It's all here, Kayla. All the theories about GEN circuitry proven out. All the details of how to apply it to the GEN nervous system. Great-grandma Fulki—she was a gene-splicer before there were gene-splicers. She worked on the genetic side and Pitamah developed the electronics."

A hollow place opened inside her. "Fifteen years before the prophets' divine inspiration."

"Pitamah told the truth. He and Great-grandma Fulki created the GENs. The tattoo on his face . . ." He looked away a moment, then back at her. "It was active once. Like a GEN tattoo."

She squeezed her eyes shut, unable to bear the way the foundation of her beliefs had been shaken. When she felt Devak's fingers tuck a strand of her rebellious hair behind her ear, she forced her eyes open.

"You shouldn't," she protested. But why not? All the rules had changed today. She didn't know what was right anymore. What did it matter if she let a trueborn touch her?

"I don't care," he whispered, echoing her thoughts. Then to her utter shock, he bent toward her and brushed his lips against hers.

She felt herself dissolve into nothing but air. She forgot the tattoo on her cheek, forgot the enigmatic Zul and the tangled weave of frightening events the old man and his Kinship had drawn her into. There was only Devak and her, protected by the emotions that knotted them together, feelings she should renounce that nevertheless lifted her heart again.

She placed her hands carefully on Devak's shoulders, felt his warmth through his thin korta. His palms curved against her face, his mouth soft against hers. It wasn't like any kiss a GEN boy had stolen from her in a Chadi alley. Those had been trivial, mechanical. Like a spent chaffhead compared to a lush spill of trueborn roses.

She shifted, trying to move even closer to him. In her clumsiness, she bumped the table, knocking the sekai to the floor. The clatter of the reader against the floor jolted them apart. He stared at her, wide-eyed, stunned.

"Don't say it," she said fiercely before he could speak. "That we shouldn't have. That it was wrong."

His slow smile took her breath away. "How could I when I only want to do it again?"

Heat rose like twin flames in her cheeks. "Well, then . . ."

He bent to retrieve the sekai, and handed it to Kayla. The message *Mishalla is on the network* glowed at the bottom of the screen.

Devak gazed, bemused, down at the device. "How did Pitamah manage to put a networked sekai in the hands of a GEN?"

"Your great-grandfather seems to be able to do whatever he wants, whenever he wants."

Devak drew the back of his finger across Kayla's tattoo. "But not the one thing I'd most like him to do."

She shuddered, then pulled away, taking the sekai from him. Sitting at the table, she opened the connection to Mishalla.

# 24

ishalla had tried for hours to relink with Kayla after their first contact the day before. She'd fallen asleep with the sekai in her hands, then jolted awake in the morning, terrified that the Brigade would return and somehow guess that she'd changed the infant reader into a networked sekai. She'd tossed it into the crate with the other readers, swearing to herself that she wouldn't touch it again.

But as she dressed in the only clothes Guntram hadn't trampled—a threadbare white blouse and a heavy woven skirt more suitable for winter than spring—the sekai drew her like a magnet. Every time she made her way through the playroom, she'd fish the reader from the crate, tap the network icon in hopeful expectation. Each time the message was the same—the network function had been blocked. She'd toss the sekai back in disgust.

At first, terror hunched on her shoulder that the Brigade had somehow detected she was on the network and had jammed her connection. But they would have come for her immediately and she heard no heavy boots outside the crèche door.

By late afternoon, she gave up trying. She dragged through her duties, soothing cranky, hungry children when the evening meal delivery was late, then parceling out their sparse provisions. She managed to coax Amila into allowing her to carefully peel back the bandage and smear antibiotic cream on what looked like an angry red burn. Afterward, the little girl ate at the table, but she kept her eyes on her sweetened kel-grain, spooning it up without enthusiasm.

During the meal, one of the sekais started beeping, an irritating triple trill every few minutes, no doubt signaling it was losing power. Too busy tidying up and washing tiny lowborn hands, she ignored the electronic complaint. She'd find the offending reader after the children were in bed. She shut her ears to its summons as she recited story after story from memory. Even Amila sat up to listen.

Finally, she got the children down, Amila scrunching herself into her corner in the playroom again. Mishalla hummed a lullaby to the stubborn little girl, relieved to see her relax. She didn't like how red Amila's skin looked around the bandage. Had the inflammation spread? Could it be infected despite her treatment? She was about to check it again when the sekai resumed its beeping.

With a huff of exasperation, Mishalla pushed to her feet and went in search of the misbehaving sekai. She sifted through the messy pile, searching for one with a telltale flashing red light. Then she spotted the networked sekai, saw the message blinking across the screen, and her heart lodged in her throat.

# tankborn

## KAYLA IS ON THE NETWORK

Mishalla quickly opened the connection. She grinned with giddy happiness when Kayla's face appeared on the screen. "I thought you'd forgotten about me."

Mishalla could see the chagrin in Kayla's face. "I couldn't get the network function to work before now."

"It doesn't matter." Mishalla sat on the floor. "We're connected now."

"I heard that you're right there in Sheysa. So close." There was just the slightest rebuke in Kayla's eyes.

"I wanted so much to come home on Restdays, but they wouldn't give me a pass."

Kayla's faint censure vanished. "I should tell you what's most important first. You've been taken off the Grid."

"That's what Pia said. I think I've been fogged somehow so the Grid can't detect me."

"Not fogged," the cultured tones of a trueborn voice cut in, then a trueborn boy's face replaced Kayla's.

Mishalla jolted and nearly terminated the connection. "He's okay," Kayla's voice assured her. "Devak wants to help us."

"You've been removed from the Grid completely," Devak said. "You're as undetectable as any trueborn or lowborn."

"Anyway, you were safe at first," Kayla put in, taking back the sekai. "The Grid was fooled into thinking you were where you were supposed to be. But now the monitors know you're missing. We're fixing that tonight. Doing some kind of ghost thing to make it seem you're back on the Grid."

"What about the children?" Mishalla said, changing the subject to the thing that had been worrying her most.

"There must be something we can do for them."

"I'll tell Zul tomorrow. He'll find a way to get them back to their parents."

Who's Zul? she wanted to ask, but Devak interrupted. "It's time, Kayla."

"I have to go," Kayla said. "Maybe we'll see each other soon." With that tantalizing promise, her face vanished from the screen.

As she sat there, savoring those few moments with Kayla, she heard Pia's familiar *rap-rap-rap* on the door.

Tossing the sekai into the crate with the others, she hurried to let Pia in. The officious woman bustled inside, her usual enforcer shadow, Juka, slinking in after her.

"You took one last night," Mishalla said, not quite keeping the edge from her tone. "Are you here to take another?"

Pia gave her a sharp look. "What business is it of yours, jik?"

"Every time you come and go, you upset the children." Mishalla gestured at Amila. "That wound doesn't look good."

Pia's eyes widened in alarm. "You didn't take the bandage away?"

"No," Mishalla lied. "But maybe a medic should have a look at it."

Pia strode over to where Amila dozed lightly and lifted the edge of the bandage. Amila whimpered, a soft keen that thankfully didn't build into a full-fledged scream. Mishalla angled to try to see the wound herself, but Pia shifted to shield the little girl from Mishalla's view.

When Pia stepped away, the bandage was back in place. "Need to do a head count." She marched off toward the sleeproom. After casting Mishalla a narrow-eyed glare, Juka followed.

Stewing over Pia's habitual rudeness, Mishalla didn't register the angry whispers from the sleeproom at first. She sidled closer to the wall that divided the rooms, relying on her enhanced hearing to pick up the conversation despite the barrier between.

". . . not in charge here," Pia said.

"I'm only saying," Juka said, an edge to her voice, "we have to jettison this plan before Guntram reports that jik."

"After all we went through to collect this many! Do you have any idea how much these children are worth?"

"We've made a pile of dhans already," Juka said. "That's all I wanted out of this, so I could buy myself some adhikar."

"I've got a deal going on an adhikar parcel myself," Pia said. "Nearly enough acreage to jump to high-status. Without the dhans those lowborns will bring, that deal will fall through."

"Once Guntram's report filters up to the Council level," Juka said, "they'll find out that Director Manel changed the jik's Assignment without authorization. Then they'll figure out that this crèche was never approved. A high-status like Manel will find a way to squeak through without a speck of drom dung on him. And a demi like you might not serve much time. But a minor-status like me, an enforcer to boot . . ."

"Why not take these over to where the others are?" Pia asked.

"Don't like it," Juka said. "Mixing them like that. Clients might get squeamish seeing them side by side."

Pia huffed with impatience. "Well, we don't have to lose all of them. Guntram doesn't even know about the others."

"Just these then," Juka said.

A pause, then Pia said, "You're right. We should cut our

losses. No point in taking that kind of risk. But we'd better tell Ansgar first."

"I don't like leaving it too long if we can't track him down."

"We have all night," Pia said. "Guntram won't report until the morning."

"I suppose. With all of us working, a couple trips to the Sheysa River is all we'd need to take care of them."

Mishalla gasped, stepping back in reflex and stumbling on a forgotten shape block.

"What's that noise?" Pia asked.

Mishalla moved as quickly as she could away from the adjoining wall just as Pia emerged from the sleeproom, Juka behind her. Their gazes flicked over her. Mishalla clutched her hands into fists, the kel-grain she'd eaten an hour ago threatening to come back up.

Finally Pia spoke. "We're moving the crèche."

Panic welled up inside Mishalla. "You can't move. That'll be terrible for the children."

Juka closed the distance between them, hooked a leg behind Mishalla's, and swept her to the floor. Mishalla hit hard, pain bringing tears to her eyes.

"We've been generous with you, jik," Juka snarled at her. "You'd best keep your opinions to yourself."

Fear cut off Mishalla's breath. She struggled to clear her throat. "When are we moving?"

"You'll know that when we return," Juka said.

Pia and Juka marched out after that, the enforcer shooting one last dark glare at Mishalla before leaving. The moment the door closed behind them, Mishalla struggled to get her aching right leg under her. She limped over to the crate of sekais, fumbling through them for the networked one.

But when she thumbed the network icon, over and over, Kayla didn't respond. She and the trueborn boy had gone to do their "ghosting" trick and left the sekai behind. Tears of despair burned Mishalla's eyes and she wanted to fall in a heap and sob. But that would do nothing to save these poor, doomed children.

Clutching the sekai, Mishalla paced the playroom, fighting to hold her terror at bay. She had to get a message to Kayla somehow. Get that trueborn boy of hers and the mysterious Zul here now to save these children.

But how, when they wouldn't answer Mishalla's summons?

What about Eoghan? What if she could somehow reach him via the network? But she knew only his given name, not his surname, or his family designator. She'd never thought to ask him. How would she find him on the network?

But Ilian . . . sudden realization stabbed her. The datapod upload had carried his embedded, encoded signature. Could she use that to contact the lowborn?

Only if that datapod upload had included enough information for her to figure out what to do. She wasn't a tech GEN like Kayla's brother. She would have to try by rote, instructed by what had been streamed into her annexed brain.

She bent to the sekai, relaxing rather than concentrating, letting whatever knowledge had been packed into her mind to emerge. For endless moments she waited, hopelessness nibbling at her. Then her autonomic functions took over, and she tapped at the sekai screen, entering the access ID for Ilian.

She waited, breathless. He'd had a sekai that day at Streetmarket, but he might not have it with him now. Or if he had it with him, he might ignore a summons from Mishalla. Even worse, he could report—

*Mishalla, is that you?*

She stared at the text floating on the screen. Now that she had the link, what should she say? She decided simple was best.

She found the keyboard icon and laboriously typed out, *I need help.*

There was a hesitation so long she feared he wouldn't respond. Finally, the message appeared. *I'll be there quick as I can.*

The connection broke off. She replaced the network display with one of the children's stories, and buried the sekai in the pile. Then she paced again, her leg pleading for rest, her anxiety driving her to keep moving.

Just as she thought she couldn't bear another moment of suspense, a knock sounded on the door. Quieter than Pia's. Certainly not the Brigade, who would have bypassed the lock and noisily stormed inside. She rushed to open the door.

Joy nearly brought her to her knees. Eoghan stood there, dressed like a trueborn in a lavish korta and cape, his brilliant smile setting rockets off in her heart.

He stepped inside and threw his arms around her, squeezing the breath out of her. When the door shut, she saw Ilian behind him, a bundle in his arms. The pieces started to fall into place.

She gave Eoghan a little push away from her. "You two know each other after all?"

"We come from the same village," Eoghan told her.

"And you never told me? When Ilian accosted me at Streetmarket?" She slapped Eoghan on the chest with both hands. "When I was so frightened of what had happened. You could have explained." Another slap, even harder. "And where have you been all this time?"

Eoghan looked offended. "I've been busy with important work."

"More important than me?"

Now Ilian laughed. "When he hasn't been whining about how he missed his dear, sweet Mishalla, he's been helping me steal trueborn datapods. And helping me load them with the programming that's pulled you and a lot of other GENs off the Grid."

Mishalla rounded on Ilian. "No one tells me anything, or if they do tell me, it's never enough. You give me mysterious messages and cryptic uploads. You tell me I can help Shan when you've said nothing about what's happened to him or how I can possibly help him. Everything is secrets with you two."

Eoghan stepped closer to her again. "We need you tonight, Mishalla. We have an important mission."

"And we shouldn't be involving her at all," Ilian said. "You can do your job alone, Eoghan, like we planned. Mishalla already did her part getting you into the crèche in the first place."

Iciness settled in Mishalla's belly. "That was the only reason you came here? And took me with you to Streetmarket? For your mission?"

"No," Eoghan said.

"Yes," Ilian said over Eoghan's denial.

Ilian grabbed Eoghan's shoulder and gave him a shake. "We don't have time for lovers' quarrels."

"I have a problem more important than your mission," Mishalla said. "An enforcer's been here, and Pia's afraid his report will lead to an investigation of the crèche. She doesn't want to take the chance that the Council will discover what's going on here. She's coming back tonight. To take all these children and drown them in the Sheysa."

Her news stunned them both into horrified silence. As she told Ilian and Eoghan what she'd overheard, she was gratified to see that she'd known something they hadn't.

"But these aren't all the children they're still holding," Ilian said. "They might plan to do the same with the others."

"Pia said they wouldn't," Mishalla said.

"And you trust her?" Ilian asked.

"I overheard her. She said they're worth a lot of dhans," Mishalla told him.

"That makes no sense," Eoghan said, "if they're only stealing them to scare off the families like Zul thought. It's the land the lowborns were on that's worth something, not the children."

"Even still, Eoghan, you have to move tonight," Ilian said. "While there's still a chance to find Shan and all the other lowborns. Zul needs to confirm where they're staging the children before Pia and Juka move them on."

"Who is Zul?" Mishalla demanded. "He knows about this already? Why hasn't he helped these children before now?"

"Because the Kinship has to move carefully," Ilian said. "They didn't know that Pia would panic. And they'd like to know if it's only Pia and Ansgar or if it goes higher up."

"Pia and Juka kept mentioning a high-status trueborn," Mishalla said. "Director Manel."

Both Ilian's and Eoghan's jaws dropped. They stared at one another a moment, then Eoghan said, "We'll have to tell Zul."

"It wouldn't surprise me if he already knows," Ilian said. "He's probably just waiting for proof."

"In any case, I want Mishalla with me tonight," Eoghan said. "And not just because we need her to help us find the other children."

"If you're intending to save the children who have come through this crèche, I want to help," she said. "But I can't leave these little ones here alone. There's no telling when Pia will be back."

"Ilian will stay with them," Eoghan said. "We'll only be gone an hour or so."

"But you can't let anyone in," Mishalla told Ilian.

"We can trust Celia," Eoghan said. "She's not Kinship, but she'd die before letting Pia take these children to the Sheysa."

"And I'll be right at Celia's side." Ilian handed Mishalla the bundle he carried. "You'll need to wear this."

She felt the richness and weight of expensive fabric. She'd not seen anything nearly so fine in all of Streetmarket.

The urgency in Ilian's and Eoghan's eyes matched her own. "I'll go change."

In her quarters, she quickly stripped off her skirt and blouse and threw on the dress Ilian had brought. It felt like heaven against her skin, the color a rich emerald, gems glittering along the neckline.

This was a trueborn's dress. How in the Infinite's name had Ilian and Eoghan come by it?

She nudged her feet into sandals, then she did what she could to tidy her hair into three quick braids she twined together. There was no changing the vivid red color, though.

When she returned to the playroom, she got another shock. Eoghan's green eyes were now as dark as any trueborn's. What looked like a high-status bali glittered in his right ear.

"Special lenses. And I have a bali and another concealer for you."

She shivered as he pressed the false blue bali to her ear. He seemed to take far more time smoothing the concealer on her face than he had the day they went to Streetmarket.

Ilian looked her over. "You'll pass. You're certainly pretty enough."

Eoghan gave his friend a dark look. "We should go."

Mishalla looked back at Amila, still hunched in the corner. "If she wakes, she'll be terrified. She barely trusts me."

Ilian moved to Amila's side and hunkered down beside the sleeping little girl. "I'll take care of her."

Mishalla and Eoghan slipped out into the darkness together. "How do we know where the children are being kept?" Mishalla asked as they started along the row of warehouses.

"The Kinship passed on to us what they think is the location. That's what I'm part of. Me and Ilian and Zul are all in the Kinship."

"So the children are there? All the ones who came in and out of my crèche?"

"We hope so."

"Are we going to free them?" Mishalla asked. "Get them back to their parents?"

"Not you and me," Eoghan said. "But the Kinship will send people in and do their best to find their homes again."

"Soon, I hope. Because I really don't trust Pia."

Up ahead, the night patrol emerged from between two buildings. Mishalla sucked in a breath, fear washing over her. She would have tried to run back toward the crèche if Eoghan hadn't taken her hand and held it tight.

"Stay with me," Eoghan murmured.

The patrol, two lowborns in yellow Sheysa uniforms, approached. A few meters away, they nodded deferentially to Eoghan and with only slightly less courtesy to Mishalla before passing.

Eoghan waited until the night patrol was well out of earshot. "As far as they know, I'm a high-status trueborn, and you're a minor-status."

"With red hair."

"Not unheard of. And, like Ilian said, you're certainly pretty enough."

Her cheeks warmed at his compliment. They continued on into the night, passing warehouse after warehouse, each one as featureless as the last. It grew gloomier the farther along they walked, and the wet dankness of the Sheysa River drifted toward them.

She couldn't resist asking the questions that had niggled at her all those long lonely nights since Streetmarket. "Do I mean anything to you? All that time you spent with me at the crèche, you taking me to Streetmarket—was it just to pull me into this plot of yours? Did you care about me at all?"

He hesitated and she thought he would refuse to answer. But then she heard footsteps and saw two lowborn men pass through the holo trees. They looked tired and their coveralls were stained with work. Late shifters cutting through the warehouses on their way to the shantytown beyond.

Eoghan waited until the men had vanished down an alley, then turned his artificially-darkened eyes on her, his brown gaze alien to her. "I was sent to you because we needed you. And I took you to Streetmarket so you could meet Ilian. But

I like you, Mishalla. Truly. I want us to be together."

"That can't happen. No matter how many concealers you press on my cheek."

He looked away as they reached the end of the row of warehouses and turned the last corner. The Sheysa River rippled along in the murk, its musty scent and creeping flow of water adding to the oppression in the air.

"We've seen high-status trueborns in and out of here, which gave us the idea of trying to infiltrate ourselves." Halfway down the building, Eoghan stopped at a shadowy doorway inset in the wall. "There's a lowborn watching over the children. I have a bribe for her. But I'm going to let her do the talking as much as possible. I'm hoping she won't be able to tell a high-status accent from a lowborn's playing the part."

"What do I do?"

"Stay quiet. Best to let me do the talking."

Mishalla glanced at the door. "Then this is another crèche?"

"Yes."

"Why two? Why not take the children directly from mine to whatever lowborn shantytown they're dumping them at? Why bring them here in between?"

Even with the dark lenses and dim light, Mishalla could see the troubled look in Eoghan's eyes. "I don't know. That part doesn't make sense to me either. Everyone in the Kinship thought your crèche was the staging area, then we heard about the other one."

"Could it be this crèche is bigger?" Mishalla suggested. "Maybe there are other smaller crèches like mine that they gather up the children from, then collect them in this one. It might be less suspicious if they relocate a bigger group less often."

"Maybe," Eoghan said, sounding unconvinced. He knocked and took an imperious stance. An old lowborn woman swung open the door, her gray hair a fluffy halo around her face, her crafty expression anything but angelic.

"Faria?" Eoghan snapped out the syllables of the woman's name with the clipped economy of a high-status trueborn.

The lowborn seemed convinced. "Finally here, are ya? Gettin' late. Wondered if you'd come."

Faria rubbed the pad of her thumb across her fingers, cackling when Eoghan placed a fat roll of dhans in her hand. Without waiting for an invitation, he grabbed Mishalla's wrist, pulling her inside beside him and shielding her from the old lowborn. As they stepped into the lighted room Faria gave Mishalla's fiery hair a once over. Mishalla could see the calculation in the woman's pale gaze. No doubt she wondered what a high-status trueborn was doing with such a minor-status companion.

The ten meter by ten meter space was a playroom, nearly identical to the one at her crèche. Presentiment fingered its way up Mishalla's spine. The near identical set-up seemed strange—the same plasscine crates filled with the same toys, stacked in the exact same way. The same scuffed table and knee-high chairs, even the same pattern on the faded rug.

But maybe all crèches were furnished the same. Still, a sick feeling settled in her stomach when she spied the doorway set exactly where the entry to the sleeproom was in her crisis crèche.

Eoghan had spotted the sleeproom too. His back turned to the old woman, he snapped out, "Where are they?"

To Mishalla's ears, it was a passable trueborn accent. The

old lowborn woman wagged her chin toward the doorway. "Yonder. Asleep. Thank you not to wake 'em."

Eoghan towed Mishalla through the sleeproom doorway. Here was a difference. As she'd guessed, there were more children here in a larger space than in Mishalla's crèche. There were more than twenty beds and cribs in neat rows rather than the ten that filled Mishalla's crèche sleeproom.

The old woman stood expectantly in the doorway. Eoghan reached in a pocket and came up with a small vac-seal. He tossed it to the lowborn. "Leave us," he said gruffly.

Her eyes bright with anticipation, Faria hurried off to her quarters, shutting the door behind her.

"What was that?" Mishalla asked, pitching her voice low.

"A lifter," Eoghan told her. "Minimal dose. Won't take her far or very high, but it'll keep her busy long enough."

Eoghan thumbed the illumination control up slightly, chasing some of the shadows from the sleeproom. Then, with his hand on the small of her back, Eoghan urged Mishalla along the first row of beds.

Mishalla saw the glimmering tattoo on the small cheek of a second-year. "She's a GEN. Why would a lowborn be caring for GENs?"

Eoghan seemed as baffled by it as Mishalla. "Maybe it's a mix. The lowborns we're looking for and some GENs, too."

"But underage GENs belong to the state," Mishalla said. "Stealing them would mean a big prison sentence. And what would that have to do with opening more adhikar?"

"Let's keep checking the beds," Eoghan said. "If there are any lowborns here, I want to know if they came through your crèche."

They proceeded to the next bed. Another GEN, this time a boy, maybe a half-year older than the first. The child whimpered in his sleep like Amila had and rubbed at his tattooed cheek.

They moved on, pausing at each of the next two cribs to see tattooed GEN babies. Then three more beds with GEN toddlers, sound asleep.

The last bed in the row was far enough from the ceiling illuminators that its occupant was poorly lit. But even though he'd snuggled deeply into his blanket, it was clear the eighteen-month-old's left cheek was unmarked. And with a sudden shock of recognition, Mishalla realized she knew him.

"It's Shan. He's been here all this time."

"Then there's at least one lowborn here."

She couldn't resist reaching for the little boy, smoothing his dark curls from his face. The light caress disturbed the toddler's sleep, and Shan shifted with a whine. He turned away from Mishalla, the blanket falling away and exposing the right side of his face.

Mishalla stumbled backward, groping blindly for Eoghan. He looked as sick as she felt.

A GEN tattoo had been installed in Shan's cheek.

She hurried along the other children's beds. "That's Cas. There's Wani. They were in the crèche my first week."

"Do you know any of the others?"

She shook her head. "Maybe they went through the crèche before I arrived, or there's another crèche. Who turned these lowborns into GENs? And why?"

Whatever answer Eoghan might have given her was cut off by a ruckus from the outer room. A woman's voice carried into the children's sleeproom. "Where's Faria?"

Heavy footsteps, then a male voice, tantalizingly familiar, rumbled in response, "High as the skyway. Should have brought in a minor-status, not a lowborn, Pia."

Pia! Come here to check on her valuable stock. Mishalla clutched at Eoghan's arm. "There's no way she won't know who I am!"

The male voice grew louder along with his booted footfalls. A moment before he appeared in the sleeproom, fear froze Mishalla in her tracks as she realized who the man was.

Ansgar.

*Don't let him know me. Please, dear Infinite, don't let him recognize me.*

"What the denking hell are you doing here?" he demanded.

Eoghan stepped in front of Mishalla, blocking her from view. She could see his fingers tapping at his wristlink behind his back. "What business is it of yours, enforcer?"

"Captain," Ansgar said. "And even a demi-status captain has authority over a high-status." He edged to one side, trying to get a better look at Mishalla. "Do I know you?"

Curse her red hair, the way it blared like a klaxon. They should have found a way to color it, to cover it. Not trusting her voice, Mishalla shook her head.

As Ansgar continued to stare at her, Eoghan again shifted to block Mishalla. "No one told me they would be babies. How can I get any work out of a GEN so young?"

Ansgar fixed his pale gaze on Eoghan. "After you commit to a purchase, they go back in the tank. The gene-splicers accelerate their growth so that this time next year you'll have an eighth or ninth-year. Good for everything but the heavy work."

"But if they keep aging," Eoghan said, "I won't get more than a couple decades labor out of them."

"They only grow fast like that for a couple more years," Ansgar said. "They'll look like fifteenth-years by then and the acceleration switches off. Takes a while for their minds to catch up, but they'll work hard enough. But if you want one of these jiks, you'll have to take it up with Director Manel, not me."

Eoghan nodded and edged past Ansgar, keeping his body between the captain and Mishalla. She could feel Ansgar's hard stare burning into her as they traversed the outer room. Mishalla promised herself she would breathe once they'd escaped the crèche.

They were nearly out the door. Eoghan had his hands on her shoulders and was guiding her toward escape. Mishalla could feel his fingers pressing into her collarbone, could hear her heart racing in her ears.

The cool night air roiled against her face. The first knots of tension began to loosen themselves. Her mouth began to curve into a smile of relief.

"I *do* know you." Ansgar's declaration burst from the crèche like an explosion. His gloved hand fell on her wrist and he wrenched her away from Eoghan.

The rough leather of his glove scraped her right cheek. She felt the concealer give way, felt the sting of pain from his roughness.

"You're a denking jik from Chadi sector." Ansgar's head swiveled to Eoghan. "Does that make you a jik-lover? Or . . ."

Ansgar tried the same trick on Eoghan's cheeks, left first, then right. The captain was even more brutal than he'd been with Mishalla, his wristlink scratching Eoghan's face. With a last assault, Ansgar knocked the bali from Eoghan's ear.

"Not a jik, but no trueborn, I'll wager. Denking hell, doesn't matter." Ansgar pulled restraints from his belt. "You're both under arrest."

# 25

**D**evak drew Kayla to the open door of her quarters. "The last of the lights are out. Senia's long gone to her shantytown. We'll go inside, wait outside Pitamah's room. If Father's still awake, we'll be able to hear."

She pulled away from him to slip Pitamah's journal back inside the cupboard. Her habitual stealth drove home to Devak the starkest difference between them—what they risked with their disobedience.

As she turned to leave the cottage, he stopped her. "Whatever the Kinship has planned for the GENs, whatever freedom—I want it for you, first. I want it for you, now."

Her gray eyes were dark in the dimness of her quarters. "There are others more important than me."

"But you're the only one I care about."

He kissed her, just a brief touch of his lips against hers. It had felt so shocking the first time, but now it felt right, perfect. Anjika, who had once seemed to own his heart, faded into insignificance, overcome by the realness of Kayla.

He released her hands, smiled at the daze in her wide gray eyes. Then he urged her out the door.

The air was cool and moist, the stepping stones faintly lit by the first two moons. He overrode the back porch motion-sensor lights with his wristlink, so they had to feel their way along in near darkness as they approached the house. Since Kayla was less familiar with the path than he was, he stayed close to her, catching her arm when she stumbled.

They crept into the house via the red door and ascended the back stairs. Pitamah's door was ajar, which would make it easy for Kayla to slip inside, if needed. They leaned against the wall on either side of the door, and Devak strained his ears to hear anything in the silence.

He watched thirty minutes tick by on his wristlink, then nodded at Kayla. He led the way down the hall, figuring his body might block his father's view of Kayla long enough for her to escape to Pitamah's room. But his father seemed to be well and truly asleep and his mother still in the grip of her drug demons. They reached his father's office safely.

Devak entered the code for the door lock, wincing as the lock release seemed to echo down the hallway. He opened the door and they slipped inside.

Devak quietly shut the door behind them, then skimmed on the ceiling illuminators. He let out a huff of relief. "We can talk as long as we keep our voices down. Father put some sound-proofing between his office and their sleeproom so he wouldn't disturb Mother."

Kayla scanned the blank walls of the empty room. "Where's the Grid?"

She wasn't a tech GEN, so she wouldn't necessarily

recognize the holo projection boxes that jutted out here and there. The workstation that ran the length of the wall opposite the door didn't look like much either. It was little more than a shelf, only wide enough to set down a sekai or wristlink. The external device interfaces set every twenty centimeters or so along its length were small enough to escape notice.

With a brush of his fingers on the nearest box, he activated the holo projection system. The sensors picked up the well-practiced sweeps of his hands that initialized the holographic keyboard and a display that nearly filled the wall. With a combination of keyboard entries and manipulation of the holographic screen, he brought up the windows he'd need to interface with the system.

"This is a false wall," he told Kayla. "There are a series of chained processors behind it for backend computation and storage for the database. Even though Father is only director of the western territories, GENs from the Northeastern and Eastern Territory are included in his database."

"So he can track them too, if they stray into the wrong territory," Kayla said.

"Yeah. Redundancy." It had seemed like a sensible notion before. Now it seemed sinister.

He gestured toward a half-meter by half-meter grille in the corner. "That's the access panel to the physical system."

He typed at the keyboard and the password entry field opened in the center of the display. "There's a biometric passkey, too, like with those files on Pitamah's sckai. Father entered my retinal scan and thumbprint as authorized passkeys. He didn't exactly give me the passwords, but I can get them."

"How?" Kayla asked.

"A program that I shouldn't have," Devak said. He took off his wristlink and aligned the back to one of the external interfaces on the workstation.

"The password changes every minute. I stole the code for the password program one time when Father left me alone with the Grid."

He should have felt shame at his actions. But he didn't, not after seeing his father take those dhans, hearing him selling off GENs to the highest bidder.

Trueborns always talked about Assigning GENs. But wasn't it really true that they were selling them? Like a drom, or a new wristlink? So that instead of being Assigned to a job, they were sold like an animal or a thing. For the first time, that felt shameful, far more than breaking into his father's system.

After a few minutes work, the program on his wristlink found the right password. The screen changed to display retinal and thumbprint scanners. He leaned close to an eye-level box behind the scanner graphic and the sensors there took his biometric data.

He pulled over the float chair. "The password and passkey will only get me into the operational system. There's another layer of protection to get into the backend programming. I'll have to hack into that level."

"Will your program do that?" Kayla moved to stand behind him, some of her long hair falling forward to tickle his neck.

He pressed his shoulders against her fingers where she gripped the chair back. "Different program. More like an algorithm than a program, something that needs my interaction. Pitamah showed me how."

"When?"

"Three or four years ago." Devak broke through to the next level of security. Using the keyboard to interface with his wristlink, he started up a tool he'd written that would cycle through passwords for the next level. "When his legs gave out completely he started teaching me about breaking through security."

"When he couldn't come in here himself," Kayla said.

"He could still. And he has, although I never knew before now why exactly he was accessing the Grid. But it's become harder and harder for him to do it on his own." Devak broke through to the next level of security. "I thought he'd taught me how just to give my brain something to work on."

"But he was getting you ready."

"To take his place."

"Like your father has been. Training you to replace him."

About to type in another command, Devak's hands froze above the keyboard. "Both of them pushing me where they wanted me to go. Except . . ." He turned to Kayla, his gaze moving over the lines of her face. She seemed to grow more beautiful to him every day.

Under his scrutiny, her cheek darkened at the border of her tattoo. "What?"

"They've managed to push me exactly where I want to be. Here, now. Helping you."

Her gaze dropped, but she smiled. Devak continued his give-and-take with the Grid system, following the security pathways to the level at which he could upload an override. This was what he enjoyed—riding the twists and turns through complex computer code, parsing the logic as each page spilled into the display window, contemplating how he could tweak this command here and that mathematical operation there to change the processing.

It was minor-status work, something he'd never be allowed to do once he took his father's place. If he took his father's place.

As he spotted the exact Grid template the upload would have to overlay, Kayla pointed to the monitor. "That's it. It looks just like what's in my annexed brain."

He turned the float chair to face her. "I never thought before now—datapod uploads are like someone putting thoughts in your mind. It seems so wrong now."

"It's only in my annexed brain, a part I wouldn't be using anyway. And this time it's going to help me and Mishalla and other GENs."

He used what was already on the datapod first, plugging it into one of the jacks. Faster than he could watch, the windows arrayed within the holo display rippled through the code change, characters flashing on the screen. When the update had finished, all of the windows prompted with the same message: *Additional files needed. Please enter.*

He released the datapod's extendibles from the system and turned to Kayla. "I know this hurts."

"We don't have a choice."

"Will you do it yourself? So I don't have to hurt you?"

"Yes."

He readied the datapod for a download. "You put your thumb here." He pointed out the control. "Apply just a little pressure on it once it's against your cheek."

She took the device and put it into position. Her flinch told him when the extendibles pierced her skin. As the green ready light glowed, her eyes blanked just as they had before in

Pitamah's room. It was as if Kayla had gone on holiday, like his mother did with her vac-seals. A chill shuddered down his spine at that thought.

Finally, after what seemed far too long, the ready light faded from green to red. The datapod's extendibles retracted and he caught the device before it fell. To his relief, the life returned to Kayla's eyes.

He slipped his wristlink back on his arm, then snapped the datapod into an interface on the workstation. The datapod upload displayed in one of the windows on the holo screen, finishing moments later with an *Upload complete* message.

He ran a comparison between the current version and the previous and found the sections that had been upgraded. He downloaded that into the datapod, then handed the device to Kayla.

With the upload of the Grid changes, she stayed conscious, barely reacting to the extendibles' bite. She caught the datapod herself this time.

"You keep it," Devak said.

She tucked it into her hidden pocket. "I guess we wait."

"It wasn't much code," Devak said. "It probably won't take long."

Devak drew Kayla over to the corner by the access panel and they sat together on the floor. He wove his fingers through hers, nudged up her sleeve so he could see the intriguing patterns on her arm.

"I've downloaded GENs before, seen them go blurry the way you did. But I've never asked how it feels."

"The first time, it scared me. But it's really like I fall asleep," she said.

"When was the first time?"

A sort of grim sorrow washed over her face. "Captain Ansgar downloaded me that day he reset poor little Tanti. I thought he was about to reset me, too."

"But he didn't."

She shook her head. "Something Skal said stopped him. I thought later it was because I was Assigned to your father, an important trueborn. But now I wonder if the Kinship had something to do with it."

"The reason you fall asleep is because the datapod has to take control for a download. That puts you offline."

Alarm flickered in her face. "But when the datapod takes control, it can only read my annexed brain, right? Not my bare brain."

"Even if it wasn't forbidden by the Edicts, there's no circuitry pathway to your bare brain. So there's no way a datapod can access it."

She let out a little huff of relief. "My nurture brother—the younger one, Jal—he's a tech GEN. He told me the trueborns figured out a way to read our bare brains too."

"He was just teasing you." He lifted his hand to her right cheek, dabbed the blood away with his thumb. "Do you have some thoughts you don't want me to know?"

Her cheeks darkened again and she shrugged away from him. "The Grid updates are finished processing." She pressed the datapod to her tattoo.

This time the download from Kayla's annexed brain was briefer. She gave him back the datapod and he loaded its contents into the Grid backend.

"I should do a sanity check." Closing the hack he'd

performed, he used the conventional menus to access the Grid. He entered first Kayla's name, then Mishalla's. "You're in your quarters and Mishalla is in the crèche."

"I thought the Grid didn't pinpoint GENs so exactly."

"It doesn't usually, but it can. I used a triangulation command."

"So, it's put us back on the Grid. And for me at least, it's been fooled into thinking I'm somewhere I'm not."

Exiting from the Grid, he brought up a search tool. "I want to see what I can find in my father's files."

He entered the lowborn names and sectors he'd overheard his father talking about with his visitors. Two files matched his query.

"This one's encrypted." He tapped the screen. "I could decrypt it, but that would take some time. But this one I can read."

He selected the file name and it opened. It contained a table, the columns labeled *name, age, location,* and *skill set.*

"There's Shan, in the middle there." Kayla leaned closer to read. "These all look like lowborn names and shantytowns."

"But this is in the Assignment folder," Devak said. "As if these were GENs being allocated for Assignments."

"But that doesn't make sense. Why would you—" She straightened. "Did you hear that?"

It registered now—the quiet closing of a door, footsteps in the hall moving nearer. Stopping outside the door.

Devak looked frantically around the room. "The access panel!" He tugged the grille free of its mag latches and Kayla dove into the tight space. Devak replaced the grille.

As the door rattled, Devak swept the file he'd been reading onto the datapod, then rapped out a sequence to log off and shut down the screen. He moved the float chair in front of the access panel to further conceal Kayla. He caught the glint of her eyes through the grille, the glitter of her tattoo.

His father stepped inside, clearly surprised to see him. "What are you doing in here?"

"I . . . I was . . ." That was all Devak could muster.

His father frowned. "I was headed downstairs and saw the lock wasn't activated. I thought I'd forgotten to set it."

Denk it, he should have locked the door behind them. He reached behind him and palmed the datapod.

"What happened to the GENs in Sheysa?" Devak asked, hoping to divert his father.

"As you said. All where they should be. The lowborn supervisor persuaded the Brigade to leave them since he'd be short-staffed otherwise."

The fail-safe Pitamah mentioned? Was the supervisor part of the Kinship?

His father's gaze narrowed. "You weren't accessing the system, were you? Did Zul give you the password again?"

That gave Devak an opening to tell part of the truth. "It wasn't his fault, Father. I wanted to check on those GENs. I was pretty sure there was a glitch in the system and it looks like there was. Those GENs are all back on the Grid now."

"Show me," his father said, quickly activating the system again, using his own eye and thumbprint scan.

Devak brought up the Grid access screen again and typed in the four GENs' names. As he had with Mishalla and Kayla, he triangulated down to their exact locations, one at a time. "See? All in their quarters, safe and sound."

His father's brow furrowed. "Did you change something in the system?"

"No!" He'd said it louder than he'd intended and his father gave him a sharp look. Devak forced himself to smile. "I just checked it, like I said. And there they were."

His father stared at the display for so long, Devak feared he'd inadvertently left behind some clue, some sign that revealed the truth. He forced himself to breathe evenly.

And clutching even harder at his gut, his awareness of Kayla, hiding behind the access panel. He was certain he could hear her breathing, her heart pounding. Surely his father would hear it too, would throw the float chair aside and find her there.

But then his father took a step back. "You're right. They're legitimately on the Grid again. Thank you for checking." His father swiped a hand across the HP box and shut down the system. "Let's go."

"Where?"

"You, to bed. Me, downstairs for a glass of tea."

"But I hoped to search the Grid for other anomalies. You wouldn't have to wait with me. I could do it on my own."

"You've solved the problem with the Sheysa GENs. Anything else can wait until morning."

His father's pointed gaze prodded Devak out of the office. Pulling the door shut, his father engaged the electronic lock.

"In future, ask permission before using the system. You know you haven't the authorization for some of the confidential information."

"I will, sir."

"And I'll take that datapod."

The breath froze in Devak's chest. "What datapod?"

"The one I lent you earlier today. I saw you slip it in your pocket."

His brain seemed to seize up. He could only muster a bare whisper. "I can't."

"Why not?"

He snatched an idea at random from his tumbling thoughts. "I lost mine at the coffee house. I was hoping to keep this one instead."

His father's jaw worked, as if he was chewing over Devak's transgression. "Have you purged my data from it?"

"Yes." Not quite a lie, Devak figured, since he'd wiped his father's datapod before he gave it to the blond lowborn.

"I'll dock your allowance for the value of it."

"Of course," Devak agreed, his body sagging in tentative relief. "Thank you, sir. Good night, then."

But his father didn't move. "Good night."

Devak turned away, forcing leaden feet to pace out the route to his sleeproom door. He didn't go inside. After turning the corner, he stationed himself just out of sight of his father. He heard his father's footsteps go down the front stairs, then the faint clattering of movement in the kitchen.

It seemed an eternity until his father returned, his tread creaking on the loose step, growing louder as he continued down the hallway. Then he stopped, long enough that Devak chanced a surreptitious glance around the corner. His heart dropped to his gut when he saw his father outside his office door. Keying in the door lock code, stepping inside, activating the illuminators.

In those brief moments, when he was certain his father

would discover Kayla, impossible plans spun out in Devak's mind. He'd overpower his father before he could contact the Brigade, then he'd take Kayla as far from Foresthill as he could before he ran out of fuel credits for his Bullet. They'd hide in a GEN sector somewhere and he'd bleach his hair, paint a denking tattoo on his cheek if he had to, to blend in.

But then his father deactivated the illuminators and backed from the room. Devak ducked behind the corner again before his father saw him, then listened intently for the latching of his father's sleeproom door. He spied around the corner to be sure the hall was empty. Then he rushed to the office door.

Devak tapped in the lock code. He didn't hear the lock release. He tried the handle, but it didn't move. The door was still locked.

He tried the sequence again, pressing each key with deliberate care. Maybe he'd just tapped the wrong button, or had held it too long and it had entered two digits instead of one.

Still no click, and the handle wouldn't move. Horror stole over him as he realized his father had changed the code.

There was an emergency override that Kayla could use inside, but she wouldn't know the sequence for it. He didn't dare knock on the door to get her attention; he'd risk waking his father. He could pass a note under the door, but what could he use? The door was nearly flush to the floor; he would need something slim enough to fit under it. His sekai was too thick. He could tear a page from one of Pitamah's paper books. But would she see it in the darkened room?

He remembered Pitamah's sekai, the one his great-grandfather had given to Kayla to use. As slim as it was, it would slide under the door, and the light from its display would be enough to catch Kayla's attention from behind the grille. He doubted she'd move from her hiding place without a signal from him, but she'd certainly notice even a faint glow in the pitch dark room.

Moving as quickly and as silently as he could, he raced for the back stairs. In the garden, he avoided the thump of his feet on paving stones, running instead across the damp lawn.

He felt only the briefest awkwardness at invading Kayla's quarters as he grabbed the sekai from the table. He took off toward the house at a dead run, questions harrowing him. What if his father was still troubled by Devak's intrusion in his office? What if he went back to check the system more thoroughly? What if Kayla made a noise—drew in a breath, sighed in discomfort—and his father found her?

Through the red door, up the back stairs, down the hall past Pitamah's room. A sudden halt at the corner to be sure the door to his parents' sleeproom was still shut and the hallway deserted. Then he padded down to the office.

Tapping out a message on the sekai—*Use emergency code!*—then the four-digit sequence, he knelt to push the sekai under the door. It was so thin, it was flexible enough that it resisted his pressure. He had to use the palm of his hand to get the carpet fibers out of the way and make enough room for the sekai.

Then he got to his feet and waited, ticking off the time to the beat of his heart, certain it was taking far too long, that Kayla couldn't see the sekai's glow. She would stay there until morning when his father would find her. Or rather, he'd find Devak first, because no way would he leave Kayla unprotected.

When the latch finally did release, it seemed to ring through the house as loud as a shockgun explosion. Kayla opened the door, the sekai in her hand. He threw his arms around her, holding her as tight as he could. He could feel the power of her embrace along his back, knew that she used only a fraction of her strength.

Then he pulled her into the hallway and locked the door with the familiar code—which his father had thankfully not changed when he changed the unlock code. They crept away past his parents' sleeproom, to the garden where they ran pell-mell to Kayla's quarters.

They ducked inside, shutting the door behind them. He drew her into his arms again and pressed his mouth to the tangle of her hair.

"You should leave," she murmured against his chest. Her warm breath sifted through the thin uttama-silk of his korta.

"How can I let you go?"

Moving to sit on her bed, he pulled her into his lap. He bent his head to kiss her, again and again, until the bleak emptiness of his life dissolved in a haze of pleasure. By slow degrees, he lowered her to the bed, the feel of her warm body an indescribable joy.

He kissed her again, his fingers working under the hem of her shirt. Before he'd explored more than a few inches, she stopped him with her firm grip. "We can't."

He nuzzled her neck. "Why not?"

"You know why. We've done too much already."

He kept his hand at her waist. "You can't make me leave you." Except she could. One effortless throw and she'd have him on the floor.

Still, she sighed and relaxed against him. "Just a few minutes more."

He cushioned her head against his chest. Pushing up the sleeve of her shirt, he drew a finger across the myriad colors on her arm. He listened to her breathe, inhaled the elusive fragrance of her. Dreamed of a time when they could be together, that a miracle would take that mark from her cheek.

The darkness of the space, the warmth of Kayla against him, conspired to make his eyelids heavy. A thought floated into his mind that he ought to get up, return to the house. The next moment he drifted off to sleep.

**K**ayla woke in a sudden panic, realized she'd slept past her internal alarm. Then her panic escalated to full-scale terror when she registered the significance of the warm weight at her waist—Devak's arm, resting heavily as he slept.

She shook him, hissing, "Devak!"

"Ow!" He shrugged away from her too-tight grip. His bleary gaze raked the room. "Denking hell. What time is it?"

"Late enough that Senia might come looking for me."

He scrambled off the bed. "There's no way I can get to the house with no one seeing."

"They can't find out you slept the night with me."

He paced the floor. "What do we do? I have to find a way out of here."

"Can you fit through the window? Go out through the alley gate?" Standing on the bed, she shoved the window open. The stink from the neighbor's faulty incinerator rolled into the room in a noxious cloud.

Devak stood on the bed beside her, his gaze measuring

the width of the narrow window. "I don't know if my shoulders will fit."

"Maybe go out the door, then, hope they don't—" She sucked in a breath. "Did you hear that?"

The sound of the red door slamming echoed across the yard. Kayla ran for her own door and cracked it open. "It's Senia! She's coming this way!"

Infinite plague the lowborn woman. Kayla's heart froze solid in fear. She shut the door again, a moan of terror escaping from her throat.

"Help me," Devak said. "Lift me up. If I go feet first . . ."

Hurrying back to the bed, she wrapped her arms around him, hefting his torso so he could feed his legs through the window. He kept his grip on her as he squirmed through, his purple korta riding up past his waist. In the midst of their dire straits, Kayla's gaze fixed on that swath of smooth brown skin.

Senia pounded on the door. "Are you in there, jik?"

Anger flashed across Devak's face. "I told her—"

"Never mind. It doesn't matter!"

With an impatient huff, he stretched his arms above his head. His body filled the window. As Senia pounded again, he pulled Kayla close and pressed a quick kiss to her mouth. Kayla could hear Senia trying the door latch.

"Help me," Devak whispered. As he squirmed backward, Kayla pushed. Just as he dropped, something ripped. A fragment of purple cloth waved in the redolent breeze.

Kayla jumped off the bed as Senia swung open the door. The lowborn woman's nose twitched. "How can you jiks stand that stink? I suppose you're used to it." Her crafty gaze narrowed on the window. "What is that stuck there?"

Kayla stood in her way. "It's nothing."

Senia tried to dodge around her. "Looks like a torn bit of cloth. From a flashy pair of leggings, maybe. Or a shirt. Who have you had in here? Who just escaped through that window?"

Kayla's lungs emptied of air. Senia couldn't possibly suspect the truth, else she'd be running to call the Brigade. Kayla lifted her chin. "How is it any business of yours?"

"I'm not the least bit concerned about your trashy GEN ways. I only care that you're late," Senia said. "The old man is asking for you."

Kayla tamped down her anger, leaning across the bed to pluck the swatch from the window frame. She slid the window shut. "Tell Zul I'll be there soon."

Senia's eyes grew small and mean. "As if I'd do a jik's bidding. I've had enough of the old man. Had to bring him his breakfast myself since Master Devak saw fit to leave early."

With a sniff, Senia turned on her heel and marched back to the house, her full skirts billowing after her. Kayla shut the door and scrambled quickly into fresh leggings and a shirt, running to the washroom to relieve herself and wash the sleep from her face.

As she stared into the washroom mirror's shiny metal surface, the reality struck her. Devak had spent the night with her. They'd slept in each other's arms, something she'd never done with a GEN boy. Scandalous to have done it with a trueborn, in the full view of the Infinite. Could He see her even now in the mirror?

It didn't bear thinking about. She set her mind to tidying her hair, wrestling it into a braid. Ducking into the shack for the sekai, she took off at a run to the house, slipping inside the red door more decorously. Senia gave her an evil look, but Kayla ignored it, making for the stairs.

Just as she'd climbed the first few steps and out of Senia's line of sight, Kayla heard the rattle of the front door. She shrank against the wall.

Mrs. Manel's hard voice drifted into the stairwell. "Where have you been?"

Devak answered, "Out with friends."

"All night?"

"What would it matter to you?" Devak said. "You were having your own party, weren't you?"

Kayla winced at the crack of a slap to Devak's face, could almost feel it on her own cheek. Tears burned her eyes in empathy.

Footsteps—Devak's, she guessed—started up the front stairs. Mrs. Manel shouted, "Your father will want to speak to you when he gets home," but there was no answer from Devak.

Kayla hurried up the stairs herself, reaching Zul's door just as Devak reached his own room. He sent her a fleeting smile, then blew her a kiss down the hall before disappearing into his room.

She pushed into Zul's room, rattled and confused but filled with a dangerous joy. The old man was not only awake, but propped up against the pillows. Even if Senia was willing, the slight lowborn woman couldn't have lifted Zul up.

Kayla set the sekai on the dresser. "You sat up in bed on your own?"

His broad smile creased the tattoo on his lined face. "And fed myself." He gestured at the remains of a bowl of kel-grain on the bedside table, his wristlink dangling on his arm. "Just as well. That mean-spirited woman would have set my breakfast down and let me starve."

Kayla nudged the door shut, then leaned against it. "Devak read the journal. Most of it, anyway."

"Then you know your prophets—"

She put up a hand to stop him. "The idea didn't come to them first, I see that now. But maybe we didn't interpret the liturgy right. Or maybe part of it was lost like those pages out of your journal."

"Those pages weren't lost. I tore them out. Some final equations. Guesses as to how the original programming went wrong. I'd intended to destroy them so Pouli and Cohn couldn't take the study to an operational phase." He shook his head. "Dr. Pouli got hold of the pages before I could shred them."

Unease settled inside Kayla at the mention of the foremost of the three prophets. When the door nudged against her, she stepped aside in a daze, letting Devak in.

"Devak, bring up breakfast for yourself and Kayla, then we'll talk."

By tacit agreement, they waited until Devak returned with two steaming bowls of kel-grain. The hot cereal was heavily sweetened, but Kayla could barely force down more than two or three bites.

Once they'd stacked the bowls on the dresser, Devak sat beside her on the bench and caught her hand, making no attempt to hide their linked fingers from his great-grandfather. Zul said not a word in reproach.

"Your Grid session went well, I presume?" Zul asked.

"The updates are in," Devak said, leaving out the more terrifying parts of the story.

"Do you want to know the truth, Kayla? Beyond what's in the journal?"

Would he tell her about Chaaya? Clear up the reason for the error in her emergence date? As much as she feared what he might say about the prophets, she wanted to know those other truths. The veil had been ripped partly aside. Why not hear the rest of it?

She swallowed against a dry throat. "The mark on your face—is that a GEN tattoo?"

"Similar. A precursor device. Installed in the ten study subjects, including Fulki and me. Our intention was to provide an exterior connection to the brain and nervous system to send messages and programming. We'd hoped to prod the body into fighting off the Abeni and Geming viruses."

"What went wrong?" Devak asked. "Did everyone in the study die of the plague like Great-grandma Fulki did?"

"None of them died of the plague. Not even Fulki." An old grief passed across his face. "The circuitry caused structural changes to the body. In some cases, the motor neurons degenerated, in others they calcified. Caused a complete breakdown of the central nervous system in all but one of the volunteers."

"You," Devak said.

"Inexplicably, it worked in me, at least partially. Enough that I was neither killed by the plague virus nor the process we'd used to fight it. Still, it left me with only rudimentary motor function. The chronic weakness."

"But how did you get from trying to cure the plague to creating GENs?" Kayla asked.

Zul's expression grew grim. "Your prophets. Gupta was experimenting with the frozen embryos we'd brought from Earth. The embryos had been intended for repopulation if an epidemic like Abeni or Geming wiped us out. Someone let slip to Cohn and Pouli that the neural circuitry we were testing might be tolerated better if it could be incorporated at the embryonic stage."

"Who told them?" asked Kayla.

"Me. In a weak moment, after Fulki died." He scrubbed at his face. "An off-hand remark to Gupta. He was Fulki's cousin. I thought I could trust him."

"You started that journal seventy-eight years ago," Devak said. "But the first GENs weren't created for another thirteen years."

"The first *successful* GENs," Zul said. "There were years of failures that didn't make it into the history. Embryos that never developed past the blastocyst stage, malformed fetuses. Ghastly deformities that killed full-term babies soon after birth. But Pouli and Cohn kept trying."

Desperate for a hole in Zul's story, Kayla spiraled back to his first claim. "You say GENs were your idea. And I can see that you must have paved the way for the prophets. But *they* did the work."

"Not they. Only Gupta. Pouli and Cohn were incompetent frauds. They could never have achieved success without Gupta as their willing dupe." He narrowed his gaze on Kayla. "And I could have done the work, if not for the immorality of it."

"You think GENs are immoral?"

"Not GENs. Trueborn enslavement of them is."

"Servitude to trueborns is in the liturgy," Kayla said.

Zul's dark gaze hardened. "Because they wrote it. Your so-called prophets."

"Of course they did. The Infinite whispered to them—"

"No," Zul said. "Pouli and Cohn made it up. All of it, created out of whole cloth. The GEN creation tale, their own status as prophets."

Kayla shook her head. "You may not believe the liturgy, it might be different from your own faith, but GENs accept it as the Infinite's word. Transcribed by the prophets."

"Transcribed . . ." Zul made a rude gesture. "Gupta told me how it went. Once they finally started producing viable GENs, Pouli and Cohn were worried about controlling them. Every attempt to lock in that control with programming failed. The Monitoring Grid would only be so effective.

"So Pouli had a brilliant idea—create a GEN religion. Weave the three of them in as prophets. Establish as liturgy the supremacy of trueborns. Make it seem noble for the GENs to replace the lowborns as the most despised. Then use that faith to ingrain in the GENs that their enslavement was ordained, even glorious. Pass their false religion down from nurturer to nurtured."

Nausea roiled in Kayla's belly. "That would be evil. The Infinite would never allow it."

"They created your Infinite, Kayla."

"No," she whispered. "The Infinite isn't made up. He's real." Wasn't that His hand she could feel on her heart?

"Real for you, maybe." Zul wove his trembling fingers together and rested them in his lap. "Pouli and Cohn's religion would have fallen apart eventually. GENs would have started questioning. But then the two of them were killed by a lowborn assassin. Gupta took his own life shortly after. He, at least, had had a conscience." Zul barked a harsh laugh. "The only thing more effective than a live prophet is a dead one.

Your prophets became saints."

In her mind's eye, Kayla groped for the Infinite's hand. "If you thought it was so wrong for Pouli and the others to create slaves, why didn't you stop them?"

"Because it didn't start out that way. They were just playing with DNA at first. Or so I thought." Zul's gaze flicked over to Devak. "You know how we all came here? How we settled out into trueborn and lowborn?"

"The trueborns paid their way to Loka," Devak said. "The high-status were rich enough to have the ships built. The demis bought the supplies to get us here and start the colony," Devak said. "Minor-status paid some, but mostly were the brain-power for the ship design, the stasis pods, the preservation of human and animal embryos and DNA."

"And the lowborns worked off their passage," Kayla added, "serving the trueborns until we came along."

"All true," Zul said. "The problem was the lowborns thought all their hard work on Loka ought to have equalized things. They'd labored their fifty years as promised—why weren't they trueborns?

"But the trueborns were horrified by the idea of the impoverished masses climbing up the status tree. The Congress found excuses to keep the status quo. Too much economic instability due to food shortages or the bad winter or the latest plague. The Congress would increase wages a few tenth-dhans to mollify the lowborns, but even still the unrest led to rioting and then full-blown insurrections."

"Like thirteen years ago when my brother was killed," Devak said.

"Yes, and thousands of lowborns were killed as well," Zul

said. "Riots and insurrections alike were brutally quashed by the Brigade. And each time someone in Congress would make the same promises to the lowborns—a path to adhikar and full citizenship. But with only adhikar-owning trueborns in Congress, it never went any further. This went on for over two centuries, long after the fifty years of servitude the lowborns had committed to."

"How do the GENs fit in?" Kayla asked.

Zul frowned. "When Pouli learned of my research and Gupta's, he saw the potential in it for a third, even lower class of beings on Loka. These new creatures could be controlled exclusively by the trueborns. They would serve multiple purposes—provide cheap labor for trueborns too fine to labor themselves, give the lowborns a people to feel superior to, and provide a potential force against future insurgencies. If another insurrection arose, they could fight the lowborns."

"GENs were first Assigned as enforcers during the last insurrection," Kayla remembered.

"Dozens of able-bodied GENs were reset and realigned as warriors," Zul said. "Sent into the lowborn shantytowns to kill."

It would be horrible to be realigned that way, to have her strength turned against innocent lowborns.

"You've asked what's special about you," Zul said, looking up at Kayla. "You may not like what you find out about yourself."

"Pitamah," Devak said. "Stop dancing around the truth."

"Is this about Chaaya?" Kayla asked, hope springing up inside her that Zul would finally confirm her guess.

For the first time since she'd met him, Zul looked puzzled. "What about Chaaya?"

Her hand shaking, she reached for the sekai. "I saw the

list. And I heard about Chaaya's DNA maybe being used for GENs when she died sixteen years ago. And I thought maybe her DNA was used for me."

"Is that what you thought?" Zul asked gently.

"I thought that's what was special about me and Mishalla. Especially after seeing us both on that list." She brought up the file and handed him the sekai. "And that note about Chaaya in the journal made me wonder if that was the connection. That I could be related to you. A sort of great-granddaughter."

Her voice faded at the end as she realized she might have just offered this high-status trueborn the most despicable of insults. That a relation of his was a GEN.

But he didn't look insulted, he just looked sad. "I'm afraid you misinterpreted the note. Chaaya was my eyes and ears in several GEN sectors. She was seeking out certain GENs for me. Special GENs."

He studied the sekai's display. "Devak, did you click the link beside Kayla's name?"

"She asked me to, Pitamah. So I figured out your passkey."

"That's fine. I don't mind. But you saw her emergence date?"

"The year is wrong," Kayla blurted. "And it says something stupid about me being in the birth records."

If anything, his expression grew even sadder. "I would welcome you as a long-lost great-granddaughter, if that were true. I would erase what's in this list if it would change the truth."

"I see now, I wasn't made from Chaaya's DNA." Grief cut through her. "But that link to the birth record—it's wrong."

"Kayla." Zul cut through the confusion clogging her brain. "I know it seems impossible to accept. You were born—"

"No."

"—but there was something wrong with you. An imperfection. A genetic defect."

She saw the flaw in his story. "But the gene-splicers destroy defective GENs and start over. I'm here, so what you're saying can't be right."

"You're here because you didn't start out as a GEN."

Of course she'd started out as a GEN, because she was a GEN now. She shook her head in confusion. "I don't understand."

"Sometimes, trueborn babies are born with defects," Zul said. "Missing limbs or mental deficiencies."

"I know," Kayla said, "and they go into the tank."

"They do," Zul said. "But sometimes, despite best efforts, a defect can't be corrected using ordinary procedures."

"I've heard about that," Devak said. "That some children die."

"Yes, some do. Even more before we had the tank," Zul said. "But even then, some would survive. They'd be shipped off to an adhikar kel-grain farm or drom ranch. Where no one would notice their artificial limbs or facial deformities or mental failings. But then twenty years ago or so, the gene-splicers discovered something interesting about the GEN circuitry—it could be installed in a child as old as four."

Kayla's skin crawled. "What does that have to do with fixing defects?"

"With the circuitry, the body could be programmed to repair itself in ways it couldn't on its own," Zul said. "In some cases, the animal DNA would need to be added in—to regenerate limbs, for instance. Not every defect could be corrected. But far more than what could be done in the tank alone."

"But, Pitamah," Devak said, his expression troubled. "They wouldn't do that to trueborn children."

Zul locked his frail hands together and stared down at them. "It takes a great deal of dhans. A goodly portion of a trueborn's adhikar to bribe the gene-splicer. Nearly as much to smuggle the new GEN into a nurture home."

Devak looked horrified. "The Judicial Council wouldn't let this happen."

"They'll stop the parents if they can before the procedure." Zul said. "Take the child and place it with a more tolerant family. But if it's already been converted to a GEN . . ."

"No trueborn family would take the child," Kayla said bitterly.

She felt so sick, she thought she'd lose the little breakfast she'd just eaten. She groped for Devak. He dropped onto the bench beside her. "Did you know?" she asked him.

He enfolded her hand in both of his. "No."

"Then I was one of those children?" Kayla asked.

Zul nodded.

Kayla clutched Devak's hand like a lifeline. "Did they break me down? Make me into embryos? Am I only part of the original me—whatever her name was?"

Zul tapped on the sekai, entering keystrokes for a few moments, then he held the reader out to her. When she didn't move, Devak took the sekai from his great-grandfather, then read from the screen.

"Elana Kalu," Devak said, showing her the display. The name sent a shiver through her and he drew her closer. "Only one record for your ID, so who you are now is the same person you were then. The same body, anyway." He whispered that last slim comfort.

"Your original parents kept you long enough," Zul said, "they must have tried to correct the defect. Over and over."

"But they gave up in the end, didn't they? Once I was nearly a fourth-year, they must have realized they'd be stuck with a defective child. Easier to pay to put me in a gen-tank, make me a GEN."

Zul offered no defense of those faceless parents.

Not faceless. She could still picture the woman in her dreams. "I've had nightmares. For years. Another mother standing over my bed. Then someone carrying me away." Remembered fear roiled in her stomach. "I tried to reach for my mother, but I had no arms."

Zul's bleak expression told her she'd hit her target. "No arms," she gasped out, "I had no arms, so they built these in the tank."

"But you can't possibly remember," Zul said. "They would have sedated you before they put you in the tank. Then reset you once the circuitry was in place. Elana's memories should have been wiped away."

"But I do remember! I can see the woman's face, see the hands of the man who took me. I screamed, tried to get away from him—"

Suddenly it was the hands of that faceless man holding her, not Devak's. She wrenched from him, her arms alien to her, like a piece of someone else stuck on her body. Almost ripping her sleeves with the force of pulling them up, she struck her left arm with her right hand, once, twice. At the first sting of pain, anger boiled up and she hit herself again, left arm, then right, striking over and over until she hurt almost as much physically as she did inside.

# tankborn

"I hate them! I hate them!" She hated all of them—her clumsy color-blotched arms, the parents who gave her up to the gene-splicers, the Infinite who had allowed them to do it. The Infinite who had abandoned her.

When Devak grabbed her, she nearly struck him too, but at the last instant regained enough self-control to hold back. Aching inside and out, she collapsed into his embrace, sobbing.

After a long while, she eased away from Devak, wiping the tears from her face. Her fingers stuttered as they passed over the familiar faint lines of her tattoo.

"Is that why my DNA mark is on my right cheek? Because I was something else before?" A sudden realization stunned her. "Was Mishalla born a trueborn too?"

"Yes," Zul told her. "Both of you. From minor-status families, but trueborn even so."

Trueborn. She touched her right earlobe where she'd once worn a blue bali. She could have had a hope, a prayer, a scrap of a chance with Devak. If they'd been able to fix her eleven years ago. Or if they'd let her live her life as she'd started it.

No use thinking about it now. It would only break her heart.

"What was Mishalla's . . ." She didn't want to say the word *defect*, didn't want to apply it to her friend. "Her leg, I guess. It's never been right. I always wondered why they made a GEN that way. So, are we human, then? Because we were once trueborn?"

"To my way of thinking, every GEN is human," Zul said. "The animal DNA means nothing to your humanity. Your time in the tank is inconsequential. When we created the first GEN prototypes, Jemali, Hala, and I devised the acronym Genetically Engineered Non-natal. A discrimination between someone gestated inside a woman's womb versus inside a gen-tank. Pouli and Cohn changed it when they took over the project. Their version of the acronym—non-human—went into their cursed liturgy and that's what everyone believed." Zul fixed his dark eyes on her. "You're built with human DNA, in human form, with only a little assistance from the animal DNA. You're no more non-human than I am."

While she wrestled with the overwhelming revelations of the last several minutes, Zul's wristlink beeped softly. He turned the device to read from its display. His face paled to a frightening gray pallor.

His hands dropped to his lap as if he hadn't the energy to hold them up. "Your friend, Mishalla, has been taken."

**27**

Ansgar pushed Mishalla from the illegal crèche, her arms tied painfully behind her back, the restraints digging into her wrists. He shoved her to the walkway outside and her bad leg gave way so she banged her shoulder against the wall. When he dragged Eoghan out, Eoghan's expression was defiant, but he had the sense not to try to fight the captain.

Ansgar dumped Eoghan ten feet from her along the walkway, too far apart to allow them to talk without being overheard. The Brigade captain stripped the wristlink from Eoghan's arm, then tapped at its display. Eoghan smiled as Ansgar scowled with frustration then dumped the wristlink into his pocket. Eoghan had the audacity to wink at Mishalla.

He kept his steady gaze on her, his eyes green again. One of his lenses had fallen out when Ansgar had muscled him outside. The Brigade captain had then ordered Eoghan to take out the other one. Both their false balis were gone. Equal parts fear and bravado shone in Eoghan's face.

Juka arrived, out of breath after running to check the

crisis crèche on Ansgar's orders. The enforcer took a position halfway between Mishalla and Eoghan, although her shockgun was trained on Mishalla.

They'd hustled her out here so quickly, she'd hardly had time to be scared. Or maybe it was just that her mind had shut down—reality seemed foggy and distant. She could do nothing to prevent whatever would happen next, and it seemed like too much effort for her shock-hobbled brain to react.

Then Ansgar bent over her, his datapod in his hand, and stark terror sliced through her. He was going to reset her! She kicked to scramble back from him, but he caught a handful of the bodice of her dress and trapped her.

Tears didn't even have time to wet her eyes before he slapped the datapod to her cheek. How long before her mind emptied, before she lost herself? Seconds seemed to drag into forever as the extendibles bit her cheek, as Ansgar stared down, watching the datapod.

She didn't feel any different. She still knew her name, remembered her nurture parents, recalled Kayla and every childish prank they'd played on her brother, Skal, could feel the restraints cutting into her wrists. She could still smell the rank Sheysa River just beyond and Ansgar's closer stink.

"Denking hell?" Ansgar muttered.

Pia stormed from the crèche, grabbing hold of Ansgar's arm. "I told you not to reset her! After all the tricks the director had to go through to get her here, it would take forever to get another."

With an impatient, painful jerk, Ansgar disengaged the datapod. He shook off Pia. "The reset didn't work. Did you upload a neural system block?"

"Why would I need to? I know how to control a jik. We don't need her to be reset."

"She knows far too much. And what she doesn't know, she'll guess. We have to keep this contained."

"But that's exactly it," Pia said. "We threaten her with destruction, not just realignment. So she'll never return to her god's hands. And even if she did talk, who would believe her?"

"We can't take that chance," Ansgar said. "I can give her back to you after, but she'll have to be realigned."

Pia huffed with impatience. "Fine. But while we're at it, have the gene-splicers dumb her down. I'd just as soon she's not inclined to be so nosy."

Panic gripped Mishalla at their casual discussion of resetting her. *You won't know the difference,* she reminded herself. *You won't be you anymore.*

Ansgar nodded over at Eoghan. "That doesn't solve the problem of the lowborn."

"Give him the same treatment as our charges in there." Pia gestured inside the crèche.

"Can't turn him into a jik. Doesn't work on anyone older than three or four. Might as well kill him."

Eoghan scarcely reacted to Ansgar's edict. He stared harder at Mishalla, as if to will her to—what? Try to escape? Even if she could struggle to her feet, she'd be taken down by the shockgun before she was more than a few paces away.

Pia stopped Ansgar as he put his hand on his sidearm. "Don't do it here. Then we have a body to dispose of. I'd rather do that where no one will see us." Her glance flicked from Eoghan to Mishalla. "Besides, what if there's more to this than a curious lowborn and his jik-whore? Maybe we ought to find out what we can from him. From both of them."

Ansgar gave Eoghan a considering look and Eoghan stared back, stolid, brave. Eoghan wouldn't easily give up what he knew and Mishalla's heart broke thinking of what Ansgar might do to him to extract that knowledge. Then the captain's mouth curved in a faint smile, a glittering anticipation lighting his eyes, and Mishalla's heart squeezed even more tightly.

And what about her? Ansgar might not be satisfied with what he could download from her annexed brain. He'd enjoy hurting her to extract what he could from her bare brain. Now twin terrors clawed at her—fear for both Eoghan and herself.

Ansgar raised his wristlink to his mouth as he strode back inside the crèche, Pia dogging him. Mishalla leaned back against the wall, her body aching from the inside out.

The night air had cooled, dampness from the Sheysa River settling on her face. As she sat slumped against the wall, moisture collected, trickling down her right cheek. The pricks left by the extendibles stung and itched maddeningly. She shifted to lower her face to her knee, started to rub her itchy cheek against her skirt.

Juka waved the shockgun at her. "Keep still, jik."

She didn't even think, just let her anger push her to her knees. "Don't call me that."

"I'll call you what I like," Juka said, stepping closer to press the shockgun to Mishalla's forehead. "Sit down."

"Mishalla," Eoghan called out. "Do what she says."

Mishalla tossed her head, the weapon's barrel moving with her. "A shockgun blast would be easier, wouldn't it? Easier than whatever they have in mind for us."

"Mishalla," he said more softly. "Please don't."

# tankborn

Her bravado faded with his plea. She retreated against the wall, false courage giving way to a sick numbness. From inside the illicit crèche, she could hear the fitful cries of one of the children.

Pity and despair washed over her. All those babies, stolen from their families, turned into GENs. Tattoos installed on their faces, GEN circuitry laid over their neural pathways. A hideous violation of their sweet young bodies.

All her life, she'd been taught about GENs' special place on Loka, that her servitude would someday place her in the Infinite's hands. She'd held tight to that future hope, knowing that only GENs would reach the Infinite's blessedness, not lowborns, certainly not trueborns.

Yet here were these children who were a hybrid of lowborn and GEN. Surely their Lord Creator would reject them. And how could the Infinite know their names when he'd never whispered the instructions to create them? The Infinite knew every gene-splicer in the regulated, Council-run gen-labs. Did He see the outlaw gene-splicers who performed this evil? If He did, why didn't He stop them? If He didn't, if He wasn't all-seeing, then these children were doomed to an afterlife without a paradise.

It had been bad enough thinking the children had been stolen to clear out space for trueborns. It had been a small comfort believing they'd be taken to safety in a lowborn shantytown. But to know that her crèche had only been a handy holding pen for stolen children before they were sent to be made into hybrids like this was horrifying.

"Please—you won't kill them now, will you?" she pleaded with Juka. "The ones at my crèche?"

"Surprised you even care, jik, considering the way you left them alone tonight."

Mishalla shared a quick glance with Eoghan, saw his triumph. Ilian had somehow escaped, no doubt alerted by whatever message Eoghan had sent out. Otherwise Juka would have discovered him when she'd checked the crisis crèche and he'd be restrained here with her and Eoghan.

But that meant no one was now caring for the children. No one to soothe Chak with silly lullabies. No one there to explain to Amila that her cheek hurt because the gene-splicer botched the tattoo installation.

She heard the sound of a lev-car engine, something larger than a Bullet, smaller than a pub-trans. Lights illuminated the sticker bushes along the Sheysa River, then doused. Pia and Ansgar emerged from the crèche.

Ansgar wrenched Eoghan to his feet while Juka did the same, just as roughly, to Mishalla. Her bad leg had stiffened from its cramped position and each step sent a jolt of pain from knee to hip. She was just as glad to feel the pain. Once Ansgar pulled what he needed from her, Mishalla would be no more and would be feeling nothing. She'd be in the hands of the Infinite.

Around the corner, a sixteen-passenger Jahaja multi-lev waited. She and Eoghan were muscled inside and shoved into seats across from each other in the back. Ansgar, Pia, and Juka settled themselves just behind the operator, four rows up from Mishalla and Eoghan.

The cab lights shut off as the Jahaja powered up and rotated to face back the way it came. As they raced down the long row of warehouses, they sped past the crisis crèche. To Mishalla's relief, she spotted Celia, her Restday substitute, at the door. So they'd sent someone to care for Mishalla's charges after all.

The multi-lev wound its way through the quiet Sheysa streets then up onto the skyway, picking up speed. With Pia and the enforcers four rows up murmuring their own quiet conversation, Eoghan leaned across the aisle toward Mishalla. The barest flick of his head brought her nearer, and she pressed her left cheek to his, so their mouths were close to each other's ears. To their captors she and Eoghan might only look like two lovers comforting one another.

"I'm sure Ilian didn't go far, wherever he's hiding. I'm sure he was still watching the crèche until Celia got there. He'll sound the alarm for us," Eoghan murmured. "Someone will get the children to safety. And they'll come for us."

"How? We don't even know where we're going."

"Through you, I'm hoping," he whispered. "The datapod upload from Ilian that day in Streetmarket took you off the Grid, made you untraceable. But I'm hoping Zul will know a way to reverse that so he can find you. The second upload put the neural block on your circuitry. Until Ansgar figures out the override code, he can't reset you."

"But what about you? What if we're separated? If you're not with me, how will they find you?"

"As long as you're safe, it doesn't matter."

"It matters to me!"

She spoke a shade too loudly, snagging the attention of Juka. As a skyway light flared across the enforcer's face, Mishalla could see Juka watching them. Making a deliberate show of it, Mishalla reared back a little to kiss Eoghan on the mouth. Juka's lip curled in disgust and she looked away.

Mishalla matched her cheek to Eoghan's again. "By the time they find us, it'll be too late. You, dead. Me, as good as. I have to tell you . . ." She shut her eyes against the tears, then said the words on a breath. "I love you, Eoghan."

In the silence that followed, she thought her heart would stop. Misgivings tumbled through her mind—that the attention he'd given her had been a tool, a way to persuade her to cooperate in this venture. He'd only pretended to care about her.

Then his lips brushed her ear. "I love you too, Mishalla."

She pressed more tightly against him, the ache of her arms tied behind her inconsequential. The bright gem of Eoghan's love would sustain her over the next hours or minutes left to her. She would go into oblivion knowing that he loved her.

Propped up against him, she dozed, exhausted by fear. She jolted awake as they were making their way back off the skyway. Off to the east, the first faint light of the sky hinted at Iyenku's dawn. Her internal clock told her she'd slept a little over an hour.

The dim glow of lights marked a lowborn shanty at the base of the skyway pillar, but the operator of the Jahaja turned away, navigating the shadowy streets until he slowed at a narrow drive cutting through thick trees. Real trees, as best she could tell, their imperfections more beguiling than the faultless symmetry a holo forest would have had. Maybe even Earth trees, an impossible trueborn extravagance. One of the trueborn preserves?

From the corner of her eye, she caught movement, and turned back to see a creature in the shadows. Too big to be a rat-snake. She scraped her memories of childhood sekai stories to come up with an improbable identification. A recreated Earth creature, a raccoon, waddled between the trees before vanishing.

Her heart ached at the beauty of the trees, of the creature. That she would see it at the end of her short life filled her with grief. Would there be anything like it in her new, realigned life?

The Jahaja pulled off the pavement onto a rougher track, its suspension engine struggling to smooth out the bumps and potholes. Mishalla stared out the window as they jounced along, hoping for another glimpse of something real and alive. But whether it was the approach of dawn or the multi-lev's roar, whatever other gene-splicer creations that lived here stayed out of sight.

When the Jahaja stopped in a small clearing walled in by trees, alarm clamored inside Mishalla. Nothing here, no one to hear them cry out. Maybe they'd changed their minds, intended to dump them here, out of sight.

She turned back to Eoghan, edging as close as she could. "I love you," she repeated. Fear choked back anything else she might have said.

Juka and Ansgar manhandled her and Eoghan out of the Jahaja toward a tall, dark thicket of trees and brush. Made stupid with terror, she didn't notice the familiar hum of a holo generator, didn't see the lines of the structure it screened until she tripped on the first step.

Now she felt the roughness of plasscrete under her feet, could just distinguish the camouflaged walls of the house from the real forest behind. Ansgar typed a code into a hidden security pad and she heard the clunk of a lock releasing. Plassteel bolt no doubt, and plasscrete door. All but impenetrable when the lock again engaged. A last little shred of hope for escape died.

They all but dragged her and Eoghan across an empty room to another door. A flight of stairs led below ground level. Mishalla stumbled on the first few steps, barking an ankle on the sharp edge of a tread. Her hands brushed against the step before they yanked her to her feet again. Actual stone. The air smelled dank and close, and she wondered if maybe a new house had been built atop an old cellar.

The plassteel door they opened at the foot of the stairs looked new enough, as did its formidable locking mechanism. Juka's shove into the room caused Mishalla to stumble again, this time to her knees when she couldn't break her fall with her restrained hands. She hissed in a breath at the sting of pain.

She looked back over her shoulder, expecting Eoghan to be tossed in with her. But she caught only a glimpse of him before they shut and locked the door.

"No!" she screamed into the darkness. "Eoghan!"

She heard him call her name, barely audible. Once, twice— then if he cried out again, she couldn't hear it. She screamed, "Eoghan!" once more, but the blackness of the room seemed to swallow up the sound.

She knelt there for a long while, too overwhelmed to think what to do next. She forced herself to focus on Eoghan, on seeing him again. On the two of them finding a way out of here, to help those lowborn children.

Awkwardly, falling once when she lost her balance, she struggled to her feet. She turned toward where she thought the door was, then with her back to the wall, felt her way along it. Finally, she found the edges of the jamb.

Her fingers were so numb from the restraints, she could barely wrap them around the handle. Of course it was locked— she couldn't budge it so much as a millimeter, especially with her hands still tied behind her. No leverage. But she had to try.

A noise echoed in the cellar outside, the concussion of it rattling the solid door. Like an explosion. Or like the blast of a shockgun.

Terror ripped Eoghan's name from her throat. She endured several seconds of silence as she waited for whatever the next horror would be. When a fist pounded on the door, Mishalla startled and jumped away.

"Where's Eoghan!" she called through the door.

"Give it up, jik girl!" Juka yelled. "The lowborn boy is dead."

Juka's words were nonsense. Mishalla couldn't bring herself to believe them. "Ansgar was going to question him."

"That idiot lowborn tried to go for Ansgar. The captain took him down."

"You're lying." She had to be. Yet Mishalla had heard the shockgun blast.

"You're next, jik. He's found a way to reset you."

Mishalla shook her head as her knees gave way and she crumpled to the damp stone floor. Heavy footsteps approached, growing louder. Then the door swung open.

# 28

"Devak!" Zul barked out. "Break into your father's office again. Override the Grid ghosting patch and get us a true location for Mishalla."

"Father changed the door code last night," Devak said.

"I installed a code capture device months ago," Zul said. "Pull off the box and jury-rig it with your datapod to access it."

Devak hurried out. A few moments later, Kayla heard Mrs. Manel shouting at Devak as he hacked the new door code, then her pounding on the office door when Devak locked himself inside.

While Devak worked, the old man used his wristlink to talk to his friends Jemali and Hala, asking them to hurry to the Manel house. Zul ordered Kayla to retrieve the carrysak from his dresser drawer, the one he'd brought home the day Kayla visited Quila.

"We'll find her, Kayla," Zul said.

"But will they have reset her already?" Kayla asked.

"We installed a reset block that would have slowed them

down. You got the same block with your upload. But it's a fairly simple fix to bypass it. Hard to be sure after all these hours."

No hope for Mishalla, then. Nothing left of her but a shell.

Devak returned, waving the datapod. "She's in an isolated corner of Tellik sector. Just across the border from Sheysa in a forest preserve."

"Can you tell if she's been reset?" Kayla asked, dreading his answer.

"Only that she's still alive."

"Eoghan would have been with her," Zul said. "If he can do anything to keep Mishalla safe, he will."

"If the enforcers haven't killed him," Devak put in.

Kayla clung to a small sliver of hope. Moments later Jemali and Hala arrived, the two old men storming past Senia's and Mrs. Manel's objections and up to Zul's room. The small space suddenly became very crowded. Devak and Kayla shoved the bench to the wall again, then Devak ceded it to Hala and Kayla while he stood in a corner.

Hala seemed not the least bit worried about sitting next to her. Of course it wouldn't matter to him. Hala, and Jemali as well, had worked with Zul to create the first GENs. They knew the original name before the prophets changed it. So, to them, GENs were human.

Jemali dumped the contents of the carrysak on the bed—dozens and dozens of circular vac-seals about the size of Kayla's palm. Clear liquid filled each one.

Jemali dropped his own carrysak beside the pile. "You'll probably kill yourself, old man," Jemali said as he sorted through the drug packets and plucked two familiar blood-red vac-seals from the rest.

Devak took a step closer. "What are you doing, Pitamah?"

Jemali spared a glance over his shoulder for Devak. "He intends to have me administer a double dose of crysophora."

"Both at once?" Devak said, alarmed. "You won't survive that!"

"What else can I do?" Zul asked. "We not only have to save the GEN girl, there are the children to rescue."

Kayla eyed the haphazard pile on the bed. "What's in the rest of those vac-seals?"

"They were meant to be your freedom, and Mishalla's," Zul said. "But circumstances have changed." He gestured imperiously at Jemali. "Come, we have no time to waste."

Devak grabbed Jemali's arm to stop him. "We know where Mishalla is. You said you know where the children are. Let the rest of us do this, Pitamah. We'll free Mishalla and the children."

"It's more complicated than that, Devak," Zul said.

"Don't be a stubborn old fool!" Devak cried. "Why risk your life if you don't have to?"

Zul's head swung up and he bellowed at Devak, "Because it isn't just a matter of finding the children! It's what we have to do *after* we find them. They've been changed, Devak. Changed into GENs!"

"I don't understand," Devak said.

"The ones who have been stealing lowborn children— we thought they only wanted to clear the lowborns to create adhikar for minor-status trueborns. Instead, they've been installing tattoos on the lowborn children's cheeks and neural circuitry inside their bodies. Converting them into GENs like they did Kayla when she was a fourth-year."

Devak stared, stunned. "Who would do that, Pitamah?"

Zul didn't answer, but Kayla could see the realization in Devak's eyes, the pain that the truth caused him.

"It's Father," Devak said. "He's neck deep in this evil scheme."

"This scheme earns your father triple his government salary," Zul said. "Your mother's habits have been draining the family wealth for years. Your father fears you'll all lose your status if he has to drain the Manel adhikar further."

"And that justifies what he's done to those lowborns? I'd rather be minor-status." Devak sank to the foot of his great-grandfather's bed. "What do we do?"

"We change them back. I change them back. I'm the only one who knows how to use what's in those vac-seals, and how to monitor the process to restore them." He glared up at Jemali. "Can we get this over with?"

"Kayla," Jemali said. "I'll need you here at his side, in case he collapses."

But as Kayla rose, Zul said, "No, I don't want the young ones here. Don't want them to see."

"I've seen you take it before," Devak said. "Seen mother get sicker than you were."

"This will be different," Zul said. "You and Kayla get the AirCloud ready. I'll be right there."

Devak stared at his great-grandfather a long while, then rose reluctantly. Kayla followed him from the room.

Hala caught up with them just as they reached the front stairs. "If this doesn't go well, Jemali will have to stay with him. The three of us will at least get the GEN girl and the children out of harm's way. We'll figure out what to do next depending on whether Zul is . . ."

*Dead*, Kayla finished in her mind. She wanted to rush back

inside and tell the old man goodbye. But maybe it was too late.

Kayla heard Senia in the kitchen. Mrs. Manel opened the door to her room as they walked by, her eyes fogged and unfocused. She didn't say a word as Kayla used the front stairs. They reached the docking garage without challenge. Kayla climbed into the back of the AirCloud and Devak backed the lev-car into the street.

"Just as well Father's not home," Devak said. "If I'd seen him, I might have hit him."

"I might have helped you," Kayla said.

Devak reached through the two front seats to take her hand. "If Pitamah dies—"

"Don't say it."

"If he dies," Devak said more firmly, "we'll have to find someone to take his place. Within the Kinship. To help us save those lowborn children."

"What about Jemali and Hala? They were part of the original team. Don't they know as much as Zul?"

"If they did," Devak asked, "why would they agree to drag Zul out of his bed, risk his life with the crysophora? Why wouldn't they just do the work themselves? I think Pitamah has kept a lot to himself."

That was certainly true. The old man liked his secrets. Or maybe he felt forced to keep them, didn't want too many people knowing he had a sort of GEN circuitry installed in his body.

Motion from the house caught Kayla's eye. Her breath caught in her throat as Zul emerged, Jemali and Hala on either side. Zul was walking on his own, although with his friends' assistance to keep his balance. He'd applied another concealer to the tattoo on his cheek.

# tan̨born

Kayla hurried from the AirCloud to meet the old men at the foot of the porch steps, relieving Hala of Zul's heavy carrysak. Devak had the lev-car door open, ready to settle Zul into the front passenger seat. Kayla climbed in the back again, the carrysak beside her.

They started off toward the skyway, Jemali and Hala following in their WindSpear. Kayla leaned forward to speak to Zul. "Will the children still be there? They won't have moved them?"

"We have someone watching the crèche," Zul said. "He'll let us know if they evacuate the lowborns."

Devak accelerated as he pulled onto the skyway, passing other slower moving lev-cars. "Why did Father do this, Pitamah? Why turn lowborns into GENs?"

"Another piece of the puzzle," Zul said, "that I should have solved before now. You know we used up the original embryos from Earth twelve years ago or so."

Devak nodded. "And the gene-splicers started creating artificial embryos. Made from other cells converted into stem cells." Devak glanced apologetically at Kayla. "Cells from GEN bodies."

"The success rate for the artificial embryos is lower," Zul said. "Works fairly well if material from a young GEN is used, but it's not profitable to destroy young, healthy GENs for their cells. There are enough older GENs to recycle, but their genetic material often degrades before the embryo forms. The gene-splicers have tried to keep it under wraps, but fewer and fewer GENs are being successfully gestated each year."

"Tala says when she first started her nurturing Assignment twenty years ago," Kayla said, "she'd get a new child every other

**337**

year, or third year at most. But in the last ten years or so, she's gotten fewer babies and some of them were sickly and died."

Devak whipped past a pair of WindSpears before pulling back into his lane. "GENs are dying in the tank, but the lowborns still produce plenty of healthy children, so that's who they took to make new GENs."

Devak glanced over at Zul. "What I don't understand is why Father didn't stop Mother. Why not send her off to one of those places where she wouldn't be able to take any more vacations? Or put her in the tank so she wouldn't want it anymore?"

"He did," Zul said. "When you were younger. You might not remember her being gone, sometimes for a week at a time, sometimes for a full month. She'd stay clean a little while. But your brother's death broke her, and she always went back to the BeCalm and crysophora. Eventually, the treatments and the bribes to keep them secret were costing your father more than the drugs themselves. So he gave up. Let her have her vacations."

Devak turned his attention back to operating the lev-car as traffic slowed, then stopped entirely. Up ahead, enforcers were detouring traffic off the skyway.

Devak lowered his window as he came even with one of the enforcers. "Is there an accident ahead?"

"Lowborn riot in Sheysa," the enforcer told him. "Started just before dawn. Any lev-car traveling in or out of the sector has to be searched."

Kayla's hand fell on the carrysak beside her. A glance at Zul told her he didn't like the idea of enforcers looking through the carrysak any more than she did. With the enforcer's attention on Devak, Kayla slid the carrysak to the floor behind her feet.

"We're headed for Tellik," Zul said to the enforcer, "and

in a bit of a hurry. Any possibility of avoiding the search?"

The enforcer made a quick scan of the lev-car, appraising Devak and Zul as high-status, dismissing Kayla as trivial. He leaned an elbow on the window. "There is a search waiver fee."

Zul passed Devak a roll of dhans and Devak peeled off several. Enough, apparently, to satisfy the enforcer. He signaled to one of his compatriots, then indicated to Devak to pull past the line of stopped lev-cars.

The slowdown had separated them from Jemali and Hala. Zul contacted them via the wristlink, told them they'd meet in Sheysa where the GEN-transformed children were being held.

They crept along the skyway, finally picking up speed once they passed the head of the line of lev-cars waiting to be searched. The skyway exit dumped them into a minor-status trueborn neighborhood of multi-housing.

Devak activated the navigation system, loading Mishalla's location from his datapod. The AirCloud took them over the border into Tellik, then backtracked to a peninsula of land that butted up to Foresthill, Sheysa, and the GEN sector, Jassa. Minor-status trueborn multi-housing gave way to a scattering of lowborn shanties tucked under the skyway. As the road narrowed, shanties gave way to brush, then exotic-looking trees. The landscape on either side grew truly wild.

"It's a preserve," Zul told them. "Earth plants and animals re-created by gene-splicers. High-status come here to connect with the Lord Creator. And to hunt." Zul snorted a laugh. "Don't know why they would have brought her here. Unless . . ."

Kayla's imagination filled in the rest. *Unless they planned to dump a body.* "Devak said she was still alive."

Devak glanced back at her. "She was when we left."

It was what? An hour since then? More than enough time for them to kill her. Kayla swallowed back the press of nausea.

The AirCloud slowed to take an even narrower dirt track that led between the thickening trees. Kayla's misgivings multiplied to a knotted throb in her belly. She wrapped her arms around herself to hold back the fear.

When the AirCloud's navigator announced they'd reached their destination, Kayla forced herself to look around. If Mishalla's body or the lowborn boy's were out there, she couldn't see them. No way would they have had time to bury two bodies.

"There's nothing here," Kayla said as she slipped from the AirCloud to help Zul to his feet. "Are you sure you got the location right?"

"Look over at those trees." Devak pointed over at a nearly uniform array of green and brown. "Hear the hum? It's a holo unit. They programmed the façade to blend with the surrounding forest, but there's a structure there."

Now she made out the lines of something man-made, not quite disguised by the holo. "Who would build a house way out here?"

"There was a warden's cottage years ago," Zul said. "They could have torn that down, put this in its place."

"No lev-car anywhere," Devak noted. "I would have expected someone to be here."

"Would they need to guard Mishalla?" Kayla asked. "If she's been reset?"

"Still, to just leave her." Zul checked around the far side of the camouflaged house, shook his head as he returned.

Zul went first, feet carefully testing the leaf-strewn ground to find where the structure began. Devak followed closely to one side, Kayla to the other. When they reached the periphery of the holo projection, Zul's reaching arms vanished into the false image. He nearly tipped forward as he stumbled. On either side, Devak and Kayla steadied him.

"Step," Zul said.

Still holding Zul, they took the three plasscrete steps through the holo image, the projection prickling along Kayla's skin. Now she could see the door, the solid, windowless walls.

"Plasscrete door, electronic lock," Devak said, running a hand over the locking panel.

"Can you decode it, Devak?" Zul asked.

"Maybe. It would take some time."

"Then we attempt civility first." Zul knocked on the door. No response. He'd raised his fist to knock again when footsteps approached from inside. The lock released and the door opened.

A small, officious demi-status woman eyed them suspiciously. "What do you want?"

"We're looking for someone," Zul said.

"No one here but me," the woman told him.

Zul tried to see past her, but the woman narrowed the opening of the door so that only her face showed. "You have to leave," she said. "This area is restricted." Before any of them could react, she slammed the door shut. With a *thunk*, the lock engaged.

"Mishalla has to be here." Kayla pounded on the door in frustration.

"She's not going to answer again," Zul said. "Devak will have to try the lock."

Kayla wrapped her fists tighter. "Why unlock it when I can break it down?"

She pounded on the door again, testing its strength. The door was plasscrete, the bolt itself likely plassteel, and stronger than the door itself.

It would be better if she could kick it in, but the strength was in her arms, not her lower body. She had only her fists.

Using both hands interlaced together as a club, she slammed them against the door, just above where she guessed the bolt was thrown. It hurt and she knew she'd be bruised. But she felt some give. She pounded again and again, blasting at the door with all her anger—against the parents who gave her up, the gene-splicer who changed her, every enforcer who'd ever slapped her.

When the door began to crumble, she moved lower, just below the bolt, continuing her assault. When it finally gave way completely, swinging inward, she would have fallen with it if Devak hadn't grabbed for her.

They stepped inside, past the dust and the rubble of the door. The trueborn woman cowered in the entryway, sidling away as they pushed inside.

"Where is she?" Kayla demanded.

The trueborn woman's blue eyes glittered with arrogance. "You don't talk to me that way, ji—"

Devak slapped a hand over the woman's mouth. "And you won't say that word. Where's Mishalla?" Devak demanded. "The GEN girl. Where is she?"

The demi woman didn't answer, but her glance flicked across the empty room to a door slightly ajar. Kayla was almost disappointed it wasn't locked—she would have liked to knock down another.

Zul pushed the door open the rest of the way and palmed

the illuminator control. "It's a cellar. Part of the original house from the looks of it."

The demi woman's fingers drifted to her wristlink. "Devak!" Kayla called out.

Before the trueborn woman could send out the alarm, Devak twisted her arm behind her back and stripped the device from her. He muscled her toward the cellar. "You'll show us where Mishalla is."

"It wasn't me," the demi woman whined as Devak all but dragged her down the stairs. "Ansgar forced me to work with him."

Mention of the Brigade captain sent a shock through Kayla. "Ansgar's enforcement sector is Chadi. What would he be doing in Sheysa?"

"Earning what he couldn't make with a captain's allotment," Zul said. "Another of my grandson's accomplices. Willing to do anything for dhans and a little adhikar."

At the foot of the stairs, they faced another door, this one of more formidable plassteel. There was a second door set in the wall farther down.

"Which one?" Devak asked.

The demi woman pointed to the nearer door. "The ji— GEN is here. The lowborn there."

Kayla pounded on the door. "Mishalla! It's Kayla. We're here to get you out!"

When there was no answer, Kayla confronted the trueborn woman. "Did Ansgar reset her? Is she still Mishalla?"

Sullen and reluctant, the demi nevertheless answered Kayla with Devak's tighter grip as encouragement. "He thought he'd figured out the override, was in there with her maybe an hour. I didn't see her again after."

"Where's Ansgar now?" Zul asked.

"Lowborn riot. He and Juka both went and left me here." That last came out bitterly. "The notification came in while he was with the GEN. He couldn't risk not turning out, not when the alert extended to Chadi and Foresthill-based Brigades."

Kayla turned her attention to the door. "Solid plassteel. Even I can't break this one down."

Devak gave the demi woman a shake. "What's the door code?"

"I don't know. I swear!" she insisted when Devak shook her. "It was Ansgar's idea to bring them here. He knew about this place, not me."

Kayla fixed on the locking control panel. "Devak, if you could get to the guts of the electronics, could you jury-rig it like you did your father's lock?"

"Maybe."

Kayla dug her fingers into the edges of the panel and wrenched the cover from the stone wall. The circuitry inside sparked as she snapped the connections. She moved to the other door and twisted off its locking control panel as well.

Devak passed the demi woman to Kayla so he could focus on the task of unlocking Mishalla's cell. The trueborn woman eyed the stairs as if plotting escape. Kayla held her tight enough to remind her of the strength that had battered down the front door.

Devak bridged the broken circuitry with his datapod, interfacing with his wristlink to restructure the locking mechanism logic. "Think I've got it," he muttered a moment before the bolt released.

Devak pushed open the door. Her priorities shifting to Mishalla, Kayla's hold on the demi woman slackened. The woman snatched her arm free and took off up the stairs.

Kayla made to go after her, but Zul stopped her. "Where can she go? The AirCloud is secure. She'll need either us or Ansgar to get her out of the preserve. With the lowborn riot, I doubt Ansgar will be returning anytime soon."

Devak had found the external control for the illumination in Mishalla's cell. Kayla's friend lay curled up on the stone floor, facing the far wall. Her red hair was a tangled spill across the rough stone and her hands were tied behind her.

"Mishalla?" Kayla crossed the cell with hesitant steps, kneeling beside her friend. Her hand trembled as she laid it on Mishalla's arm. Relief washed through Kayla as she felt Mishalla's warmth. *Alive, at any rate.*

Reset, she wouldn't recognize her own name. Kayla remembered the way Ansgar had ordered poor Tanti to rise. With a tug, she snapped the restraints around Mishalla's wrists, then shook her friend's arm. "Please, get up."

Mishalla stirred then, turning toward Kayla. Opened her eyes. And stared, unseeing, up at Kayla.

# 29

**D**evak went down on one knee beside Kayla, put his arm around her. Kayla had been fighting tears, and Devak's touch nearly lost the battle for her.

She wove her fingers in Mishalla's, gave one last hopeless try. "Are you in there?"

Mishalla blinked, her gaze fixing on Kayla. But not empty as it had been moments ago. Mishalla's brow furrowed and bit by bit, life seemed to return to those hazel eyes.

She whispered something, then swallowed as if her throat was parched. When she finally spoke, the words were thready. "You're not a dream?"

Mishalla pushed herself up, sat staring at Kayla. "This isn't the After? Is it really you?"

Kayla put gentle hands on Mishalla's shoulders. "Is it you? Ansgar didn't reset you?"

Mishalla shook her head. "No. Yes." She laughed, the sound watery with tears. "No, he didn't reset me. Yes, it's me."

Kayla let her own eyes spill over as she pulled Mishalla into a careful embrace. They both wept like a pair of tank-babies.

When they were done, Kayla helped Mishalla to her feet, supporting her friend when her bad leg gave way. Mishalla still looked dazed and unbelieving.

Behind her, Devak brushed Kayla's arm. "I'm going to see what I can do about opening the other cell."

Mishalla leaned heavily against Kayla. "When I first heard your voice, I thought it was a hallucination. After what Ansgar did, I hurt so much, everything shut down. I couldn't even think."

Kayla glanced back at Zul, lowered her voice. "What did he do? He didn't—"

"He didn't molest me. He would have had to touch me for that. He hit me. Used the shockgun on a low setting." Tears tracked down her cheeks again. "Juka said Ansgar killed Eoghan. I love him, Kayla. We just found each other."

Devak shouted from the other cell. "Pitamah! Come quick!"

Zul hurried to answer Devak's summons, and Kayla followed more slowly with Mishalla. What Kayla saw in the other cell sent her heart plummeting—a dark-skinned boy lay sprawled on the stone floor, the blackening of a shockgun strike along his side.

Devak cushioned the boy's head. "This is one of the lowborns who stole my datapod."

"In the service of the Kinship," Zul said.

Then the boy groaned, and Mishalla wrenched free of Kayla's hold. Her leg betrayed her, taking her to her knees, but Mishalla seemed intent only on taking Eoghan's hand.

"He's alive, thank the Infinite," Mishalla murmured.

"But gravely injured," Zul said. "Not much I can do for

him here. We have to take him to Jemali."

Kayla picked up the wounded Eoghan while Devak helped Mishalla up the stairs. They made it to the AirCloud, but the demi woman descended on them as Kayla was loading the unconscious lowborn into the back seat.

"Take me back to Sheysa," she demanded. "That lowborn's good as dead anyway. Leave him here and take me."

"As if we'd value a rat-snake like you over him? You can wait for Ansgar," Zul said. "Although he may be a long time coming after I notify the Judicial Council what he's been up to."

They shut the doors to the AirCloud, then Devak circled back the way they came. The demi woman shouted at them as they pulled away, her words inaudible, her face twisted with anger.

Eoghan sat between Kayla and Mishalla, barely conscious, his face tipped into Mishalla's thick red hair. Kayla could see the ugly black wound on his side, its charred edges rimming a two-by-ten centimeter slash of red. She'd seen worse shockgun strikes, but not many. And none of those wounded had lived—they'd been GENs, and the medics saw more value in salvaging the non-humans' genetic material than in saving their lives.

Devak loaded the location of the crèche into the navigator, then programmed in a detour around the blockade in Sheysa. Their indirect route took them through Jassa, a GEN sector. GENs lined the streets, watching them pass. The GENs were accustomed to supply trucks rumbling down their narrow streets, not sleek AirClouds. And certainly not AirClouds with GENs inside.

Zul spent most of the trip on his wristlink. Kayla could only hear his side of the conversation, but she worked out that he'd called the Southwest Territory Judicial Council. He explained about the kidnapping and conversion of the lowborn children, and reported the names of those involved that Mishalla had told him—Captain Ansgar and an enforcer named Juka, and Pia Lanton, the demi woman they'd seen at the preserve. Zul's voice broke just a little when he identified his grandson Ved as the mastermind of the scheme.

When he was done, he told them, "An enforcer from the Council detail will arrest Pia. They'll be adding a charge of trespassing since she entered the preserve without permission." He glanced over at Devak. "They'll send someone out for your father as well. Quietly."

"I'd just as soon have the whole neighborhood know what Father's done, Pitamah."

They crossed the Sheysa River over a footbridge barely wide enough for the AirCloud, its supports trembling under the force of the lev-car suspension engine. As they topped the rise of the riverbank, they saw the plumes of smoke rising beyond the warehouse district.

"Stay along the river as best you can," Zul said. "We don't want to get mixed up in that."

They jounced along the uneven gravel surface. She caught a glimpse down an alleyway of a crowd of lowborns battering at the door to a warehouse loading dock.

"The crèche that Eoghan and I went to last night is up ahead on the right," Mishalla said, the first time she'd spoken since they'd left the preserve.

As they neared the end of the row of warehouses, Kayla spotted a Jahaja multi-lev docked up against the building, Jemali and Hala's WindSpear docked beside it. Although the AirCloud still glided along at a good fifty kilometers per hour, Mishalla fumbled with the door release, panic draining her face of color.

"Ansgar was in that multi-lev," Mishalla moaned. "He'll find me. I can't—"

"He's not here," Zul said soothingly. "He's busy with the riot. That's a different multi, one the Kinship brought to transport the children."

Mishalla shook so hard her teeth clattered. "He took us to the preserve in a Jahaja. I thought . . ." She drew a long, deliberate breath.

Kayla pointed to an open doorway, almost indistinguishable between the warehouses. "Is that it?"

"Yes," Mishalla said. "That's where Shan is, and all the other lowborns that were converted to GENs."

As Devak docked nose to nose with the WindSpear, Jemali emerged from the crèche. Kayla lifted Eoghan from the AirCloud.

She called to the trueborn medic. "We have an injury."

Jemali hurried over and took a quick look at Eoghan's wound. "Bring him inside."

Mishalla followed at their heels. "You can help him?"

"I'll do what I can," Jemali said.

They passed through the crèche's playroom where close to twenty GEN—no, lowborn—children slept on the floor or played with colorful shape-blocks and toy lev-cars, Hala watching over them. One of the little boys brightened when he saw Mishalla, running toward her as fast as his sturdy legs could carry him.

The boy flung his arms around Mishalla, crying, "Up, up!"

Tears streaming down her face, Mishalla lifted the boy, cradling him against her shoulder. With a shock, Kayla recognized that small face. It was Shan, Quila's son. The boy she'd seen in the shantytown on her Assignment day. Now with a GEN tattoo on his face.

Jemali led them into the caregiver's quarters, where an old lowborn woman sat tied to a chair in the corner. "Lay the boy on the bed," Jemali said.

Once Kayla had settled Eoghan atop the rumpled bedclothes, she stood back to give Jemali room. Mishalla sat opposite the medic, as close to Eoghan as she could, Shan snuggled in her lap.

The lowborn woman scowled at Jemali. "I don't want that filthy jik-lover on my bed."

"It won't be your bed any longer, Faria," Jemali said, piling bedclothes over Eoghan. "Not once you've been turned over to the JC."

"I can't believe the Judicial Council will do anything," Kayla said. "Not when it's only lowborns who've been hurt."

"Zul has some leverage if they don't take action," Jemali said. "He can threaten to make public the looming GEN shortage. The trueborns would panic at the loss of their workforce. The lowborns would likely riot at the possibility of their small gains taken away, not to mention outrage over their children stolen and converted to GENs. Zul will make sure the Council punishes all of them, including Director Manel, grandson or no."

Jemali gently peeled back Eoghan's korta. "A dead-on hit would have killed him instantly, so we have the small comfort of a peripheral strike."

"What about Mishalla's part in this?" Kayla asked.

Mishalla lifted her worried gaze to Kayla. "I didn't know anything about it."

"But you were involved," Kayla said. "What if they mix you into the same kettle of kel-grain?"

Mishalla didn't have an answer for that. So easy to put the blame on a GEN.

Devak poked his head into Faria's quarters. "Mishalla, Zul's asking for you, if you feel up to it. The children are terrified and he'd like you to keep them comfortable while he administers the treatment."

Mishalla gripped Shan more tightly. "What treatment?"

"He's going to change them back, Mishalla," Kayla said. "Take away the GEN circuitry and tattoos."

"He wants us too, Kayla," Devak said. "The procedure's complex. He needs us sanity-checking the process."

"I don't want to leave Eoghan," Mishalla said.

Jemali had pulled a scanner from his carrysak and was running it slowly along the wound. "It'll take me some time to determine how deep the tissue damage goes. I'll tell you the moment I know something more."

Mishalla looked doubtful, but she leaned down to press a kiss to Eoghan's cheek, lingering there a moment. As they walked through the playroom, several of the children tracked their passage, uneasy and tearful, as if they couldn't bear even one more gram of distress.

"Better to leave Shan here, if you can," Kayla told Mishalla. "Watching Zul's treatment might upset him."

Mishalla set Shan down beside a crate of toy lev-cars, whispering a promise that she'd be back soon. She pressed a toy WindSpear in Shan's hand, then brushed a kiss on his forehead. The sleeproom was packed with cribs and small beds, Zul standing beside one of the beds, a sobbing second-year boy struggling in his arms. The vac-seals had been spread across the bed in neat rows.

"Mishalla, thank the Lord Creator," Zul said. "This poor child is terrified."

Mishalla gathered up the second-year. "This is Cas. Always a bit of a crybaby. Bad luck you picked him first."

Zul directed Kayla and Devak to the vac-seals. "When we produced these, we didn't have the resources to include the identity fail-safes of white market medicinals. So no color-coding or the capacity for sequence lock-in. It's just my bare brain keeping them straight."

He pointed to the top row. "I apply them in order, one from the first set, then the next, et cetera, until all six vac-seals have been administered. There's a time lapse between applications. Five minutes, six minutes, four, two, three." He indicated each row in turn. "I'll need your inner clock, Kayla, to keep us on track."

Zul went on, "I want you two to study the IDs on each row and to memorize the sequence and the time lapses. Devak, enter the numbers and sequence in your wristlink as backup. Kayla can use mine." He unclasped the device and gave it to her. "But don't mindlessly rely on the wristlink. It's essential I keep the order straight. I do it wrong, and at the least, the process won't work."

"At worst?" Kayla asked.

"I kill one of these children," Zul said grimly. "You can see why we have to do one at a time."

Mishalla sat with Cas on an adjacent bed while Kayla scanned the vac-seals, first across the rows to be sure the numbers were identical, then down the columns to be sure there were no repeats in each child's dosage. She entered the IDs as she went while Devak did the same.

"Good, then," Zul said, the first signs of post-crysophora fatigue showing in his face. "Let's get started."

But before he could reach for the first vac-seal, they heard Hala shout from the other room. Throwing out an order to Mishalla to stay put, Kayla took off for the playroom at a run, Devak right behind her. They came face to face with Ansgar.

The captain jabbed his shockgun in Kayla's direction. "What the denking hell are you doing here?"

"Setting things right," she said, gauging the distance between her and the enforcer. Maybe close enough that she could get to him before he fired off a shot. He would take her down, but it would give Devak a chance to overpower Ansgar.

She edged closer. "The Judicial Council already knows about you. About the others, including Ved Manel."

"This has nothing to do with you, jik. You go on back to your Assignment and maybe I won't report you for a location violation."

"I'm not going anywhere." She took another step closer. "We're going to restore these children to what they were before Director Manel's hack gene-splicers put their hands on them."

"I can have you reset, just like that," Ansgar said, brandishing his shockgun. "Who's going to believe the word of a GEN over a trueborn?"

"I would." Devak moved up beside her, which she'd just as soon he didn't do. She wanted herself between him and danger.

"She works for my family. She's here on my business."

Ansgar's eyes widened and now he looked scared. "You're Devak Manel?"

She took another stride closer. "You may be in his pay, captain, but I don't think Ved Manel would appreciate you blasting his son with your shockgun."

"But he denking well wouldn't care if it was a worthless jik."

She lunged for the captain just as he raised the shockgun. She felt the excruciating sting of it just below her right shoulder, felt her arm grow numb and useless. She struck out with her other hand, trying to knock the weapon away, but he dodged her and aimed the shockgun between her eyes.

As the cool metal pressed against her skin, emotions tumbled inside her—anger at Ansgar's cruel grin, grief that she would have no future at all with Devak.

She took one last breath.

As Kayla waited for oblivion, Devak knocked the shockgun clear. In nearly the same moment, Ansgar dropped at her feet. She stared down at him, stunned, swaying in reaction to the pain in her arm. Devak stepped past the prone Ansgar to support her in his embrace.

A familiar cheerful voice called out to her from the doorway of the crèche. "Looks like your Assignment is going well."

"Skal?" She shook her head, trying to rattle some sense into it. "How did you . . . what happened?"

He waved his shockgun. "Not so bad for a low-power GEN model. Might not put him down for long, but it puts him down nevertheless."

Skal ambled over and yanked Ansgar's arms behind his back. "He won't know it was me. Which means I'm still useful to the Kinship."

"But how did you know?" Kayla asked.

"We were both called in to the riots. I got notification that he was mixed in with this." He glanced around the room. "It's true, then. They tried to turn these poor kids into GENs."

"Not tried," Kayla said. "They've done it. With your help. Those aptitude tests you were doing got Shan kidnapped."

Skal shook his head. "I never reported what I learned about Shan. Ansgar took him anyway."

Zul came to the sleeproom doorway. "If you two are finished playing thieves and enforcers, we have a job to do here." He gave Skal a nod of acknowledgement.

"In a minute, Pitamah," Devak called out. "Jemali has to look at Kayla's shoulder."

As Devak tugged her along after him toward the caregiver's quarters, Kayla called out, "I want to hear the rest of this, Skal." He smiled and waved her off.

The feeling had come back in her arm with a vengeance by the time Jemali pulled away from Eoghan to attend to her. "Mostly epidermal damage," he said, passing his scanner across the black slash. "Some nerve damage. Your GEN healing capacity should put it right soon enough."

He sprayed some kind of deadening agent on the wound and sent her back to Zul. Along the way, she had a few moments to think about what she'd felt under the threat of the shockgun, the rush of emotions for Devak. She was just as glad to have the work with Zul to take her mind off the confusion inside her.

In the sleeproom, Zul had pulled up a chair to sit opposite Mishalla. He had the first vac-seal in his hand. "Ready?"

Putting aside Ansgar and her near-death, she reviewed the sequence in her mind. "Ready."

The moment he took Cas's arm, the little boy screamed. Kayla heard the sympathetic cries from the playroom.

"Will it hurt?" Mishalla asked.

"Not the application. The process will wipe him out. He'll sleep the rest of the day."

Kayla didn't take her eyes off Zul as he pressed one vac-seal after another into Cas's arms, with Kayla counting the time for him. Zul alternated which arm he used, but when he'd finished, Cas's tender skin was puffy and inflamed.

"This will deactivate the circuitry inside him, and his body will eventually assimilate it. The tattoo will lose adherence bit by bit and will slough off in a matter of days. We'll bandage it, and his parents will have to keep him hidden until it heals."

"How will you find these kids' parents?" Kayla asked. "I'm guessing Ansgar and Pia didn't keep records of every child they stole."

"Lowborn Kinship members in the villages have been reporting when and where a child has been stolen. Not enough reports to match the number of children here, but we'll keep asking."

Mishalla laid the sleepy Cas in one of the beds. "Not to mention the ones who were bought already and put back in the tank. This is bad enough, but to have them grow to eighth and ninth-years in one year, then put to work. How will we find the others?"

"Once we round up everyone who's involved in this scheme," Zul said, "one of them will tell us where the tank farm is hidden."

"But the growing process will have started already," Mishalla said. "Their own parents might not recognize them."

"We'll do the best we can, Mishalla," Zul said.

Mishalla sighed. "At least we're helping these babies." She left to fetch another child.

# tankborn

Kayla looked down at the vac-seals arrayed across the bed. "These were meant to transform GENs. Not these poor lowborn children. How had you planned to choose which GENs?"

"We know several more like you and Mishalla. That's what the list on my sekai was—potential candidates. GENs who started as trueborns. The process works best on GENs whose circuitry wasn't installed at the embryonic stage."

"How did you know it would work?" Kayla asked. "That it wouldn't hurt these children?"

"We've tested it," Zul said. "Not as widely as we should have to be completely sure it's safe. A few dozen GENs in all, spread across the western territories. Only a handful of those were children, babies who weren't handling the GEN circuitry well and were in danger of being reset or recycled. The young ones actually did the best."

"Where are they now?" Kayla asked.

"Safe."

That was all Zul would say.

Kayla counted the doses again. "Twenty left. How many children still to be treated?"

"Eighteen more," Zul said.

"Which leaves two doses of your magic potion unused." Kayla rubbed the crook of her own arm with the heel of her hand.

"One for you," Zul said. "One for Mishalla. Just as well we have enough to spare for you considering how long it will take to manufacture more. After the treatment, you won't pass as a trueborn, unfortunately. A bali can detect the changes the GEN circuitry caused to your cellular structure. You'll have to be a lowborn."

Even still, to be a lowborn. The realization all but took her feet right out from under her. *To no longer be a GEN.* To live as she wished, to have her own life. Would the Infinite approve? Had this been His plan all along?

Mishalla returned with Shan, and Kayla had to put her world-shattering thoughts aside. She had to focus on the methodical. Vac-seal one, then two, then three. Alternate arms, count out the minutes between. Finish with Shan, put the boy to bed while Mishalla retrieved another lowborn baby.

The careful, timed pace meant the process dragged on for hours. The crèche grew quieter as each child fell into exhausted sleep. Zul's energy faded more with each patient, until Kayla had to support him in his chair.

With the last child dosed, Devak insisted Zul take a short rest. They moved one of the sleeping boys to double up with another to clear a bed. After extracting a promise from Devak and Kayla that they'd wake him in ten minutes, Zul lay down, his long legs hanging off the end. He immediately dropped off to sleep.

Mishalla all but collapsed on the bed where Shan slept, beside the twelve remaining vac-seals. Kayla made a quick check of the playroom and caregiver's quarters. No children hiding in the corners. Skal had apparently cleaned things up—both Faria and Ansgar were gone, along with the GEN enforcer himself.

Kayla returned to the sleeproom to sit with Devak cross-legged on the floor, propped up against one of the cribs. She leaned against him, savoring his closeness. She'd all but dozed off when a blond lowborn boy strode into the sleeproom carrying a dainty dark-haired girl.

"It took some doing," the boy said, "but I managed to talk Celia at the crisis crèche into letting me take this little one for medical care."

"Amila." Mishalla held out her arms and the lowborn boy gave her the little girl. "Kayla, Devak, this is Ilian."

"We've met," Devak said. "Eoghan's partner."

"Sorry, trueborn," Ilian said, although his apology didn't sound very convincing. "You also have me to blame for the Sheysa riot. First thing I could think of to pull those enforcers off Eoghan and Mishalla. My boys might have gone a bit too far, but it got the job done."

Mishalla carefully peeled the bandage from Amila's right cheek. "When I saw it before, I thought it was a burn, but now I can see the tattoo pattern."

Ilian bent to brush Amila's hair from her face. "After I saw this, I guessed it was worse than just kidnapped lowborns. Then I got Eoghan's message." He looked up at Mishalla. "He'll be okay?"

"The medic did what he could, some kind of mods at the genetic level to speed the healing. Something you usually have to do in the tank." Mishalla, holding Amila close, said to Kayla, "Zul can fix her too, right? With his magic stuff?"

At the mention of his name, Zul roused, pushing himself up with an effort. He blinked bleary-eyed at Amila. "Another child?"

"Amila," Mishalla said. "You have two doses left. You can use one on her."

Kayla felt Zul's gaze on her, but she smiled up at Mishalla. "Yes. It's good that we have extra."

Kayla helped Zul into his chair, stood at his side as he

took Amila through the regimen. With each step, the little girl stared at Zul in a kind of angry terror.

And as each minute ticked by, as Kayla let her internal clock count the time, she could think of nothing but that last dose of the treatment. Mishalla didn't know that she and Kayla had both been candidates, that Zul had intended to give each of them a dose. Kayla could offer herself up for the last treatment and Mishalla would likely accept it—after all, Kayla was Zul's caregiver. It would make sense he would choose her.

So when Zul finished with Amila and turned to Kayla, she could just hold out her arm, turn her back on her life as a GEN. She could live her life as a lowborn.

But she and Devak could never be together. She couldn't ask him to turn his back on being a trueborn. But Mishalla and Eoghan, they might have a chance.

Zul gave Amila the last vac-seal and the little girl finally drifted off. Kayla took Amila from Mishalla and laid the child on the bed Zul had napped in.

"Stay there, Mishalla," Kayla told her friend. "You're next."

"Kayla—" Devak said, but she waved him off.

"Next for what?" Mishalla asked.

Kayla took Mishalla's hands. "This treatment was meant for GENs, to disable our circuitry, to take us permanently off the Grid. To let us live our lives on our own terms. What happened to these children changed that. But there's one dose left, just for you."

"But what about you?"

"They'll make more, won't they, Zul?" She glanced over at the old man.

He inclined his head slightly. "It will take time, but yes."

How much time? Kayla wondered. Years? Despair threatened to bubble up inside her. But she knew this was the right choice.

"You and Eoghan can be together. Travel far away to another sector where no one knows either one of you. Be safe."

"What if I don't want it?" Mishalla asked.

"You do. I know you do." Kayla turned to Zul. "Are you ready?"

He hesitated a moment, then picked up the first vac-seal. "This will be harder for you than the children. They bounce back quicker."

"You'll be fine," Kayla said, drawing her friend's arm out straight.

She watched Mishalla's face as Zul applied each vac-seal, clinging to Mishalla's hand. When it was finished and Mishalla's head lolled on Kayla's shoulder, she carried her friend to Faria's quarters to lay her beside Eoghan.

Eoghan stirred as Kayla pulled the covers up over Mishalla, his startling green eyes opening. "Mishalla? Is she—?"

"Mishalla's fine, Eoghan. You just both need to rest."

Devak met her at the door to the children's sleeproom. He took her hands, an indecipherable message in his dark gaze. "Pitamah wants to speak with you." He walked away.

Ilian had gone. Zul sat on the one empty bed, leaning against the wall. He patted the space beside him.

"The Kinship is going to place you in a new Assignment," Zul said. "We think it's safer all around."

The air left her lungs. A new Assignment. She and Devak separated.

Zul went on, "Ved will be prosecuted for the kidnapping and assault of those lowborn children. I'll do everything in my power to be certain he's convicted. His punishment will likely include the loss of adhikar. So the Manels will lose status. The family fortunes will be changed."

"I'm sorry. For Devak. For you."

He waved off her concern. "I had hoped you would fill your new role as a lowborn. But a GEN will have to do. We have a number of fictitious GEN identities inserted in the Grid. We'll change your designator ID to one of those and alter your internal ID as well."

"And then what?" she asked, the hollow place inside her growing deeper.

"You remember that GEN I mentioned to you before, the one who was to transport the information on the datapod that Quila gave you? Before she was reset, we'd intended to team her with Risa Mandoza, a lowborn member of the Kinship. Risa operates a supply truck throughout the Central Western and Southwest Territories. You'll take the other GEN's place. Tote kel-grain kegs, fibermix sacks and such for Risa."

"Still toting," she said with a sigh. "I thought I was done with that."

"You'll gather information. More DNA packets like the one you brought from Chadi so the Kinship can create more of the treatment. And you'll keep a sharp eye out for the lowborn children Ansgar and his crew defiled and sent to trueborn homes. The ones we couldn't help today."

At least she'd have a real purpose. Something to take her mind off her loss of Devak.

"I made the right choice," she said, "giving it to Mishalla."

"You made the most courageous choice I've ever seen a person make." He took her hand, patted it gently. "You'll have your chance. I promise you."

She didn't ask when that would be. Asking wouldn't make it happen any faster.

She left the sleeproom, scanned the playroom for Devak. Not there, or in Faria's quarters with Eoghan and Mishalla. She stepped from the crèche and found him standing by the Sheysa River.

He heard her approach and reached out a hand for her. He folded her into his arms. "I wanted it to be you," he murmured.

"It had to be her. She and Eoghan have a chance."

"We would have too."

She shook her head, her tattooed cheek rubbing against his chest. "Even if I'd taken the treatment, I couldn't pass for anything but a lowborn. You couldn't possibly be with me."

"I would be a lowborn for you," Devak said urgently. "I would be a GEN for you."

"No. You—we—can do more for now just as we are. Find the rest of the kidnapped children. Bring more people into the Kinship." She reached up to cradle his face. "Change the minds we can."

He drew his fingers across her tattoo. "Kayla, you mean so much to me."

She smiled as her heart filled. She went up on tiptoe to kiss him. "Me too."

He kissed her back. "We'll be together someday. No matter what happens."

"No matter what."

They walked along the riverside, watching Kas follow its brother sun Iyenku below the horizon. As they sank, the suns painted the smoky sky orange, then crimson, then deep purple black.

"Always," Kayla whispered, then leaned in close for one last kiss.

# epilogue

**K**ayla swung down from the cab of Risa Mandoza's supply truck, then leaned back in to wave goodbye. "Thanks again for the ride. And the loan of the dress." Risa had not only lent the delicate pale green gown, the lowborn woman had helped Kayla fit it to her smaller frame.

Dark-haired Risa smiled across the bench seat at Kayla. "Couldn't let you attend a wedding in your everydays. Pick you up in what? Four hours?"

"See you then."

Kayla slammed the door shut and stepped back as Risa's Jumba rumbled off. She'd come to very much enjoy the lively lowborn woman's companionship in the three months since she'd started her new Assignment. They made a game of their relationship in public, Risa treating Kayla with derisive scorn, Kayla responding with sullen GEN anger. But in private, they were fast friends and both devoted to the Kinship.

She scanned the guests milling around the chairs set up in Plator sector's central green as they waited for the wedding

# tankborn

ceremony to begin. She wouldn't expect Mishalla or Eoghan to be in view; they were likely cloistered in the striped tent that had been set up on the far end of the green. But Ilian ought to be nearby, ready to stand up for his friend.

Mishalla had wanted Kayla beside her, but that would have opened too large a sack of sewer toads. Kayla wasn't the only GEN in attendance—Mishalla had indiscriminately allowed several into her circle of friends here in Plator. But even in a sector like this, where minor-status trueborns and lowborns mixed freely, asking a GEN to stand up for her at her wedding would draw notice. And Kayla worked very hard to avoid notice.

So instead Mishalla had asked Quila, the lowborn woman and her husband having relocated to Plator after their reunion with Shan. Quila and Mishalla had struck up a friendship, based at least partly on Quila's gratitude to Mishalla for her part in returning her son.

Kayla finally spied Ilian up front beside the dais where the ceremony would take place. Beside him, a Speaker of the Word of the Lord Creator thumbed through his sekai screen. During those sessions when Kayla borrowed Risa's wristlink and spoke to Mishalla, her friend revealed that she was just as glad not to have an Intercessor of the Infinite perform a joining for her and Eoghan. After Kayla had revealed to Mishalla the truth about the so-called prophets, Mishalla had lost what little faith she'd once clung to. She worshipped the Lord Creator now.

Kayla could not turn her back on the Infinite so easily. The prophets may have invented her faith, but who was to say it was not with the Infinite's guidance. Kayla still felt His touch on her heart in her dark moments. She refused to abandon Him.

Kayla threaded her way through the crowd of lowborns and occasional GENs, sometimes nodding at the familiar faces of those she knew to be part of the Kinship. With only minutes before the start of the ceremony, people had started moving toward the chairs, the lowborns in front, GENs taking seats in the back.

Mishalla was gorgeous in a pale yellow gown, Eoghan beside her handsome in a midnight blue korta and cheras. They crossed the short distance from the tent to where the Speaker stood, the betrothed couple dazzling the guests with their brilliant smiles.

The ceremony, its ritual unfamiliar to Kayla, nevertheless tightened her throat with emotion. Mishalla and Eoghan would love, honor and cherish one another until death parted them. Thanks to the blessing of the Kinship's gift, Mishalla would be able to keep those promises.

There would be no children though. Jemali had confirmed for Mishalla that her trueborn uterus—and Kayla's as well—had been altered in the tank. Enough tissue for the girls to cycle, but not nearly enough to grow a baby. Mishalla and Eoghan had soothed that pain by taking in two of the unclaimed lowborns from the illicit crèche. If the parents were never found, they'd raise the little boy and girl as their own.

Wiping away tears, Kayla stayed in her seat with the other GENs while a crowd of lowborns surrounded Mishalla and Eoghan. Mishalla had promised Kayla a few private moments as soon as she could break away after the ceremony. She'd just have to wait.

As she'd waited for Devak these last three months. For even so much as a word from him.

# tankborn

At the Kinship meetings Zul smuggled her into, the old man told her that Devak's world had been turned upside down. Ansgar, Pia, Juka and the gene-splicers Ved had hired had been promised lighter punishment if they confessed to everything they knew about the director's scheme. The Council sentenced Devak's father to ten years in a Far North prison and forfeiture of all of his personal adhikar.

Enraged at Ved, Devak's mother had sold the Foresthill house and gone to live with a sister in Sona. She'd cut off all ties with her son.

Zul and Devak lived in Two Rivers now, their pooled dhans and adhikar just enough to maintain a small home and to cling to their high-status rank. Of the ones Devak had known in Foresthill, only his boyhood friend Junjie still spoke to him.

According to Zul, Devak's only spot of joy was learning that his old nemesis, Livot, had been tangled up in Ved Manel's scheme as well. Demi-status Livot's Bullet and high-status clothes had come courtesy of the dhans Ved paid him to scout out likely lowborn children. That was why Livot had been at the river the day Kayla had met Devak.

The crowd around Mishalla had dwindled, so Kayla got to her feet. About to make her way up to the dais, something made her turn to where a lone figure stood at the far edge of the green. She couldn't see his face from that distance, but she would know that slim body and the proud set of those shoulders from a hundred kilometers away.

Devak.

It was like that first day when she saw him across the river and wondered if he'd wave goodbye. Then, it had been a ridiculous notion that a high-status trueborn would acknowledge a GEN. But so much had changed since then.

He lifted his hand as if to call her to him. Reached in her direction.

Kayla reached out too, imagining their fingers touching, remembering the warm feel of his skin. They stood that way for several long seconds.

Then Mishalla called her name and Kayla turned to her friend. When she looked for Devak again, he'd gone.

Holding that moment in her heart, Kayla went up to the dais to congratulate her newly-wedded friend.

# author's note

*Tankborn* took a long and circuitous journey from its roots to the book you're holding in your hand. The original germ of the story started as a screenplay called *Icer* that was written in the mid-80s. *Icer* was optioned to a production company, was shown around Hollywood, but was never produced. Off and on, I considered novelizing the story, but never got around to it.

Then I became enchanted with young adult fiction. A notion popped into my mind to adapt *Icer* as a young adult novel. I plunged in, completely turning the story inside out and upside down, preserving almost nothing except the idea of genetically engineered slaves and only one character name—Kayla's.

Somewhere along the line, the concept of a caste system crept in, inspired by my long-ago conversations with an Indian-born co-worker named Azad (yes, I co-opted his name for Devak's brother). I'd been fascinated by Indian society and that caste system for decades and was delighted to finally weave that into a story.

After many iterations and re-writes, continually fine-tuning Loka's society, economy, and religion, the world became as real to me as my own. I hope you enjoy your visit to Loka, and enjoy sharing the lives of Kayla and Devak, Mishalla and Eoghan.

# acknowledgements

No book springs fully formed from the pen (okay, the word processor) of an author. Even the most brilliant writer, after plowing through multiple drafts, needs fresh pairs of eyes to find what's working and what isn't, what's missing and what has to go. I was lucky enough to have three pairs of eyes help me polish *Tankborn* to a beautiful shine.

First, the dynamic duo of my agent, Matt Bialer of Sanford J. Greenburger Associates and his assistant, Lindsay Ribar. They coached me through the process of readying *Tankborn* for submission, fine-tuning, clarifying, and eliminating the throat clearing, as Matt would say.

Stacy Whitman, editorial director of Tu Books, pushed me to take *Tankborn* to the next level (and several more above that) with her persistent, on-point questions and eagle eye. I like to think that between us, we took a good book to great.

Finally, a special shout-out to Nina Lourie, Lindsay's intern at SJGA, who pulled *Tankborn* from the slush pile in the first place.